ME, 'BOLO.'
YOU, 'HAMBURGER.'

Aghrracht gestured at the holo image with a razor-clawed forehand. "The worlds of this cluster are rich . . . fabulously wealthy. And ripe for hunting."

"These creatures have no soldiers or warriors? No *hunter packs*?" asked Sh'graat'na.

"They have soldiers," Aghrracht said with a dismissive hiss. "Their organization, however, is predicated on defense rather than offense . . . the tactics of omnivores and plant eaters. Our scouts encountered only a single weapon in their sweeps that offered any serious challenge to our pack tactics."

She gestured, and the human on the holo vanished, replaced by . . . a machine.

Judging from the scale set in one corner of the image, the thing was huge, a thousand *crucht* long at the very least, more of a mobile fortress than a deadly fighting machine.

"Our scout packs encountered this machine on the second world they investigated. It proved a formidable foe, armed with plasma and laser beam weapons, as well as a variety of missiles. It destroyed a number of our hunters before it was overwhelmed and disabled at last. I dare say, these devices will add a certain spice to our campaign, the challenge we all hunger for."

"Robots?" Kha'laa'sht snorted noisily and with utter disdain. "What kind of opponents can such be for us?"

"The locals call them *Bolos*," Aghrracht replied.

ALSO IN THIS SERIES

The Compleat Bolo by Keith Laumer

Bolos,
Created by Keith Laumer:
The Honor of the Regiment

The Unconquerable

The Triumphant
by David Weber & Linda Evans

Last Stand

BAEN BOOKS by WILLIAM H.
KEITH, JR.

Diplomatic Act (with Peter Jurasik)

Created by
KEITH LAUMER

BOLO BRIGADE

WILLIAM H. KEITH, JR.

BOLO BRIGADE

This is a work of fiction. All the characters and events
portrayed in this book are fictional, and any resemblance to
real people or incidents is purely coincidental.

A Baen Books Original

Baen Publishing Enterprises
P.O. Box 1403
Riverdale, NY 10471

ISBN: 0-671-87781-X

Cover art by C. W. Kelly

First printing, May 1997

Distributed by Simon & Schuster
1230 Avenue of the Americas
New York, NY 10020

Printed in the United States of America

PROLOGUE

She strode into the place of the hunting circle, iridium-sheathed slasher claws *click-click-clicking* across the steel deck with each confident step. Her ceremonial robes, colored a deep, blood-blue, were thickly encrusted with platinum braid, silver and gold scale, lead inlay, uranium gorget and wristlets—the heavy-metal emblems of her rank and wealth. Her entourage of males and brooders took up their positions to either side of the circle gate, their vertically slitted eyes blinking in the twilight with a savage, reptilian intensity.

Her name was Aghrracht the Swift-Slayer, and her line was one of the richest and oldest of Zhanaach. Her rank and her title—within Malach culture the two concepts were identical—was *Ghaavat'ghavagh*, a gargled snarl best translated as *Deathgiver*.

Aghrracht's Second approached, offering ceremonial challenge with a piercing hiss, then genuflecting with stooped carriage, upraised snout, and bared throat. Aghrracht's jaws gaped wide, then snapped shut in the ritual nip, closing lightly on her Second's vulnerable jugular. For a moment, she felt the lifebeat of the other's pulse beneath the pressure of her jaws; gently, almost reluctantly, she released her grip.

1

"Welcome, Deathgiver, to the circle of your plains," the Second said. "Kill and eat!"

The place was, in fact, a large, circular room aboard the huntress ship, but projections on smoothed bulkheads and curving overhead gave the illusion of open veldt, the ancestral hunting grounds of Aghrrracht's matrilineal line on far-off Zhanaach. Malach tended to be as uncomfortable with closed-in spaces as they were with solitude; by human standards, they were both claustrophobic and monophobic—a psychological legacy of their evolutionary roots as pack-hunters on the open plains.

The others of her hunting circle regarded her with slitted, ruby eyes, their flat heads carefully held a few *taych* below the level of her own.

"The scout packs have returned," Aghrrracht announced, with her customary lack of preamble. "They have found fresh prey within the target cluster. Soon we will run the Gift to ground, and then we shall kill and eat."

The others in the circle stirred, some lifting throats in obeisance, most watching with guarded expressions through ragged, vertically slit pupils. "Kill and eat!" several said together in ancient litany.

"Kill and eat. Sha'gnaasht gives us the right."

"Honor to the prophet of true divine science, Sha'gnaasht the Skilled Tracker!" the others intoned, all speaking now in solemn chorus. "Honor to Sha'gnaasht!"

Aghrrracht gestured with a razor-clawed fore-hand. A holoprojected image appeared at the circle's center, a shivering, strangely articulated creature, the image part of the recorded data transmitted by the scouts. The thing was bipedal but with legs awkwardly jointed backward from the digitigrade stance of the Malach. It possessed only two arms, but those were gangly, outsized things, oddly placed, with too many digits on the wide hands and with vestigial claws only at the tips. The head was round and blocky on a stub of a neck, the eyes small and close-set, the mouth a thin slit with an omnivore's pathetic excuse for teeth and no feeding tendrils at all. The creature's unarmored hide looked as soft and as invitingly tender as the velvet skin of a *goregh*.

"A specimen of the cluster's dominant organism, taken by our scouts," Aghrracht said quietly. "Unarmored. Weak." She paused before delivering the final adjective with the sibilant modifier that was the Malach's equivalent of a shrug of dismissal. "*Solitary.*"

Several approving hisses and whistles sounded from the watching circle. The image shifted ahead to a later stage of the creature's interrogation. Its limbs had been splayed on an examination table, its torso opened up, revealing the arrangement of organs within the body cavity. One—presumably one of the hearts—continued pulsing behind a cage of flat, white bones; the blood that spilled from the cavity as the creature writhed against its bonds was bright red.

"Odd-colored blood," Sh'graat'na the Prey Wounder observed.

"Is it good to eat?" Kha'laa'sht the Meat Finder wanted to know.

Aghrracht opened her left hind-hand, a gesture of negation. "Incompatible body chemistries," she said. "Regrettably. Their blood chemistry is based on an iron-bearing molecule, which is why the blood is red. Several of their proteins would be poison to us. But the worlds of this cluster are rich . . . *rich.*" She closed both fore-hands, signifying both affirmation and approval. "It is as our cosmologists predicted. As in the Zhanaach Void, early-generation stars are metal-poor. Only the youngest have elements heavy enough to allow planetary formation, and those have few resources. Late-generation suns, however, are almost invariably circled by planets heavily laden with metals. By our standards, the inhabitants of these worlds are fabulously wealthy . . . and ripe for hunting."

Sh'graat'na gestured at the holo image, where the specimen's struggles were rapidly fading into death. "These creatures have no *greschu'u'schtha?*" The word was a complex one, carrying shades of meaning suggesting military camaraderie, the high morale that comes from comfortable crowding, and a sense of triumphant purpose. "No soldiers or warriors? No *hunter packs?*"

"They have soldiers," Aghrracht said, with a dismissive hiss. "Their organization, however, seems divided between soldiers and non-soldiers . . . a strange concept. Their hunter-thoughts are predicated on defense rather than offense . . . the tactics of omnivores and plant eaters. Our scouts encountered only a single weapon in their sweeps that offered any serious challenge to our pack tactics."

She gestured, and the now-still form on the examination table vanished, replaced by . . . a machine.

Judging from the scale set in one corner of the image, the thing was huge, a thousand *erucht* long at the very least. Unlike Malach war machines, it was inelegantly squat, cumbersome in appearance and ponderous in its movements, more of a mobile fortress of some kind than a deadly fighting machine.

"Our scout packs encountered this machine on the second world they investigated. It proved a formidable foe, armed with plasma and laser beam weapons, as well as a variety of missile and close-in point-defense weaponry. It destroyed a number of our hunters before it was overwhelmed and disabled at last. It was, however, pathetically slow. Those armored belts you see are driven by sprocketed wheels . . . in effect creating its own road or track, but its speed is limited to, we estimate, no more than two *t'charucht* per *quor*. Our hunters ran rings around it, wearing down its defenses, destroying its armor, until it was vulnerable to attack at slasher claw range."

"Like dismembering a swamp-mired *gr'raa'zhghavescht,*" Kha'laa'sht said with a satisfied snap of razor-edged fangs.

She never failed to take each opportunity of reminding her pack sisters of her spectacular *gr'raa* kill, during her Ritual of Ga'kirascht, many years before.

"Like the *gr'raa'zhghavescht*," Aghrracht said, closing a hind-hand in agreement, "these machines are solitary, intended purely for defense, helpless against hunter-pack tactics. Still, I dare say, these devices will add a certain spice to our campaign, the challenge we all hunger for."

"We should name them," Zhallet'llesch the Scent Finder—and Aghrracht's Second—said. "To honor valiant opponents, however mismatched they might be against us."

"According to the scout packs," Aghrracht said, drawing herself up and opening her pupils wide for emphasis, "the cluster's inhabitants have a name for them already. Apparently they are robots of a sort, fighting independently."

"Robots?" Kha'laa'sht snorted noisily and with utter disdain. "What kind of opponents can such be for the Race of Sha'gnaasht?"

"Dangerous, if we do not treat them with appropriate respect," Aghrracht replied. "The locals call them *Bolos*."

CHAPTER ONE

"I've heard all about you, Lieutenant," the general said with blunt disapproval. With a stubby but carefully manicured forefinger, he tapped the file folder, thick with service record printouts, in front of him on his desk. "I've heard *all* about you and that affair at Dahlgren, and let me tell you that I don't like what I've heard one damned little bit!"

Lieutenant Donal Ragnor remained at attention, wondering if the general's point-blank attack required a response . . . and if so, what kind of response. *No excuse, sir* was the proper and expected reply to a superior officer's direct challenge to a junior's behavior, but Donal had arrived on Muir only hours ago and, so far as he was aware, had done nothing to get himself in trouble.

"I find myself shocked, sir, *shocked*," the general continued before Donal could offer any reply at all, "that you are still in military service at all!"

"I love the military, sir," he said, as the man behind the broad, hardwood desk paused to draw breath. "I would never think of leaving it."

That, of course, was not entirely true. He'd thought long and hard about just that, during the long months leading up to the court martial. He'd thought about it even harder after the court's verdict had been read in.

"Harumph!" General Barnard Phalbin, evidently, was not used to subordinates interspersing thoughts of their own into one of his tirades. He hesitated, as though wondering where exactly he'd been in his speech before being interrupted. He regarded Donal a moment longer, lips pursed, eyes narrowed in a manner appropriately menacing for interviews with know-it-all junior officers. "Harrumph," he said again. "Ah, that is . . . it takes more than *not thinking* to make a success of one's self as a career officer, let me tell you!"

Donal allowed his focus to drift past Phalbin's glowering visage and across the trophy display on the wall at his back. The general prided himself on his long career in the military. That much was clear from the mementos, awards, and holographic pics that were scattered about his lavishly appointed office. Most of them clustered on that wall, where they provided an appropriately impressive backdrop to the general's desk, surrounding a large holo of the Cluster's current governor, Reginald Chard. There was a moving holovid clip of the general shaking hands with President Alvarez of Dreyfus, another of Phalbin as a young captain receiving a plaque from a general in an Imperial uniform, still another showing him standing on a dock next to a grinning Prince Philip of Farmarine, rod and reel in hand, an exotic-looking game fish hanging head-down between them. The plaque was an award for outstanding efficiency by then-Captain Phalbin in his posting as base logistical officer on Siegfried. Nearby was the gold trophy for first place in the annual Imperial war games on Aldo Cerise.

That last was interesting. Donal had read Phalbin's bio on the journey out from Sector, and there was no indication that the general had ever actually been in combat. But then, the Aldo Cerise war games had the reputation for being something on the order of a gentlemanly diversion over the weekend.

No, that was probably unfair. True, Phalbin had the puffy face, the narrow and somewhat beady eyes, the studied look of dim concentration that might attend a not-too-bright pugilist . . . but appearances *could* be deceiving.

"I fail to understand, Mr. Ragnor," Phalbin was saying, "why Sector should see fit to burden me with your presence. It's not as though we need additional manpower just now. Quite the contrary, in fact. Things in the Cluster are quiet, have been quiet for decades, now. A young officer of your, um, *impetuous* nature is likely to find duty here somewhat on the boring side. I will not have the good order and discipline of my command upset by a junior officer's impatience."

"I've been hearing rumors about unfriendly neighbors out this way, sir. A new race, moving in from . . . from somewhere out beyond the edge of the Arm. My impression was that Sector HQ thought—"

"As you say, Lieutenant, those are *rumors*. Unverified. And unverifiable. I've discussed the issue at length in several of my quarterly reports."

"I've read them, sir."

"Then you know my feelings on the matter. I, after all, am *here*, smack in the center of these so-called alien incursions, and I assure you that there have been no reliable reports, nothing solid that would lend the least bit of substance to these wild stories. Some ships have disappeared along the borders of the Strathan Cluster, yes. What we are dealing with is probably a statistical fluctuation . . . or possibly a dishonest ship owner or two making fraudulent claims on his insurance."

"Eight ships of various classifications vanishing from long-established routes within the space of eighteen months," Donal said. "Reports from Starhold and

Endatheline of settlements raided and burned. Seems like more than statistics to me, sir. Or an insurance scam."

"Harrrumph!" Phalbin's pudgy hands gathered up a stack of file folders from one corner of his desktop and neatly reshuffled them, stacking them with millimeter precision in another corner. "Well, as to that, I might even allow that there are some small-time pirates operating on the fringes of the cluster. That, of course, would be the Space Service's jurisdiction."

"And what do they say, sir?"

The fat lips pouted. "That they are overextended as it is. That they cannot spare a task force unless there is more concrete evidence of an alien incursion. Predictable, of course."

"Of course." Donal had read those reports as well.

"Can't say I blame them, actually. In any case, there are no alien invaders coming from out beyond the edge of the Galaxy because there is no place out there for them to come from. That's clear enough, is it not?"

Donal opened his mouth, ready to contradict Phalbin. The gulf between the galaxies was not completely empty, and the old and half-magical phrase "the edge of the Galaxy" was meaningless. There could be no well-defined edge to the Galaxy's arms when in fact they gently trailed away, the local star density only gradually petering out into the near-emptiness of the galactic halo. Likely, there were suns in the gulf halfway out to Andromeda, too thinly scattered to be detectable, isolated one from the next by light millennia, rather than the five- or ten-light-year average spacing between suns within the galactic arms.

But Donal rethought what he'd been about to say and closed his mouth with a snap. Talking without thinking—in particular, spouting off to his superiors without thinking—had gotten him in deep hot water more than once in the past. It had landed him here, for one thing . . .

and there might very well be worse assignments than Bolo Tactical Officer for the Strathan Confederation.

"You were about to say, Lieutenant?"

"Ah . . . just that what you were saying is perfectly clear, yes, sir," he said. Better not to antagonize the man who was going to be his superior for at least the next four years.

Four years, out here on the ragged edge of nowhere. *God,* he thought with a fresh burst of anger tinged with despair. *Did I really deserve this?*

"Harrumph," Phalbin grunted with comfortable self-satisfaction. "Quite. We are remarkably self-sufficient out here in the Cluster. The Confederation is organized as an autonomous border district, you understand, with its own legislative body, constitution, and military. We need little from the Concordiat. We want less. That is why I really can't understand why they sent you *here. . . ."*

As Phalbin continued to expound on how little the Confederation military actually needed a supernumerary like Donal Ragnor, the lieutenant stole a sidelong glance out of the big window that dominated Phalbin's office.

It was a status symbol, a *real* window of transplas rather than a wallvid, one occupying most of two full walls in the general's corner office. It looked out over the Kinkaid Spaceport and, across the sundance-sparkling waves of Starbright Bay, to the city of Kinkaid itself, capital both of Muir and of the entire Strathan Confederation. Phalbin's eagle's eyrie, fifty floors up, gave an excellent view out over the spaceport which was the Confederation military's particular responsibility on Muir. The starliner *Rim Argent* still stood needle-slim in her landing pit on the port's field, her silver-blue finish dazzling in the late afternoon light of Muir's sun. Donal had come in on that liner, grounding less than half a dozen hours ago, and he wondered wryly if it was too late to wangle passage aboard her back to Gaspar where he'd come from.

Not that he could, of course. Muir was the end of the line, so far as Donal Ragnor was concerned. The end of the line . . . and if he was not careful, the end of his career.

At least he would still be working with Bolos. *The Dinochrome Brigade* . . .

"Perhaps, General," he said carefully, when Phalbin had paused to draw breath, "they felt I could benefit from a tour under your command."

"A nicely turned answer, Lieutenant, but not one, you understand, that I am bound to accept as completely sincere."

"Sir, I didn't mean—"

Phalbin held up one pudgy hand. "No excuses, now, Mr. Ragnor. You have a history, I understand, of always knowing the right thing to say. You have, too, the reputation for going over your commanding officer's head when there was something you wanted, going over . . . or around, or under or through, for that matter, in a manner entirely inconsistent with the niceties of proper military protocol. I will tell you right now, however, that while you are here, you will answer first to Colonel Wood, who commands your Bolo unit, and then to *me*, as commanding general of all ground military forces throughout the Cluster. You understand the TC out here?"

Donal nodded. He'd done his homework. "You've got command of all ground forces in the Cluster, though the units out on the other thirty-some worlds are more like regional militias. A brigade-level Bolo unit, the 15th Gladius." The term "Dinochrome Brigade" was sometimes applied to all Bolos everywhere, which could get confusing. Generally, a *real* brigade numbered about twenty Bolos.

"The key idea there, Mr. Ragnor, is that *I* am in charge here. I will have my eye on you, Lieutenant, of that you may be assured. I will tolerate no trouble makers in my command. Possibly they didn't know how to handle insubordination back at Sector, but I promise you that I do! Do I make myself clear?"

"Perfectly clear. Sir."

"Very well." Taking a pen and a memo block, the general scribbled a note, tore it off, and handed it to Donal. "There's your temporary authorization. Check in with the BOQ . . . ah, you're *not* married, are you?"

"No sir." *Not any more. . . .*

"Then check in at the bachelor officers' quarters and get yourself settled in. After that, report to Colonel Wood. He'll get your permanent papers and security ID." Phalbin leaned back in his chair, giving Ragnor an appraising look. "How long have you been with Bolos?"

Was this a test? Phalbin would know that from Ragnor's service record. "Almost ten years, sir."

"You like 'em?"

Donal nodded slowly. "Yes, sir. I do." When Phalbin didn't say anything more, he went on, more confidently. "They're easier to get along with than most people I know."

"Bolos," Phalbin said, "are double-edged weapons. They can be as dangerous to the user as they are to the enemy."

"I don't think—"

"I know, I know," the general said, holding one hand up. "I've heard all of the arguments, Lieutenant. Bolos have enough safety cut-outs that there's supposed to be no way they could possibly turn on their owners. But I always say, the fancier the plumbing, the easier it is to stop up the works. Or Murphy's Law, if you prefer. If something can go wrong, it will . . . and at absolutely the worst possible time."

"Sir, there has never been a case of a Bolo turning against its own side. Never. Quite a apart from the programming safeguards, Bolos, the self-aware Marks, at any rate, are too loyal to their regiment, to their cause, to the humans working with them."

For the first time, Phalbin's face actually creased in a

smile. "You speak of these, these machines being *loyal*? Really, Lieutenant. You astonish me. Forward the Dinochrome Brigade! Perhaps we should simply dispense with the human factor entirely and turn the fighting of all wars over to our machines."

"I believe, sir, that that was precisely what the original AI designers must have had in mind when they developed the self-awareness circuits for the Mark XXs. Bolos are a lot better at fighting than people are."

"Which is why we must keep them on a short leash, metaphorically speaking, of course." He scowled then and seemed to be searching his meticulously ordered desktop for something more to do. "Harrrumph. I am not in the habit, however, of discussing strategy or policy with junior officers. You are dismissed, Lieutenant."

Donal snapped off a crisp salute. "Yes, *sir*." He wheeled in a sharp about-face and strode from the office.

It was night by the time Donal had checked in with the BOQ desk . . . or as close to night as it ever got on Muir. After arranging for the delivery of his luggage off the *Rim Argent*, he strode out onto the parade ground in front of the officers' quarters, staring up at the unfamiliar, glorious sky.

That sky over Muir's nightside hemisphere blazed with stars fairly jostling one another in a glowing mob of radiant embers, a dazzling, close-crowding swarm of stars that very nearly banished the night, sending rainbow-hued reflections dancing across the waters of Starbright Bay. Most shone in ruby or orange hues and provided light enough on a clear night to read by. The Strathan Cluster was ancient, a clotting of old Population II stars left over from the Galaxy's earliest beginnings, giving the swarm a distinctly orange cast. Repeated supernovae among those teeming ancients, however, and the passage of the cluster through the Galaxy's dusty plane with each orbit about the Galactic Core, had given birth to a scattering of younger Population I stars, suns with elements heavier than hydrogen and helium, and with heavy metals enough to spawn planets of their own.

Such was Muir, an earthlike world, fourth from the F9 star men had named McNair. Donal glanced at his fingerwatch; it was still the middle of the afternoon work period, whatever the sky might say. The planet's short, nineteen-hour day did not meld well with human habits, and so the working day was divided into six-hour watches that ignored the rising or setting of the local sun. With an hour and a half remaining in the afternoon watch, Colonel Wood should still be in his office.

The Bolo brigade had its own compound, tucked away in one corner of the sprawling Kinkaid Base complex. The sign above the main gate read 15TH GLADIUS; the motto, inscribed beneath, read, in illiterate Latin, *IN COGITUM VICTOR*. An unemptied garbage can with a missing lid rested against the fence nearby.

He showed his pass to the sentry at the gate, noting the man's scuffed boots, wrinkled uniform, and general I-don't-give-a-damn air. A second sentry was visible through the window of the guard hut, his feet up on the desk as he lovingly studied a nudie magazine.

"You with the Fifteenth, son?" he asked after the sentry gave Phalbin's scrawl a cursory glance and started to wave him through.

"Yeah," the man said. As Donal held him pinned with a hard, cold stare, he slowly seemed to become aware that something was wrong, then did a double-take on the insignia on Donal's collar. "Uh, I mean, yessir."

"Do you know who I am, soldier?"

"Uh, nossir."

"And yet you were about to let me just waltz into a restricted area."

"Uh, I mean, that is, uh—"

"Save it." Donal considered the unhappy man, who

was now standing approximately at attention, beads of sweat chasing one another down the side of his face. He was tempted to call the corporal of the guard, even put the man under arrest . . . but it seemed pretty clear that morale in the 15th was shot.

And he didn't want to take out his feelings in the aftermath of his interview with Phalbin on the first unsuspecting private he happened to meet.

"For your information, son," Donal told the sentry, "I am Lieutenant Ragnor, the new Bolo tactical officer. I could have you put under arrest for dereliction of duty, but I'll tell you what I'm going to do instead. You tell your friend in there to get rid of the contraband, and then the two of you man your post like your lives depended on it . . . because they do. You hear me?"

"Yessir!"

"I'll be making inspection rounds later, and I'd better find you both on the ball!"

"Yessir! Thank you, sir!"

"Carry on!"

As he strode away, though, he thought wryly that the kid still hadn't properly checked his ID. And when he was almost out of earshot, he distinctly heard one of the sentries tell the other, "Sheesh! *He's* not gonna last long!"

I've got news for you, son, he thought. *I'm going to be here four more bloody long years.*

CHAPTER TWO

I dislike this feeling of vulnerability. My maintenance crew have removed both port-side tracks in order to carry out a routine check of the hydraulic suspension system and at the same time have manually deactivated all weapons systems, both primary and secondary. Worse, they are carrying out similar repairs on my brother unit, Bolo 96875, an oversight that in my opinion has seriously compromised our effectiveness, carrying out this partial shutdown despite the clear directives laid out in the Bolo General Maintenance Instructions requiring a methodical and step-by-step approach to active Bolo repair protocols. Such an approach is designed to provide an element of redundancy and backup in case of a sudden change in the current tactical situation. If the situation required rapid movement or response of any kind from either my brother or me, we would be unable to comply with orders.

I devote .073 seconds to a review of the current tacsit, scanning all available base files, systems checks, and communications traffic for the past twelve-hour period. The situation remains unchanged, with the alert status set at Code Five [Green] and all traffic flagged as completely routine. Still, the intelligence gleaned from the comm reports relayed from Wide Sky, Endatheline, and Starhold three standard days ago is disquieting. Surely any suggestions of unidentified spacecraft in orbit, of civilian reports of unusual surface activity, of civil and military intercepts of unknown coded radio transmissions, should be aggressively investigated.

However, the local military hierarchy have not been particularly diligent in keeping me or my brother unit supplied with timely intelligence. In fact, all we have had to rely on for the past twenty-seven standard years has been the daily departmental intelligence briefing, uploaded each day to all commands and departments by a purely automatic server. It is entirely possible that the disturbing reports of activity by an as yet unknown and potentially hostile intruder within the boundaries of Confederation space have been investigated and cleared, but that the relevant data has not been uploaded into my files. This would be consistent with the lamentable lack of interest Muir Military HQ has shown in the Bolo facilities throughout our deployment in the Strathan Cluster.

I receive an incoming comlink query on the private channel. Bolo 96875 wants to talk.

"Unit 96875 to Unit 96876," he says. "We have a visitor. Coming in the front gate."

The base security cameras are easily accessed through the computer network, which we penetrated some time ago. Through Camera 27, mounted inside the guard shack, I can now see the two sentries currently on duty, discussing a third man walking away from them. "Sheesh," one of them says to the other, shaking his head. "He's not gonna last long!"

The object of their discussion is a man wearing the uniform of a Concordiat lieutenant, walking away from the guard post and onto the Bolo facility. I compute a 79.22 percent likelihood that this is, at last, a new commander.

"That could be a new tactical officer," Bolo 96875 says, echoing my thoughts.

"Possibly," I reply. "However, there are two billets open for TOs at this facility."

"I am accessing the base personnel files."

Bolo 96875's electronics suite has been upgraded more recently than mine, and he is slightly faster than am I at penetrating secure communications lines. Within .054 seconds he has retrieved the files and is downloading them into temporary storage.

It takes .021 seconds to scan completely the data enclosed in the personnel records and military history files, confirming that Lieutenant Donal Ragnor has, indeed, been transferred to this command as a Bolo Tactical Officer. I feel considerable curiosity as to which of us he has been assigned to.

In the guard shack, one of the men assigned to sentry duty returns to his desk, picking up the magazine he has been reading. The interest male humans have for images of unclad female humans, both in flat photo and holo, never ceases to amaze me. Most humans, I have learned, do not take the business of war seriously at all.

I wonder what kind of a commander this Lieutenant Ragnor will be.

Lieutenant Colonel Victor Wood was a small, fussy-looking man with a neatly trimmed mustache and light brown hair turning silver above the ears. His office was considerably smaller than Phalbin's, lacked the trophy wall, and possessed a much smaller window—a wallvid, this time, with a static view overlooking Kinkaid.

As Donal walked into the office, ushered through the door by a dour-faced secretary, the colonel was speaking into a small, hand-held computer transcriber, watching his words flick across the screen on his desk.

". . . in view of this, it is the recommendation of this office that alternate sources of the necessary supplies be found outside of official channels, unless such purchases are expressly prohibited by civil or military law." He clicked off the mike and looked up.

Donal came to attention and rendered a salute. "Lieutenant Donal Ragnor, reporting for duty, sir. My record files have already been uploaded to Brigade HQ."

The colonel gave him a once over, then nodded. "Welcome to the end of the Galaxy, Lieutenant," he said. "I won't bother to tell you which end I mean, since I'm sure you've figured that out for yourself."

"Thank you, sir." He wasn't entirely certain how to answer; the colonel's words, while friendly enough, carried a sharp and bitter edge, warning Donal that he was on somewhat shaky ground. Wood's face was flushed, his voice very lightly slurred. Donal wondered, with some alarm, whether the man had been drinking.

"So, tell me," Wood said. "What brings you to this dizzying nadir of your military career?"

"I . . . I don't consider it to be such, sir."

"Mmm. Or, as our illustrious and beloved commanding general might put it, 'harrumph.' It seems to me I read something about a court martial. . . ."

Donal sighed. "Yes, sir. I . . . let's just say I didn't get on well with my former CO. But I assure you that I—"

Wood held up one bony hand, shaking his head. "Leave it, son. Leave it. I'm not really interested in what happened. You're here, and we'll both have to make the best of it, eh?"

Turning in his chair, he made a keyboard entry on his desk computer, then studied the information that came up an instant later. Donal couldn't see the screen from where he was standing, but he assumed that the colonel was accessing his service record.

"Mmm-mm. Thirty-six T-years old. Sixteen years with

the Concordiat Army. A little old for a lieutenant, aren't you?"

Donal wasn't sure how best to answer, so he remained silent. He'd been passed by for promotion more than once in the past sixteen years, as good an indicator as any that his future options within Concordiat service had been sharply limited, and growing more so. After the court martial, in fact, he'd been given a choice: resign his commission, or accept a reserve commission and temporary reassignment to the Strathan Confederation. Technically, the Confederation was independent, but the Concordiat still had a vested interest in the military forces and equipment now under Confederation control.

Especially the Bolos.

"Bolo officer," Wood said, still reading.

"Yes, sir."

"You like Bolos?"

"Yes, sir. I do."

"But you don't like ROEs."

Donal considered that question a moment. "There certainly is a need for Rules of Engagement, sir. I think, though, that operational guidelines *can* become a straitjacket. When that happens, the ROEs should be flexible. Not cast in durachrome-jacketed flintsteel."

Wood chuckled. "You'll find out about *that*. Just don't ever try to blame your own inadequacies and inefficiencies on the ROEs. Believe me, I've tried. The general won't stand for it."

ROEs—Rules of Engagement—were an ancient military concept, one designed to make certain that the politicians who ran things didn't find themselves in a shooting war by accident. Generally, they ran to ideas like not being allowed to fire unless you were fired on first, though they could get considerably more complex. Donal wondered what ROEs he'd be facing here.

"What units did you work with?" Wood asked him.

"Third Batt, Nineteenth Regiment. The Invincibles. Later I was transferred to the Fourth of the Sixty-third."

"What Marks?"

"Most of my service was with Bolo Mark XXVIIs and XXVIIIs. When I was with the Invincibles, of course, I was working with old Mark XXIIIs." He grinned and shook his head. "Strictly third-line stuff, of course. Three hundred years old, some of them were."

"Well, you'd best get used to that third-line stuff, Lieutenant, because we don't have anything so modern as a Mark XXVIII out here."

Bolos—those monster, land-traveling juggernauts descended from the primitive and strictly non-cybernetic tanks of thirteen centuries ago—were formidable fighting machines no matter what their Mark. A bullet, after all, was just as deadly to an unprotected man whether it was fired from a hyper-kinetic mag-pulse railgun or from a black-powder musket.

Still, Donal felt a renewed stab of disappointment. "Yes, sir. I'm aware that the 15th Gladius Brigade is made up of old Mark XVIIIs," he said.

The words came out tight and clipped. The Bolo Mark XVIII had been introduced in A.E. 727, almost six centuries ago. A good machine in its time, the Mark XVIII *Gladius* had been front-line equipment throughout the Concordiat for over a century after its introduction, a ten-thousand-ton general-purpose behemoth with a fusion-powered 60cm Hellbore as main armament. Mark XVIIIs had been the first of all Bolos actually able to engage warships in planetary orbit from the surface.

"Fourteen Mark XVIIIs, to be precise," Wood said with a curt nod. "Which is what remains of the original brigade that was shipped to the Strathan Cluster four hundred years ago. However, you won't be working with them."

"Oh?"

"All fourteen Mark XVIIIs are stationed off-planet,"

Wood said, "but there are two more on the roster. You're being brought in to serve as TO for our pair of Mark XXIVs."

Donal felt the tight knot in his gut relax slightly. For him, the thrill of working with Bolos lay in the very special relationship between a human tactical officer and those combat machines that possessed sentience, even a measure of self-awareness. The older Mark XVIIIs, though possessing voder circuits and able to communicate with their human operators, could not be considered intelligent, were no more self-aware than a typical high-speed computer . . . or a coffee-maker, for that matter. Not until the psychotronic breakthrough with the Mark XX in 851 or so were self-directing and self-aware Bolos possible; the Mark XXIV, which had appeared in 1016, had been the first truly autonomous and strategically self-directing Bolo and the first to evolve personalities that, on some level, could at last be considered "human."

"You have two XXIVs?" Donal asked.

"Yes. Both based here on Muir. The others are scattered all over the damned cluster." He didn't sound happy about that. Indeed, Lieutenant Colonel Wood did not sound happy about much of anything.

"An interesting brigade mix." Bolos were generally deployed in brigades of like-model machines . . . if only because a variety of Marks made for unpleasant logistical headaches.

"Not my idea, believe me. The Mark XXIVs were brought to Muir just before the Cluster gained autonomy from the Concordiat. That would have been . . . I guess about two hundred years ago, now. Of course, the Concordiat military forces are still concerned about where their babies have gone. That's probably why they insist on sending us transfer officers like you."

"There are still those who think self-aware Bolos are . . . a threat. Even to their owners."

"Aren't they?"

"It depends on who their owners are, I suppose. But Bolos are loyal."

"Hmm. Maybe. But I'm not entirely sure they understand the concept of politics. There are still wars between various human factions, from time to time, you know. Bolos have been used against humans, so we know their loyalty isn't to the human race."

"Their principal loyalty, Colonel, is always to their unit. And to their commander. It's the same way with most human soldiers I know."

"Maybe." Wood shrugged, apparently indifferent. "You might have an argument with the general on that."

"I, ah, gathered as much."

"In any case, we're down by two Bolo TOs for the Mark XXIVs. You'll be filling both billets."

Donal's eyebrows crawled up his forehead.

"I know, I know," Wood said. "But, well, you'll find priorities different out here from the Concordiat. The 15th is considered a support brigade, not line. General Phalbin is strictly a conventional forces man." He spread his hands, helplessly. "Look at me. A brigade command calls for a brigadier general, usually . . . or a full colonel at *least*. They gave the 15th to me because it really isn't that important a command. Get used to that fact, son. You'll find things pretty boring around here, and you won't have any more trouble bossing two Bolos than you would with one."

"I'm . . . surprised at that. Sir."

Wood shrugged. "General Phalbin admits that Bolos might have a certain defensive value, certainly."

"Good lord. Is that why the Mark XVIIIs were deployed on different planets, scattered throughout the cluster?"

"That's about the size of it, son. Look here." He touched a control on his desk, and the wallvid to his right faded out, the city view of Kinkaid replaced by a knotted tangle of tightly packed points of colored light. "You've seen a map of our cluster?"

"Yes, sir. Back at Sector, when I first got my orders."

The Strathan Cluster was a midget as globular clusters went, with several thousand stars packed into a ragged sphere less than fifty light years across. Like others of its ilk, it orbited the galactic core; in this epoch, it chanced to be passing through the plane of the Galaxy and lay embedded deep within the nebulae and younger stars of the trailing edge of the Eastern Arm.

The image in the wallvid was computer-generated, the close-packed, old, and metal-poor Population II stars plotted in red, the younger and more widely scattered Population Is in yellow and green. Some of the systems, the green ones, also bore identifying tags of alphanumerics. The whole rotated slowly, showing the three-dimensional relationships between the populated systems scattered about and among the beehive of thronging, cluster stars.

"The members of the Strathan Confederation are in green," Wood said. He touched a control on his desk, and one of the green stars momentarily pulsed brighter. "That one's McNair . . . and Muir, of course. McNair IV. Hanging on the ragged edge of damn-all, with nothing beyond but empty."

Donal pursed his lips but said nothing. Muir had been first of the Strathan Cluster's worlds to be colonized by humans, during the last great wave of colonial expansion along the outlying fringes of the Eastern Arm centuries before. Beyond the cluster, the Arm dwindled away into emptiness. Muir's sky might blaze with crowded suns; but beyond the cluster's ragged boundaries, looking outward from the Arm into the intergalactic night, lay parsec upon empty megaparsec of void, where suns were hauntingly few and far between.

He wondered if the cluster's location at the end of the Eastern Arm preyed on men's minds here. Phalbin had sounded preoccupied by the emptiness beyond the close, familiar spacelanes of the civilized Galaxy. Wood seemed almost morbidly so.

"Muir is, technically, at any rate, the capital of the entire Confederation, thirty-six inhabited suns scattered through a volume of some one hundred twenty thousand cubic light years. Communications and travel between those suns, though, can be a mite difficult." White lines appeared throughout the map, a webwork connecting the green points. "Navigation gets tricky in that star jungle. We depend on automated interstellar beacons. When we lose one of those, we can lose contact with some of the other confederacy worlds for months, even years at a time.

"Our strategic difficulty, of course, is maintaining any kind of coherent political order over the thirty-six inhabited systems that make up the Strathan Confederation. The Confederation Armed Forces are responsible both for protecting us from hostile forces and for keeping the peace on all thirty-six worlds, but it's obviously a lot easier to rush troops to a trouble spot than a Bolo or three. The Mark XVIIIs were split among the most important worlds a long time ago, and no one's ever bothered moving them."

"Oh, great," Donal said under his breath. A scattered brigade, and uncertain communications. That was just *wonderful*. . . .

"We could do more, of course, with more help from the Concordiat," Wood continued, with a sour look that suggested he took Donal's presence on Muir as far too little, too late. "But I gather that the Concordiat is having troubles of its own. We'll get no help from *that* quarter."

There could be no answer to that statement. Since the Terran Concordiat had first encountered the out-reaching probes of the Melconian Empire several years ago, relations had been steadily deteriorating. War was coming to the Concordiat, a paroxysm that some were already referring to somewhat apocalytically as "the Last War." The Concordiat's full attention was fixed, not on the Galaxy's remote outer rim, but inward, toward the teeming suns of the galactic core, and the Melconian threat.

"Have you heard anything about the rumors, sir?" he asked, probing. "About a new and hostile race from outside?"

"Shoot, Lieutenant. Hang out at the bars in the Kinkaid Strip long enough and you'll hear every wild kind of story there is." The slur that Donal had noted earlier was growing more pronounced now, and the colonel seemed to be having some trouble focusing on his visitor. "I've heard all kinds of rumors. You can pretty much take your pick."

"General Phalbin thought the whole idea could be discounted. He thinks there's no place out in the Gulf where hostiles could come from."

"There isn't."

"Sir, you must know as well as I do that the space between galaxies isn't completely empty. There are planet-bearing suns in the halo. There *must* be. They're just scattered too thinly to be worth our sending a survey to check them out."

"Sure. But they're *so* thinly scattered that it'd be impossible for any race that'd evolved intelligence out there to be able to develop FTL. If the next nearest star's a thousand light years off, you're not gonna be anxious to go calling on your neighbors. You'll stay at home and contemplate your navel instead." He shrugged heavily. "Besides, most stars out there are poor in heavy elements. Not that many solid planets to begin with, y'know? And even terrestrial planets out there are probably pretty poor in easily extracted iron or copper or any of the other metals you need to develop a technic civilization. So any intelligent species out there is gonna be stuck in the Stone Age, right?"

Donal didn't argue the point, but he was far from convinced. He'd learned long ago that it was risky trying to rationalize the psychologies—or the likely attitudes and actions—of non-humans. If nothing else, they didn't think like humans, which made them unpredictable.

"In any case," Colonel Wood concluded with another shrug, "it's not up to us to worry about it, right? We sit here, we follow orders, and we wait for our twenty years to be up so we can get the hell out of this stinkin' outfit and back to a civilian job that makes some kind of sense."

The colonel swung his chair away, appearing to lose himself in a glum and somewhat bleary contemplation of the slow-rotating map of the cluster still displayed on his wallvid. The interview clearly at an end, Donal turned to leave.

As he touched the door switch, however, he glanced back once more in time to see Wood pulling a bottle out of one of his desk drawers, unscrewing the lid, and knocking back a hefty chug of the dark amber liquid inside.

It was, Donal thought, a less than auspicious start to his new posting.

CHAPTER THREE

The maintenance team tasked with completing the checks on my port-side suspension have evidently decided to take an extended break. Six of them are seated in a circle beneath the overhang by my aft port-side drive wheel and are engaged in a strangely ritualized series of social behaviors centered on the element of chance as applied to fifty-two small cardboard rectangles printed with various numerals, symbols, and icons. The rest are standing around the six, watching and exchanging pointed comments among themselves.

Bolo 96875 has explained at length to me the nature of "games," as enjoyed by humans, but I confess that I do not as yet understand the interest humans have in the subject. The concept is similar in some respects to various simulations—"war games," in fact—designed to test battle plans, tactics, and strategies on various levels. Indeed, the ancient human game "chess" is a useful tool in sharpening strategic understanding, and I have enjoyed playing it with several humans and with Unit 96875 in the past. What this wild shuffling and collecting of pasteboard cards can have to do with combat tactics or strategy, however, I have not yet discerned, despite many seconds of thought dedicated to the problem.

In any case, the game carried out beside my stripped-down wheel train seems to have been enjoined purely for the recreational diversion of Tech Master Sergeant Blandings and his men, not in preparation for any military endeavor. I cannot ignore the fact, however, that the completion of my repairs and my return to full combat capability must have an extremely low priority among the humans charged with maintaining my efficiency at peak levels. This affects me in a manner that humans might think of as emotional, though it does not and cannot reduce my efficiency as would almost certainly be the case with humans.

I wonder why they bother to maintain me at full awareness levels. Sometimes, I believe that the fact that I have not been set to autonomous standby reserve power levels has left me with too much time to think. . . .

A door at the end of the vehicle bay opens; through Security Camera 16, I can see that it is Lieutenant Ragnor, arrived, no doubt, to inspect his new command.

I doubt very much that he will be pleased with what he finds here.

Donal was not at all pleased with what he found inside the vast and cavernous vault of the Bolo Depot Vehicle Bay. There were no guards posted by the door through which he entered, and no Bolo security check point, though a small security camera mounted on an arm extended from the ceiling swiveled to track him as he walked across the ferrocrete floor toward the nearer of the behemoth war machines parked inside. At least someone was aware he'd just entered what ought to be the most secure installation on this entire base. Trash was littered about the floor, including crumpled beverage cans and wads of paper, discarded rags and shavings from a metal lathe, bits of candy bar wrapper and a jumble of discarded computer printout.

He saw a small group of people far off across the floor, huddled in the shadow of the near Bolo. Disgusted, he strode toward them.

The Bolo dominated the huge room, filled it like some immense idol of cast iron and chromalloy in a cavern shrine. A second Bolo rested close by, mostly obscured by the first, but Donal's eyes were held captive by the closer machine as the humans gathered in its lee threw its size and bulk into sharp perspective.

It was enormous, a building . . . no, a small, wheeled *mountain* of metal eighty meters long and towering a full twenty meters above the floor. Mark XXIII Bolos possessed two main armament turrets, fore and aft; the Mark XXIVs had been pegged back to a single MA turret, but that one low, flatly angled structure mounted a 90cm "super" Hellbore, a two-megaton-per-second beam weapon easily the equal of anything carried by the Space Arm's largest and most powerfully equipped dreadnoughts. Despite the modifications in hull and armament, the Mark XXIV was only a thousand tons lighter than its evolutionary predecessor; each of the Bolos in the depot's main vehicle chamber massed a full fourteen thousand metric tons.

Only as he drew closer did smaller details separate themselves from the larger bulk of armor. Staggered, bulbous swellings in the hull both above and below the side overhangs housed batteries of antipersonnel weapons. Nine secondary turrets, each sporting the stubby snout of an ion-bolt infinite repeater, were arrayed along each flank like the broadside turrets of a battleship. Hexagonal blocks of antiplasma reactive armor appliqués were everywhere, scattered around sensor ports, antenna arrays, field coils for disrupter shielding and battle screens, and secondary flintsteel armor block. The entire machine had been painted in subdued patterns of splotchy green and brown, a somewhat traditional and no doubt unsuccessful attempt to provide a measure of camouflage for a vehicle that was far too large to hide anywhere, even in the thickest forest. Skirts and tracks had been removed from both the fore and aft wheel train assemblies. The entire unit had been lifted just clear of the floor on massive hydraulic jacks rising out of the floor; each of the interleaved wheels in the Christie-mount chassis was over five meters tall, a vertical cliff of smooth metal very nearly three times the height of a man.

Work lights had been strung from the left hull overhang, illuminating a group of soldiers and technicians who seemed totally absorbed in a six-handed poker game.

"Call," one of the men challenged.

"Ah!" another, with the insignia of a tech master sergeant on his sleeve, said with mock disgust. "All I got is two pair."

"Read 'em an' weep, boys!" the first man said, laying out his cards. "Full house!"

"Beats me," another player said, slapping her cards down.

"Me too."

"Shoot. Busts mine."

"Y'got me."

"Ha! Love it!" The man with the full house began raking piles of Confederation scrip toward his side of the circle. "Come t' poppa, baby!"

"Hold it right there, Willard," the master sergeant said, grinning evilly. "I said I got two pair."

"Hell, Sarge," Willard replied, looking up. "A full house beats a crummy two pair any day of the week!"

"Not when what I got is one pair of jacks, along with *another* pair of jacks!"

Willard groaned and relinquished the pile. The sergeant cackled wickedly as he began scooping up his winnings.

"I do hope I'm not disturbing anything important," Donal said casually, walking closer to the edge of the light.

"Who the hell are—" Willard started to say, but then his eyes fastened on the rank insignia on Donal's collar and widened. "Comp'ny!" he snapped. "Atten-*hut!*"

The group scrambled to attention, some remaining on the floor just long enough to scoop up fistfuls of Confederation cash before making it to their feet. A sudden hush descended over the vehicle bay, heightened by the soft rasp of breathing men. Donal stepped into the light; the men, though standing at attention, were facing in several directions, rigid, eyes fixed ahead, as though terrified of betraying the slightest movement.

"I am Lieutenant Donal Ragnor," he said quietly, looking from face to face, reading the emotions he saw there—fear, surprise . . . and a lot of resentment.

The group numbered sixteen—eleven men, five women— some in greasy dungarees, some in military-issue shorts and T-shirts, three of them in civilian clothing. As he noted facial expressions, he noted, too, details of hair too long, of jewelry, of personal adornment. Willard, he saw, wore a neck chain with a large ankh hanging from it outside his partly unbuttoned dungaree shirt. One of the women wore a faded olive-drab T-shirt with a collar so torn and stretched out it exposed rather more of her substantial upper chest than was strictly permitted by military regs. One of the men wore dangling earrings in the fashion currently popular with the Kinkaid party-hard set.

"I have been assigned as Tactical Officer to this pair of Mark XXIVs," he continued after a moment. "I gather this is my maintenance company."

"Fifteenth Gladius Bolo Maintenance and Transport Company, Muir Detachment, Tech Master Sergeant Blandings reporting," the sergeant said. "*Sir!*"

"Is this everyone?"

"We have four on the sick list," Blandings rasped out, "seven more back in the barracks or somewhere, and, uh, three who, uh, well, I guess they're AWOL. Sir."

"You *guess* you have three men absent without leave?"

"Three men have not reported for duty since last week," he said stiffly. "Sir."

"Mmm. How about the rest of you. Is *anyone* doing any work around here?"

"Sir, this is our down period. Recreational, you know?"

Donal nodded, as though considering this. With one toe, he nudged one of the piles of cards scattered on the floor, sliding a queen off of the three of hearts. "I wouldn't want to think," he said quietly, "that any of you men were actually *gambling*. As I understand it, that's strictly contra-regs. Am I right?"

There was no immediate reply, though several sets of eyes exchanged worried glances. Donal stepped in front of Sergeant Blandings, staring for a moment into a seamed and experienced face. He looked down at Blandings' hands, both of which were clenched into white-knuckled fists clutching bundles of money. Slowly, he removed his service hat and held it out. "In here."

"Sir—"

"In here!"

Reluctantly, Blandings dropped both fistfuls of bills into the hat. Turning, in place, Donal extended the hat to each of the other men holding the games' stakes. "You know," he said thoughtfully, "if I don't see you with any money in your hands, I can't bring charges against you for gambling. Right?"

One by one, the men dropped handfuls of bills into the hat, until it was nearly overflowing. "This," Donal said when the last man had made his contribution, "will make for a nice enlisted men's fund, don't you think?"

"It was just a friendly little game, sir," Blandings said, resentment in his voice.

"Uh-huh." Donal glanced up at the huge, trackless road wheels rising at his side. "What's the word on this Unit? Why is it down by two tracks?"

"Suspension train maintenance, sir. Routine."

"But why *two* tracks? The drill is to pull 'em one at a time."

"Shoot, sir," Blandings said. "It's more efficient this way, y'know? We do one whole side, then we do the other. Get the job done in half the time."

"Mmm. And how long has this Bolo been up on the jacks?" Blandings started to reply, and Donal spoke again, cutting him off. "I *will* be checking your maintenance logs, Sergeant, so give it to me straight."

"Uh . . . about seven or eight days, sir."

"For a job that normally logs thirty hours. Doesn't sound like half the time to me."

"Well, it's not like there's a rush on, is it?" one of the men, a skinny kid who must still have been in his teens, piped up. "I mean, what's the hurry, huh?"

Donal whirled on the kid, eyes blazing. "The hurry, son, is in whether or not we're gonna be ready if hostiles decide to jump us! What's your name?"

"Uh . . . Kemperer, sir. Private First Len Kemperer."

"Well, Private Kemperer, let me tell you something. Right now, this machine wouldn't be able to defend us from an army of little old ladies armed with tea pots and galoshes, much less a *real* threat."

"Is there a threat?" the one they'd called Willard wanted to know. His eyes were wide. "I mean, sir, we haven't heard any—"

"I suppose hostiles in this part of the Galaxy always warn you before they hit you, huh?"

"Take it easy, Lieutenant," Sergeant Blandings said. Donal recognized the tone, that of a mother whose kids are being scolded by a stranger. These *were* Blandings' people, after all, and he would resent an outsider dressing them down or bringing them grief. "This isn't the Concordiat, y'know."

Donal studied the sergeant for a moment. "No, Master

Sergeant. It isn't. And I suppose you resent Concordiat officers being dropped on you like unpleasant surprise packages. But when it comes to Bolos, especially the higher Marks, like this one, Concordiat Bolo Command likes to make sure their property is being taken care of. Your Bolos are a *loan*, Master Sergeant. A very long-term loan, perhaps, with no payback . . . but those Bolos are still on the Concordiat military's records, and Bolo Command still feels a certain responsibility for them. That's why they insist that tactical officers like me are assigned to keep an eye on them. You have no idea how dangerous this machine could be if it is not properly maintained and serviced."

"Shoot, sir," a short, skinny corporal with greasy black hair said. "Ol' Freddy here won't hurt us. We're buddies!"

Donal stared the man down. "You don't really know what you're playing with, do you?" He jerked a thumb at the massive bogie wheel behind him. "With two megatons-per-second firepower, one of these Mark XXIV units could level Kinkaid in the blink of an eye, without even working up a sweat. If that AP cluster mounted up there above your head was armed, and if the unit security programming got it into its one-track mind that you were hostile, there wouldn't be enough of your miserable carcass left to scrape off the floor with a spatula. Bolos work superbly when they're properly cared for. Looking at this one . . . and at the condition of this vehicle depot, I seriously doubt that it has been cared for properly. If its psychotronic functions have become unstable, it could be deadly."

"Ah, all the self-protect hardware was disabled, Lieutenant," Willard said. "It would have t' be, y'know? If we wanted to even get close to this monster."

"I see. And what does the Bolo have to say about it?"

"It's a *machine*, Lieutenant," Sergeant Blandings said, shaking his head. "It's not like ol' Freddy's alive, y'know?"

"How long have you worked with . . . 'Freddy'?"

"Long enough," Blandings replied. He eyed Donal appraisingly. "Look, Lieutenant. You're ticked, I know, about how we're kind of laid back, here. But this ain't the Concordiat. Things are different out here, less hectic, y'know? Things'll go a lot smoother if you kind a', well, hang back and get a feel for the big picture."

"Don't make waves, is that it?"

"Sure. That's it, Lieutenant. Don't make waves!"

"From what I've seen here, Master Sergeant, we *need* a fair-sized tidal wave to sweep this pigsty clean. I'll tell you what I'm going to do. Since my arrival was such a surprise, and because neither of us wants to get off on the wrong foot with the other, I'm going to take your advice and hang back."

He could feel the ease in the tension, see eyes exchanging sly winks, mouths quirking in tiny, secret grins.

"I'm going to hang back," he continued, "until First Hour, First Watch tomorrow. At that time, I'll come back, *officially*. At that time I will expect to see this vehicle bay looking like a military facility and not like a Kinkaid back alley." He glanced up at the massive wheels at his side. "You will also have the port-forward track remounted on this machine."

There was a sudden outburst from the others, groans, complaints, and protestations.

One of the women looked especially angry. "Hey! What gives you the right to come in here and—"

Donal pulled out a small, flat, gray case, the transport container for a crystal memory pack . . . a set of programs and memory feed instructions for a Mark XXIV Bolo. "This gives me the right. I'm the new Tactical Officer for both of these machines, and that means you will care for them according to *my* specifications and directives. Do I make myself clear?"

More protests sounded. "Sir," Blandings said, shouting

to be heard above the noise. "Uh . . . maybe you don't know how our schedules work on Muir, yet, you bein' new to the planet, and all." He glanced at the chrono set in a ring on his forefinger. "We're just wrapping up the afternoon watch now. Then it's a sleep period. First Watch starts in just six more hours. My people couldn't possibly—"

"I *know* how your watches work on Muir, Master Sergeant," Donal said coldly. "Six hours is exactly right."

"But we can't clean this whole bay in six hours and remount a track too! And we need to sleep, and get somethin' t' eat, and mebee have some private down-time, and—"

"Obviously, Master Sergeant, you will need to decide which of those activities you've just listed for me are expendable, and drop them from your schedule in order to get the job done. What is *not* expendable is having this facility look like a military installation instead of a combat zone . . . nor do I want my Bolos sitting around helpless on their bare road wheels in case of an enemy surprise attack. Those two are your priorities for the next six hours. Do you read me?"

Blandings' jaw worked for a moment, before he managed a harsh, "Yes, sir."

"I will expect you all to be presentable, in the proper uniform of the day." He looked at the woman in the ill-fitting T-shirt. "That's in the proper and properly worn uniform, incidentally. Jewelry will be regulation. We'll worry about details like haircuts and such later, after we've sorted out the more important stuff." He nodded toward the Bolo. "If any of you have any questions, I'll be in there."

"Sir . . . in the Bolo?"

"Evidently, Master Sergeant, I have some work to do before I *officially* arrive as well. If you need me in any unofficial capacity, you know where to find me.

Otherwise . . ." He let his face slip into a grin at least as fiendish as the one displayed by Blandings earlier. "I'll see you all at Hour One!"

Without another word, he turned and strode toward the front of the Bolo.

CHAPTER FOUR

I have, of course, been listening to the conversation taking place beneath my left side, and I find myself somewhat at a loss as to how to interpret it. This new arrival, Lieutenant Ragnor, certainly has a military bearing and tone of voice that speak well of his leadership abilities.

Even so, haircuts and proper uniforms have nothing to do with a unit's ability to perform well in combat. My military reference library has 724 distinct references to different units throughout recorded history that, while both professional—as opposed to guerrilla units or rebels—and elite in terms both of their effectiveness as soldiers and of their morale, did not bother with formal uniform codes and regulations or, indeed, gloried in an absence of such regulations. Rogers's Rangers, Merrill's Marauders, the United States Navy SEAL Teams, and the Terran Cobra Units are four obvious and well-known cases in point. It is possible that Lieutenant Ragnor is simply what they call a stickler for regulations, a by-the-book officer who will enforce a narrow interpretation of the regulations without markedly reducing the very serious defects in morale, in priorities, and in matériel extant at this facility.

39

I am also concerned because of the apparent disregard for security exhibited by the personnel charged with my maintenance. This newcomer could easily be an enemy agent, and he should have been challenged at the depot's entrance. As it is, I will have to challenge him inside my fighting compartment, which leaves me vulnerable. Nor is this a good way to meet the man who may well be my new commander.

Still, I have very little latitude now in the courses of action open to me. I await developments.

Donal walked around to the front of the Bolo, glancing up at the massive armored cliff of the glacis rising fifteen meters above his head, then stooping to make his way beneath the slanting overhang of the huge machine's prow. The belly hatch had been left standing open—another violation of any strict interpretation of the Bolo maintenance field manual directives—and the crew access ladder lowered. Light spilled from the open hatchway, illuminating a rectangular patch beneath the vast machine's ventral plate. Several smaller access plates had been removed between the massive, erect cylinders of the depot's hydraulic jacks, and the wiring and mechanical workings of the Bolo's left-side suspension system were exposed. Tools were scattered on the floor, along with bolts, fasteners, and spare parts, and he had to watch where he stepped. Crouching low—the Bolo cleared the ground by only a meter and a half—he made his way to the ladder and scrambled up into the fighting compartment.

The command deck fighting compartment was an evolutionary holdover from the distant past, like a human's vermiform appendix. Once, a thousand years before, *men* had ridden these machines into battle, serving their guns and manning their steering controls. Long after Bolos had become totally autonomous, with no need for human supervision at any level, the big machines retained these vestiges of organic control. A massive, thickly padded shock-mounted seat filled much of the chamber, which was made hazardous by wiring clusters and feedlines, conduits and piping snaking everywhere across the uncomfortably low ceiling. There were no windows or vision ports, of course, this deep within the Bolo's inner workings. Instead, a toroidal vid display, now blank, circled the chair completely, providing all-round vision for the chamber's occupant. Several small computer displays were positioned at different points around the seat, but there were no visible controls. Bolos were generally given their orders by voice command.

"Warning," a voice said from an unseen overhead speaker. It was a neutral voice in the tenor range, lacking any expression or emotion that Donal could detect. "Access to this Unit is restricted. Please identify yourself."

A red light gleamed from a dilated aperture in a small box high up in one corner of the compartment, painting a ruby-red spot squarely in the center of his forehead, and Donal was uncomfortably aware that the snub-snout of a high-power antipersonnel laser was trained directly at the aim point.

"Lieutenant Donal Ragnor," he replied slowly, making each word carefully distinct. He'd not been exaggerating with the corporal outside; a neglected Bolo could be dangerous if the programming—*especially* the programming dealing with self-defense and threat assessment—had become corrupted. That sort of thing didn't happen often unless the Bolo's higher psychotronic centers had been exposed to more ionizing radiation than was healthy for them, and he doubted that there was in fact a problem. Still, it didn't hurt to be damned careful in how he answered. "Bolo Command, Concordiat Army Reserve, on temporary assignment to Bolo Command, Strathan Confederation Military Command. Service number 2524-265-17821."

"Please face the computer display for laser and retinal scan verification."

A white dot winked slowly in the center of the computer terminal. Leaning forward, he stared at the dot, holding his face motionless and expressionless. There was a green flash, and a gridwork of lines glowed against his face, recording each crease, each angle, each plane of his somewhat craggy face. A computer-painted image of his face appeared on a second screen to his right, rotating to show his head from every angle, revealing dark brown hair, squared-off jaw, gray eyes, somewhat disapproving quirk to the corners of the mouth. As he continued to stare at the blinking dot, a green light flashed from a small retinal scan unit mounted on top of the display terminal, dazzling him, leaving him blinking for a few seconds against the drifting purple blurs obscuring his vision. Another screen lit up, showing the twisting, interlacing red streams and tributaries of the blood vessels at the back of his eye. The Bolo, he knew, would be comparing both his facial features and his retinal prints with the records he'd uploaded to headquarters that afternoon.

"Identity confirmed," the voice said, as comparison points flickered rapid-fire across the retinal scan image, and the word MATCH flashed on. "Good afternoon, Lieutenant Ragnor. Bolo Unit of the Line 96876 FRD awaiting orders."

"Good afternoon, Bolo Unit," Donal said. He was relieved to note that the laser's aiming light had winked out and the weapon's muzzle had retracted and the aperture closed. Slowly, he pulled the computer memory transport case from his uniform pocket. "I have complete files on myself, a copy of my orders, and an intelligence update for the entire Eastern Arm here."

"Thank you, Lieutenant. We have already taken the liberty of downloading your files and orders from the base communications net, but an intelligence update would be most welcome. Our only source of outside information, including data with a bearing on the local strategic situation, is the daily intelligence briefings that are both simplistic and incomplete."

"I . . . see." The Bolos had been eavesdropping on electronic communications? Was that part of their built-in need for as full an intelligence picture as possible? Or had someone ordered them to do that?

Opening the case, he extracted the program pack, walked over to a drive slot, and slipped it in. With a faint whir, the Bolo digested the encrypted data stored within the pack, patterns of spin and polarization in the crystalline lattice of its atomic structure that could carry one hundred terabytes of data. The news Donal had brought from Sector HQ, however, was much less, a few thousand bytes at most.

The Bolo paused for several seconds, as though digesting the data. Donal pursed his lips, recognizing one of the games routinely played by high-Mark Bolos in their relationships with humans. A Bolo could download megabytes of data, assimilate it, and draw conclusions from it in something like a few hundredths of a second. Most humans, though, with their ponderously slow organic brains based on electrochemical exchanges of ions, found it disconcerting to have a machine that replied to a question immediately, without apparent thought. They'd been programmed to hesitate at appropriate points in a conversation simply to comfort their human associates. Sometimes he wondered what Bolos thought about working with humans, when humans thought and acted so much more slowly than they did. For a Bolo, speaking with a human must be somewhat akin to a man speaking with an exceptionally slow-witted boy, one who took several hours simply to respond to a question like "How are you?"

"I note," the Bolo's voice said after the deliberate pause,

"that there have been several reports of potentially hostile activity in this sector, as well as twelve anomalous events that could be attributed to hostile activity, all within the boundaries of the Strathan Cluster."

"That's right."

"Have these reports been investigated?"

"The Confederation Military Command has . . . I think, satisfied itself that these reports are nothing more than statistical fluctuations or possible pirate activity."

"We would like to see the intelligence that allowed the CMC to draw this conclusion."

So would I, Donal thought wryly. *But I haven't seen that much intelligence here to begin with, military or otherwise.*

"I'm afraid I don't have access to that information," he told the Bolo. "We'll just have to trust our bosses and hope they know what they're doing."

"If we are to judge their efficiency by past experience," the Bolo said, "we cannot find your statement particularly reassuring."

Donal gave a low, slow exhalation of breath. If he hadn't known better, he would have attributed that last comment to an attempt at understated humor on the Bolo's part, something that, clearly, was flatly impossible. And its use of the word "we." That was an interesting datum as well, indicating that the two machines routinely exchanged information.

He dismissed the thought, however. There were more serious and immediate concerns. It was important that he find out if slipshod maintenance had affected this machine's operating systems at all.

"I'm curious," he said. "Why did you let me get all the way in here? I should have been challenged as soon as I entered the Bolo Vehicle Bay. Your security safeguards just now wouldn't have meant much if I'd been carrying a small fusion bomb in a bodypack."

"Normally, I would have challenged any unknown personnel entering this facility from a remote unit at the vehicle bay entrance," the voice said. Though still emotionless, it almost sounded hurt to Donal's ears, an electronic reluctance to accept the unfair aspects of an unjust universe. "However, that particular subroutine was disabled some time ago by the local Bolo command authority. Further, my antipersonnel clusters and both primary and secondary weapon fire control centers have been taken off line. This Unit is unable at present to move or engage in combat."

"I understand. Your maintenance crew is carrying out routine servicing."

"Affirmative."

"They should not have disabled both of your port-side tracks simultaneously."

"The procedure currently being employed is in violation of the directives specified in the *Bolo Depot Maintenance Manual*, FM-8327-B7." There was a heavy pause. "I am most concerned, however, with the fact that both Bolo Units are at less than full operational capacity at the same time. Would it be possible, Lieutenant, for you to correct this oversight?"

Slowly, Donal raised his head, staring with a growing, numb disbelief at the main computer display. Had the Bolo just taken the initiative in the conversation and asked him a *question*?

"*What* did you say?"

"I asked whether it would be possible to correct the oversight of the maintenance team. If hostile forces attacked at this time, I would be unable to respond effectively. My companion unit, Bolo Unit of the Line 96875, has been similarly immobilized, with primary and secondary weapons taken off line. If this facility were to be attacked, as the lieutenant himself pointed out a few minutes ago, we would be unable to offer a worthwhile defense. I heard you direct the maintenance team to replace one of my tracks, in accordance with standing maintenance directives. I further recommend that one of the two Units stationed here be returned immediately to full operational capability as a precautionary measure."

Donal was already typing out a string of commands on the keyboard, initiating a series of level-one diagnostics. The Mark XXIV, he knew, was the first Bolo capable of evolving a "human" personality . . . though just what that actually meant was something the AI experts and psychotronic technicians were still arguing about, even now. Many cyberneticists, even yet, preferred to believe that Bolo id integration circuits and personality centers mimicked self-awareness but did not in fact grant it.

The problem was that the Mark XXIV still had the built-in inhibitory safeguards designed to prevent the huge combat machine from going rogue, either due to battle damage, or because of so-called "psychotronic senility" due to poor or improper maintenance. It had a much greater degree of freedom outside of combat status than the older Mark XXIIIs, but it could not engage its full abilities—or achieve truly autonomous operation—outside of full Battle Reflex Mode. In a very real sense, the Mark XXIV in Standby Mode possessed only a fraction of the intelligence and virtually none of the autonomous decision-making capabilities that it could access in combat.

That this one had decided to ask a question, to lead the conversation, to actually attempt to manipulate its own environment, was nothing short of astounding.

Donal continued running the autodiagnostic series.

"I assure you, Commander," the machine voice said, "that with the exceptions already mentioned, I am in satisfactory operational condition. My power plant is on standby and I am running on base-supplied power, but I could go to full autonomous operational status within

10.54 seconds. My psychotronic circuitry and personality centers are functional within normal parameters."

Even as the Bolo said the words, the results were coming up on the display. There was nothing wrong with the machine that Donal—or the diagnostic programs—could see.

But the Bolo should not have asked that question. And something else. Though it could be programmed to use first-person singular, most Bolos of this Mark referred to themselves in the third person, as "this Unit." He'd heard this one call itself "I" several times, and he doubted that it had been programmed to do so by the maintenance team at this base.

More disturbing still was the fact that the Bolos had been intercepting communications feeds on the base. It was important now that he find out definitely, one way or the other, whether that eavesdropping was something that had been programmed into them, or something the Bolos had worked out for themselves.

What the hell was going on here?

"Lieutenant?"

"Yes?"

"You have not answered my question."

"Uh . . . sorry. You kind of caught me by surprise." He frowned, thinking fast. "They call you 'Freddy'?"

"Affirmative. It appears to be derived from the three-letter code used to designate Bolo hull style, power plant, and main armament, in my case, 'FRD.' "

"Right."

"My companion is known as 'Ferd' or 'Ferdy' for the same reason."

"I understand. Okay, Freddy, here's the way it stands. As you heard, I told them to remount one of your port-side tracks immediately. That'll give you some mobility, in a pinch."

In fact, a Bolo could operate without tracks—it could

even blow them entirely during an emergency in combat and run directly on the flintsteel road wheels, but traction was seriously reduced, as were speed and maneuverability.

"I agree," Donal continued, "that we ought to have only one of you down at a time, ideally, but it's going to take several days to get one of you entirely reassembled, right?"

"I would estimate sixty-one point five standard hours at a minimum, Commander."

"Right. If I ordered that on Ferdy, say, you would be left as you are. So, that's sixty-some hours before they can start work on you. Then, once they're done with you and have you back in one piece, they have to go back and take Ferdy apart, starting all over again.

"Now, believe me, I was tempted to order them to do just that, but I also have to take into consideration the morale of the maintenance crew. I have reason to think that morale is quite low in this unit. As the new supervising officer, I have to be careful. I don't mind coming on like a hard taskmaster, but I can't afford to make too many enemies or to look like a complete fool. It would be different, of course, if we were expecting imminent hostile action. But, frankly, they're right. There are no immediate threats to the Confederation's military security, nothing at all save some unsubstantiated rumors. We have time to go one step at a time, to get both of you Bolos back to full operational status, and to build up the morale of the maintenance company."

"I see, Commander. This is an aspect of working with humans that I had not previously considered."

"Now, you tell me something."

"If I can, Commander."

"You said you downloaded my files from base communications feeds."

"That is correct."

"Did someone tell you to do that?"

"Affirmative."

Donal began to relax, just a bit. If the Bolo had been under orders . . .

"Unit 96875 suggested that we do so," Freddy continued, "and showed me how to do this."

"Unit 96875 . . . showed you."

"Affirmative."

"Did a human originally tell either of you to do this? Or was it part of your original program package?"

"No, Commander. But it seemed like a good idea at the time."

That response rocked Donal back in his seat, not because of the humor, which would have been unintentional on the Bolo's part, but because of the implicit statement that Freddy and Ferdy were capable of independent and creative thought . . . that they could so much as have an idea of their own in the first place. Bolos did not have ideas, not when they were at anything less than full battle mode, and even then their ideas tended to be military ones, ideas drawn from historical records and carefully designed strategic and tactical algorithms on how best to overwhelm and overpower an opponent on the battlefield.

He was going to need to take his time in studying this. *And what if the damned things have gone unstable?* he thought. *If the inhibitions have started to erode, independent thought might be the first clue we have to the fact.*

And with Bolos, as with humans, when one set of inhibitions was gone, others were sure to follow. What, he wondered, would be next? The inhibitory software that impelled it to obey its commanding officer? The electronic inhibitions that told it that Kinkaid was a friendly city and not a military target?

His posting to Muir, he realized, had just taken on a new and somewhat frightening urgency.

CHAPTER FIVE

Kill and eat!

Schaagrasch the Blood Taster gripped the padding of her seat restraints, ruby eyes squeezed shut as the Hunterpod shrieked blood/kill defiance across a sky swiftly changing from black to burning pink. The pod was thrumming now with the vibration of atmospheric entry; glowing LED readouts in the near-darkness of the control center registered an external hull temperature of nearly three thousand *nachakt*, higher on the leading edges of the pod's sleek, aerodynamic surfaces.

This was always the hardest part, she thought, trying to stave off the growing panic in mind and hearts. Only the bravest and most dedicated of Malach hunter-killers could endure the claustrophobia of a combat pod descent, the terror of being trapped—*trapped*—inside a tiny egg of black metal and ceramics, hurtling out of the sky at twenty times the speed of sound. Deceleration thumped and clawed at her strapped-down body, accompanied by a feeling of suffocating heaviness that amplified the feelings of being shut in, of being buried alive. . . .

During training, back on golden, warm Zhanaach, she'd heard stories about Malach hunters who'd been driven insane during such enclosed, fiery descents. *Use the death panic,* her instructors had told her. *Concentrate on the fact that soon you will be free, and then let the madness consume you . . . and your foes!*

Reflexively, Schaagrasch flexed her slasher claws, feeling their silk-smooth glide across scaled flesh in hands and feet as they extended, retracted, then extended once more.

Use your fear. . . .

How? Fear was a black, gibbering madness looming at the back of her head. She longed to whirl and slash, but the straps held her tight. How much longer?

Altitude . . . almost 310 *tairucht*, with the atmosphere thickening outside.

She wished she could see, even if there was nothing to see, but the Hunter was completely encased in its heat shield, its external sensors shut down. She could imagine well enough what it must look like outside, though, with the black, stub-winged hull of the pod enveloped in pink-orange flame. The vibrations continued to build in intensity, the thrumming growing to a jackhammer pounding that sounded like it would shred the pod's paper-thin hull at any moment.

This was awful . . . *awful*, eight times worse than any training exercise she had ever endured. She could *feel* her sanity shredding away, like the ablative outer hull ceramics. In a moment, she would lose all control, and her berserker's rage would demolish the Hunter's control center and end her life.

Schaagrasch wondered how the rest of her Hunter Pack was faring. . . .

They were walking along the old stone mole above Galloway Harbor. Stars filled one half of the sky, the blaze of color that was Strathan Cluster; the emptiness of the Gulf filled the other. Alexie Turner still wore the formal gown and holo accessories demanded by the dinner she'd been attending, her blond hair piled high beneath a sparkling tiara projecting a cloud of stars above her head. Frank Kirkpatrick, smooth, oily, and slick, was handsome enough in a greasy way in his dinner jacket and formal kilt, but with a face reddened by anger and too much alcohol. They made an unlikely couple.

"But surely you see how important this project is to our people," Legislator Kirkpatrick told her.

"No, Mr. Kirkpatrick," Alexie replied. "I do not. I see how it will profit you and your friends, but I don't see how it will help Wide Sky."

He stiffened, scowling. "That is most uncharitable of you, Alexie. *Most* uncharitable. Why, in new business and engineering contracts alone—"

"Most of which are being handled by Sky Development, I believe?" She was pretty sure that Frank Kirkpatrick was squarely in the hip pocket of Sky Development, the engineering and construction contracting firm that wanted to build a brand new spaceport smack in the middle of the Tall Trees District. Not that Wide Sky *needed* another port. Hell, they had trouble keeping the one they had busy and in good repair; but the landowners along Highway 60 stood to make a lot of money when the warehouses, bars, and joy houses started going up along the new port access strip.

"You still haven't learned how to do it, Alexie, have you?"

"Do what?"

"How to play the game. Enjoy the give and take. The quid pro quo. You help me, I help you—"

"I can't imagine anything that you have, Mr. Kirkpatrick, that I could possibly want."

"I assure you, Miss Turner," Kirkpatrick said, suddenly coldly formal, "that if you could see your way clear to side with us—a friendly word in the right ear, you know— it would be very much worth your while."

"I don't believe your friends could meet my price."

His eyebrows went up, as though he'd just seen a glimmer of hope in an otherwise dark prospect. "Then you have a price? And just what might your price be?"

"My personal integrity as Deputy Director of this colony," she said. He frowned, baffled, and she laughed. "You see, Mr. Kirkpatrick, if I sell out to you, I won't have it anymore. Integrity is like virginity. Once gone, gone forever."

"I . . . don't understand."

"No, sir. I didn't think you would."

He shook his head. "Look, never mind all that. If I can convince you that a new port would be good for Wide Sky, for our economy, for our industry, would you—"

"Mr. Kirkpatrick," she said, suddenly feeling very tired. "I really do have other things on my mind, just now. We haven't heard from Endatheline for almost two weeks now, and in view of those fragmentary messages . . ."

He shrugged. "Communications difficulties, no doubt. You know how often the relays go down for one reason or another."

"They *said* they were being attacked, and then something about their Bolo. That doesn't sound like communications difficulties to me."

"Major Fitzsimmons—"

"I *know* what Fitzsimmons says, Mr. Kirkpatrick. He never has liked Bolos. Or trusted them."

"Who does? Outdated Concordiat junk, if you ask me. Dangerous things that should have been retired years ago. The thought of ours going nuts, going rogue in downtown Galloway . . ." He shuddered.

"We don't know that that was what happened on Endatheline," she said firmly.

He chuckled. "You don't think it was mysterious invaders from the Gulf, do you? Like Sam Carver and his crowd of yokels?"

"It doesn't seem likely," she conceded. Carver headed

up a delegation of citizens from the Sea Cliffs District, who'd demanded a government investigation into the mysterious sightings and disappearances along the east coast in the past few months. A full-fledged invasion scare had been spreading throughout the outlying districts.

"Well, then, you see?" Kirkpatrick favored her with a broad and condescending grin. "There's nothing to worry about after all! Likely, Endatheline's Bolo blew a circuit board and went on a rampage. Once they get the thing shut down and repair the damage, we'll hear the full story, I'd bet. And when we do, you can bet we'll have a measure passed in the House like that," he snapped his fingers, "calling for dismantling our own Bolo before the same thing happens here!"

"Maybe," she said. "But if Sam and his neighbors turn out to be right, I think we're going to want to bring a few more of the things out here, not shut them down. Any invading force that could take out a Bolo, even old ones like the one we have . . ." She let the uncomfortable thought trail off.

"Well, we'll just have to wait and see, won't we? Now, to get back to what I was saying, you *must* see—"

"Oh, honestly, Mr. Kirkpatrick! I will not stand out here and have you badger me about your damned friends' plans to pave over the Tall Trees District!"

Turning abruptly, she stalked away, leaving him standing on the mole.

Alexie had never wanted to be a politician, even though she'd been raised in an environment that fairly reeked of smoke-filled rooms and power-brokering, behind-the-scenes deals. Her father had been Alexander Jefferson Turner, a five-term legislator and three times elected Director General of the Wide Sky colony. Sometimes she thought it was precisely *because* her father had been the colony's DG that she'd decided not to go into politics.

She knew first-hand how rough—and how dirty—that game could be.

Her father had been an honest man, at least so far as she could tell, but the Mannheim banking affair had broken just before the conclusion of his third term as Director, and the ensuing scandal had swept quite a few prominent politicians out of office besides A. J. Turner. The strain of that battle, coupled with an ailing heart, had killed him in the end. When the Reform Party had started running mud spots on all of the vid channels, though, attacking not only her father's policies but his character as well, Alexie had weighed in as the Common Sense Party's legislative representative from the Mount Golden District and fought back. Somewhat to her surprise, she'd found support for her father and his name still strong across all of Wide Sky; a backlash against the vid muddies had swept her into office, and five years later, she'd accepted her party's nomination as Deputy Director General of Wide Sky. When Vince Stanfeld was elected DG, she found herself—as her critics liked to say—one heart beat away from the directorship of the planet.

She was still angry, angry at Kirkpatrick and angry at herself for allowing him to get under her skin. She reached the stony beach at the head of the mole, jumped down onto the wave-rounded pebbles, and walked out a few meters, breathing deeply, trying to think.

Footing was uncertain here, and she stooped to remove her dress shoes. Smooth, wet stones clacked beneath her bare feet with each step, and she waded out until silk-warm water swirled past her ankles with the surf.

Alexie loved Wide Sky. The beauty of the place was haunting . . . and during the summer months in the southern hemisphere, like now, the night sky was stunning, the reason for the world's name obvious. Unlike the McNair-Muir system, snuggled away within its beehive swarm of suns, Wide Sky was located just outside the Strathan Cluster proper, precariously balanced, as some locals liked to say, between the glory of the cluster and the emptiness of the Great Gulf.

To the east, the Strathan Cluster glowed in somber red, orange, and yellow hues, stretching from the horizon three quarters of the way to the zenith, with the Galaxy's trailing spiral arm a mist-silver tumble of stars and frosty light beyond, the whole casting a gleaming shimmer across the waves of the bay as they rolled gently in with the slow-rising tide. West, though, only a handful of stars were visible, and those were mingled with soft, unfocused smudges of light, other galaxies, inconceivably distant.

There were those who said that Wide Skyers tended toward melancholy, that living on the thin, cold edge of the Gulf made them solitary and just a little strange.

She snorted at the thought. Strange they might be in their independence and in their disdain for the norms of socially mandated convention, but most Wide Skyers she knew tended to be a gregarious lot, as though huddling together helped to hold out the chill of the Ultimate Night. There was a piece by the Strathan poet Sharon Kimberly that she quite liked.

> Balanced, we
> On cusp of night
> Between stark glory of the stars
> And darkened folds that swallow light
> That show how small our lives.

There was a lot more, committed once to memory, but she couldn't remember it all now. Wide Sky's spell at once reminded its inhabitants of just how small they were . . . and reaffirmed the importance of friends, of neighbors, of family, of all the good human values that kept you warm and held the Night at bay.

Her eyes picked out one bright, orange-hued pinpoint of light, all alone in the emptiness, the sun of Endatheline, just eight light years distant. Endatheline hung even a bit further out into the Gulf than did Wide Sky, on the outermost frontier of the Strathan Confederation. It had been settled a hundred years earlier by colonists from Wide Sky and Thule, and its people had that same hard-headed practicality, the same stubbornness, the same love of independence and self-reliance that most Wide Skyers did.

What's going on there? she wondered, staring at the lonely star. If she couldn't quite believe Sam Carver's stories of alien invaders, neither could she believe the story about a Bolo running amuck. She'd seen Bolo Unit 76235—"Algy," they called it—often enough at the Galloway military base. The machine was an immense assembly of metal and ceramic armor atop four sets of tracks, guided by a sophisticated computer. Bolos—at least the older Mark XVIIIs, like Algy—were not self-aware, could not be considered intelligent in any but the vaguest and most artificial sense, and certainly did not "go nuts," as Kirkpatrick had suggested. As impressive as the thing might be, she could not imagine a Mark XVIII suddenly turning against its human masters any more than she could imagine the same act by an toaster, or some other automated piece of kitchen hardware.

The first meteor streaked in from high in the west, a brilliant speck of yellow-orange light trailing white fire. In utter silence, it flashed almost directly overhead, traveling southeast, vanishing in seconds behind the Granger Hills. The second followed almost in the glowing wake of the first, and it was flanked by two more. Long seconds later, she heard something like a roll of thunder, following the apparitions from one side of the sky to the other.

"My God," Kirkpatrick said. She started. She hadn't realized he'd followed her down onto the beach. "It's like fireworks."

Three more meteors followed, dazzling, tiny flares of arc-burning light that dazzled the eye and momentarily robbed the Strathan Cluster of its glory.

"What is it," Kirkpatrick asked. "A meteor storm?"

"Those weren't meteors," Alexie said. Three more blossomed alight, following the rest in perfect V-formation. "Those are spacecraft!"

"They can't be! We're not expecting that kind of traffic at Skyport!"

She arched one perfect eyebrow. "Oh, really? Then maybe we won't be needing that new spaceport facility after all."

"But what *are* they?" he demanded.

"Military maneuvers of some kind, I imagine. Goodnight, Mr. Kirkpatrick."

She walked away over faintly clacking stones, leaving him on the beach. She really wanted to be rid of the man and disliked the fact that he seemed to be pursuing her. Had her opposition to the new spaceport project really hampered Kirkpatrick's friends that much?

Another train of meteors—or atmosphere-entering spacecraft—blazed overhead, followed seconds later by the rumble of distant thunder.

Explosive panels blew free with a spine-rattling thump and the winged entry pod disintegrated in a radar-obscuring cloud of burning fragments, giving Schaagrasch the Blood Taster her first decent view of the target world. Her altitude was now twenty-five *tairucht*, still well above the few scraps of cloud, high enough that the far horizon showed just a hint of a curve against the glow of the sky. The Pack had descended on the planet's night side, but ocean and rolling hill country and forested mountain alike were softly illuminated by the sphere-swarm of blood-tinted stars hanging above the eastern horizon.

With her vision restored, her claustrophobic panic

subsided, giving way to the hot, pulsing eagerness of
pre-battle lust. Schaagrasch's eyes were best equipped
to handle light at the red end of the spectrum, her
vision extending well into the infrared, so to her the
landscape below was bathed in the pearly light of a
shimmering, golden sunset, where a human would have
seen a bloody, late evening dusk. The Hunterpod's
computer helped her, painting geometric symbols and
the twisting worm characters of the Malach alphabet
across her viewscreens. Most of the landscape below
was wilderness and ocean, a shocking waste of valuable
resources; radar and more subtle electronic senses
identified the sprawl of a population center, the glow
of industrial heat spillage from a factory complex, the
bright, hard pulse of ground-based search and traffic-
control radars. Something that might be a spaceport
lay north of the city, inland from the sea. Something
else—a military base of some sort—was sandwiched
between spaceport and coastline. A dozen of the
phoneme symbols meaning "active radar site" winked
in that area; someone down there was quite interested
in the objects screaming down out of the thin, cold
reaches of the planet's upper atmosphere. There'd been
no hostile fire yet, however. Surprise, evidently, had
been complete. Hunters were at their most vulnerable
during the transit from orbit to ground.

The Hunter, freed now of the embrace of its entry
packaging, was flattened enough to provide considerable
aerodynamic lift at transonic speeds, a lozenge shape of
ebon black ceramics and durasteel edged with down-
curved, manta's wings. A twitch of Schaagrasch's right
fore-arm fired small control jets, swinging the sleek shape
left toward an expanse of wooded, hilly terrain north of
the military site. A blur of trees and rugged ground swept
past her field of vision; scant *erucht* above the rocks she
fired her main air-breathing jets, decelerating sharply,

as G piled upon G and her speed bled away in jets of superheated steam.

Then she struck the ground, bellying in with a grinding crunch and a geysering cascade of rock and earth. She felt the savage, flesh-ripping joy of completion, of success. She was down, safe, intact . . . and still as sane as she could be after her enforced confinement.

Battle-lust surged within her, hot and pounding and urgent. She began searching for an enemy against which she could turn it.

CHAPTER SIX

For a moment there was no sound save the sharp, intermittent *ping* of cooling metal and briefly, the sonic-boom rumble of another pod arrowing in overhead. The Hunter had excavated a small gully as it slid into the ground, blasting a crater into the spot where it had finally come to rest. With a whine, panels at the rear dilated wide, aerodyne pods split open, and the Hunter rose from the steaming pit on skeletal steel-and-ceramic legs that unfolded beneath it like jointed, telescoping stilts.

Fully combat-deployed, the Hunter stood perhaps five times the height of an adult Malach, the manta-body sleek, armor-plated, and wedge-prowed, a shape much, in fact, like a Malach's head, bristling with the spikes and needles of its main and secondary armament clusters. The legs were digitigrade, like those of organic Malach, the joints thrust backward, the feet splayed into durasteel-sheathed slasher claws. The paint scheme was a light-drinking black that eliminated shadows and made the machine's overall shape difficult to discern in daylight, and nearly invisible at night. That paint drank radar frequencies as easily as it drank light; Hunters were difficult to see, and even more difficult to track and target-lock.

The military base spotted from the air lay approximately twelve thousand *erucht* to the south, uncomfortably close by the standards of Malach mobile warfare . . . but if the Hunter Pack had truly achieved surprise, that closeness might translate into advantage if they could slash and gut the local defenders before they could organize a proper defense.

Pivoting on spindly legs, Schaagrasch scanned the immediate area. A number of autochthons were approaching from the southwest, and she moved swiftly to meet them.

For the Malach warrior, the Hunter was a kind of second body. Suspended inside a close-fitting harness, her body closely embraced by thousands of sensors and position feeds, she could walk, run, stoop, and leap, her movements in the harness translated into movements of her teleoperated steed. A striding gait against the enveloping pressure of her leggings became the ground-eating sprint of the Hunter; thrusts and movements of her arms and gestures of her hands and claws aimed, locked, and fired various of her weapons or triggered the bursts of superheated air that could send the Hunter sailing along in low, gliding leaps. Cameras and other sensors embedded in the heavily armored outer hull gave her very nearly all-round vision inside the control cell, and her computer gave constantly updated enhancements of the view, blended with identifying alphanumerics to help her sort rapidly through the torrent of battle information.

At the moment, light levels were low, though not uncomfortably so. There was more than enough light from the sky to navigate by, though Schaagrasch cut in full infrared imaging to provide the maximum informational input.

Smashing through a thick-growing wall of tangled

vegetation, she emerged at the top of a low ridge, her legs angled sharply back to keep the Hunter's body just a couple of *erucht* above the ground. Movement snared her full attention, along with the flare of color signifying multiple heat sources. The autochthons were scrambling up the ridge from the opposite side, two eights of them, at least, so many that it was difficult to sort them out one from another, their body heat showing as strangely shaped blobs of color against the cooler background. Schaagrasch saw nothing she could distinguish as a weapon, but the capabilities of this species were still less than perfectly known. With a twist of her head and a double blink of her eyes, she targeted the group, now fifty *erucht* distant. A forward thrust of her left hand, third claw extended, triggered a single bolt from her *kaigho*.

The word translated as "fang-slash" and referred to the first, satisfying lunge-and-rip designed to disembowel or cut the leg tendons of large prey, rendering it helpless. A relatively short-ranged weapon, it discharged a dazzling pulse of electrons, a Malach-made bolt of lightning that scrambled unhardened electronics, melted armor, and charred flesh. The flash was dazzling, the thunderclap deafening as autochthons were scattered in every direction, some of them gloriously ablaze, some squeaking in terror or pain. In an instant, Schaagrasch was upon them, standing astride a tumble of charred and still-smoking corpses, lashing out with one clawed foot to slice one of the screaming wounded in two, bringing the foot down atop the writhing, partly burned body of another. Four of the autochthons not caught in the *kaigho*'s killzone fled in panic down the slope. She turned and lowered the Hunter's snout; a movement of her second claw, right hind-arm, triggered her mag gun, flinging a buzzing swarm of flechettes through the screaming survivors and cutting them into bloody shreds.

Kill and eat!

Schaagrasch paused momentarily, among the torn and scattered bodies. Odd little creatures, with blood that was altogether the wrong color. Killing them was not quite as satisfying as she'd anticipated . . . a psychological effect, she knew, of the fact that the color red did not trigger the same urges and mental channelings as the color blue-green. It left her with the gnawing, hungry need to keep striking, keep slashing. She needed to find more autochthons to kill.

She had read the reports of these scout packs and watched vid records of the vivisection of several captives. They were oddly made, to be sure, erect and tailless, with too few limbs, with an omnivore's teeth, with only a single heart, and with digestive organs unprotected and easily opened. She gave a short, hard snort of derision. These had been unarmored and apparently unarmed. Had they been juveniles? Where were their Guardians? She turned in place, surveying the surrounding hills and forests. There must be more to sate her blood-hunger.

New movement to her right caught her attention; another ebon-hulled Hunter topped the ridge, flat, weapon-heavy hull bobbing in mechanical mimicry of an organic Malach's search-and-track body language. A second machine followed. Schaagrasch's electronic overlays identified both: Krakuscht the Never-Tiring and Ureskchagh the Sinews-Cutter. The sight thrilled Schaagrasch, kindling the sharp joy of *UrrghChaak*, the Blood-chase. In military operations like these, the hardest part might be the waiting, but the most dangerous in a tactical sense was those critical few moments after landing, when the Pack was scattered and unable to coordinate effectively. Now, though, two of Schaagrasch's companions had joined her. Both strode forward, tipping the prows of their machines high in a salute acknowledging Schaagrasch's greater rank and social status.

"You have killed," Krakuscht said over the Hunter Pack's radio link. "The first taste is to you!"

Contemptuously, Schaagrasch scattered wet body parts with a flick of one huge, clawed foot. "*Gnedissh*," she said. "Trash. There is nothing here worthy of the Pack."

"The military base is that way," Ureskchagh said, indicating the south with a twist of her Hunter's body. "There will be Guardians there."

"Then we will kill and eat," Schaagrasch said, the *UrrghChaak* pounding behind her eyes, bringing anticipatory blood-taste to her jaws.

"*Shch'kaa uroch!*" the others bayed. "*Kill and eat!*"

It was still night when Alexie reached downtown Galloway in her turbo-electric LaRouche, but the city center was lit more brightly than it usually was for the Grounding Day Festival, and there was a large crowd congregating at the Town Hall. Evidently, the Council had appropriated the old grange hall in Galloway and set it up as a temporary command center, a clearing house for information as well as a place where the citizens of outlying districts could come to make their reports and sound off about the government's incompetence.

Howard, her secretary, had called Alexie on her private comm while she was still driving home, to tell her that she was needed at the grange as the Director General's personal representative; Director General Stanfeld had been caught out of town by the emergency, at the antipodes, in fact, visiting the fishery cities at Scarba.

Alexie envied him. *He* didn't have to face this mob of screaming, shouting, frightened people. Theoretically, she didn't either—that's what undersecretaries and public relations spokespersons were for—but when she'd arrived and seen that crowd battling to get up the steps and squeeze into the main hall, she'd known that this was one task she couldn't delegate to anyone else. She just wished she'd had time to go home and change into more businesslike clothes first.

She'd gone in through the private entrance in the back; there was no way she'd have made it in through the front, that was certain. Inside, she'd found a harried-looking Major Streven Fitzsimmons in a heated debate with Sam Carver. "And furthermore," Fitzsimmons was bellowing as she walked in, "if you don't exercise your authority over these yahoos out front, I'll have you put under military arrest."

"What charge, Major?" Carver said in a low voice that carried plenty of unspoken menace.

"Obstruction of government business! Rioting! Disturbing the peace! Any charge I damn well feel—"

"That is *enough*, Major!" Alexie snapped.

Fitzsimmons jumped, whirling around, looking guilty. "Ah, why, Alexie! I didn't know—"

"Obviously." She looked at Sam, a tall, rangy, and ruggedly good-looking rancher with piercing blue eyes. She'd worked with him before, starting back when he'd been on her father's re-election committee, and liked both his refreshing directness and his honesty. "What's the word, Sam?"

"We're being invaded and this uniformed jackass wants *verification*."

"Well, it's standard procedure, Alexie," Fitzsimmons said with huffy dignity. "We can't simply accept every wild story that comes in here!"

"Looks to me like you have a fair amount of verification out front, Fitz," she told him. "Why don't you go out there and talk to them, maybe get them to start telling their stories one at a time. Instead of stonewalling them for a change."

Fitzsimmons opened his mouth to reply, caught a hard look from Alexie, then closed it again. "Very well, ma'am," he said. "But you know how these wild rumors get started.

One drunken rancher thinks he sees something, and the next thing you know half the planet's seen Melconian invaders!"

"What do you think, Sam?" she asked the rancher as Fitzsimmons stalked off. "Is it a drunken story? Or Melconians?"

"Neither. I heard it first from Fred Noyes, and he's never touched a drop in his life. You remember Fred, don't you?"

"Yes. . . ."

"He called me two, two and a half hours ago and told me a space ship had landed in the Sea Cliffs District, and could I please bring some of the boys over to have a look-see. He told me he thought the thing had crashed, said he and a bunch of his neighbors were heading out to try to find it."

"Did they?"

Sam's jaw hardened. "More like something found them. I went out there with about twenty boys maybe an hour later and found Fred up above Dreyden's Gulch. At least, I *think* it was Fred. I thought I recognized his jacket."

"My God! What happened?"

"If I didn't know better, I'd say Fred and his neighbors ran head-on into a small army. Some of them were burned to a . . . well, it was pretty bad. Flamers, maybe. But it looked like a hit from a small-caliber Hellbore. And then there were the others . . ." He stopped, and shuddered.

"Go on. What did you see?"

"I can't really describe it. I've never seen the like. Some guys were just torn apart. I mean that literally. Some had been . . . I don't know. Run over. Stomped on. There was blood all over the place."

He looked shook . . . and for Sam Carver to be shook, it had to be bad. "So what did you do?"

"Some of the fellas wanted to track the things. I can't say I was all that eager to catch up with whatever had done that, but it looked like they were headed south, toward Camp Olson."

"Wait a minute. 'Things'?"

"We saw their tracks, Alexie. Big critters, too. From the looks of it, there were several ships that landed, and landed pretty hard. They must've dropped these things off and took off again, though, 'cause we didn't see any sign of them."

"How big, Sam?"

"We measured one print left in soft dirt. It was splayed, like this." He held his hand up, the first and second fingers held together and apart from the third and fourth, in a V-shape. "Measured better'n two meters from the back of the heel to the tip of the toe."

"An . . . an *animal* track?"

He shook his head. "I don't think so. The markings looked, well, artificial. Like the foot had been made of cast flintsteel with ridges, like on the bottom of a sports shoe. No, if I had to guess, Alexie, I'd guess that we're looking for something like a small Bolo on legs."

"Who? Melconians?" News from the Concordiat was slow to reach the Confederation and often was distorted along the way. Still, the Strathan News Network had been running stories on the trouble brewing with the Melconian Empire for months now.

"I don't think so," Sam replied. "We've got most of the Concordiat and half the Eastern Arm between us and where those guys are supposed to hang out. I can't believe the Empire'd swing all the way around, something like fifty thousand light years out of the way, to come stomp on *us*. Especially when their quarrel is with Terra. No, I think this is something else."

"We'll have to get our Guard unit mobilized right away," she said. "If this is the start of an invasion—"

"Fitzsimmons didn't sound all that eager to check it out."

"The Guard works for the government," Alexie said. "Not the other way around. I'd better get on out there, though, and talk to the people."

"It'll help, Alexie," Sam said quietly, "just knowing that *someone* in the government doesn't automatically assume that they're all drunk or idiots. I'll tag along, if I can."

"Ms. Turner!" Sally Vogel, her chief aide, hurried down the passageway behind her. "Ms. Turner!"

"What is it, Sally?"

"We've got a vidcast from Camp Olson. I think you'd better see this . . . and Major Fitzsimmons, too."

"What is it?"

"They say they're being attacked, ma'am. By *things*!"

Alexie felt a cold twist of dread in her gut. "Come on," she said. "Let's go see."

Schaagrasch emerged from the treeline high atop the ridge overlooking the enemy military base. All sixteen pack members had assembled by now, a pair of eights deployed in standard slash-and-feed formation. A million years before, on the sere and sun-baked veldts of Zhanaach, Malach hunter packs had deployed the same way when stalking herds of *grelssh* or the ponderous but dangerous *gr'raa'zhghavescht*. Two eights would make the approach. One, the senior pack, would hold back, observing, feinting, distracting, perhaps driving; the other was the *kaigho,* the fang-slash that cut tendons and crippled the prey. At the proper tactical moment, the senior eight became the *cha'igho*, the final, disemboweling slash with major claw that brought the prey down, gasping its last.

It was the same today, for all that the Malach now rode Hunters and battled prey far more deadly, intelligent, and tenacious than any lumbering *gr'raa'zhghavescht*. Schaagrasch had ordered Chaghna'kraa the Blade-Fanged to lead her eight down the slope, striking into the enemy compound from the west. Schaagrasch waited and watched with the others, as fires winked and flickered among shattered buildings, and smoke began staining the pearly glow of the predawn sky.

Schaagrasch was curious about whether or not one of the autochthons' mechanical *gr'raa'zhghavescht*—the things they called Bolos—was going to make an appearance. She'd read the Deathgiver's report of the preliminary Malach scouting raids on two other outlying worlds inhabited by these curiously weak and fragile creatures. On the world code-named *Zsha'h'lach*, the Warm and Soft One, a machine similar to the primitive tanks used by the Malach themselves centuries ago had destroyed several Hunters. According to reports, the war machines were heavily armored, operated on fusion power, and possessed a deadly and hard-hitting array of weaponry, including plasma and ion beam weapons, heavy-caliber howitzers, and vertically launched missiles. It had not yet been ascertained whether the things were piloted by crews, were teleoperated by remote control, or were autonomous robots operating according to programmed instructions.

The single specimen on Zsha'h'lach had been destroyed, unfortunately. Schaagrasch's orders included a level-four directive—low priority—to capture one of the machines if possible, in order to better ascertain the sophistication of the autochthons' military technology. She would not risk her Pack to fulfill those orders, but if she saw the opportunity . . .

She was, in fact, pretty sure that she saw a way that the thing might be done. Her pre-invasion briefing had included extensive vid and sound files on every aspect of the Zsha'h'lach operation, including a step-by-step, bolt-by-bolt account of the battle with the artificial *gr'raa*. The things were slow, like their namesakes, and ponderous, with poor maneuverability in tight quarters. The Pack that had brought down the machine on Zsha'h'lach had done so by moving in close, to claw-slashing range, in fact, and engaging the thing in battle at point-blank range, so close that the more powerful ion and plasma weapons couldn't be brought to bear.

The trick, of course, was in getting that close in the first place. She hoped that one of the machines was, in fact, operating in this region and that she would have the opportunity to test herself against the best they could throw at her Pack.

She was looking forward to the challenge.

"We're sending out the Bolo now!" Static fuzzed the big vidscreen, breaking up the army captain's face. When Alexie could see him again, he'd turned away from the camera and was shouting at someone out of its field of view. "Damn it, I don't *care* about authorization, Lew! Get that thing moving, stat!" He turned again to face Alexie. "Ms. Turner, we've been hit pretty hard. We'll hold 'em if we can, but frankly, things are not looking good."

Major Fitzsimmons crowded himself past Alexie's chair, leaning over to put his face into the vid pickup's field. "Captain Hemingway! What the devil's going on back there?"

"Oh, Major!" the captain said. "I already told the DDG. We're in deep trouble here. Enemy war machines of some kind. Stilters, big ones. Look, I'll patch in a view from one of our externals."

The captain's face winked off the screen and was replaced by a blurry shot of flat-bodied, jet-black stalkers entering the base compound. From the way they towered over the nearby buildings, each stood ten meters tall, with triangular bodies studded with wicked-looking spikes or muzzles that might have been weapons of some kind. Hemingway's descriptive word "stilters" was apt; they walked with a delicate, almost mincing grace, like enormous, ornamental flightless birds of some kind . . . save that these were the size of a house, and where they walked, they left utter and complete devastation in their steps. Alexie watched, wide-eyed, as several soldiers ran past the camera; a blue-violet beam lanced from the nearest machine, sparkling as it burned a thread of illumination through a drifting haze of smoke, and a one-story building exploded in flame and whirling splinters of wood.

"They hit us a few minutes ago," Captain Hemingway's voice continued, speaking over the vid scene of fiery devastation. "Eight of them, though we have reports of more moving around on the ridge above the camp. They came through the west fence, laying down a barrage of beams and missiles that—"

Another burst of static buzzed and hissed, dissolving the picture in a storm of crackling, electronic snow.

"What is that?" Fitzsimmons said. "Why is it doing that?"

"Particle beam," Sam Carver said at his back. "Either a proton cannon or an electron beam. It's like lightning. Puts out all kinds of electrical interference."

"*I* know that," Fitzsimmons said, a bit testily. "What is this civilian doing in here?"

"I asked him," Alexie said. "He might have some insights into what's happening that we would miss."

"We seem to have lost contact, ma'am," the communications tech said from his console. The screen continued to display an uninformative blanket of white noise and snow. "They're just . . . gone!"

"Did he say who the attackers were?" Fitzsimmons wanted to know.

"He didn't know, Major," Alexie told him. "I've never seen anything like that. Have you?"

"N-no," Fitzsimmons said.

"I think we know now what it was that knocked out Endatheline," Sam said.

Fitzsimmons turned sharply. "That's right! Their Bolo couldn't stop those things there. We should warn Hemingway right away!"

"I think we're too late, Major," Alexie told him. "If he's already deployed his Bolo, there's not much we can do."

"I don't think we're going to raise Camp Olson again," the commo tech said. "I've been trying, but they're off the air. No carrier wave, even. Either their transmission mast is down, or. . ."

"Or what?" Fitzsimmons demanded.

"Or that last particle bolt fried Captain Hemingway and his radio."

"I guess," Alexie said quietly, "it's up to their Bolo, now."

CHAPTER SEVEN

```
LOAD SLFDIAG/LEVEL 3
    ELAPSTIME: .04 SEC
RUN SLFDIAG/LEVEL 3
    POWER SYS: 72.5%+
    DRVTRAIN: OP
    NAV: ONLINE
    TRACK/SENS: ONLINE
    SUSPENSION: FNCTNL
    TAC/COMM: ONLINE
    SYSOP: OPTML
    MAGSCRN: ONLINE
    WEAPSYS: ONLINE
END SLFDIAG/LEVEL 3
    ELAPSTIME: .13 SEC
    >>ALL SYSTEMS ON-LINE, FUNCTIONING AT OPTIMAL LEVELS
LOAD NAVPROG
    ELAPSTIME: .03 SEC
RUN NAVPROG
    >>MOVING
RUN THREAT ASSESMNT
    MULTIPLE CONTACTS/IR/VIS/RADAR
INITIATE PRIMTRACSEQ, SUBRTN 76
    >>DESIGNATING PRIMARY TARGET ALPHA, BEARING 311,
```

RANGE 71 METERS
ELAPSTIME: 5.72 SEC
ARM WEAPONS

Schaagrasch watched the enemy combat machine's
approach with a keen and hungry interest. This was more
like what she'd been waiting for, a challenge worthy of
her Hunter Pack. Eight hundred *erucht* long at least,
the thing must have massed thousands of *klaatch*.
Emerging from a heavily armored and partly buried
bunker of some sort, it moved clumsily on enormous,
cleated tracks, making its own road as it ground along
cracking, splintering, crumbling asphalt.

That datum alone was important. The asphalt surface
of the compound had been poured *after* the *gr'raa* had
been stored in the bunker. Did they never exercise with
their equipment? Engage in sham wars and training?
Yes. Very interesting indeed. . . .

Chaghna'kraa shrieked the order for attack, and her
eight closed on the monster war machine. A small, flat
turret spun rapidly, tracing, then spat flame, flinging a
large-caliber howitzer shell into Hunter Fifteen with
precisionist accuracy. The explosion all but engulfed the
Malach Hunter's body, rocking it back on deeply flexing
legs as it absorbed the concussion. The smoke cleared,
and the Hunter continued its charge, main batteries flaring
at wavelengths invisible to the Malach eye but picked
up and superimposed on Schaagrasch's combat screen
as dazzling white bolts of energy.

It was difficult at this range to see how effective Malach
fire was against the alien armor, though spectroscopes
mounted in Schaagrasch's sensor suite detected the glow
of titanium, iron, carbon, and an eight or two of other
elements, boiling away into the air in a superheated mist.
The Hunters' weapons were striking home, and they were
doing damage. The question was whether they would

damage the armored *gr'raa* enough to incapacitate it before all of Schaagrasch's Hunters were dead.

As planned, four of Chaghna'kraa's Pack hung back, hurling bolt upon bolt of energy into the huge and slow-moving prey, while the other four rushed in from four different directions. The *gr'raa's* main armament turret, flat and fast-traversing, spun in the blink of an eye to loose a searing torrent of white-hot plasma, fusion-fired and star-hot. The blast stripped the outer armor from Hunter Ten's hull, leaving scoured, gray-streaked metal and a charred and smoking hole. Hunter Ten loosed a barrage of laser and particle beam fire in reply before a second plasma bolt penetrated the break in its armor, setting off a chain of internal detonations as stored munitions exploded.

The final blast was an eye-searing flash that volatized Ten almost completely, leveling nearby buildings and sending a black and roiling cloud mushrooming into the sky.

"Closer!" Schaagrasch commanded over the tactical channel. "Get closer! Use your *va'xachat!*"

The name was that of a Zhanaachan lifeform, an insect-like flyer respected for its fierce attack, high speed, and evolution-honed habit of laying eggs deep inside a parasitized host, a trait shared by many species on the Malach homeworld.

Flame spat from one of the Hunter's launch tubes, hurling a silvery penetrator on a burning rocket's trail. Triggered by proximity, the *va'xachat's* outer casing flared into white hot plasma, channeled and shaped by powerful magnetic fields into a dazzling lance of starfire, stabbing at the *gr'raa's* armored flank. A neat hexagon of the *gr'raa's* armor exploded violently, disrupting the plasma lance before it could strike the target, and the penetrator within detonated with a spectacular but harmless blast.

Reactive armor—plates of sandwiched high explosives

designed to disrupt incoming beams of plasma, molten metal, or coherent radiation. Well, the briefing had mentioned that, and Schaagrasch had been expecting it. Reactive armor was only good for one strike, and then it was gone.

By now, scant seconds after the engagement had begun, the lumbering *gr'raa* was completely engulfed and surrounded by white flame. Nine ball-turret-mounted ion cannons along each side kept up a steady, sweeping barrage, hosing the circling Hunters with deadly accuracy; the single main plasma weapon in its flat, quick-shifting turret tracked and fired, tracked and fired, with a relentless precision that was at once machinelike and personal. The powerful magnetic shields and beam disrupters built into the Malach Hunter hull metal could shrug aside one, possibly two direct hits from those terrifying discharges of raw, lightning violence, but then defenses were overwhelmed, screens fell as field guides melted away or tripped out on overload, and the hardest, diamond-weave carbon shell could endure that hellish firepower for only the briefest of measurable instants. Two Hunters were gone . . . now three, and the enemy *gr'raa* seemed hardly to have been hurt at all. Still, Schaagrasch waited, studying the circling firefight with narrow-slitted eyes.

Hunter Fourteen fired a *va'xachat* from a greater range, almost twenty *erucht* . . . too far, it turned out, as an antimissile battery blazed, vaporizing the penetrator before it reached the enemy machine's side. A turret spun and a *gr'raa* howitzer round exploded against Fourteen's left leg, the shell too massive and fast to be shunted aside by the Malach's defensive shields. Bits of metal spun away; Fourteen took another step, wobbled, then fell as the leg collapsed beneath its weight.

Four down, half of Chaghna'kraa's octet.

But Schaagrasch had already learned what she needed most to know. The enemy was incapable of layered strategies or flexible defense with multiple combat vehicles. They were relying on this single behemoth, with no hidden reserves . . . or they would certainly have deployed them by now, before their combat machine sustained significant damage. The armor and weapons displayed were identical to those of the artificial *gr'raa* on Zsha'h'lach, massive, dense, and covered over with both reactive armor plate and less substantial magnetic fields, but it *was* vulnerable to the Malach tactics evolved to counter it.

Time to bring in the second octet. Schaagrasch barked an order, and her eight broke from cover, sprinting at a full run down the slope, smashing through the compound fence, storming into the enemy sanctuary.

"*Va'xachat!*" she yelled. "All Hunters, coordinated fire, as close as you can get!" She had the *chaak'sha'*, now, the blood-taste that was so vital a part of *UrrghChaak*.

The enemy machine spun, a remarkably graceful maneuver for so large and clumsy-looking a vehicle, accomplished by reversing the double set of tracks on one side while keeping the tracks on the other side moving at full throttle. As the *gr'raa* whipped around with deliberate malice, one massive set of treads caught Twelve just as it was trying to angle in closer, crushing one leg with a violent *pop-pop-crack* and sending the flat and angular hull bounding across the pavement. Another Hunter took a direct hit from the *gr'raa*'s main weapon— the second that it had sustained in as many seconds— and the forward third of its hull disintegrated in a violently expanding cloud of metallic vapor.

A seventh Hunter, Number Six from Schaagrasch's octet, was torn into flaming shreds by a rapid-pulsed trio of plasma bolts, but the rest loped across open and fire-torn ground, circling, seeking weakness, a Hunter Pack in fact as well as name, seeking to drag down their titanic prey. *Va'xachat* flared and stabbed, most of the projectiles cut down in mid-flight by lightning parries of the *gr'raa's* point-defense weapons, more exploding harmlessly in the subtle web of the prey's magnetic shielding. But even magnetic force screens couldn't deflect the full fury of nuclear violence that stabbed and slashed in dazzling pulses of raw, sun-hot plasma. Mag screens overloaded and failed; reactive armor detonated. In seconds, a dozen bare spots in the giant's flanks had been scoured away, and the circling, snapping Hunters began targeting those exclusively.

When a *Va'xachat* exploded into plasma, a needle-slender penetrator remained at its heart, hard driven by a powerful rocket motor, shaping the energy lance with magnetic fields as it hurtled along its core. Magnetic screens sheathing the target might distort the lance fields or deflect the highly charged plasma, but the electromagnetic pulse or EMP of the blast was powerful enough to overload all but the most powerful mag screens locally. When the lance struck reactive armor, of course, it was disrupted by the back-blast and the penetrator detonated harmlessly against unyielding flintsteel. If the lance touched a spot just scoured clear of outer, reactive armor plate moments before, however, it was hot enough to boil its way down through a slasher claw's breadth of flintsteel; the penetrator struck home an instant later, firing a second plasma bolt from its tip, widening the wound and peeling the inner armored hull open, a white-hot, glowing doorway for the mininuke main charge coming through close behind.

No physical armor, no matter how it was cast, packed, or laminated, could more than briefly resist the detonation of a tenth-kiloton fission device, With the detonation delayed until the penetrator had already plunged deep into the target's protective shell, the blast was sharply focused in two directions, in . . . and out.

One penetrator, fired into a partly molten spot at point-blank range by Hunter Eleven, exploded deep within the armored monster, the blast spilling from the *gr'raa*'s side, a volcano's eruption in roiling white flame. The backblast caught Eleven in the side, toppling the Hunter over in a thrashing of wildly scissoring legs, even as internal explosions rippled through the massive enemy combat machine. One secondary turret was ripped out of the *gr'raa*'s flank and sent spinning end-for-end across the compound.

Eight Hunters down, an octet's worth . . . a high price indeed.

But Schaagrasch could already tell that the tide was turning in the Pack's favor.

LOAD SLFDIAG/LEVEL 4
   ELAPSTIME: .023 SEC
RUN SLFDIAG/LEVEL 4
   POWER SYS: 62.51%-
   DRVTRAIN: OP, REDUCED CAPABILITY:86%
   NAV: ONLINE
   TRACK/SENS: ONLINE
   SUSPENSION: FNCTNL
   TAC/COMM: ONLINE/JAMMED
   SYSOP: OPTML
   MAGSCRN: ONLINE, REDUCED CAPABILITY: 81%
   WEAPSYS: ONLINE
      INFRPTR 2, 5, 6 DSTRYD
      INFRPTR 3, 10 DMGD, 50%
END SLFDIAG/LEVEL 4
   ELAPSTIME: .23 SEC
   >>MAGNETIC SCREENS FAILING; HEAVY DAMAGE SUSTAINED TO ARMOR; HULL BREACH AT 3 POINTS.
   >>FIREFIGHT ELAPSED TIME: 17.7 SECONDS W 8 KILLS
   >>STRENGTH OF ENEMY FIREPOWER AND ARRIVAL OF ENEMY REINFORCEMENTS REDUCES CHANCE OF SUCCESSFUL ENGAGEMENT TO 45%

❖   ❖   ❖

Dust and smoke swirled about the artificial *gr'raa's* massive hull as it reversed direction yet again, thundering down on Schaagrasch's Hunter now with astonishing speed. Schaagrasch stood her ground for a long moment, pouring fire into the advancing juggernaut, watching that massive armor absorb everything the Malach Pack leader could throw at it. Ion bolts from the enemy's side turrets sizzled and snapped; Schaagrasch felt the jarring thud as a triplet of well-aimed shots slammed into her machine, rocking her backward. At the last possible moment, she triggered her belly jets, soaring forward and to one side, skimming across the shattered pavement as she twisted in flight, savaging the *gr'raa's* already savaged left flank.

As the huge machine thundered past, a smoking, quaking cliffside of black and blast-shredded metal, she fired another penetrator from a range of less than six *erucht*. The projectile flared almost the instant it left the muzzle of her *va'xachat* launch tube, plunging into armor already ruptured and torn, sending the penetrator striking deep into the metal beast's vitals. When the mininuke detonated, a long instant later, the flash seemed to illuminate the enemy machine from within, setting off a rippling chain of internal explosions that jolted the *gr'raa* and spun it part way around.

The *gr'raa* screamed, tortured metal giving way. With a rending clatter of shattering links, the left-forward track fragmented, bits of metal ringing off pavement and the sides of Schaagrasch's Hunter like hot metal hail. One of the road wheels jounced free in a spray of mounting bolts, striking the ground on its spun monocarbide rim and rolling wildly across the pavement.

The machine kept moving, however, the rims of its remaining wheels striking sparks and black fragments from the hard pavement as they clashed and grated across the surface. The Hunter Pack, sensing in the prey a potentially fatal wound, redoubled their efforts against the *gr'raa*'s left front quarter, pouring round after round into the already smoking and blast-torn road wheels, laser and particle beam fire clawing at the spinning wheels, as *va'xachat* penetrators melted their way through relatively thin armor laminate and mininukes flashed and shrilled in a thunderous cacophony. A thunderous barrage of laser and particle beam weaponry swept across the heavily armored blisters on the machine's hull that housed its radar, IR, and optical sensors. Enough hits, enough heat, and the prey's eyes would be gouged, blinded for the kill. Additional weapons—beams and missiles with tactical mininuclear warheads—slammed viciously into the fast-rotating turret that housed the machine's main gun.

At the same time, two of Schaagrasch's surviving Hunters, Two and Sixteen, managed to concentrate their fire against the enemy's remaining port-side track, slicing away great chunks of flintsteel plate with powerfully focused particle beams. The track parted, shattering into separate cleated links as the machine pulled into another hard turn, leaving the broken track stretched out on the ground behind. Inside the fighting compartment of her Hunter, Schaagrasch angled her head far back and loosed a piercing, barking ululation, the victory cry of a Pack Leader tasting blood.

```
LOAD SLFDIAG/LEVEL 4
    ELAPSTIME: .023 SEC
RUN SLFDIAG/LEVEL 4
    POWER SYS: 21.05%(-)
    DRVTRAIN: OP, REDUCED CAPABILITY: 42%
    NAV: ONLINE
    TRACK/SENS: 12%
    SUSPENSION: FNCTNL AT 52%
    TAC/COMM: ONLINE/JAMMED
    SYSOP: LOGIC ARRAY INTEGRATION AT 87%
```

MAGSCRN: ONLINE, REDUCED CAPABILITY: 53%
WEAPSYS: ONLINE
  INFRPTR 2, 3, 5, 6, 9 DSTRYD
  INFRPTR 10, 15, 18 DMGD, 40%
END SLFDIAG/LEVEL 4
  ELAPSTIME: .23 SEC
  >>MAGNETIC SCREENS FAILING; HEAVY DAMAGE SUSTAINED
  TO ARMOR; HULL BREACH AT 7 POINTS
  >>SERIOUS DAMAGE TO OPTICAL AND IR SENSORS
  >>FIREFIGHT ELAPSED TIME: 21.4 SECONDS W 8 KILLS
  >>STRENGTH OF ENEMY FIREPOWER AND ARRIVAL OF ENEMY
  REINFORCEMENTS REDUCES CHANCE OF SUCCESSFUL
  ENGAGEMENT TO 12%

If Schaagrasch was cataloging the weaknesses of the enemy's defenses and technology, she was also critiquing the battle plan that had pitted her Hunter Pack against this foe. With half of her attacking force gone now, and heavy damage to several other of her machines, it was blood-spoor obvious that sixteen Hunters were not enough to guarantee success against one of these lumbering, mechanical *gr'raa*. They might be slow, and they might be stupidly deployed singly instead of in more efficient pack formations, but their armor made them tougher than a *gna'shadath* in its shell, and their firepower was devastating—powerful, precise, and lightning fast. She spoke rapidly, her words picked up and recorded by the Hunter's computer for immediate transmission to base, directing that no less than half an eight of eights ever be allowed to engage one of the enemy *gr'raa* in open battle.

She paused then, considering various possibilities. Malach never failed to learn from their experiences in battle . . . and for that reason they never assumed that the enemy would fail to learn either. It was possible that the enemy did not deploy more than one *gr'raa* at a time for the simple reason that they were expensive, each a profligate investment in raw materials. Still, the enemy was certain to recognize the appalling weakness of their single-machine approach and modify their tactics. It would be best to assume that very soon now, the enemy would begin deploying their *gr'raa* in groups of two or more.

She recorded that thought for the Deathgiver as well . . . along with the recommendation that the optimal deployment in future would be a full eight of eights in any single operation.

No enemy *gr'raa*, no *group* of *gr'raa* numbering fewer than an eight, would survive for long against a Hunter Pack of sixty-four. . . .

This one, she knew, was nearly done for. Its main weapon had taken repeated direct hits, until the turret's outer armor was sagging and misshapen, until the muzzle of the plasma gun had been sheared away by the detonation of a mininuke at point-blank range. Schaagrasch re-entered the fight, lunging forward with a full-powered volley of particle-beam and missile fire. The giant prey swung sharply right, blinded now, its radar emissions almost randomly probing. Hunter Two fired a *ghava'igho*, a tenth-kiloton mininuke that arrowed into the pavement just ahead of the prey, detonating with a dazzling flash twenty *erucht* ahead of the huge machine. The *gr'raa* continued forward, slowing somewhat, as though it sensed danger, but unable to see the sudden yawning crater in front of it. With shattered chunks of pavement flying, it rumbled out over the edge of the crater, tried to stop as it sensed the heat-softened pavement yielding beneath its weight, reversing as the ground suddenly gave way . . . then dropping heavily into the steaming, radioactive pit in a thundering cascade of rubble and crumbling earth.

The prey was trapped now, wheels and remaining treads thrashing helplessly as it ground back and forth in the smoldering crater, gears clashing, smoke boiling from a dozen savage, red-hot rents in its hull. Hunters, black, sleek, and hungry, closed in for the kill. . . .

```
LOAD SLFDIAG/LEVEL 4
    ELAPSTIME: .19 SEC
RUN SLFDIAG/LEVEL 4
    POWER SYS: 02.10%-
    DRVTRAIN: REDUCED CAPABILITY: INOPERABLE
    NAV: OFFLINE
    TRACK/SENS: INOPERABLE
    SUSPENSION: NONFNCTNL
    TAC/COMM: ONLINE/JAMMED
    SYSOP: LOGIC ARRAY INTEGRATION AT 11%
    MAGSCRN: OFFLINE
    WEAPSYS: INOPERABLE
END SLFDIAG/LEVEL 4
    ELAPSTIME: 1.3 SEC
    >>MAGNETIC SCREENS: CRITICAL FAILURE; MASSIVE DAMAGE
    SUSTAINED TO ARMOR; HULL BREACH AT 7 POINTS
    >>OPTICAL AND IR SENSORS INOPERABLE
    >>FIREFIGHT ELAPSED TIME: 28.5 SECONDS W 8 KILLS
    >>CHANCE OF SUCCESSFUL ENGAGEMENT NULL
LOAD ESCAPE/EVASION SUBROUTINE 329
SYSTEM FAILURE/ABORT, RETRY, CANCEL
LOAD ESCAPE/EVASION SUBROUTINE 329
SYSTEM FAILURE/ABORT, RETRY, CANCEL
LOAD ESCAPE/EVASION SUBROUTINE 329
SYSTEM FAILURE/ABORT, RETRY, CANCEL
LOAD ESCAPE/EVASION SUBROUTINE 329
SYSTEM FAILURE/ABORT, RE—
```

CHAPTER EIGHT

Conditions have indeed improved considerably over the past five standard days, and this improvement is clearly due to the intervention of our new Commander. My port-aft track has been replaced, and the maintenance work on my port-forward suspension was completed in only 42.4 standard hours. While I have detected a certain amount of grumbling among the maintenance crew personnel, they have resumed a regular work schedule, and I can at last anticipate being returned to full combat status within two more weeks.

Messages intercepted through base communications continue to worry us, however. Unconfirmed reports of hostile or unknown spacecraft in three systems—Starhold, Endatheline, and Wide Sky—have increased dramatically in both number and frequency. Endatheline has been out of communication for the past 15.72 standard days, and 2.74 hours ago, Unit 96875 reported that all communications—including SWIFT relays—between Muir and Wide Sky had also been interrupted. We reported the matter to our Commander and continue to await developments.

He, meanwhile, has been invited to one of those incomprehensible social engagements occasionally held at the Governor's Residence.

❖ ❖ ❖

Donal arrived precisely at the beginning of Third Watch, as specified in the invitation, but it was clear that the party had been going on for some time already. The Governor's Residence was ablaze with light, so brightly illuminated in fact that the stars of the cluster overhead were washed out, and the emptiness of the Gulf kept at bay. Richly dressed guests stood about on the covered patio or strolled along the tree-lined drive leading up to the house. From a low bluff the house overlooked the bay, sparkling with the reflected hues of lights both from the mansion and from the city of Kinkaid, which sprawled along the horizon on the opposite shore.

Stepping off the public flier and onto the broad, plascrete landing pad, Donal was immediately greeted by a gray-and-gold-uniformed servant, who discreetly checked his invitation, then smiled, bowed, and gestured with a pleasant and professional "*This* way, if you please, sir."

The title "Governor" was clearly a holdover from an earlier era, when the Strathan Cluster was first being colonized by human explorers moving out along the Eastern Arm toward the Galaxy's outer rim. The Cluster had been independent for two centuries, now, but the Confederation retained most of the ranks, titles, and formalities of the original thirty-six colonies. The changeover from dependent to independent status had been entirely peaceful; if anything, most citizens of the Confederation had *resisted* the idea of self-government, favoring a central government that was remote and unconcerned with the affairs of their day-to-day lives.

It was interesting, Donal thought as the servant led him through a tall and richly paneled door, how the people of Muir, at least, clung to the illusions of the past. Governor Reginald Chard was as powerful an autocrat as any human ruler in history, ruling a world of half a billion people while answering solely to a small and largely docile advisory council and to a legislative body that did little but rubber-stamp his proclamations and wrangle with the popular representatives and local district managers. Besides this, he was the senior member of the Strathan Confederation Council, a benign and relaxed dictatorship embracing thirty-six worlds. Despite the Confederation's independence, however, there was still the pretense that Muir and the Strathan Cluster were merely extensions of the whole of human-ruled space.

It was, he realized, a kind of game, a way of fooling themselves into believing that they were part of something larger . . . and more secure.

The grand reception hall of the Governor's Residence was alive with glittering light and color, as each movement, each gesture of each elaborately bejeweled woman, of each elegantly dressed and bemedaled man, reflected the blaze of lights overhead in kaleidoscopic radiance. The floor itself had been set to display an immense portrait of the Galaxy, a simulation of the broad spiral viewed face-on, as though seen from a vantage point ten thousand light years above the core.

Perhaps, Donal thought wryly, it wasn't a game after all. It was as though the people here on this lonely outpost of humanity were unconsciously trying to hold the Ultimate Night at bay, to fill their small, enclosed bubble of a universe with light and forget the emptiness of the Void. By standing, walking, or dancing across the image of the Galaxy, they seemed to be trying to lay symbolic claim to its three hundred billion stars, as though one could own an ocean and all of its treasures and secrets simply by taking its photograph.

"Drink, sir?" Another servant, this one in white, offered him a glass on a silver tray with a precisely measured bow. Donal accepted the drink with a nod. He was greeted in friendly fashion by several men and women just inside the hall. A whirl of introductions left him a little lost, trying to fit names with faces as he fielded the usual pleasantries. When did you arrive in Muir? What do you think of Kinkaid? Where were you stationed in the Concordiat?

One of the women in the group was memorable, even if he lost her name almost as soon as it was given to him. She was blond and intense and quite pretty in a clinging and somewhat insubstantial fluff of iridescent blue and starpearls, and she'd seemed determined at the time to give him every opportunity to steal glances down her low-cut décolletage. Something about the way she kept folding her arms beneath her generous breasts and leaning forward as she looked up into his face with those alluring blue eyes seemed to be body language enough to constitute a full-blown proposition.

Donal knew that he would have to tread carefully, though. Customs varied from world to world throughout human space, and a display of near-naked female breasts might not be the invitation here that it was on other worlds.

Within a few moments, though, the conversation had turned to other things—the weather on Muir and the advent of thorsh-hunting season—and he'd politely taken his leave, wandering away from the group to a spot off to one side of the reception hall, where he could watch the glittering assembly with a measure of anonymity.

Donal had been on Muir for almost a week now and still knew very few of the local people. Most of his time, during both on-duty hours and off, had been spent working with the two Bolos in Vehicle Bay Four, trying to ascertain just how far their test responses and psychotronic measurements might have drifted from the baselines listed in the manuals as normal. The problem was far from solved. Both Bolos showed a high degree of stability, and most of their answers to his test questions were dead on . . . but every once in a while one or the other would come back with an answer that couldn't even be charted, and that worried him. It was like the old story about the behavioral scientists who put a chimpanzee in a room with a locked box of food and various tools to see how the animal would handle elementary problem-solving. When they squinted through the peephole to watch, however, what they encountered was the large, brown eye of the chimp, peering through the peephole from the other side in an effort to study *them*. It was eerie, and more than a little disturbing.

"So tell me, Lieutenant," a woman said, stepping close to him from his right. "How do our social functions here in the Cluster compare to those back in the Concordiat?"

He took a sip of his drink, working on an answer. The woman . . . Lina? Tina? Something like that . . . was one of the people who'd greeted him on his arrival . . . the memorable one, with the generous and nearly naked breasts. From the wry and somewhat calculating expression on her face, she seemed to have set her sights on him for some reason and claimed him for herself.

"Actually, ma'am," he said at last, smiling, "I never attended assemblies like this all that much, so I'm not really much of an authority. Still, the people here are the nicest I've run into in a long time."

"I'm not *ma'am*," she said, laughing. "*Lina!*"

"Lina." He took another sip of his drink and tried to keep his eyes from straying down the front of her gown. "Anyway, I like what I've seen so far."

"My, and aren't *we* the diplomat, now!" she exclaimed, twinkling as she lightly slapped his chest with an "oh, go on" gesture. "I declare, we must have a refugee from the Corps Diplomatique Terrestrienne here!"

"No, no," he said. "Not at all. In fact, my big mouth usually manages to get me into trouble. Not very diplomatic at all."

"Well, that *does* sound intriguing!" She laughed, a rather scratchy squeak and cackle that was not nearly as attractive as her face. "It makes you a man of mystery! You know, the word around Kinkaid is that you fled some sort of trouble back in the Concordiat."

"Really?"

"I've *heard* that a woman was involved."

"How interesting."

"But then, I also heard that you tried to warn some people about the Drozan, but they didn't listen."

"I can't imagine where you got your information."

"There was some sort of a cover-up, and a court martial. Something about you saying your commanding officer had a fat head."

He sighed. "If that were true, it wouldn't be the first time. Like I said, I have a big mouth."

"Mmm." Those blue eyes regarded him steadily for a moment, as though searching out chinks in his armor. ". . . and . . . are you married?"

"I was. That was a while ago, though."

"Oh, I'm *so* sorry." But he could tell from her eyes that she wasn't sorry at all.

He shrugged. The memories weren't so painful now. Not as much, anyway.

Donal felt a light touch at his elbow. Turning, he found himself face to face with Lieutenant Colonel Wood.

"Miss Brodly," the colonel said gravely. "Lieutenant. Please excuse the interruption."

"Yes, sir," Donal said, drawing himself up a bit straighter.

"Why, Colonel Wood!" Lina said. "I haven't seen you in weeks! When are you coming over to my place again? You promised to tell me all about your—"

"Um, yes. If I may borrow your companion, Miss Brodly? Lieutenant? The governor would like to see you now."

"Ah!" Donal exclaimed, delighted at the interruption.

He set his glass on the empty tray of a passing waiter, then bowed to the woman with formal gallantry. "If you would excuse me, Tina?"

"It's *Lina!*"

"Sorry to take you away from the young lady," Wood said as they crossed the soft-glowing, milky curdle of one of the Galaxy's spiral arms. "But Governor Chard likes to meet all newly arrived officers. And he *is* your host."

"Oh, by all means, sir. Duty, and all like that, of course." He suppressed a shudder. The woman had such a predatory, such a *hungry* look. Not that he minded the attentions of a pretty young woman, necessarily, but he still hadn't gotten his bearings on this world, and he didn't want to take a misstep on unfamiliar ground.

He wondered if the local social life here was somewhat stunted by the rarity of new faces. It was the only reason he could imagine that explained such interest in a low-ranking newcomer like him.

Governor Reginald Chard was a thin, sharp-faced man with white-blond hair and the expression of someone who has just tasted something unpleasant. He was talking with General Phalbin, but he turned and gave Donal a thorough once-over as he approached with Wood. "Ah," he said, extending his hand with a deliberate air of condescension. "You must be our newest expatriate from the civilized worlds. Welcome to the Cluster, Lieutenant."

"Harrrumph," Phalbin added. The general momentarily buried his nose in the wine glass he was holding. When he emerged again, he shook his head. "Not as though we need these puppies from the Concordiat, eh, Governor? Coming out here like lords of creation to tell us what to do. Ha?"

"Now, now, General," the governor said, smiling. "Be gracious. This gentleman can't help his orders, and he certainly can't be held responsible for the, ah, perceptions of his superiors."

Donal was stung. "I assure you, General," he said, voice sharp, "that my only interest here is in the Bolos. I wouldn't dream of telling you what to do."

"You seem to be making a fair start over in the Maintenance Depot, young man. I hear you've been shaking things up over there. Rocking the boat, as they say." He took another long and thirsty swallow from his rosé. "It is generally expected that a junior officer newly posted to an unfamiliar command will take his time to settle in, to, ah, get the lay of the land, as it were. . . ."

Obviously, someone had been complaining about the way he'd been running things. It was, he supposed, to be expected, though he would have thought the complaints would have gone to Lieutenant Colonel Wood, not all the way up the line to the commanding general.

This was not the time or the place to discuss brigade politics, however, or the problems inherent in going outside the chain of command. "Perhaps, sir," he said carefully, "we should discuss this at another time."

"Absolutely!" the governor said, face creasing in a broad smile. "Come, come, General! I throw these affairs so we can get away from the stress of the daily grind, you know. Can't keep your nose in your work all the time. Got to come up for air once in a while and see what the world has to offer, eh?" He sipped his drink, then gestured with the glass, taking in the glittering room. "So. Lieutenant. What do you think of our little corner of the Galaxy?"

"I'm afraid I haven't had the chance to get out and see much of Kinkaid as yet, Governor," he said. "Your night skies are certainly spectacular."

"Yes indeed, they are that. Some people who come out here find them disturbing, you know. All that emptiness out there."

"I can imagine. Still, that's all in the head, isn't it? What does it matter if the next nearest star is four light years away, or four thousand? As long as you have a good piece of ground to stand on right here."

"Well, well, General!" Chard said, turning to Phalbin. "Our newest officer is a philosopher as well!"

"That was neatly put," Phalbin said, grudgingly. "But it takes—eh?"

A gaudily uniformed aide, gold aiguillettes spilling from her left shoulder, moved to Phalbin's side and whispered something in his ear. He started as though pinched. "What? When?" he demanded.

The aide whispered something else, and Phalbin shook his head. "Who would have believed it?"

"Is there trouble, General?" Chard asked mildly.

"Um . . . harrumph, well, possibly. Possibly. Governor? May I see you privately for a moment?"

The two men stepped aside, conversing in low and urgent tones. Donal looked at Lieutenant Colonel Wood, one eyebrow cocked higher than the other in an unvoiced question.

"Probably running short of wine," Wood said, a mildly acid edge to his voice. "They're wondering if they have to break out the good stuff they were saving for themselves."

"You don't much like this posting, do you, sir?"

"Is it that obvious?" He shrugged, then took a sip from his glass. "I wonder, sometimes, how in God's name humans can imagine they're the pinnacle of creation. I seem to remember reading something, somewhere, about a notion called 'survival of the fittest.' "

Donal chuckled. "Don't think we're going to make it?"

"Frankly, I'm astonished we've made it this far." He studied the governor and the general for a moment with evident distaste. "Any evolutionary system that allows people who can't see past the end of their nose to rise to positions of power . . ."

"Are you talking about the governor, sir? Or General Phalbin?"

He shook his head. "Forget I said that. But it's damned frustrating, sometimes. I keep wondering what happens when we come up against a race that's smarter, faster . . . and just plain *meaner* than we are."

"I always thought humankind was pretty nasty, sir. We've had the evolutionary monopoly on nastiness so far, anyway."

"The only trouble is that too often somebody has to come along and smash us in the face a few times before we wake up and recognize that there's a problem at all."

"The rumors? About something out in the Gulf?"

He shrugged. "Probably just that. Rumors. But God help these people if there's ever a *real* threat to our security. Everyone spends so much time worrying about covering his own tail that we could find ourselves in real trouble someday, and with no one to blame. The cold, dead hand of Darwin doesn't distinguish between social classes, and it damned well doesn't wait for openings in engagement calendars."

Donal guessed that Wood had been trying to get something out of Phalbin or the governor, an appropriation, perhaps, or access to needed supplies, and had been refused. A coldness brushed across the back of his mind, raising his hackles. For the past week he'd been deluging Wood's office with requests for service and maintenance parts for the Bolos. Had those requisitions been turned down? Ignored? Had Wood been called on the carpet because of them?

"Trouble with the hierarchy, sir?"

"Mmm. Let's just say that—" He stopped abruptly. Phalbin and the governor were coming back. Phalbin was glowering; Chard looked rattled. "Bad news, Governor?"

"The base is going on alert, Colonel," Phalbin said bluntly. "You'd better inform your men."

"I'm sorry to have to end the evening's festivities," Chard added. "But this is . . . distressing."

"What is it, sir?" Donal asked. "If we're going on alert, it would be nice to know what's threatening us."

"That's just it," Chard said. "We don't know. Nothing but vague and panicky guesses. Fear-mongering. Hysteria—"

"It has just been reported," Phalbin said, cutting in, "that a large and definitely hostile force has landed on Wide Sky. We haven't been able to learn anything, save that the enemy force appears to be a species unknown to us, and possessing superior technology and firepower."

"Superior technology?" Donal asked, eyebrows raised.

"Superior enough to destroy the Mark XVIII that was based there," Phalbin said. "It seems one of your vaunted Concordiat Bolos, Lieutenant, didn't even have sense enough to know it was outclassed. They took it to pieces in just seconds."

Wood pursed his lips and gave a low whistle. "Where did they come from?"

"Unknown at this time," Phalbin said.

Chard shrugged. "It's possible, I suppose, that they are from the Void after all."

"*Highly* unlikely, sir." The general pursed his lips and gave Donal a swift, sidelong glance. "Undoubtedly we are dealing with raiders, refugees, perhaps, from strife somewhere within our Galaxy."

"Melconians, possibly?" Wood asked. "Seeking easier targets?"

"Possibly." Phalbin looked at his drink, as though attempting to divine the answers there. "They are a long way from home, if they are."

"Apparently," Chard went on, "we lost all contact with Wide Sky several hours ago. Our last message from them indicated that the military base there was on the point of being overrun. Evidently, their SWIFT equipment was captured or destroyed."

"Could have been the relays between here and there, too," Phalbin said. "This deep inside the Cluster, SWIFT needs relays every few light years just to keep up the signal strength."

Chard's eyes widened. "Eh? But that means they might be on their way here. Knocking out our faster-than-light comm links could be the prelude to an invasion."

"That's why we're going on alert, of course. Not that invasion is all that likely. . . ."

"I understand we've also lost contact with Endatheline, General," Donal said casually. "Seems a bit much to expect mere raiders to knock out two of the other worlds of the Cluster in such short order, don't you think?"

Phalbin's face darkened, and he was about to say something curt, but Chard spoke first. "What's your point, Lieutenant?"

"That we could make better decisions if we knew exactly what this threat was. Who they are, what they want." He looked at Phalbin. "And where they come from."

"And how would we do that, Lieutenant?" Phalbin said.

"By going there, of course," Donal said. "I volunteer."

"He's got a point, you know," Chard said. "We need to know what the hell is going on out there."

"Yes, sir, but—"

"If it's just raiders or bandits, riffraff like that, we won't need to alarm people here unnecessarily. I'd hate to upset the political status quo."

Phalbin digested this. "You would go by yourself, Lieutenant?"

"Yes, sir. Well, I'll need transport, of course. I don't think we want to wait for the next freighter or passenger liner due in-port. Maybe a military courier or a mail packet—"

"There's a regular Space Service courier run scheduled for two days from now," Wood said. "We might even bump that up a day."

"Could you leave tomorrow, Lieutenant?" Phalbin asked.

"Certainly. And a courier would be ideal. Fast enough to keep out of trouble if things are bad in Wide Sky orbit. I could at least get close enough to use standard radio or use a SWIFT link-up without having to go through the relays. One way or the other, we'd know."

"What about your work here? With the Bolos?"

"Frankly, General, there's not a lot more I could get done staying here." There'd been some foot-dragging with the depot crew, certainly—not to mention someone taking detours around the usual chain of command— but work on the Bolos was pretty close to back on schedule now. And the way things seemed to work around here, Donal was beginning to think he'd prefer to get the intel he needed to work with himself, rather than wait for it to trickle down the line from someone else. It was surprising, he thought, how quickly he was getting excited by the prospect of getting out of Kinkaid and off of Muir for a few days. He grinned. "If you send me, General," he said, "I'll promise not to submit any more parts requisitions until I get back."

"Harrumph," Phalbin said . . . but then he managed a quirk of a smile. "We *do* need to know what's happening at Wide Sky. Very well, Lieutenant. I'll write up your orders. But let me remind you, this won't be an annual leave. No paid vacations. I expect you to go in, see what's happening, talk to the local authorities if you can raise them, and then get back here, at once."

"Yes, sir." He frowned.

"Something, Lieutenant?" Wood asked.

"Just a thought, sir. You people should probably make plans in case I don't return."

"Eh?" Chard said. "What do you mean?"

"Sir, from what we've heard, we have hostiles out there who eat Mark XVIII Bolos for breakfast. If I don't return on schedule, well, you'd better just assume that I've run into something really nasty out there. Something that you're going to want to be prepared for when it reaches Muir."

"Pleasant thought," Wood said.

Donal gave him a thin smile. "Just thinking about Darwin, sir. And the survival of the fittest."

CHAPTER NINE

Work continues unabated to get both Bolo 96875 and me fully back on-line, but I sense that in some inherently indefinable way that work has taken on a new sense of urgency. This, we agree, must be related to the new reports—and the sudden SWIFT silence—from Wide Sky, and we both feel a quickening that in an organic life form would be interpreted as growing excitement.

Using our private channel, we have discussed at length the apparently easy destruction of the Mark XVIII Bolo stationed on Wide Sky. Though Mark XXIV Bolos are far superior in every way to older and more primitive marks, we agree that the unknown hostiles on Wide Sky must possess either an impressive weapons technology or a considerable numerical advantage, or both, to have so easily defeated even a Mark XVIII. The Gladius may be old, limited both in overall intelligence and flexibility, and verging on obsolescence in many areas, but it would still require several direct hits or extremely near-misses by multiple nuclear warheads in the half- to one-megaton range to disable it, and its antimissile defense system is very nearly the equal of my own. The reports that we have intercepted, that a Mark XVIII was disabled in a firefight lasting something less than thirty seconds, are disquieting.

This, we assume, is the reason that our new Commander has boarded a military courier and left for the Wide Sky system. This is regrettable. While we understand our Commander's desire to acquire military intelligence first-hand, his departure could adversely affect the efficiency of the maintenance crews working to bring us back on-line. He does seem to have instilled in them a willingness to continue their work in order to get the job done quickly, but I detect a sullenness in some individuals that could interfere with the schedule.

The work proceeds so much more smoothly when Lieutenant Ragnor is present. I hope he returns soon.

Though Bolos are not subject to such emotions as loneliness or worry, both Bolo 96875 and I believe that our full availability and functionality will be necessary in the very near future, and Lieutenant Ragnor's presence may be directly necessary to achieve this.

"What is this?" Tech Master Sergeant Georg Blandings said, hands on hips, feet apart as he leaned over the edge of the Bolo's main deck and bawled at the group of men and women eight meters below. "A holiday? Nobody said you people could stop workin'!"

Private First Class Len Kemperer glared up at him, arms crossed. "Aw, c'mon, Sarge! Give us a break! The old man's gone! An' when the cat's away, and all like that—"

"Can it, Lennie," Blandings said. "We've got a sched to keep, and we're gonna keep it."

Corporal Debbie Hall laughed. "What's with you, Sarge? You going hardliner on us all of a sudden?"

"Maybe it's time someone did," he growled. "Now listen up, and listen sharp. You might not like the new CO, and you might not agree with him . . . but he is the Man and we're gonna play it by the book, see? I got my orders, which means you got *your* orders, and by Bolo you guys're gonna carry 'em out. Y'hear me?"

"Sheesh, Sarge!" Corporal Steve Dombrowski ran a hand through his greasy hair. "The guy's tryin' to work us to death! We can't get all of these torsion suspension assemblies balanced by Third Watch! It's inhuman!"

"Yeah, Sarge," Hall added. "Cut us some slack, huh?"

"Look!" Blandings yelled, his voice echoing off the high, wide ceiling of the depot. "I don't wanna hear it! The lieutenant's not gonna like it if he gets back and finds these babies still high and dry with their tracks off and their suspensions in pieces! He'll be very unhappy, and that means *I'll* be unhappy . . . and you just don't know how unhappy that's gonna make *you*! Now get the hell to work!"

The maintenance crew grumbled, but they went back to their jobs.

Thirty light years from Muir, the KR-72 Lightning-class courier made the final preparations to emerge from transpace. Donal shifted uncomfortably in his acceleration seat. Glad as he was to escape the confines of Muir, he would be happier still when this journey was complete. He glanced to his left at the courier's pilot. Commander Kathy Ross, he imagined, would be glad to be rid of him too.

The KR-72 Lightning was the product of fairly recent advances in ship-design technology. FTL-capable, it could make the thirty-light-year hop from Muir to Wide Sky in a little less than a week, though the cabin was so cramped that Donal wasn't able to move around very much during that time. He slept in the bridge acceleration couch reserved for supercargo, leaving its close embrace only to use the tiny fresher at the rear of the cabin, or to prepare a self-heating meal packet from the stores locker. Kathy Ross, he learned, a hard-eyed, black-skinned, gray-haired woman of about fifty, liked her command precisely because she got to spend so much time alone—and having to share with a passenger a compartment that was small for one person was decidedly not her idea of a good time.

Externally, the courier *Black Flash* was a space-black pencil with broad, down-canted delta wings, a sneakship designed to penetrate enemy-patrolled space without being detected. While not invisible to radar or infrared scans, the ship had been crafted with stealth in mind. On radar, the Lightning appeared no more than a meter or two across, a chunk of nondescript space debris. Heat from its fusion power plant was cycled through wing-array dissipaters that minimized the IR track. In an emergency, heat could be stored, then channeled through the laser weaponry for dispersal. The Lightning's chief claim to fame was in her speed and maneuverability. The cranky, high-powered little ships served throughout the Concordiat and beyond as express carriers for packages or non-electronic mail, and as military scouts.

"Twenty seconds to normal space," Commander Ross said. She sighed, extended her long, slender arms above her head, and stretched.

"And then you can be rid of me," Donal said with a tight grin.

"I won't say it's been fun, Lieutenant," she replied. She wrinkled her nose. "The air purifiers in this bucket really aren't up to handling the stink of *two* people, you know." A sharp warbling sounded from the swing-pivot console in front of her chair. "Ah! Here we go!"

Outside, the glowing murk of transpace exploded into myriad, rainbow-hued streaks, each of which steadied almost at once into more familiar objects: a scattering of stars, isolated and cold; a local sun, glowing warm orange off to the right; a pair of largish moons showing three-quarters-phases to the left; and, dead ahead, the gorgeous, half-phase glory of blue and white and green that was the earthlike world of Wide Sky. A viewscreen mounted between the two bridge seats was set to display a view aft and was filled with the teeming suns of the Cluster. It was a silent reminder that they were now well beyond the warmer, friendlier skies of the Strathan Cluster's heart.

Another warning chirped from the console.

"What's that?" Donal asked.

"Proximity alert," Ross replied. "We've got ships . . . big suckers, and lots of 'em."

"Uh, oh." He'd been afraid of this. Wide Sky's space arm was limited to a handful of aging patrol cutters, a couple of light frigates, and eight or ten corvettes assigned customs duties. And freighters and free traders weren't so common in the Cluster that they ever showed up in fleets. "You got a visual?"

"Coming up."

The view aft winked off and was replaced a moment later by a long-range optical scan of a ship, an unknown ship, all curves and bulges, spike antennae and deadly looking weapons turrets. Most of the ship was rust-brown, though traces of an old and sand-blasted paint scheme were still visible—what might have been a black-and-yellow tiger-stripe pattern. A sense of the scale of the thing was evident when a tiny fighter or ship's boat passed in front of the behemoth; the scale sharpened when Donal took a closer look and realized that the second vessel was a corvette or a small escort of some kind, a warship far larger than any fighter. The big vessel was at least a kilometer long, easily a match for the largest battleship in the Concordiat Space Arm.

"I've got sixty-four ships of various masses on my scope," Ross told him. "Eight are monsters like that one out there . . . seven huge ships and one even huger . . . a *big* mama. Twenty-four are big, but low power readings. I think they must be transports of some kind. The rest are probably warships."

"Interesting," Donal said. "I wonder if the fact that those numbers are all factors of eight means anything?"

"Like a base-eight numerical system? Maybe. So what?"

He shrugged. "Anything we can learn about these people . . ."

"Well, I think we're about to learn how they receive unexpected guests," she told him. "I've got bogies vectoring for an intercept. Hang on!"

With the inertial dampers full on, there was no sensation of movement, but the view through the forward bridge window spun wildly as Ross applied full thrust.

Long minutes passed, with no further change in the view ahead save the gradually accelerating growth of Wide Sky as the Lightning plunged across the dwindling kilometers. Commander Ross kept her eyes on her instruments, especially on a small, three-D radar display that showed the relative positions of *Black Flash* and the pursuing vessels. As the blips slowly shifted on the small display, Donal could see what Ross was doing— accelerating hard along one vector until the other ships had started moving to block her, then kicking in a brutal side thrust, jamming the courier into a new vector that took advantage of the displacement of the blockading forces,

Even the courier's damping fields couldn't entirely block the effects of that savage thrust. Donal was slammed against the side of his couch, and his vision blurred. Something like a giant hand clamped down over his head and shoulders, squeezing until he couldn't breathe, until his heart thumped with a laboring beat in his ears and his vision was tinted red. A groan sounded from somewhere aft, a groan that shifted gradually to a shriek of tortured hull braces and plates, and it seemed as though no ship ever made could tolerate such stress.

Then they were through a gap in the enemy defenses five thousand kilometers wide, and Wide Sky was flattening out ahead of them into a blue, cloud-swathed curve of sunlit horizon beneath a jet-black sky.

"I'm surprised they didn't fire at us," Donal said, finding his voice at last.

"They did. We have sixteen missiles tracking us right now, and from the rads they're emitting, my guess is that they're nukes."

"Can you lose them?"

"We'll never know it if I can't."

Something struck the *Black Flash*, a savage blow from beneath that rattled Donal's bones and would have thrown him out of his seat had he not been strapped down. At first he thought they'd been hit, but he saw the truth a second later, as Kathy Ross gripped the flight controls with both hands, fighting to bring the little ship's nose higher.

They'd just hit atmosphere.

Even from the edge of space, the signs of wide-scale, planet-devastating warfare were painfully, starkly clear. Over the world's night side, where oceans gleamed beneath the Strathan Cluster's pale glow, Donal could see the sullen, throbbing orange smears of enormous fires, partly masked by palls of ebon blackness, the glare of burning cities showing through the smoke and ash clouds as if through dirty cotton. On the day side, the cities were invisible, but the clouds over certain locations had an ugly, charcoal cast to them, vast plumes of black spreading downwind from the funeral pyres of a space-faring civilization.

He found Galloway, Wide Sky's capital . . . or what, at any rate, had once been the capital. From the records he'd studied on the way out from Muir, the place scarcely rated the name "city." None of the population centers on Wide Sky had been larger than eighty or ninety thousand people, and most were small clusters of a few homesteads . . . villages, in fact, in distinctly rural settings. As far as he could tell, all of the larger population centers were gone now, smashed to rubble and the wreckage set aflame.

Using the *Black Flash*'s long-range optics, Donal zeroed in on what was left of Galloway, riding the planet's terminator on the line between night and dawn. Parts of the city were still burning, and strange machines were laboring in the ruins. It was difficult to see from orbit precisely what was happening, but advanced computer enhancement yielded scenes, viewed from overhead, of a variety of long-legged labor or combat machines demolishing the wrecked shells of buildings, stacking up huge piles of pipe, wiring, steel beams, and junked vehicles, and loading the debris onto transports.

There were hundreds of those last, space-going barges, actually, equipped with contragrav to let them settle slowly, with clumsy yawings and driftings, all the way down through the atmosphere to the ground to receive their loads of scrap metal.

Scrap metal? The invaders, whoever they were, seemed to be frantically ferreting out and grabbing the stuff, in any shape or form. Whole buildings were being demolished; wiring, especially, seemed highly prized, for Donal could see vast coils of copper wiring stacked adjacent to the barge landing sites.

"We need to call in the Concordiat Space Arm," Donal said, more to himself than to his companion. The Strathan Cluster Confederation had a defense treaty with the Concordiat still; besides, Terra would be extremely interested in a high-tech intruder on a human-occupied world, even this far out in the great beyond. "Trouble is, how long will it take for them to get here?"

"I'll tell you one thing, Lieutenant," Commander Ross said, snapping off a row of switches above her head. "It'll take thirty years if we have to rely on standard radio to let 'em know what the story is back on Muir."

"What do you mean?"

"SWIFT's out. Dead. No carrier. I think these guys have a way of jamming it, somehow."

So. No faster-than-light communication with Muir . . . or with the Concordiat, at least not until he could get back to Muir in person, or they could find a way to get clear of the enemy jamming effect.

"Terrific. Can we talk to anybody on Wide Sky?"

"Radio doesn't seem affected. Question is, will you end up getting through to the colonists, what's left of 'em? Or to . . . those *things*?"

Her classification of the intruders wasn't fair, obviously, since they hadn't yet seen one of them. Still, the eldritch cant and form and posture of those work machines down there spoke of an alien twist of mind, something quite outside what humans might find comfortable . . . or comprehensible. Worse was the realization that the invaders had smashed and stripped a world that was both peaceful and nonmilitary. Their army had been small, their space navy smaller. The invaders didn't seem to care about that, didn't care about anything except razing the works of man and looting them of metal.

Donal could understand her disgust.

The ship lurched violently to the side. "Sorry," Ross said. "I'm trying to throw those missiles off the scent. They're still closing."

Involuntarily, Donal glanced back over his shoulder, but there was nothing to be seen there but the doorway leading to the fresher. He felt a sudden, sharp need to urinate, but suppressed it. *Not exactly a dignified way to die*, he thought wryly. *Taken out by a nuke while you're taking a—*

The sky outside the cockpit lit up, a savage, sun-brilliant flash of white light. "Don't look!" Ross yelled, her own eyes squeezed tight shut, her head turned away even as the polarizer filters in the bridge windows tried to go black against that intolerable glare. The light faded, and Donal blinked against the fuzzy circles of purple hovering in his field of vision.

"Close one," Donal observed. "For a minute, there, I thought—"

The shock wave struck in mid-sentence, a sickening, hull-rattling shudder that nearly flipped the courier end for end. Somehow, though, Commander Ross kept the craft flying and more or less under control.

"You were saying?"

"Never mind. As long as we're still more or less in one piece." He reached for the radio mike, switching to a military frequency. "Wide Sky, Wide Sky, anyone on Wide Sky, this is the Confederation Space Service Courier *Black Flash* on entry approach from low orbit. Does anybody copy? Over."

He was answered by a faint hiss of static—a hiss that swelled to a deafening howl twice when nuclear warheads detonated in quick succession a few tens of kilometers astern. He repeated the call . . . and again . . . and yet again. Finally, he was rewarded with a faint voice, barely heard through the background hiss.

"—*Flash*, this is Wide Sky. *Black Flash*, this is Wide Sky. We have you on our radar, coming in over our south-central continent in the eastern hemisphere, altitude about one hundred twenty klicks."

Donal glanced at Ross, who nodded curtly. "That's us."

"Wide Sky, we confirm. It looks like the port at Galloway's been plastered. Where do you want us to set down? Over."

"*Black Flash*, there aren't many places left. Most of us who could move, including what's left of our ground forces, have fallen back to Scarba. That's in the western part of the South Sea, about nine thousand kilometers from your present position, on a great circle heading of one-zero-niner."

The Lightning canted suddenly to the right, nose dipping, wings struggling with the thickening air. Donal could see a bit of ionization building up outside, like a faint, pink glow spreading back from nose and wingtips. The static on the radio became sharper.

"I've got them plotted," Ross said. "We're on course. Eighteen minutes."

"Wide Sky, this is *Black Flash*. We're locked in and coming down. ETA eighteen minutes."

Another nuke detonated, washing out the radio spectrum with white noise. By the time it cleared, the ionization of re-entry was so thick that no message would be able to punch through for another ten or twelve minutes at least.

"Can we make it without taking one of those firecrackers up our tail jets?" he asked her.

"Like I say, Lieutenant. You never feel the one that—"

Another detonation lit the sky, the shock wave close behind the light that heralded its approach. The courier fluttered like a leaf, rolling wing over wing as it plummeted through shrieking air, a white plume of vapor boiling out of the shocked atmosphere as it passed.

Long and heart-pounding minutes later, Ross pulled them out of the roll. "I think we're clear," she said. "I don't see any more missiles. They all missed, detonated short, or went wild. And it doesn't look like the bad guys are inclined to follow us, either."

"That's good. I am wondering, though, how the heck we're supposed to get off this rock."

"One crisis at a time, Lieutenant. One crisis at a time. Right now I'm busy praying that this bucket holds together long enough to deliver us both to something like solid ground without smearing us all over the horizon . . . and I suggest that you do the same."

The next few minutes seemed like an eternity, but at last the Lightning punched through the ionization cloud, soaring through thin, cold air at an altitude of fifty thousand meters. Clouds, cobalt-blue ocean, and scattered land forms of green and brown swept silently beneath the delta-craft's keel. A coastline swept toward them out of the east, snow-capped mountains wrinkling up from green-ocher veldts and the darker masses of tropical forest. A world, *any* world, was such an enormous place, varied in terrain, in landscape features, in special beauties and dangers unique to itself.

"Nice job, Commander," he said, allowing himself to relax. "For a time, there, I didn't think we were going to make it."

"Don't congratulate me yet, Lieutenant. We ain't out of the woods, not by a long shot." The aircraft lurched heavily, nose coming up. It felt sluggish.

"What . . . what's the problem?"

"Can't tell. Starboard control surfaces are jammed, it feels like, and I can't pop the air brakes. The leads're melted through, I think. And the engine's dead. Can't restart. Looks like we're going down, and hard."

Damn! "How far to this Scarba they told us about?"

"Not too far. Two, three hundred kilometers, maybe. I'll get us as close as I can. Then we're going to have to punch out."

He kept quiet after that, though rivulets of sweat beaded his face and tickled their way down his cheeks. They were steadily losing altitude now, a dead-stick glider with the aerodynamic grace and precise control of a falling rock.

Ocean gleamed in the distance, just ahead of the dark purple band of the approaching nightside terminator. To the north, smoke stained the sky—another burning city.

He wondered how close they were to the human perimeter.

Another lurch . . . a kick in the seat of his pants accompanied by the screech of ripping metal. Suddenly, the air was buffeting them wildly as the courier began a lazy roll to port.

"Hang on, Lieutenant!" Ross yelled above the sudden

roar. "Can't hold her! We're punching out!" Plastic shields snapped out of the chair, embracing him in a wind-proof bubble. Thunder exploded, coupled with a wrenching, gut-sick sensation of heavy acceleration, of falling . . .

And then Donal lost all awareness of any sensation whatsoever.

CHAPTER TEN

"*C'mon*, Lieutenant!" The voice was low, the words whispered, but with sharp urgency. "Snap out of it!"

Someone slapped his face again, and Donal opened his eyes. At first he thought something was wrong with his eyes because it was so dark, but then memories began dropping into place. Kathy Ross was leaning over him, one hand holding a stim injector from a medkit, the other holding his jaw as she moved his head back and forth and peered down into his face.

Awareness returned. It was dark because it was night. The sky was clear, but with the empty loneliness of skies out on the Rim; two moons glowed with orange-gold beauty, one full, near the zenith, the other crescent-sharp, above the mountains inland. He smelled the salt spray, heard the gentle hiss of ocean surf nearby. He was lying on his back in the sand, and his clothes were wet. He tried to sit up.

"Ssst! Careful!" Ross warned, pressing him back with a firm hand against his chest. "We've got company. No fast moves. . . ."

He looked past her, at the . . . *things* moving up the beach.

Invader war machines. They had to be, because they

113

looked like nothing he'd ever seen in human space.

There were two of them, perhaps half a kilometer down the beach, both painted ebon-black but clearly visible by the moonlight and by the phosphorescent glow scattered back by the sea. Each was perhaps five or six meters tall. They stood on two slender legs, claw-footed and broad at the bottoms, narrower at the tops where they merged with the shadowed complexities of drive machinery beneath their flat bodies. The knee joints were angled backward, the opposite of human legs, with the digitigrade articulation of a bird or bipedal reptile.

In fact, they reminded Donal of birds in a way . . . of giant chickens, perhaps, picking their way through a farmyard with mincing, strutting movements.

He fought an insane compulsion to laugh. They looked ridiculous.

They also, clearly, were deadly. The upper body of each of the machines was flat, a triangle with rounded edges and slightly down-curved wingtips, a little like the stingrays or giant mantas that still swam the oceans of Terra. There was no sign of a cockpit or fighting compartment, but the blunt prow of each machine was studded with short, vicious-looking muzzles of various shapes and calibers, weapons of various types, without a doubt.

Other details became clearer as they moved closer. There were jet venturis of some sort on the bellies, suggesting at least a limited ability to fly. The feet were flanged, with three blunt toes on each, two ahead, one behind, but there was also a forward-facing claw, sickle shaped and razor-edged. He couldn't imagine what that was supposed to be for. Their movements had a smooth and curiously organic feel, as though the machines were in fact alive, or at the very least as if they were enormous, string-dangling puppets. There was a quickness to their movements, an alertness in the attitudes of the huge bodies, that far transcended the stalwart, massive, and uncompromising solidity of a Bolo.

Teleoperation, he thought. *They move as though they're wired up to living beings, moving in step with them.* That would explain why they walked on spindly legs, rather than moving on more stable and solid tracks. Humans had been experimenting with teleoperated systems for the past thousand years or so, but when it came to weapons, humanity had chosen the path leading to huge, mobile fortresses; the tanks of the early twentieth century had evolved into tracked behemoths, slow-moving, heavily armed and armored mountains of metal that could withstand damned near anything thrown at them. He couldn't imagine one of these frail-looking things lasting for more than an instant against the two-megaton-per-second firepower of a Bolo's Hellbore.

Donal knew that it would be dangerous to judge the invader machines by their silly looks, though.

Several alien designs had gone the way of legs rather than tracks. The Axorc robot hunters with their jointed crawler-legs, for instance, like great, black millipedes. Or the Yavac walkers of the spider-like Deng. Bolos had fought the combat machines of those races, and others even stranger, in the thousand years since Man had gone to the stars, and it was never smart to assume that an odd look or a twist of alien psychology indicated an inherent inferiority to human designs. These machines could be tougher than they looked. Too, reports that had made it through from Wide Sky suggested that the invaders had used mass assault tactics on the Mark XVIII. Throw enough machines at a Bolo all at once, and even the best could be overwhelmed by numbers and worn down by repeated hits.

A lot depended on what the beings piloting those things were like, where they came from, how they *thought*.

He snuggled himself a bit further back down out of

sight. Donal and the courier pilot were lying on the reverse slope of a grass-cloaked sand dune, just behind the top, looking over the crest toward the broad, flat beach where the two invader machines were walking. They were far enough off that he could take some comfort in the distance, and in the insignificance of two shadows-clad humans hidden in the dunes, but it was hard to tell what they might be able to see or not see with the instruments of an alien technology. If they had sufficiently sensitive IR scanning, the two watching humans were probably standing out against the darkness like a pair of small bonfires; a Bolo, certainly, would have had no trouble seeing them at this range.

On the other hand, the invaders didn't seem terribly interested in searching the area. They'd found one of the eject capsules from the crashed Lightning lying in the sand at the edge of the surf. Even without image enhancement, Donal could see by the light of the two moons in the sky the footprints and drag marks where Kathy Ross had hauled him up the beach, leading more or less straight to their current hiding spot, but the two invader machines seemed more interested in the wreckage of the capsule. Though it was difficult to see in the darkness, it looked to Donal as though a slender set of claw-tipped arms was reaching down from the flat, manta-body of the thing and was lifting the seat and its shattered plastic canopy from the surging waves. It drew it up, dripping, then gave it a shake. Was that machine's operator looking for the human who'd ridden inside? Or trying to figure out what it was?

One of the machines turned in place until it was directly facing them across two hundred yards of open sand. Donal felt Ross stiffen beside him, getting ready to run; he laid a hand on her arm, willing her to be still. It looked . . . it *felt* as though these invaders simply didn't care about anything as small or inconsequential as humans. Certainly, if these were the combat vehicles that had done in a Mark XVIII Bolo in less than half a minute—more, if these were the machines that had actually survived an all-out assault against the Bolo—then there probably wasn't much a couple of isolated soldiers could do to hurt them.

Another much larger and slower machine appeared on the beach, lumbering along on four jointed, massive legs toward the pair of bipedal combat walkers. Straddling the junked ejection seats, it dropped multiple clawed arms from its belly, grasped the wreckage, and hauled it up inside. After a moment more it began waddling away, leaving the biped invaders where they stood. There was something about their manner now, an agitation, that worried Donal. They turned away from the two humans and seemed to be scanning the horizon to the southeast.

Could they have spotted something in that direction? A ship perhaps, or . . .

Both walkers pivoted suddenly, fixing their attention on one small part of the sky. A moment later, a howl sounded out of the southeast, and the walkers turned slowly, weapons tracking the dark sky out over the ocean. Then Donal saw them, a pair of shapes hurtled in toward the beach, wave-skimming, afterburners glaring in star-banishing cones of blue-white light. The two invaders opened fire, dazzling beams of light slicing across the night; one of the aircraft—they looked to Donal like old, K-100 Gremlins—exploded in a dazzling spray of burning fragments while it was still far out over the water.

The second Gremlin managed to loose one missile before its port-side wing was sheared away and it pancaked into a dizzying tumble toward the water. The missile exploded far short of its intended target, vaporized by a particle beam of some kind, Donal thought. The aircraft hit the water several kilometers out to sea, exploded in a white flash, and sank.

"Oh, my God . . ." Ross said quietly.

One of the walkers was striding off down the beach, following the big four-legged machine. The second walker stood on the beach alone for a moment. Suddenly, with no warning, it pivoted to face the hidden humans once more.

Something in the aggressive way it twisted about warned Donal. "Duck!" The two slid down the reverse slope of the dune, scrabbling deeper into the cool embrace of the sand. With the suddenness of a thrown switch, the night above them flared into noonday brilliance, a harsh, actinic blue-white light that burned their eyes even through tight-shut eyelids. The thunderclap that accompanied the light shrieked in Donal's ears, threatening to lift him from the sheltering sand, clawing at his consciousness.

And then the night was dark and silent once again.

Dazed, he sat up, brushing sand from his uniform. Kathy Ross sat up beside him, blinking. "Look . . ."

He followed her gaze. The entire top of the dune they were hiding behind had been fused, the grass scoured away cleanly by the white hot beam, the individual grains of sand melted together into a cracked and irregular cap of dirty, frosted glass that extended in a ragged zigzag along ten meters of the dune's top. The stuff was still hot. Donal could feel the heat rolling off the surface in waves, and as it cooled, cracking and popping sounds emanated from the glassy mass.

The walkers were gone, and only the churned-up footprints they'd left at the water's edge remained to show they'd been there. That, and the fused glass at the top of the dune.

"Well," Donal said, trying to keep the shakiness out of his voice. "What now?"

Ross let out a deep sigh, her hands hanging limply at her side as she stared wide-eyed at the spot where two high-performance aircraft had just been swept from the sky. "We need to go *that* way," she said, nodding toward the southeast, and the moons-gleam on the ocean's empty horizon. "Scarba is out there."

"In the middle of the ocean?"

"Wide Sky's got these fishing centers," she explained. "The biggest one is called Fortrose. They're kind of like cities raised on enormous, sea-going platforms. Scarba's the name of the island chain where they're anchored right now. I gather they usually follow certain fish on long, deep-ocean migrations, harvesting as they go, and the Scarba Chain's where the fish are. I guess when the invasion came—"

"They became a sanctuary," Donal said, completing the thought. "Yeah." He looked at her. "You've been here before?"

"A time or two. Used to work for a free trader who pulled his circuit throughout this part of the Cluster." Turning, she looked up at the star cluster, hanging low in the western sky. "Wouldn't mind seeing his rattletrap old freight hauler now. *Nefertiti*, her name was."

Donal moved his hand closer to the fused glass, experimentally testing the heat. "What do we have in the way of emergency gear?" he asked. "I wasn't much aware of what happened after you hit the eject button."

"Not much," she admitted. "Those seats are fitted with emergency packs. You know, first aid kits, survival radios, stuff like that. But after we touched down, I was kind of busy getting you out of your pod and dragging you ashore before you drowned. Your eject pod was smashed open when it hit, and was filling up with water."

"Thanks," he said, seriously. He tried to picture Kathy Ross battling the surf to haul his inert body out of the partly exposed seat in the eject pod. He outmassed her by twenty-five kilos, at least.

"No problem. But, well, by the time I'd hauled your tail up onto the beach, I saw those . . . things coming. I dragged you the rest of the way up the beach and over the dune. You started moaning and coming around a few minutes later."

"So. No radio?"

"I'm afraid not. That four-legged stilter has them now."

"Then," he said slowly, "Maybe we'd better start walking."

"To an *island*?" She laughed, and there was a brittle edge to the sound.

"It would help if we knew if the bad guys were everywhere except those islands . . . or if there are still some hold-outs on the mainland we could reach."

"If there are," Kathy said, "they might not be around much longer."

"Well, damn it!" Donal exploded. "We can't just *sit* here!"

His thoughts were racing. He'd *seen* the invaders now; that fact was just beginning to seep down into his conscious awareness. He'd seen them in action, and he knew that they posed a deadly threat to the Strathan Cluster. The power behind that brief bolt of energy—he was pretty sure it had been a particle beam of some kind—had been enormous, at least the output of a small fusion reactor. If the invaders attacked in massed groups, the way the message from Wide Sky had implied, even a Mark XXIV Bolo might have a tough time against them.

They had to find a way to warn Muir. . . .

"You know," Kathy said suddenly. "That's exactly what we're going to do."

"Huh? What?" His thoughts had wandered far enough that he didn't know what she was talking about. Had he spoken aloud about the need to get the news to Muir? "What are we going to do?"

"Just sit here." She pointed toward the southeast. "Look!"

Thunder rolled in the distance. A pair of dark shapes,

silhouetted against their own tailpipe flares, rocketed in low across the sea. In a thrilling instant, they boomed low overhead, separated, and circled back, looping around the area.

Gremlins! Like the two downed minutes earlier. They appeared to be flying a search pattern over the area. As one of the aircraft passed again overhead, a single bright star flashed from its fuselage, dazzling against the night overhead. Before the flare had drifted slowly into the sea minutes later, a third aircraft could be seen approaching from the southeast, a larger, slower machine with heavy lines and tilt-jets mounted on the tips of four stubby wings.

"SAR!" Kathy cried. "Search and Rescue! They came looking for the pilots of those downed aircraft!"

They stood, waving, stepping away from the cracked and cooling glass at the top of the dune so their IR signatures wouldn't be washed out by the fiercely radiating patch of sand. Another flare turned the night sky above them a flickering neon green. Donal and Kathy, taking care to stay carefully clear of the hot glass, stumbled down to the beach.

The SAR vehicle—an aging and rust-streaked T-950 Percheron—settled to the beach in a swirl of jet-blasted sand and sea spray, hatches swung open along the sides, and armored men packing massive personal weapons leaped out, forming a defensive perimeter. The Gremlins continued to fly air cover low overhead.

A young second lieutenant in bulky armor and carrying a Mark XII powergun that would have been laughably outmatched by the invaders' weaponry, trotted toward them across the beach. "You two from the *Black Flash*?" he asked.

"That's right, Lieutenant," Kathy said. "I'm Commander Ross, pilot. This is my passenger, Lieutenant Ragnor."

The lieutenant nodded; Donal noted that he had the sense—or the experience—not to salute in the field.

"Commander. Lieutenant. I'm Lieutenant Foster." He jerked a thumb over his shoulder. "Best get your tails on board the Perch, now. We don't have much time."

"We haven't seen any sign of your people on those downed Gremlins," Kathy told him as they started trotting together toward the waiting transport. "I'm sorry."

"Didn't expect to, ma'am. Telemetry indicated immediate kills on both of 'em."

"Then why—"

"We're out here looking for *you*. So were they." They trotted up the Percheron's boarding ramp with a metallic clatter. "Scarba Approach Control saw you going in and pinpointed your crash site. But we also knew some stilters were in the area, and we thought they might get to you first."

"They did," Donal told him. "But they didn't seem that interested in us. They tossed one p-bolt in our direction, like a man might swat at a fly. Casual, like they didn't really care about us at all."

They were settling into the straight-back, thinly padded chairs in the Percheron's cargo bay now, as a sergeant outside bawled at the troops to file back on board, leapfrog withdrawal. "That sounds like the stilters, all right," Foster said as he helped them buckle on their seat harnesses, then dropped into a seat facing them across the central aisle and strapped himself in. "I don't think they're really interested in anything except scrap."

"Scrap?" Donal prompted.

"Metal of any kind. Some plastics and ceramics. Mostly stuff like copper wiring, lead shielding, steel girders. They smashed their way into just about every city on Wide Sky, and as soon as we'd been booted out, they just started taking the places apart."

"We saw some of that from space, coming in," Kathy said. "They were loading stuff onto big barges or transports of some kind."

Foster nodded. "Scavengers. They're damned vultures, feeding on the dead body of Wide Sky's civilization."

"There's one difference," Donal told him.

"What's that, sir?"

"Vultures usually don't kill the body they're feeding on in the first place."

The last of the soldiers was aboard. The sergeant barked into a microphone, *"Go! Go!"* Outside, the idling hum of the Percheron's engines spooled into a shrieking howl. With a lurch and a swift-tilting deck, the transport hurled itself at the sky.

CHAPTER ELEVEN

The sun was rising as the Percheron descended toward Pad Seven on the floating city of Fortrose, giving Donal a splendid view of the sprawling, six-sided patch of green and sand-white. The structure had originally been designated as Industrial Fishery Complex Two, but the artificial island with its lagoons and palm orchards and central spires was far too much a *place* to be known only by the cold number of a catalogue designation. The fishing city covered perhaps a hundred square kilometers of ocean, a vast, artificial island of seament electrically accreted out of the water and plated out across the surface of a preform molded in slender conducting wires.

Most of the outer portion of the hexagonal cell was given over to breakwater and dunes, shielding the central habitat from storms and wave damage. At the center, near the emerald-green sweep of the lagoons, the island's habitat rose in a series of slender, spire-tipped columns of seament and sun-sparkling transplas, a city, Donal was told, that normally housed some tens of thousands of workers and their families. Unseen, plunging deep into the emerald waters below the structure's center, was the vertical support core containing the seament accreters, the thermal power generators, sub pens, fish intakes, stabilizers, and all of the rest of the technological complexities necessary to support the idyllic, upper-surface environment.

Perhaps, Donal thought, *idyllic* was no longer exactly the right word. The towers of Fortrose still gleamed in the sun like the turrets of a fairy-tale castle, but as the Percheron descended toward the landing pad, the clutter and chaos everywhere on the floating city's upper works became more and more evident. The open areas, the malls, the parks, the sandy expanses around the lagoon, even the broad, hard tops of the breakwaters had all been taken over by brightly colored tents and shantytown structures of plywood and cloth and fiberboard. The lagoon and the gated channels leading to it from the sea, as well as the outer reaches of the seawall itself, were thickly crowded with ships and smallcraft of all sizes and descriptions, from vast hordes of personal yachts, trimarans, and hover runabouts to a three-hundred-meter submarine liner surfaced and moored in the main channel.

A half-dozen space transports were moored by the seawall as well, including three of the big, spherical D-12 Conestogas that handled so much of the freight and passenger service out here along the Rim. Donal turned from the Percheron's window to glance at Lieutenant Foster, questioning, but the soldier was slumped back in his seat, powergun cradled against his chest, eyes shut in exhausted sleep. Turning back to the window, he surveyed the human sea crowding the artificial island below and shook his head. It looked to Donal as though refugees from all over the planet must have been flocking to the Scarba floating city complex for some days, now, while at the same time, star transports gathered here, a last, desperate chance for them to get off-world.

It would be up to Wide Sky's military forces, though, to buy time enough for the civilians to get clear.

Not exactly an enviable responsibility.

"Those poor people," Kathy Ross said quietly, at his side. Her face was pressed against the window as she stared down into the enormous tent city below.

"I'm surprised the invaders haven't attacked here," Donal said. "If they're as ruthless as everyone's been saying . . ."

"Maybe the invaders don't see the place as a threat," she replied. "They ignored us, after all, back on the beach . . . until it looked like we'd called in an air strike. Then they came down on us with both metal feet."

"They've attacked civilian targets before this," he reminded her. "Hell, Wide Sky didn't have much in the way of a standing army to begin with, and these monsters still started hitting every city and town on the map and taking it apart. I think we need to learn more about the enemy, about how they think, before we can start taking guesses at their motives."

Out of sight but close by, just over the curve of the horizon, Donal knew, four more of the floating cities had gathered, a slow-moving fleet that ought to make an excellent target for the invaders. He wondered again why they hadn't attacked already.

The Percheron settled to the hard-surfaced pavement of the landing pad with a dwindling shriek of belly jets and blast-swirled sand. As the cargo bay doors hissed open, he heard another, more ominous sound . . . the thunder of a large, desperate, and angry crowd.

As he jumped down from the cargo deck, he paused and looked around. Thousands of people, it seemed, most of them in rags, surrounded the landing pad, restrained—just barely—by a thin line of armed troops.

"*Do* something about the invaders!" one voice called, rising above the others. "*Do* something!" Other voices pitched higher and louder in response, in agreement.

A pair of Gremlins howled low overhead, circling the area. It was hard, on the face of it, to know whether they were watching for invaders . . . or keeping watch on the near-riot below.

A harried-looking junior lieutenant met Donal and Kathy with a salute and a gesture toward a waiting aircar. "What's with the crowds, Lieutenant?" Kathy asked.

"They want off of Wide Sky, Commander," he replied as they slipped into the passenger compartment of the vehicle and a military pilot up front spooled up the turbines. "And you know, I'm not sure I blame 'em."

It was a five-minute aircar flight from the landing pad up to a broad balcony in the tallest, central tower. Military uniforms were more in evidence up here, including more uniforms of higher ranks. The lieutenant escorted Kathy away to another suite of offices for debriefing by naval officers, while depositing Donal in a large, transplas-walled office overlooking the entire island, occupied by an overweight man in an army major's uniform and at least a battalion of aides, mostly lieutenants with a smattering of captains.

"I'm Major Fitzsimmons, CO of the Wide Sky militia here," the man said brusquely and without preamble. He looked Donal up and down, a quick and less-than-pleased evaluation. "Have a seat. I understand that you are our cavalry from Muir."

"Cavalry? No, sir. I am here to try to find out what's going on for my bosses back at HQ. They, ah, were having a bit of trouble believing in the reports they were getting from Wide Sky."

Fitzsimmons's face puckered into a wry smile. "They were, were they? Well, I can sympathize. None of us has really been able to believe in this threat. But it's real enough, as you've discovered for yourself."

"Yes, sir."

"These Dinos are deadly. Never seen anything like 'em."

"Dinos?"

"We've recovered some bodies. Not many, not as good

as their combat machines are, not as hard as they are to stop. Four-armed dinosaurs, sort of. Tough. Fast. Mean. These things are *good*, Lieutenant. Their walkers are much faster and more maneuverable than anything we have. They leave Bolos in the dust, quite literally run rings around them. Individually, they're not as heavily armored as a Bolo, of course, but they operate in close-knit packs that make them far more deadly."

Donal's eyebrows rose. "Deadlier than Bolos, sir?"

Fitzsimmons snorted. "I take it from your file that you are a Bolo officer."

There it was again. That challenge, as though admitting to working with Bolos was somehow admitting to some small, secret perversion. "Yes, sir."

"Well, simply take it from me that two-megatons-per-second firepower is not the ultimate in military strategy and tactics. Accurate placement of that firepower, and the maneuverability to survive while placing it, are of considerably more importance than the firepower itself."

"I can't refute that, sir. Bolos are designed for accurate placement, however."

Fitzsimmons waved a pudgy hand in casual dismissal. "Foolishness. These things took a Mark XVIII apart piece by piece as though it . . . I don't know. As though it was some sort of big, slow, clumsy game animal or something. Yes. That's exactly the impression I had, watching it. The Bolo was *game*."

"Bolo Mark XVIIIs aren't exactly the latest thing in military hardware, Major. The invaders would have a bit more trouble with a Mark XXIV."

He sighed. "I'm not going to argue force structures and maneuvers with you, Lieutenant. What we are facing here is unlike anything I've ever seen or heard of. We've been running computer simulations, and they suggest that we would need a far more powerful force of Bolos than the Cluster has available, simply to have a chance of matching this threat, let alone overcoming it. And now," Fitzsimmons added, with the definite air of someone who has said all there is to say on a topic, "my staff and I here would like to hear what happened to you and your pilot out there, when you got shot down."

For the next half hour or so, Donal described what he'd seen and experienced, including his up-close, almost *too* close encounter with the two walkers on the beach. Fitzsimmons and his staff were particularly interested in the *Lightning's* approach to Wide Sky, and in how Kathy had managed to slip in past the invader blockade.

"I'm really not sure," he said for at least the fifth time, when one of the aides asked for the probable upper speed of the blockaders' maneuvering envelope. "You'd have to ask Commander Ross about that."

"We have," Fitzsimmons replied glumly. He gestured at the computer terminal on his desk where, evidently, he had access to Kathy's debriefing, elsewhere in the building. "But the more points of view we can round up the better. We're going to need that information."

Donal frowned. Wide Sky had no navy to speak of; the entire Strathan Cluster couldn't muster much more than a handful of gunboats and frigates. Knowing invader ship capabilities wouldn't—

Then the reason for their interest struck him. "You're planning on an evacuation," he said. "You need to know how to get past the orbital blockade."

"A partial evacuation, anyway," Fitzsimmons agreed. "We can't hope to get everyone off, of course."

"Wide Sky has a population of, what?" Donal asked. "A hundred million?"

"Too many to cram aboard a handful of transports and passenger liners, that's for damned sure. Alexie wants to get as many of the kids and young people off as we can."

"Alexie?"

"Alexie Turner. She was the DDG." He shook his head. "Our Director General was here, as a matter of fact, when the Dinos hit. Pure bad luck. He was flying back. Caught in the air by Dino flyers. So I guess she must've inherited."

"I see. And where is she now, Major? I'd like to pay my respects."

He nodded toward a spot on the floor. "Down on the main level, at the moment. In the Assembly Hall dealing with God knows how many different civilian delegations, refugee groups, camp organizers, you name it. They're talking about who should get evacuated, and for me, I'd just as soon stay here and face the Dinos as mix it up with *that* crowd."

Donal smiled. "I know what you mean, sir."

"Anyone else have any questions of this young man?" Fitzsimmons said, looking at his aides. There was a general shaking of heads and muttered "no, sirs" for response, and the major waved Donal off. "If you hurry, you can probably catch her act, or part of it. Tell the elevator to take you to the Assembly Hall."

"Thank you, sir." Donal saluted, then turned and left the office.

Fitzsimmons, he thought, seemed to be a bit more solidly grounded in reality than the brass back on Muir. He wondered if that was a reflection of the man's basic nature, or if it had more to do with his proximity to the alien invaders.

The Assembly Hall was an enormous public arena on the ground floor of the central tower, an enclosed stadium beneath a blue-tinted transplas dome that let the morning sun spill into the auditorium but robbed it of glare and heat. The seats, he estimated, could hold several thousand people, and most were already filled by the time he entered the room.

At the auditorium's central stage, there was a round, raised platform with a table and holographic display apparatus. An older, white-haired man was addressing the crowd with all of the passion of a somewhat bored university professor giving a lecture.

"We know pathetically little about this species as yet," he was saying as Donal squeezed into the room. The man's voice, amplified by the room's electronics, was perfectly clear but somewhat on the frail side. A curved, two-story wall screen set up behind the speaker's podium magnified the man's image to titanic proportions; his name and title— Dr. Ulysee Goldman, Professor of Xenosophontology, University of Wide Sky at Galloway—was spelled out at the bottom of the screen in letters half a meter tall.

"Everything we know about them so far, in fact," Goldman continued, "has been gleaned from a handful of bodies recovered from what were probably scout machines destroyed by Skyan military aircraft, and from radio transmissions between the surface and their fleet that we were partially able to translate with the AI at the university before the invaders overran Galloway. We know that they call themselves 'Malach,' and that they organize themselves in what appears to be a strict, military hierarchy. Whether, of course, that hierarchy is a direct reflection of their entire culture, or of the fact that we are so far dealing only with their military, is unknown."

So, the invaders called themselves *Malach*. The speaker had pronounced the name with a German "ch" that turned the end of the word into a soft-palate gargle. It helped, somehow, making them less faceless and impersonal, to know their name for themselves. Fitzsimmons's "Dino" seemed calculated to deflate the enemy, to make the threat feel smaller and more manageable.

But Donal wanted to know them as they really were. The Cluster's survival might depend upon stark and uncoated truths.

"We have some graphics here," Goldman said, placing

his hand on the podium's control screen, "that may give you an idea of what we are facing."

The blue-tinted transplas overhead darkened sharply, plunging the room into near darkness as a nervous titter ran though the crowd. After a moment, however, a shaft of blue light flicked on above the table as Goldman engaged the holoprojector. Donal leaned forward in his seat, studying the figure repeated on the big screen behind the speaker. It was . . . disturbing.

The being, evidently, had followed the same line of evolutionary descent as had certain carnivorous dinosaurs on old Earth, a hundred million years before. According to the scale showing in the three-dimensional image, the thing stood at just over two meters tall . . . indeed, its flat, dragonish head would have looked down on Donal in a face-to-face confrontation. It was bipedal, with the digitigrade stance of a large bird, but the body was canted forward, level with the ground, rather than carried erect, with a whiplike tail serving for balance. The jaws were those of a predator, with razor-keen, back-curved teeth that protruded in a blood-hungry grin even when the scaly jaws were shut. A bristling of red-pink tendrils, each the size of Donal's forefinger, sprouted across its lipless upper jaw like an obscene mustache. The bone-knobbed head behind the four large and vertically slitted, gleaming red cat's eyes, however, was large and deep, plenty roomy enough for a sizable brain. Not two, but four arms were suspended from a complex shoulder girdle arrangement beneath the wrinkled neck, two small arms above with delicate, four-fingered hands, two larger ones below, more massively turned and muscled and with hands more adapted to ripping or grasping than fine manipulation. The claws were impressive, both on hands and feet; sickle-shaped slashing claws curved from loose-skinned pouches on wrists and ankles, designed, perhaps, for tearing at prey to cripple it on the run. The color was startling, overall a deep forest green above and pale gold below, but with bright ruby-red stripes picked out in scales that flashed and gleamed like jewels in the light. The creature was astonishingly beautiful, for all that evolution had crafted every muscle, every curve to the single-minded need for pursuit and slaughter.

"We put this image together," Goldman said, standing next to the glowing holo, "from the bodies we managed to recover from those few walker machines we've been able to take out. It looks more or less reptilian, though we have reason to believe that it's warm-blooded, like a bird or mammal. Dr. Duchenny, at the Wide Sky Institute, has suggested that they are evolved from paradinosaurian pack-hunters, creatures that have evolved in parallel from creatures similar to the deinonychus and velociraptor that roamed Earth during the Cretaceous era, some sixty-five to one hundred million years ago. Obviously, too, they evolved from hexapodal stock, as opposed to the quadrupeds of higher terrestrial life. We should keep in mind that the similarities to extinct terrestrial life are no doubt the result of parallel evolution . . . of organisms shaped to familiar form by similar evolutionary and environmental forces."

"Excuse me, Doctor," someone down in the front called out. "We can all see what these beasts look like. What I want to know, what I think everyone here wants to know, is where the hell do they come from?"

"If you mean have we identified a homeworld yet," Goldman replied, "we have not. However, it seems fairly clear that this is a new species, unknown as yet to humanity. This far out along the Eastern Arm, the only place they could have come from is one of the worlds of the Gulf."

A stir ran through the audience at that, and a low-whispered murmur of many voices. Goldman had their full attention now.

"Their curious . . . habit," the professor continued, "of dismantling captured ruins, buildings, vehicle wreckage, and so on in order to strip them of useful metal appears to be one predictable aspect of such an evolution. The Gulf stars tend, on the whole, to be metal poor, at least compared to those that formed within the Galactic disk. Most, of course, are ancient Population II stars, possessing no elements heavier than hydrogen or helium at all and, therefore, no terrestrial planets. A few, however, a small percentage, are either Population I suns accreted from areas enriched by rare supernovae within the Gulf, or they are Population I stars ejected from our Galaxy at some point eons in the past. In the latter case, of course, the star and any attendant planets would be identical to those we know within the Galaxy. In the former, however, planets will tend to be heavy-element poor. Elements such as carbon and aluminum will be relatively common, but iron will be comparatively rare, since the planet's iron core will tend to be smaller and buried within a thicker silicate crust. Extremely heavy elements, such as radioactives, will be scarce or even non-existent.

"We expect that this scarcity has dramatically affected their culture and their outlook on the universe, as well as their attitude toward other intelligent species . . . such as ourselves."

"They woke up cranky, you mean," someone called out from the audience, and there was an answering patter of nervous laughter.

"It may be that the Malach perceive their entire universe as raw materials for their use," Goldman went on, ignoring the comment. "They may be unable to recognize a viewpoint other than their own. At the university, we have been speculating that the Malach see *all* other species, whether intelligent or not, as prey animals of some kind, as sources of raw material for them to exploit. That, certainly, is the upshot of what seems to be happening here on Wide Sky. We are to them nothing more or less than a source of already mined, purified, and sequestered metals."

"We're not gonna let these lizards take away what we've built here!" someone in the first row shouted. He was echoed by another voice, then by another ten, then by fifty more. In a moment, everyone in the auditorium it seemed, was on their feet, shouting.

At the podium, Dr. Goldman tried to continue with his presentation, but the sound system was drowned out by the commotion. A moment later, an attractive, blond-haired woman in a severe gray business suit stepped up to the podium, took Goldman's arm, and whispered quietly to him. The professor nodded and walked away, leaving the woman next to the glowing holograph of the green-and-red-striped Malach. As she touched the podium controls, the image of the invader faded out and the windows depolarized, flooding the huge room with light once more. She then waited patiently as the commotion in the chamber dwindled to the point where she could address the crowd. From the cool detachment with which she surveyed the audience, he assumed she was Alexie Turner.

"Thank you, Professor Goldman," she said. "That information was hard won and cost us dearly. We appreciate your coming here today to brief us. And that, ladies and gentlemen, is all that we have for you today—"

The crowd noise rose again, an angry thunder as most of the people leaped to their feet, shouting down at the small, lone figure at the podium.

"What about the evacuation?" someone yelled. "What about getting people off this rock?"

"Hell, no!" another voice echoed back. "We're gonna stay and fight these monsters!"

"We came here all the way from Galloway! What's the government going to do about these Malach things?"

"Yeah! We want to know what's being *done!*"

The room exploded in noise and shouting. Men wearing the light blue uniforms of Wide Sky security appeared, standing in front of the stage in an attempt to block it off, but there were too few to stop the surging crowd. The mood in the room was fast turning ugly. Desperate people, feeding off the atmosphere of panic, might do almost anything. It looked to Donal as though the most immediate danger to the survivors on Fortrose wasn't the Malach . . . but the very real threat of mob violence. Something was going to have to be done, and fast, or that riot would kill more people than a Malach attack.

Donal took a deep breath and started forward.

CHAPTER TWELVE

It took him only a moment to assess the situation. Half of the people in the auditorium, it seemed, were trying to move up the passageways between the rows of seats to the doors and the outside; the other half were moving down toward the center stage in a blind, stumbling rush, and the surging collision of the two had completely blocked the aisles.

There was only one way to get to the podium with any reasonable speed. Donal vaulted onto the back of an empty seat in the top row, took a big, unsteady step to the back of the seat ahead in the next row down, and swiftly made his way down the slope of the auditorium's bowl, stepping from seat back to seat back, sometimes moving over people still trying to get out into the jam-packed aisles.

At the front row, he shouldered his way through the mob; his uniform won him admittance past the struggling line of security officers, and he made it at last to the podium.

A dozen men had made it past the security line and were crowding their way up onto the stage. More were crowding in behind them, closing on the lone woman at the podium. "We want our questions answered!" a hard-

137

faced man was demanding, shouting into Alexie Turner's face.

"Where's Muir?" another man shouted. "Why the hell haven't they sent us help?"

"What's the army doing?"

"What's the *government* doing?"

"Please, all of you," Alexie said. "Why don't you all—"

"Now you listen here, young lady," one of the more persistent men went on. "Your father relied, yes, *relied* on my advice, and I don't think you're wise to simply—"

"Do you need a military escort, ma'am?" Donal said sharply, his voice projected loudly enough to carry above the mob noise.

"Eh?"

"I've just arrived here from Muir, Director," he added, brushing past the persistent man and letting him see the rank insignia on his tunic.

The man's eyes widened. "You're from Muir! Help has arrived, then?"

"It's about damned time!" another man observed. "Has the Navy taken out the Dino fleet yet?"

"Nobody's taken out anything," Donal replied. "And they can't unless you let these people do their jobs!"

"I saw for myself what those monsters can do, and—"

"Do you people have a skywatch set up?"

The persistent man blinked. "A . . . what?"

"A skywatch." Donal pointed at the man. "What's your name?"

"Uh . . . Sam Carver."

"Well, Mr. Carver. You need a civilian skywatch here on Fortrose, and my instincts tell me you're just the man to organize it."

Carver's eyes narrowed, as though he was expecting some trick. "Well, I am pretty good at running things, uh, Lieutenant. . . ."

"I knew it! Now, here's what the Strathan Central

Command needs you to do, Mr. Carver. You get together as many good men and women as you can. People with good eyes. Talk to the Wide Sky MLC to see about getting electronic binoculars."

"Uh . . . wait. MLC?"

"Military Logistics Center." He shook his head, grinning wolfishly. "If you're going to join up, you'd better learn the language, don't you think?"

"Now wait, wait! I haven't joined anything!"

Donal folded his arms and gave Carver a severe look. "I thought you wanted to help, Mr. Carver. If you do, I've got a whole list of things civilian groups could do under military direction, things that need to be done for the common defense."

"Yeah, but—"

"You can organize a skywatch to keep track of aircraft and surface vessels approaching Fortrose. That will act as a backup for the city's radar net, and maybe free up some military personnel for other duties. You could start organizing guerrilla forces from among civilians who have some experience moving around in the woods. Having this many people on board this floating city is just begging the Malach to come drown you all at once, so the faster we can get most of you back ashore, the better.

"In other words, Mr. Carver, you can get off your tail and do something about your situation here, or you can sit on that fat behind and moan and complain until the Malach come and sink Fortrose out from under you. If you choose to help, you will do so under military jurisdiction, if for no other reason than that we can't have you getting in the way. That means you and your people will follow orders. If you choose to moan and complain, I hope you can swim, because the official military designation of this city is 'VLST.' " When Carver blinked confusion, he added, "That's milspeak for 'Very Large Stationary Target.' Do we understand one another, sir?"

"Uh, yeah. Yeah, I guess we do."

"What about the evacuation?" another man demanded. "We got all these transports out here. I say we load 'em up and boost for someplace safe!"

"Oh? And where would that be, Mister, ah . . . ?"

"Halliwell. Jess Halliwell."

"Mr. Halliwell, how is your arithmetic?"

"Huh? Whatcha mean?"

"The population of Wide Sky is something on the order of one hundred million, is it not?"

"I, uh, guess it—"

"When I was coming in to land this morning, I saw three Conestoga-class transports out there. That's more than you usually see in port at once. When used as troops ships, which means maximum crowding and no room for the amenities, Conestogas can carry about five thousand people. It's a one-week flight to Muir, another week back for a second load. There may be other worlds closer, but none that aren't in imminent danger of attack by the Malach. You've got other ships out there as well, but all of them together probably couldn't carry as much as one Conestoga. Let's be generous, though, and say you can carry another five thousand there. So, that tells me you can haul twenty thousand people off this planet every two weeks, which is actually pretty decent when you're trying to organize an interstellar mass migration. At that rate, how long is it going to take to move one hundred million people, Mr. Halliwell?"

Halliwell looked confused, then doubtful, then belligerent. "Look, none a' that is my business, see? I want t' know what the government is gonna do about these damned, four-eyed lizards!"

"Why, Mr. Halliwell. Weren't you listening a moment ago? We're going to *draft* you into the army."

"Now wait just a damned minute!"

"That way, we can most efficiently make use of your

skills and talents in fighting the Malach. I can't promise, of course, that those skills and talents will suit you to any task more glamorous than cannon fodder, but we all must do what we do best if we're to survive this crisis."

"I, uh, that is—"

"C'mon, Jess," Carver said, tugging at Halliwell's shoulder. "We'll go talk to Major Fitzsimmons about this."

"Shoot," someone else said. "Old Fitz isn't going to do anything. . . ."

"Yeah, but he's better than the damned Cluster Authority. Drafted! We'll just see about this. . . ."

The crowd in front of the table was breaking up, however, the most belligerent moving away more hastily than the others. Some threw Donal dark glances as they left, and he heard the name "Muir" repeated several times. In moments, Donal was alone with Alexie Turner. The auditorium was slowly clearing as the crowd kept moving up the aisles. Riot, for the moment, at any rate, had been averted.

"Well," Alexie said. She had a dazzling smile, though there were dark smudges beneath her eyes that suggested that it had been a while since she'd slept. "You must be Lieutenant Ragnor. I heard the Search and Rescue boys had found you and brought you in."

"For which I thank you, Director."

"Uh-uh. Thank *you*," she said, shaking Donal's hand. Her grip was cool and firm. "And it's still *Deputy* Director. At least until we hold an election that makes it official." She looked past Donal at the rapidly emptying auditorium. "Frankly, anyone who'd want to be Director General of this circus has probably just disqualified herself. Mental incompetence. In any case, I really appreciated your help just now."

"My pleasure, uh, Deputy Director. All part of our cheerful, friendly service."

"It's . . . a little terrifying how fast friends and neighbors can turn into a murderous riot. I've known Sam Carver for years. He used to work for my dad."

"Well, we haven't really solved anything yet, you know. After they get outside and talk things over, they're going to spot the sleight-of-hand in my arithmetic lesson just now."

"What do you mean? You got it just right. There's no way we can move a hundred million people off of Wide Sky. Even if we had the ships, which we certainly don't, we couldn't load anything like the supplies we'd need." She grinned ruefully. "And I doubt that any other world in the Cluster would want a hundred million refugees dropping into their back yards, even if we could manage it."

"No, the sleight-of-hand was in the basic assumption. A hundred million people. Pretty soon, now, Mr. Carver and his friends will figure out that, so far as they're concerned, there's no need to move the entire population, so long as *they* get away to safety."

"You mean . . . they'd just *take* a ship? Hijack it?"

"They might."

"I can't believe that of Sam."

"Well, if I were you, I'd post a heavy guard on all of the spacecraft you have parked out there, just to be sure. Effective immediately."

"Yes, you're right. We have security people guarding the ships now, but . . ." She stopped, unhooked a personal transceiver from her wrist, and spoke into it for several moments. When she replaced the unit, she met his eyes with a smile. "Thank you again, Lieutenant. I must say, you seem to be pretty much on the ball."

"We try, ma'am."

"That's been our biggest problem since the refugee crisis started," she told him. "Knowing that, once it sinks home that there is no escape, we're going to have a *real* panic on our hands."

"It's a possibility," Donal told her. "Your big problem will be the few who are smart enough to see the angles, and who are selfish enough not to care about their neighbors. Usually in situations like this, there are always a few troublemakers. The majority, though, usually manage to rally themselves in a crisis, somehow."

"I hope you're right, Lieutenant."

His eyes met those of Kathy as she approached the podium. "Ah! Here's my pilot. Deputy Director Alexie Turner? Commander Kathy Ross."

"Pleased to meet you, Commander. I gather you're the one who spread a KR-72 Lightning across half of West Continent." Her smile robbed the words of any sting.

"Mmm. Yeah, that was me. You know, I may be in violation of Wide Sky's littering laws."

Alexie laughed. "I think we can let you off the hook this time. Extenuating circumstances."

"So," Donal said. "You're trying to lift your kids off in those ships parked out there."

"Yes. We want to evacuate as many children as we can, and enough young adults to ride herd on them all. We hope to get perhaps fifty thousand off of Wide Sky."

"Fifty thousand? I was figuring you'd be lucky to get twenty thousand. Or do you have more ships available?"

"No. Except for a few at the other floating cities, this is all we could scrape together, and at that we practically had to requisition the Conestogas at gun point. But children are small, and they don't mind crowding or lack of privacy. More can be squeezed into a cabin than adults."

"You'll send them to Muir, of course."

She looked up at him through long lashes. Her eyes, he only now realized, were a deep and lustrous blue. "You seem very sure of yourself, Lieutenant."

He shrugged. "You don't have a lot of choice. And, well, my bosses are going to need some convincing back there that this crisis is real. I can't think of a better way to convince them than dropping fifty thousand kids on their doorstep. And . . . you'll be with them, right?"

She shook her head. "My place is here. With my people."

"Mmm. Seems to me your place is wherever you could be the most help to your people. And that might be on Muir, convincing Governor Chard that the Malach are a threat to the entire Cluster."

"We'll give you the information you need, Lieutenant. Including downloads of everything the people from the university have put together."

"In my experience, Deputy Director, human beings have an innate capacity for ignoring information, in whatever form, that is nothing short of astonishing."

"Um, I know what you mean. Especially if they have administrative, bureaucratic, or career-related territories to defend."

"Exactly. Quite a few careers back on Muir appear to be founded on the principle that there's nothing dangerous in the Gulf. It would be too . . . inconvenient."

"I was thinking of sending Sam Carver as my representative, actually," Alexie said. "He's not a bad sort, despite the bluster. And he was head of a pretty fair-sized citizens' group back at Sea Cliffs."

"Maybe. But it would sound a hell of a lot more convincing coming from you."

"I'll take it under advisement." She sounded genuinely torn, but it was clear she was still sure her duty lay here on Wide Sky. "Our first priority is to organize the evacuation of the children, and that's not going to be easy. We'll decide who else gets to go when the kids are taken care of."

"Aren't you two forgetting something?" Kathy asked.

"What's that?" Donal asked.

She pointed one slim index finger toward the domed

roof of the auditorium. "Our friends up there. The ones that shot us down, remember? You're gonna have a time of it trying to get three Conestogas past that blockade."

"We do have some space fighters left," Alexie said. "Major Fitzsimmons is still planning the operation with his staff, but the idea is that a sudden, surprise attack on the blockading fleet might open a hole long enough for the evacuation fleet to slip out. Once in hyper-L, of course, nothing could touch them."

"Could work," Kathy said. "I might have some ideas on the subject, too."

"I think," Donal said, "that you ought to have a talk with the major. He seemed reasonably receptive." He smiled. "Not as closed-minded as some I could think of."

"How soon are you planning on making your run for it?" Kathy asked.

"Wait," Donal said, holding up his hand. "What is that God-awful racket?"

A keening sound was wailing outside, the rise and fall stirring his hackles and goading the people still in the auditorium to push their way out even faster.

"Air raid siren," Alexie told him. "Fortrose is under attack." A moment later, a dull, heavy thump sounded from outside, followed by the redoubled screams and shouts from the crowd.

"C'mon," Donal said. "Let's have a look."

They hurried after the others as explosions rumbled and thumped from outside. Emerging through the auditorium's main doors, they found themselves on a broad and crowded plaza overlooking Fortrose's main lagoon. Most of the people in the crowd were scattering now in panicked flight, but a few clung to the safety railing, staring and pointing toward the western sky.

A pair of Gremlins shrieked low overhead, their shadows momentarily sweeping across the plaza as they passed between the floating city and the sun. Another explosion thundered as a plume of white water geysered into the sky just beyond the city's breakwater.

Eight tiny black specks strung across the sky just above the western horizon were rapidly growing, sweeping in toward the city with heartstopping speed.

Everything seemed to happen at once. As the eight invaders hurtled closer to the city, a massive Percheron on one of the city's landing pads—Donal thought it must be the craft that had rescued them hours before—began lumbering into the sky on howling ventral thrusters. A missile arrowed in from the west at the tip of an unraveling white contrail, striking the Percheron squarely in the center and detonating in a thunderous crash and rising ball of orange flame. The Percheron staggered under the impact, then tumbled back to the pad, metal crumbling and burning with a fierce white heat. Three more missiles streaked in through the air. The Gremlins banked left and right, scattering flares and antimissile scattershot. Two of the missiles detonated short of their target; the third sheared the wing off one Gremlin in a blossoming white detonation, sending the aircraft spinning wildly, tumbling out of control just above the crowded breakwater and smashing into the sea.

In another instant, the Malach aircraft were shrieking low above the city. Donal realized with a start of recognition that the vehicles were identical to the combat machines he and Kathy had seen on the beach the night before. The legs on each were telescoped in and tucked up tight against the belly, transforming the alien walkers into huge, winged fliers. Ducted venturis along the crafts' undersides held them aloft on shrieking blasts of hot plasma. Where those invisible jets touched the sea they erupted in boiling clouds of steam. As the craft drifted across the breakwater and over the artificial island, the jets kicked up swirling clouds of sand and dust, lashing the rows of carefully planted trees into whiplashing frenzies.

There was a desperate need, Donal decided, for high-powered cannon mounts or laser turrets somewhere on the city's walls or towers. A few dozen such weapons would have brought down those hovering craft in moments. Banking hard, the surviving Gremlin fired a pair of Skystreak missiles. Both impacted against the same Malach flier with dazzling flashes of high explosive, but the Malach craft kept flying, its armor scorched and charred in places but with no apparent damage to either its hull or its performance. Perhaps, Donal thought, it would take more than cannon mounts or lasers after all; those flying craft were *tough*, more like miniature airborne Bolos than traditional aircraft.

The last Gremlin fell from the sky, its tail sheared away by a beam as cleanly as a hot knife slicing through plastic. The Malach craft were circling the artificial island now, weaving back and forth in a complex pattern of multiple loops and figure-eights. A dazzling, blue-white beam like a razor-straight bolt of lightning flicked down across the lagoon, striking several boats in rapid succession. The attack stirred the milling, scattering crowd to greater panic. As flame and smoke exploded from the lagoon, people everywhere, on the plaza, on the walkways next to the lagoon, in the open, sandy areas covered by refugee tents, began fleeing wildly, running in no particular direction, guided only by a desperate need to escape the darting, airborne attackers. Several screaming men and women smashed past Donal, Alexie, and Kathy as they stood at the edge of the plaza overlook; one of them hit Alexie hard enough in the back that she nearly catapulted over the railing, but Kathy and Donal both grabbed her and kept her from falling.

"We'd better find shelter," he told them.

"It's too late for that," Kathy replied. "Look!" She

pointed. Eight more airborne vehicles were approaching on shrieking ventral jets. These were similar to the first but larger, much larger, and as they howled over the breakwater, their legs began unfolding like complex puzzles, telescoping out with clawed, grasping feet that sank into sand or grated on seament.

The Malach were landing and in considerable force.

"Come on," Donal shouted. "We have to get out of here!"

"We'll go to Cee-cubed," Alexie said.

"Command-Control-Communications?" Donal asked her as they turned from the railing and started across the plaza, angling toward the central cluster of towers.

"We call it the City Control Center," Alexie replied. "Same thing, I guess, though. It's where Major Fitzsimmons will be. And we can follow things on the big city map."

As the women dashed on ahead, Donal stopped, turning to have another look at the grounded invader craft. They were opening up now, spilling large numbers of Malach troops, and Donal felt a small shock of surprise at the sight. Only a few minutes before he'd seen the computer-generated image of a Malach in the presentation in the auditorium; there was a vast difference, however, between the simulation and the reality. These creatures, no, these *beings*, moved with the fluid grace of born predators. Their heads didn't turn, they *snapped* from side to side with the quick and alert agility of birds. Their gait could be almost comical when they walked slowly, like the mincing strut of chickens . . . but then they would dash ahead with breathtaking speed, the muscles rippling beneath their green-and-ruby-scaled hides, and there was suddenly nothing in the least amusing about them.

Each wore a complicated harness of metal and black leather; each carried a weapon, a slim, exotically curved and fragile-seeming artifact that still managed to look deadly when wielded by those long-clawed hands. They tended to hold them in the upper, slender pair of arms, saving the lower, more muscular pair for picking things up or moving debris. As he watched, a pack of eight of the Malach sprinted ahead in a tight-packed wedge, plunging into the tent city near where their lander had parked.

"Lieutenant!" Kathy yelled at him from twenty meters away. "Come *on!*"

"You two go ahead!" he yelled back, waving them on. "I'll be along soon!"

He had to see this. If he ever made it back to Muir alive, his memories of the Malach in battle would be invaluable. Not for the Confederation Military Command, necessarily . . . but for Freddy and Ferdy, the two Mark XXIVs waiting for him back at the maintenance depot. He wished he had a vid recorder; the Bolos, almost certainly, would be able to analyze the Malach attack profiles and tactics with far greater accuracy and detail than was possible for any mere human soldier.

A pair of Malach fighters howled overhead, traveling so close to the city's surface that Donal was knocked down by a blast of hot air from one of those ventral jets. Ball turrets beneath the fighters' rounded prows loosed stuttering volleys of needle-thin, blue-white bolts that sprayed across the buildings of the central towers. Glass shattered, seament exploded in the heat, sending an avalanche of rubble cascading down the faces of several of the towers and smashing onto the plaza below, close to where Kathy and Alexie had been moments ago.

"Kathy!" he yelled. "*Kathy!*" Oh, God! Had they been caught by that avalanche? He couldn't tell. Scrambling to his feet, he started forward, searching. Pain clawed at his left arm. When he looked down, he saw that the sleeve of his uniform tunic had been burned away, and the skin beneath turned boiled-lobster red. He could feel burns on his side and his face as well, but only as a kind of tightness, as from a sunburn that hadn't really started to hurt yet.

No matter. He could still function. Where were Kathy and Alexie?

Behind, above, and around him, explosions thundered and civilians screamed. For them, he thought, it must seem like the end of the world . . . and in a sense, it was the end of *this* world, at least.

The Malach had arrived to challenge Man for the mastery of this planet, and, so far as Donal could see, there wasn't a damned thing that Man could do in the way of fighting back. . . .

CHAPTER THIRTEEN

Donal reached the edge of the spill of rubble from the front of one of the city towers. Several people lay dead or wounded beneath jagged white blocks of seament or twisted pieces of metal, but he didn't see either the commander or the deputy director. He helped several civilians pull a massive block of seament off of a man with badly crushed legs. More and more civilians were rallying around, now, helping rescue the injured. Donal looked around, to see what more he could do.

Fresh screams and shouted warnings attracted his attention back to the west, toward the railing a hundred meters away, not far from the spot where he and the two women had been standing moments before. Another of the big Malach troop carriers was hovering there, an oval door in the side dilating to disgorge a small army of bipedal, green-and-ruby-scaled lizards directly onto the plaza.

A security guard had been killed in the avalanche. Part of his light-blue uniform, stained with blood, showed from beneath a pile of rubble. A military rifle lay next to one outflung, paste-white hand. Donal scooped the bulky weapon up, worked the action, and checked safety and receiver.

It was a Guiscard-DuPres-90, an accelerator rifle, a ten-kilo monster originally developed as a big-game rifle for some hunter's world deep in human space, but adapted to military use. The original design was at least seven centuries old, but that made it no less deadly. Checking to see that he had a full magazine of iron-jacketed vanadium-uranium slugs, he dropped to one knee and took aim at the advancing Malach warriors.

They were coming across the plaza in a tightly packed wedge formation. Assuming that the one in the lead, at the arrow's tip, was the leader, Donal took aim, centering the glowing crosshairs in the tiny view screen above the receiver smack between the Malach's four bright red eyes and squeezing the trigger.

With an ear-ringing crack, the GDP-90 slammed back painfully against his shoulder, the recoil and the noise both catching him by surprise. Accelerator rifles used a powerful magnetic pulse to launch a dense, iron-jacketed needle at something like Mach five. The magfield itself was silent, but the sonic boom emitted by the projectile could be startling, and the recoil—the action-reaction generated by a small slug traveling very fast indeed—slammed the buttstock against his shoulder despite the rifle's considerable mass and its internal recoil dampers.

The effect was immediate and spectacular, however. The lead Malach, which must have massed a good two hundred kilos, had been flung backward by the impact, and most of its heavy, bony dome of a skull above the eyes was missing. Malach, Donal saw, had greenish-blue blood.

The death of their leader—assuming Donal had been right in his guess about their squad organization—did not slow the others. They closed ranks and kept coming, loosing bolts of blue-white coherent light from their hand weapons as they advanced. Donal dove behind a tumble of broken seament blocks as the laser beams scored the air above his head, then came up with the accelerator rifle at the ready, drawing a bead on a second Malach and squeezing off a second, painful thump of a shot.

The high-velocity slug tunneled into the Malach's chest, between the joints of its upper set of arms. Flesh and blood could not resist that much kinetic energy dumped into soft tissue that quickly; a bubble of superheated steam and expanding, vaporized tissue literally blew the Malach's upper torso apart in a bloody green splatter. Donal shifted aim and fired again . . . and again . . .

His deadly accuracy stopped the Malach rush at last. Four of the invaders remained now, crouched on the plaza, firing at random into the people scattering away from this deadly new threat. Donal bit off a sharp curse as three women and a man died on different parts of the plaza, laser bolts searing into their backs . . . followed by four more people in another heartbeat, and four more after that. His one-man stand had generated an indiscriminate slaughter of the fleeing civilians.

Taking aim once more, Donal shot another Malach, watching the toothily grinning, green-and-red head explode under the impact of the vanadium-uranium projectile. By that time, however, twenty-four more of the jewel-scaled monsters had emerged from the hovering Malach transport and were fanning out in three groups of eight across the plaza.

Donal knew when a cause was hopeless. The enemy had apparently lost track of where he was and hadn't been able to spot where his sniper fire was coming from, but they would keep killing the civilians until they flushed him into the open, and then he would die.

Or . . . was it possible that they weren't even distinguishing between civilians and armed men? Peering around the side of his ten-ton chunk of sheltering debris, he saw eight of the Malach rush into a fleeing gaggle of civilians. Several of the aliens carried odd-looking weapons different in design from the lasers. When they fired them, they spewed unfolding nets of some gray-silver, sticky filaments that entangled a dozen running humans at a time and knocked them kicking to the ground. A couple of Malach grabbed the ends of the nets then and began dragging them back toward the waiting transport.

A prisoner snatch. Donal understood suddenly that this was why the Malach had launched their attack on the city. They weren't here in strength enough to capture Fortrose; this was a raid, one aimed at capturing a number of humans. No doubt the Malach found humans as strange as humans found the Malach, and they needed prisoners for interrogation . . . or worse.

Angry, now, Donal took aim at one of the Malach dragging away his prize of half a dozen entangled humans, shooting the dinosaurian monster through its grinning head. A flurry of laser shots replied; they'd seen him that time and were peppering his seament cover, the flashes cracking and hissing like miniature lightning bolts. Flat on his belly, his GDP-90 cradled in his arms, Donal snake-squirmed himself away from the block of rubble, staying beneath the cover of the debris spill as he sought another, better vantage point from which he could continue his one-man campaign.

When he poked his head up once more, he was startled to see that the Malach were pulling back. A line of the creatures had formed up in a ragged perimeter around the hovering transport, weapons leveled outward, while the rest—dragging along their human captives—scrambled back into the open hatchway.

One young man—a boy, really, a teenager—managed to break free of the net and scramble away. His captor grappled with him, using all four clawed arms to drag him back toward the ship. Donal snapped his rifle to his shoulder once more, taking aim at the Malach even though he knew the boy's plight, inside the enemy's perimeter, was hopeless. Before he could squeeze the trigger, he saw the boy struggling wildly, the image magnified on his targeting screen. An instant later, the Malach, exasperated, possibly, by the boy's struggles, ducked its head sharply, the jaws clamping down hard on the boy's arm, torso, and shoulder in a spray of bright red blood. Viciously, the Malach shook the body, now gone deathly limp, like a terrier worrying a rag doll. Sickened, Donal was about to squeeze the trigger again when he saw something unusual, something that made him hold his fire.

The Malach, clearly, was injured . . . no, it was *sick*. The sharply mottled green and red coloring of its scaly face had gone so pale it was difficult to distinguish between the two colors, and all four of its eyes were squeezed tightly shut. Abruptly, it vomited, took another pair of steps toward the transport, and then collapsed in a tangle of weakly thrashing limbs and twitching tail. Two other Malach, withdrawing toward the transport, stopped and dragged their stricken companion between them. As they dragged it aboard, he could make out a greenish froth bubbling from its mouth.

Interesting. That single bite it had taken out of the human captive had poisoned the Malach. That had to be a useful datum, though Donal couldn't think how to apply it at the moment. The last of the invaders, meanwhile, crowded aboard the transport, which slowly rose above the plaza on shrieking underjets, laser fire spraying wildly in every direction.

The raid was nearly over. As Donal emerged from cover, he could see that the transports that had landed elsewhere on the island were also beginning to lift off one by one, as the smaller, faster fighters continued their tight loops and turns overhead. The Wide Sky military was engaging the attackers, though there simply wasn't enough firepower on Fortrose to more than inconvenience them.

A dozen Firefly hovertanks had appeared from somewhere, sweeping past the city on high-splashing roostertails of spray. The hovercraft were fast and highly maneuverable, but they were thin-skinned and possessed only light weapons—three-centimeter rockets and half-megajoule needle-beam lasers that reflected off the Malach armor in jeweled scatterings of light. Worse, the Malach vehicles were nearly as maneuverable as the hovertanks, skittering from side to side on howling underjets as they poured volleys of laser and particle beam fire into the defenders. One after another, the hovertanks were marked down and smashed, their thin armor holed or melted away, with oily black pillars of smoke to mark the junk-pile funeral pyre of those destroyed over the island, or oily patches on the water where they'd been destroyed over the sea.

Before their destruction, one by one, the last five of the Fireflies managed to gang up on one of the circling Malach fighters, pounding at it with volleyed rockets and laser fire. The vehicle broke off its circling and limped off toward the west, trailing smoke, but it was a dearly purchased victory.

And the attack, valiant as it was, had been far too little, too late. The transports departed toward the west, howling off low over the sea, their ventral jets churning up the surface of the water in steaming gouts of spray. The fighters followed, delivering a final volley of laser and plasma bolts that shattered building facades and smashed craters into unyielding seament. Then they were gone, and the only sound was the crackle of scattered fires, the despairing calls of people searching for loved ones and companions in the rubble, and the moans and occasional heart-rending shrieks of the wounded. The alert siren, the wailing that had first attracted his attention and unheard during the thunderous cacophony of the battle, was still going.

Not that it could do any good now, save, possibly, adding to the mournful atmosphere of loss and devastation that hung above Fortrose now like the pall of black smoke that rose from a hundred scattered fires.

Perhaps an hour later, Donal found the City Control Center and there, to his tremendous relief, he found both Kathy Ross and Alexie Turner, huddled in conference with Major Fitzsimmons and a small army of aides. "Donal!" Kathy cried as he entered the room. "We thought you'd been killed!"

"I thought the same about you," he said.

She started to hug him, then drew back when he winced. "Ow!" she said, eyes widening. "What happened to your arm? And your face?"

He looked down at his arm. Blisters had formed a cluster of long, puffy sacs along the outside of his forearm, and his entire hand and arm were beet red. "It's not too bad," he lied. "I caught the edge of a Malach flier's exhaust."

"You were lucky, then," Fitzsimmons told him. "We've been getting reports of lots of people boiled to death when those things flew low overhead. They use superheated water as reaction mass, and steam burns can be pretty nasty."

"We should get you to a medic," Alexie told him.

"Nah, I'm okay," he told them. In fact, he was feeling dizzy and sick with the onset of shock, but so far he was managing to hold the worst effects at bay. He needed to talk to them first about what he'd learned. "Mind if I sit down, though?" He was dangerously close to collapse.

Fitzsimmons signaled an aide, who produced a chair. Donal unslung his rifle and slumped into the chair with heartfelt relief.

"Thanks." He fixed Fitzsimmons with a hard look. "Well, so much for hoping the Malach had overlooked your cities."

"We beat them off."

"We didn't beat anything off," Alexie told him, her voice sour. "They walked all over us and left when they'd done what they'd come here to do."

"Prisoners," Donal told them. "They grabbed, I don't know, twenty or thirty people that I could see, up on the plaza outside of the auditorium. The other landings probably grabbed more, but I didn't see what happened with them." He patted his bulky accelerator rifle, propped up next to his chair. "I was a little busy at the time."

"So far, we've had reports of two hundred twenty-one people snatched by those damned things," Fitzsimmons said. "We assume that they are curious about both humans and these cities." He cocked his head. "We had reports of someone shooting down a lot of Malach on the plaza. Was that you?"

"Probably. It didn't get us anything, though. Just made them mad."

"The reports said six confirmed kills on the plaza," Kathy said. "And another one wounded. Witnesses saw it being helped aboard the landing craft."

"Yeah. I don't know how many I shot," Donal told them. "I lost count. But the wounded one, that wasn't my doing." He told them what he'd seen through his rifle's scope, how the Malach had bitten the boy to death, then suffered an apparent reaction.

"I'm not sure how to interpret what I saw happen," he told them then. "I see two possible reasons the critter got sick."

"We were speculating here on heavy-metal poisoning," Alexie said. "If the Malach are from a relatively metal-poor world, you would expect them to have a pretty low tolerance for, well, the iron in human blood and tissue, say."

"Good possibility. Though the fact that they have a fair amount of metal trappings on those harnesses of theirs and are carrying metallic weapons argues they're not *that* sensitive. Otherwise, their skin would break out in hives just from picking up one of their weapons."

"You said you saw two possibilities," Kathy prompted.

"Incompatible proteins. Our body chemistry is based on right-handed sugars and left-handed amino acids. Assuming they're based on sugars and amino acids, like us, there's still only a one in four chance that their chemistry would be like ours."

Alexie shook her head. "If they had different proteins, that would just mean they couldn't get any nourishment from eating us. Like eating cardboard. It wouldn't necessarily poison them."

"Well, *something* poisoned that Malach soldier," Donal said. He was too tired, too sick to think the thing through now. "If you have your people do an autopsy on the bodies, it might tell you enough about their body chemistry to tell us what their weaknesses are."

"We've had people doing chemistry work-ups on some of the other bodies we've picked up," Fitzsimmons said, "but I don't think they did anything beyond a basic carbon chemistry work-up. I'll have some of our bioscience people start modeling the protein structure. That ought to tell us something about these things, anyway."

"Somehow, I don't think we're going to beat these monsters by making them take bites out of us," Kathy observed. She looked at Alexie. "I also don't think you can delay in getting your evac ships away. The Malach probably just learned one hell of a lot more about you and these floating cities of yours than we've learned so far about them. They've been here once, they'll be back. And soon."

"You're right. Of course, we've learned one vital fact." Alexie smiled at Donal. "We learned the Malach aren't superhuman. They can be killed."

"Yeah," Donal said. "But it isn't easy. I saw your Firefly hovertanks tangling with those things. They managed to damage, *damage*, mind you, one. Twelve Fireflies were destroyed in the process. You can't afford those kinds of trade-offs. Not and survive."

"What about the Bolos?" Fitzsimmons asked. "The advanced ones, I mean, back on Muir. The Mark XVIII we had here didn't last for long, and that was against just sixteen of those Malach machines. How do you think a Mark XXIV would do?"

Donal shook his head. "Impossible question to answer."

"Not that hard, surely. If sixteen Malach walkers—I guess we can't call them that anymore, since we saw them in an air role today—sixteen combat machines took out a Mark XVIII, well, how much better is a Mark XXIV? Twice as good? Three times?"

"The point is that a Mark XXIV is intelligent and self-aware, while a Mark XVIII isn't," Donal said. "Self-evident, I know, but it makes a hell of a big difference, and people don't think about it that much. The Mark XVIII, you see, would have been working off of a standard attack/defense program. That software would have been flexible, of course, to give the machine a lot of latitude in its approach, but the chances were it couldn't rewrite its own reaction code fast enough to respond to what was probably a threat unlike any in its historical archives or sim banks."

"It was destroyed in just under thirty seconds," Fitzsimmons said with a sour set to his mouth.

Donal nodded. "I know. And that's pretty amazing. These Malach machines are a hell of a lot tougher and more dangerous than they look. You know, if you people have tapes of that action, I'm going to need copies to take with me back to Muir. I'll give them to Freddy and Ferdy and see what they make of them."

"Freddy and Ferdy?" Alexie asked, her eyebrows arching.

"The Bolos. Mark XXIV, unit designation FRD." He grinned at her. "You'll like them."

Her eyebrows climbed higher. "What's *that* supposed to mean?"

"That you're coming with us, back to Muir."

"I haven't agreed to that." She shook her head. "I'm needed here. More than ever."

"If I may, Deputy Director," Fitzsimmons said, "let me point out that you can do more good on Muir than you can here."

"What is this, a conspiracy?" she demanded, "Have you two been discussing this behind my back?"

"Not at all," Donal told her. He looked at Fitzsimmons, who wore a quizzical look on his face. "I was suggesting that Deputy Director Turner would be of more use to Wide Sky if she came with us back to Muir. Her word will carry a hell of a lot more weight with my bosses in the Confederation Military Command than mine will."

"He's right, you know," Major Fitzsimmons said. "The situation here requires a military approach, not a civilian one."

"Wide Sky is a civilian-run democracy, Major. Not a military dictatorship."

"With all due respect, ma'am, there are times when democracy has to give way, temporarily, at least, to dictatorship. In cases of martial law, for example. We're going to be fighting for our lives here. We won't be able to stop and take a vote on whether or not to attack or lay low. Am I right?"

"I'll be seen to be running away."

Donal gave a tight smile. "I can't say what it'll look like to the people who stay here," he told her. "Maybe you're right. Maybe they'll think it's cowardice. Maybe the brave thing to do, though, is to say to hell with what people think, and do what you know is right."

"I respect you for your convictions, Deputy Director," Fitzsimmons added. "But you have to do what's right, not what is politically expedient."

"And running away is right?"

Donal shrugged, spreading his hands. "I know that you'll do a whole lot more for the cause of your people if you come talk to my bosses on Muir yourself. They're not likely to believe me when I tell them what's coming. The Director of Wide Sky, well, I'd guess they're going to have to listen to you."

"Deputy Director," she reminded him. "I would say that people couldn't possibly be so blind," she added quietly, "except that I've seen that sort of blindness for myself, here."

"Then you know what I mean."

"We'll need a resolution passed in the legislature. If they decide that my leaving is . . . politically unfeasible . . ."

"I imagine that issue will take care of itself," Fitzsimmons told her.

She sighed, then looked at Fitzsimmons. "You'll take care of . . . of everyone who stays, Fitz?"

"You know I can't promise safety for them, Alexie," the major replied. "Rather the opposite, I should think. But I'll do what I can. For your dad's sake. And for yours."

"I guess I have no alternative, then."

"No, ma'am," Fitzsimmons told her. "No, you don't. Because if you *don't* get on that transport when it comes time to leave, I'll carry you aboard myself. I promised your daddy I'd look after you, and by God that's what I'm going to do." He looked at Donal. "Son, you take care of getting her to Muir. You see that she gets what she needs to get the job done, okay? Or I'll know the reason why!"

Donal smiled. "Yes, sir!"

An aide called to Fitzsimmons from the other side of the room. "Excuse me a moment."

"What was *that* all about?" he asked as Fitzsimmons walked away. "About you and your dad?"

"Fitz was a good friend of my father, back when he

was Director General of the colony," she said. She sighed. "He was always kind of like an uncle. I think he still wants to look out for me, for my interests, some times."

"How long before the transports can be loaded?" Kathy asked.

"We're working on that now . . . or we were, before the attack. Last I heard, the first would be ready for boost early tomorrow. The rest by the day after that."

"It's going to be damned hard to slip past that blockade," Donal said. He sank back in the chair. His arm was hurting badly now, and he was feeling cold. "And if we do it once, they're not likely to let it happen again. I think I'd suggest waiting until they're all ready, then go in a group."

"I was suggesting the same thing, Lieutenant," Kathy told him. "And they'll need a diversion. Something to open a hole in the blockade long enough for the transports to get away."

Donal felt a small, cold stab of fear. "You have any ideas about that?"

"Yes," Kathy told them. "As a matter of fact I do."

CHAPTER FOURTEEN

The Conestoga-class transport *Uriel* had seemed small when viewed from the vantage point of a descending Percheron, high above the floating city. From here, however, as he walked out on the transplas-enclosed walkway leading from the towering white city breakwater to the ship's brow, it seemed as though the transport was the most titanic manmade structure Donal had ever seen . . . excepting, of course, the artificial island itself, and the island was simply of such a scale that words like artificial or manmade lost their meanings. The vessel measured nearly half a kilometer in diameter and half that again in length, though only the upper hundred meters or so extended above the surface of the ocean. Several Bolos could have fit comfortably within her capacious holds.

Seen close up, *Uriel* showed her age. Corrosion streaked her outer hull, where plates once painted white had dulled and blackened in ragged patches where the rust was eating through. According to the Port Authority records Donal had studied the day before, *Uriel* was over four hundred years old, having come off the starship ways at Aldo Cerise in 2614. She'd started in the Concordiat merchant service, later been transferred to

Rim, and finally been sold to the Strathan Authority in 3001. According to her maintenance records, she'd been due for retirement a good two centuries ago.

Nonetheless, she was a proud old lady . . . and she'd been called on to perform one more vital run. He hoped she was up to it.

The covered walkway was crowded, and Donal found himself being jostled a bit as he made his way toward the ship's main entry port, holding his injured arm up high. A medic had sprayed it with a sealant that kept it numb while letting the burns heal, but it still hurt when someone bumped it, and he had it in a sling. A steady stream of children, making their way slowly out from the breakwater and into the bowels of the huge transport, all but filled the passageway. Despite the jostling, the procession was remarkably orderly and quiet. Few of the kids cried, and all seemed willing to follow the adults assigned to shepherd them aboard. Indeed, the adults with them seemed more fearful than their charges.

He identified himself to the ship's officer who was ticking off names on her data pad at the entrance, then followed the signs in and up, heading for the bridge. It was chaotic aboard; the children were still well-behaved, but *Uriel's* interior was a maze of passageways, corridors, elevators, and compartments; three of the Conestoga's five immense cargo bays had been partitioned into cramped, dormitory-style living quarters, while the remaining two were crammed with food concentrates and water tanks.

It didn't take him long to get lost. Somewhat against the laws of chance, though, he found Alexie fifteen minutes later standing at the intersection of two passageways, an electronic notepad in one hand as she directed traffic with the other.

"Alexie! Thank God! I thought I was going to starve to death in this rat's maze!"

She looked at him coldly, and he saw the resentment in her eyes. She'd made the decision to come, but he knew well that it had been against what she thought was her better judgment.

"I'm glad you're coming," he told her.

Resentment changed, reluctantly, to what might have almost been a tight, tired smile. "I still feel a bit guilty," she told him. "Like I'm running away."

He gestured at the crowds of children filling the passageways around them, the handful of shepherding, scared-looking adults. "You're not running out on *them.* They need you, too."

"We'll discuss the philosophy of cowardice later," she told him, a sharp edge hardening the words. "Right now, I have to get these people checked in and in their quarters."

"They've given me a jumpseat up on the bridge." He smiled apologetically. "But I'm a bit turned around. Army, you know. Not navy. Which way?"

She jerked her thumb over her shoulder. "Down that passageway to the end, find an elevator, and take it to the oh-ten level. You'll see the signs."

"Thanks."

She was already talking with a harried-looking woman with a small army of four through six-year-olds and didn't reply.

Following her directions he found the bridge, where Captain Charles Arkin and his bridge crew were making the final preparations for launch.

"Welcome aboard, Lieutenant," Arkin told him curtly when he announced himself. He pointed to a folding jumpseat wedged into a corner of the tiny bridge between the flight engineer and the comm officer's position. "We're boosting as soon as the diversion goes up, and so we're a bit busy right now. Try to stay out of the way."

"Thank you, sir. Uh, will I be able to watch the diversion from here?"

Arkin pointed to a large, curved view screen set against the tangle of cables and conduits covering most of the dome that stretched over the crowded bridge. A larger screen was mounted lower down, in front of the seats occupied by *Uriel*'s helm and navigation officers. Currently, it showed the view from a camera mounted high up on *Uriel*'s prow, looking back into the city. From here, the damage done two days before by the attacking Malach was shocking, a collection of black, grisly scars across the once immaculate white towers of the city center.

From his position, he could also see one of the ship's repeater screens, showing the camera view from somewhere out in the city. The crowds outside were gone now, though he could make out the shadows of some thousands of people watching from the enclosed safety of some of the larger public buildings near the center of the floating city.

He checked each of the monitors, but his attention was swiftly pulled back to the one on the dome. It showed a map, a Mercator projection of Wide Sky, with the land and sea colors accurately depicted, as though taken from satellite shots. The five floating cities were plainly marked, a cluster of blue dots among the scattered archipelagoes of Scarba. A lone white dot was positioned west of the cities; as he watched, minute by minute, he could just make out its slow, westward drift.

Commander Kathy Ross, flying one of Wide Sky's surviving XK-4000s.

"Okay, boys and girls," Kathy's voice said over the bridge speakers. "Blue Hawk is moving. Punched through Mach three and accelerating. Over the ocean, heading west. No sign of the bad guys yet."

Donal's heart hammered a little harder in his chest. He'd not been happy with Kathy's plan, but ultimately there'd been no real choice. The same argument he'd used on Alexie to get her to come with him to the relative safety of Muir had been turned against him; Kathy had more experience than any of the space fighter pilots on Wide Sky, and the best chance of pulling this thing off and returning in one piece.

"This is Blue Hawk, going feet dry at zero-nine-three-five. Still no sign of the opposition."

Unfortunately, best chance was a relative term, not an absolute. Even in the relatively new XK-4000, a sleek, supercharged high-performance fighter popularly called the Starhawk, her chances of surviving against the Malach orbital blockade were far from good.

"I'm starting to pick up some activity on deep radar," Kathy's voice said. Her fighter was now nearly a thousand kilometers to the west, well past the beach where she and Donal had been shot down three nights ago. "I think they're interested."

A smaller window opened in the upper right corner of the screen, showing a three-D representation of the Wide Sky globe, its continents picked out in graphic white lines. Red dots of light circled the globe, each trailing a paler, curved red line as it orbited the planet. Kathy's fighter was marked in green, drawing a green line around the curve of the planet. Sure enough, as minute followed tense minute, the red dots could be seen to be changing course, swinging out of their orbits to converge on the fast-moving XK-4000.

The hunt, Donal thought grimly, was on.

Commander Kathy Ross took a quick look straight up through the transplex dome over her cockpit, wondering if she could see her Malach pursuers yet. There were lots of stars . . . but she couldn't see any of the telltale moving stars that indicated a spacecraft in low orbit.

She'd crossed the terminator some minutes ago and was flying over Wide Sky's night side, still hugging the surface at an altitude of less than one hundred meters. She was depending on her Starhawk's terrain-following

AI for a level of flying precision impossible for any human pilot. With the fighter traveling at almost Mach five now, a mountain or sudden change in elevation would be on her before she could possibly see it and react, even in daylight, even using the craft's sophisticated radar and IR imaging screens, located on her center console to either side of her main Computer Graphic Display.

The CGD was currently showing a computer-painted representation of the terrain she was crossing . . . a narrow valley with sheer-sided cliffs to either side. From second to second, she could feel the slight tugs this way and that as the aircraft adjusted its flight path, keeping clear of the rocky crags flashing past in the darkness to either side.

She glanced up again. Directly overhead, she saw stars . . . by chance the warm and swarming reds and yellows of the Strathan Cluster. She was glad to have a last look at that star-clustered glory; she was not at all convinced that she was going to be able to pull this off.

Still no sign of her pursuers, but she knew they were there. Every few seconds, a set of lights winked from green to red on her threat board, just to the right of her right armrest, indicating various wavelengths of weapons, targeting, and search radars. They were probably having trouble picking her out of the ground clutter at this altitude, especially since they couldn't nail her with a side-looking beam in this narrow defile, but sooner or later they would get close enough to lock on hard.

Then things would get interesting.

Suddenly, she was out of the valley and booming out over the ocean, the shock wave from her Mach five passage raising a plume of spray in her wake fifty meters high. More red lights winked on, as more Malach radars pegged her. Another glance through her canopy, up into star-strewn night. She thought she could see a couple of moving points of light up there, but she couldn't be sure.

Kathy still wasn't entirely sure why she'd volunteered for this run, even if it *had* been her idea to begin with. It had to do, she supposed, with the fact that she'd logged more hours—most of them in singleships like this one—than anyone else on Wide Sky, but that fact alone hadn't demanded that she make the offer.

But she did take intense pride in her proficiency as a pilot, even when the spacecraft was flying itself. The time would come, soon enough, when it would be her brain directing the sleek, black Starhawk, and not the computer. That, she was convinced, was where human warriors had it over the machines like Lieutenant Ragnor's Bolos. Sure, the smart ones were supposed to be able to think, but Kathy was convinced that a human brain made the difference, more often than not.

More than anything else, though, she remembered those crowds of people in their ragged tent city . . . and the hell of smoke and flame and noise when the Malach had struck.

Donal Ragnor hadn't been happy when she'd told him what she was going to do . . . not that he'd any say in her decision. She ranked him, and he'd known she was right in any case. She'd seen it in his eyes.

In the end, she'd assured him that this flight would not be a suicide mission, not the way *she* flew. She'd even been able to convince herself of that, during that long restless and wakeful night last night. All she needed to do was sucker enough of those orbiting Malach ships to chase after her, and she could do that by vectoring on Big Mama, as she'd nicknamed the huge, single transport now in far orbit around Wide Sky. If she could threaten Big Mama, boosting into an approach vector that convinced the lizards that she was attacking their largest ship, they would have to break their own blockade orbits and come after her, just in case. The damned Dinos couldn't be so sure of themselves that they would ignore such a threat.

I hope....

It was also possible that they would fry her with a single shot from long range, catching her like a moth in a blowtorch flame. Still, she had a pretty good idea now of Malach fleet capabilities. If she could survive the gauntlet, she would break out on one side of the blockade while the Wide Sky transports were breaking out on the other. The XK-4000 was one of those rare space fighters that possessed hyper-L capability. It would be a long, cramped, and hungry trek back to Muir, with stops at Endymion, Carter, and Faraway for pile recharges and life-support overhaul, but she would be able to make it.

I hope....

So many unknowns.

She checked her nav screen, comparing her position with the position of known Malach ships. Things were getting pretty damned thick up there; it was time to find herself some maneuvering room.

"This is Blue Hawk," she said, keying her com unit. "Going ballistic at zero-niner-five-one. I've got a search lock on Big Mama. Keep your eyes peeled, boys and girls. This ought to really shake those lizards!"

Savagely, she hauled back on the Starhawk's control stick, bringing her nose high until it pointed almost directly toward the Strathan Cluster, then ramming her throttle forward to the last detent.

Thunder howled and shrieked and bucked scant meters behind the thin padding of her acceleration couch and life-support capsule. The Starhawk shuddered, the stick wrenching against her hand, but she held the craft steady as she engaged full burner, punching upward through rapidly thinning atmosphere.

Acceleration flattened her breasts, crushing her, smothering her, the G-counter on her HUD ticking upward past 8.5 to 9.0, then 9.2 . . . 9.4. . . .

Ten Gs was her limit, she knew, the line at which her

vision would go and then she would black out. She kept the throttle full forward, however, and howled into the sky.

Around her, the unseen Malach ships were converging. . . .

"She's doing it!" someone on the bridge called, her voice hushed with wonder. "By God, she's doing it!"

Donal's eyes snapped open. He'd closed them momentarily, the better to imagine the sleek, black Starhawk arrowing into Wide Sky's stratosphere on the far side of the planet, some twelve thousand kilometers to the west.

"That's our window," the captain said. "All ships! Stand by to boost in ninety seconds! Engineering! Bring us to one hundred percent, standby."

"Fusion core at one hundred percent, standing by."

"Reaction mass."

"RM, check. We are ready for boost, on your mark, Captain."

"Com. Link with the other ships."

"All ships standing by, Captain. Report ready for boost."

"Navigation."

"Plot locked in, sir."

"Mooring lines."

"Mooring lines cast off. We're clear to navigate, sir."

"Clear sky."

"Flight path clear, sir. And we have a green light from the port."

"Message from Fortrose, Captain."

"Let's hear it."

"It reads, 'God speed, and good luck.' "

"How original. Acknowledge."

"Message acknowledged, Captain."

"Maneuvering thrusters."

"Maneuvering, check."

"Meteor lasers."

"Met lasers. Operational. On auto."

"Telemetry. . . ."

The checklist droned on, system and acknowledgment, a dance of professional routine. Mesmerized by the drifting points of light on the screen, Donal kept watching the secondary screen as the seconds dwindled away. Kathy's fighter was passing two hundred kilometers altitude now, well clear of Wide Sky's atmosphere and hurtling out into space.

Yes . . . she was closing on the blip representing the Malach's largest transport, as planned. *Just scare them, Kathy, then cut in full boost and get the hell out of there. You don't need to get closer than a couple of thousand klicks to scare them out of their scales, and that's all we'll need. . . .*

Someone announced the thirty-second mark . . . and then the twenty. The secondary screen showed the red dots of the Malach blockader ships now, streaming around the curve of the planet in hot pursuit of the solitary XK-4000 Starhawk. The Dino forces were definitely moving clear of the sky overhead, swarming toward the opposite hemisphere to defend against that sudden valiant, suicidal attack.

"Hang onto your breakfasts, people," Captain Arkin called. "That's five . . . four . . . three . . . two . . . one . . . and punch it!"

Thunder sounded, deep beneath the ship, a growing rumble that climbed rapidly in volume, accompanied by a steady shaking as the Conestoga's enormous Argosy-B fusion drives cut in, hurling the massive craft into a rapidly darkening sky. A massive hand clamped down over Donal's chest, squeezing him back into the hard and close-fitting confines of the jumpseat. His breath came in short gasps as his weight increased; he wondered how the thousands of kids below decks were taking the brutal acceleration.

He wondered how Kathy was doing, fighting for her life twelve thousand kilometers away. . . .

❖   ❖   ❖

Acceleration peaked at 10.2 Gs . . . a bit more than Kathy had been shooting for, but she surprised herself by somehow hanging on to the ragged, fuzzy-visioned edge of consciousness as the stars brightened and hardened and Wide Sky's night side fell away at her back. As her thrusters cut out, she felt the heart-lifting surge of zero-G.

White light, hard, actinic, and dazzling, blossomed soundlessly to her right. Some lizard fighter jock had just gotten eager and launched a hunter-killer her way, but it had detonated well short of its target. So far, none of her pursuers was close enough to pose a real threat.

But they would be soon. Her course had been calculated to punch up and through the blockade before they could react, but some few, at least, would be in orbits that gave them a decent chance of intercepting her. She checked her radar screen again, comparing it with her nav plot. Yeah . . . there were at least four Malach ships out there that would be within easy missile range in another couple of minutes. And if she changed course, there would be a handful more lizard hotshots on her tail who would be in position to cut her off.

But that was the idea, of course, to drag as many of the Malach after her as possible. She checked range to target, then looked at the graphic trajectory plot on her CGD and gave a low chuckle. Big Mama was two thousand kilometers away, and she'd nailed her perfectly with a class-one intercept vector. The only question now was, how long should she hold this course? The longer she stayed on the intercept, the more convinced the Malach would be that she was after Big Mama, and that was good for the Conestogas at the antipodes. But the longer she held this course, the closer the lizards on an intercept with her would get . . . and the less likely it was that she was going to get out of this.

But she already knew the answer to the equation. . . .

Aghrrracht the Swift-Slayer opened all four eyes. "Solitary?" she hissed. "There is only *one*?"

"Only one, Deathgiver," Sh'graat'na the Prey Wounder told her. "It is approaching at approximately three thousand *t'charucht* per *quor*. We have been scanning for support elements, assuming that this might be a diversion, but have seen nothing as yet."

Aghrracht's Second, Zhallet'llesch the Scent Finder, raised her head. "We believe the craft may be intended as *k'klaj'sh'achk*."

Aghrracht closed both hind-hands in empathic understanding. The Malach term literally meant head-crush but referred to an attack made by one member of a hunter pack against the head and jaws of some particularly large and dangerous prey. The word denoted bravery, and the willingness to sacrifice one's self so that the rest of the pack would eat.

"If she seeks death, we must help that warrior find her destiny," Aghrracht said. "Destroy her!"

"Kill and eat!" the others said in unison, hind-hands clenched.

The large command center suddenly and unaccountably felt close and warm.

Eight hundred more kilometers to Big Mama. Kathy could see the target visually now . . . a point of white light, about first magnitude, drifting slowly from her right toward her Starhawk's nose.

A warning buzzer sounded. Some lizard hotshot had just acquired a weapons radar lock. *Now it begins. . . .*

The warning tone changed pitch. "Hostile missile launch," her Starhawk's computer voice informed her with a maddening composure. "Radar lock. Impact in twenty-three seconds."

"Ordnance, radar decoy launch," she said. "Dump chaff."

She heard the thump from aft, and the AI confirmed the launch a moment later. "Radar decoy deployed," the calm voice said. "Chaff deployed. Beacon broadcasting. Impact in fifteen seconds."

Chaff, a cloud of aluminized mylar exploded aft of the Starhawk to confuse the missile's radar lock, was an ancient countermeasure, but an effective one. The decoy was also old, in principle, a fist-sized beacon that leaked signals sounding suspiciously like reflections from the Starhawk itself. Together, the two might confuse the enemy's homing missile enough to let Kathy get a bit closer.

"Missile veering to port. Impact in—"

White light flared to her left, a dazzling glare that would have been blinding had she chanced to look into that nuclear glow. She felt a prickling sensation on her skin beneath her space suit. *Damn, that was close. The lizards must be using rad-enhanced warheads, hoping for a long-distance kill.* She wondered how many roentgens she'd just absorbed.

"Hostile missile launch. Radar lock. Impact in nineteen seconds."

"You know the drill," she replied. "Ordnance, radar decoy launch. Dump chaff."

The second warhead detonated moments later in savage, blinding brilliance and perfect silence. So far, her decoys were keeping the warheads at arm's length, but she was going to be out of squawkers soon. She goosed her thrusters, accelerating hard, changing her side vector at the same time to hold her intercept with Big Mama.

The range closed, the kilometers ticking away faster now, as five more missiles arced in from astern. . . .

CHAPTER FIFTEEN

"She's going for the big Dino ship," the navigator said. She turned and gave Donal an unreadable look, then turned to Captain Arkin. "I don't think she intended to bluff it out at all. She's going for the kill."

"Damn," Arkin said. Acceleration continued to hammer at them, but as *Uriel* punched up through Wide Sky's stratosphere and into open space, the thrust began easing off. Unlike the sturdy little Starhawk fighter, the big Conestogas weren't built for heavy acceleration over the long haul, and a sustained boost at more than about five Gs might crack the hull or snap her spine.

Donal looked at the main screen, which showed the view ahead along *Uriel*'s upward curving course. Blue sky had been giving way moment by moment, first to purple, and then to the dead black of open space. They were rising from the planet on the side opposite from the Strathan Cluster, but that would not pose a major navigational problem. They would enter hyper-L, travel for a light year or so to get clear of the Malach ships, then drop back into normal space to realign for the long run for Muir and safety.

He looked back at the secondary screen on the bridge dome. Nearly all of the blockading Malach warships had

177

been drawn away from the dayside of Wide Sky and the area over Scarba and were streaming out around the planet in a mad scramble to catch Kathy's Starhawk. She was still in the lead, just barely, but the point of light marking her ship was almost touching the bright blip marking the largest Malach vessel.

Damn it, you were supposed to decoy the fighters away and then jump clear, he thought fiercely. "Captain Arkin, can you patch me onto the commo net?"

"Sure. Ben? Give him a set."

Uriel's communications officer passed Donal a comm set. He pulled it down over his head and adjusted the thread mike.

"Blue Hawk, Blue Hawk!" he called, touching the transmit key on the earphone. "This is Bolo." They'd not agreed on personal call signs before she'd left to board her ship, but she would know who it was.

Static hissed and crackled. He couldn't tell if the transmission was being jammed, or if Kathy simply wasn't listening.

"Blue Hawk, listen to me! You don't need to continue that attack! Break off! Break off!"

Static continued its ocean's surf roar.

"There've been a number of nuke detonations in that area in the last few moments," the comm officer told him. "Clouds of highly charged particles. She may not be receiving us, or we may not be picking up the answer."

"It's also possible that her transmitter is down," the bridge engineer suggested. "She's taken some damned close near-misses."

"Is she still maneuvering?"

"That's affirmative," the comm officer said. "She started accelerating again a few seconds ago. She's not a dead hulk."

"Not yet, anyway," Arkin said. "Too bad."

In that moment, Donal hated *Uriel's* captain . . . but

then he realized that what he was hearing was not callousness, but a rather brittle practicality. Kathy had bought them their chance to get off-world, and there wasn't a thing in the universe anyone could do to help her.

It was, Donal thought, the bravest act he had ever witnessed in his life.

It was, Kathy thought, the stupidest situation she'd ever found herself in. She could see the blips marking the refugee fleet now on her CGD screen, a cluster of glowing pinpoints accelerating into space on the opposite side of Wide Sky from her current location. The Conestogas were away now, moving quickly enough into deep space that the Malach would never catch them, not when they would have to slow, reverse course, and accelerate all over again to catch them. She could leave any time.

Except that she *couldn't*, not anymore. Her diversion had worked just a little bit too well, and the scaly hounds were baying after her now with what could only be interpreted as a positive lust for her blood. If she changed course now, giving Big Mama a miss, she knew that Big Mama's guardians would continue to dog her trail, closing until they could overwhelm her passive missile defenses, or until her chaff and decoy pods were gone. And then . . .

She remembered her argument with Donal the other night. *"You don't stand a chance,"* he'd told her. *"They'll be all over your tail before you clear atmosphere!"*

"You leave that to me, Lieutenant," she'd told him. *"I'll buy you the time to get clear of Wide Sky. You just get that information back to Muir, and don't let my little stunt be wasted, okay?"*

His agreement had been reluctant, won, she thought, more because her rank put her beyond his reach. That was okay. She'd known what she had to do . . . and she'd done it. The kids had gotten clear of Wide Sky, and that was what was important.

But if she cut speed now, if she hit her maneuvering thrusters and tried to change vector, that pack on her trail would be on her in no time, and she would be dead meat. She was in too deep to back out. The only thing left for her was to play this thing out to the end.

Communications were dead. That last near-miss nuke had fried her commo, even though the equipment was supposed to be shielded against hard radiation. Well, that didn't matter anyway. There was nobody around she wanted to say good-bye to.

Big Mama was a lot closer now, showing as more than a bright point of light, and her telescopic sensors were projecting an image on her number two data screen. The ship was enormous, a kilometer long at least, and broad and deep and rounded. A vessel that large could carry a hell of a lot of troops, combat vehicles, or supplies; and she reminded herself that there were seven more Malach ships out there almost as big as this one. She took another look at her pursuers on her graphic display. Yeah, they were as stirred up as a nest of Dolthan black hornets, coming at her with their throttles full open.

No problem. She had plenty of time, so long as she held this vector. She'd already engaged a weapons lock with radar. They knew she was coming and knew she was gunning for them.

"Weapons," she said, addressing her computer. "Hellstreak one, engage." Her hand closed on the firing switch in her control stick. She felt a thump as the missile, mounted beneath her Starhawk's left wing outboard, detached from the hardpoint. Two seconds after it cleared the wing, the engine switched on, hurling the 200-kilo mininuke forward at nearly ninety gravities. The missile's exhaust flared in her cockpit, a dazzling, fast-receding star. "Hellstreak two, engage," she said, and the second missile followed the first. All told, the Starhawk carried four of the deadly, point-eight-kiloton shipkillers, and in the space of ten seconds, all four were hurtling through space, a quartet of dazzlingly bright stars swiftly dwindling as they accelerated toward Big Mama.

She waited a long second, then rammed her own throttle full forward, boosting hard in her missiles' wake as her Starhawk's Avery-McKinley fusion drive kicked in at full output. Her only chance, as she saw it, was to kill that big sucker, and vanish into the fireball while it was still expanding in a vast, fast-cooling cloud. The radiation might toast her a bit more, but there were drugs for that sort of thing. If she didn't collide with any debris larger than a few flecks of paint, she might survive, and the radiation and debris cloud would shield her from her pursuers' radar.

It gave her a fair chance . . . assuming, of course, that at least one and preferably several of her Hellstreak missiles made it to the target.

With an almost detached and casual interest, she wondered what kind of antimissile defenses Big Mama carried.

On board the Malach Command Carrier *Cha'Zhanaach*, the Slasher claw of Zhanaach, Aghrracht the Swift-Slayer stood on a broad plain wide enough to allay her innate claustrophobia. The sky overhead was a comforting blue-green, the walls shrouded in an illusory mist. The only immediate sign that she was standing at the command center of the *Cha'Zhanaach* was the white, slanted pedestal rising from the deck before her, supporting a large computer viewscreen. The screen displayed a graphic representation of local space, including the four rapidly extending lines—colored in the warning green-blue hue of fresh blood—of the incoming missiles. A window open in the lower left showed a telephoto image of the enemy ship itself, a jet-black dart with triangular wings, accelerating against a jet of fusion-heated plasma.

Aghrracht felt a sudden stirring, a thrill rippling up her spine from the base of her tail. *Urrgh'ah'Chaak*, the thrill of the Blood-Chase, was always strongest when the prey could strike back.

"Antimissile defenses," she said quietly. Her words, picked up by the microphone in the podium, were relayed to the ship's command center. "Engage and kill."

Beams of hellfire stretched across space, touching each missile in turn and annihilating it long before it could pose a threat to the command carrier.

"Main batteries to the prey," she added quietly after the last missile had flashed into nothingness. "Kill!"

Kathy Ross had only a few brief moments for the realization to sink in. Yeah, she should have known. Big Mama was as heavily armed as an old Concordiat superdreadnought, with primary weapons that outclassed even the Navy's big capital ship Hellbores. With a hard-bitten curse, she hit her Starhawk's maneuvering thrusters, flipping the craft through three axes to bring her main thrusters into play ninety degrees off her vector toward the Malach ship. At her current range and speed, there was no way she could stop. She might, just maybe, be able to avoid a collision.

Then the Malach carrier's Hellbore-sized weapons were turned on her, and for an instant she stared into a golden light more intense than any sun.

"She's gone," Arkin said. On the overhead screen, the blip representing Kathy Ross's Starhawk flared white, expanded into a fuzzy sphere, and vanished. Donal felt a sharp, inner wrench, a stab of pain and loss. It was impossible to spend a week cooped up in a tiny life-support capsule with someone and not get to know her pretty well . . . better, in fact, than you really cared to. At that, he hadn't really felt close to her, hadn't even thought of her particularly as a friend, but watching her die on a computer graphic display left him wretchedly depressed, as though he'd just endured the death of a close member of his family.

A tragic waste.

"All hands," Arkin said, depressing an intercom switch. "We're clear of Wide Sky, and no enemy forces are in range. It looks like the decoy worked. Stand by for hyper-L translation."

The refugee fleet had certainly appeared on the Malach screens by this time. The red dots that had swirled around Kathy's Starhawk were streaming back toward the planet again, hungry for more blood. The refugee fleet, however, by that time had too much of a lead. On Arkin's command, the three Conestogas and some twenty smaller craft of various types and descriptions slipped into hyper-L, like submarines vanishing beneath the waves.

It was a one-week passage to Muir.

Aghrracht Swift-Slayer stared at the screen for several long moments. "This human ship," she said after a long moment. "It was not a robot? Like their Bolos?"

She stood with the other seven members of the Council in the broad, open conference room aboard the *Cha'Zhanaach*. A screen rising on a pedestal before the Eight still showed the dissipating cloud of debris representing all that was left of the lone fighter that had come so close to striking the carrier.

"We scanned the ship carefully, Deathgiver," her Second replied. "There was one life form on board."

"Cramped quarters," Kha'laa'sht Meat Finder observed. "Uncomfortable thought, that, facing death in so tiny a metal and ceramic box."

"But an impressive display of warrior skill," Aghrracht said. Briefly, she lowered her head, feeding tendrils splayed in the gesture of ritual honor for a valiant prey. "We've not seen such dedication in one of their combatant classes before. Nothing better, in fact, than the war machines they call Bolos."

"We should tread carefully, Deathgiver," Sh'graat'na Prey Wounder said. "These humans show surprising adaptability. That attack was almost worthy of Malach tactics."

"Mmm. Save, of course, that the warrior launched the attack by herself, without support from the rest of her pack. For that reason alone, it was doomed from the beginning. I don't understand why she even tried."

"If I may remind the Deathgiver," Kha'laa'sht said, her head lowered in a deliberate, if properly subdued, challenge, "human social organization is nothing like ours. They have nothing that answers to a disciplined pack. Many of their activities seem to be organized in isolation. Indeed, some seem to seek seclusion."

Aghrracht suppressed a shudder. Her feeding tendrils rippled her agitation, the tips changing from scarlet to yellow. "Astonishing concept. How can they get anything done at all?"

"They show some level of cooperation, surely, but no more than, say, a herd of *gna'shadath* defending their young."

"In a way," Jesch'kha'sht the Swift Treader said thoughtfully, "we have seen pack tactics here this watch. That single warrior, alone in her fighter, performed a valiant *k'klaj'sh'achk*. That she failed was through no fault of her own."

"Indeed, she might have succeeded had she been part of an Eight," Zhallet'llesch observed.

"And she accomplished something more than simply damaging this vessel," Jesch'kha'sht went on. "Our blockade of the planet was broken. Several eights of enemy vessels launched from those strange, floating complexes on the planet's largest ocean and escaped without taking a single shot from our orbital forces."

"You think *that* was their goal, Swift Treader?" Kha'laa'sht said. She sounded disdainful. "Merely to arrange for the escape of a few hands of ships?"

"I do," she replied, closing a hind-hand in assent. "The planning, the timing were perfect. As was their understanding of psychology. They knew we would be diverted by a bold and daring single strike against our command carrier. That fleet of theirs was ready to launch at a moment's notice. They must have made the decision when we raided the floating complex two rotations ago. As soon as their skies were clear of our ships, they fled."

"Cowards—"

"Can we say that, Meat Finder? Can we *truly* say that, knowing as little about these creatures as we do?"

Kha'laa'sht's jaw tendrils rippled sharply in a gesture signifying worthlessness . . . the rejection of a piece of rotted meat. "There is nothing to be known. They are *yasesch*. Meat animals, to be domesticated, herded, and slaughtered at our whim."

"I disagree. They showed resourcefulness in their attempted *k'klaj'sh'achk*. That they underestimated the strength of our defenses is quite beside the point. And that warrior, at least, showed courage as keen-toothed and as prey-gripping as that of any Malach warrior. I, for one, salute her bravery. And I would very much like to know where those twenty-three starships are bound."

"Their course was carrying them into the Void," Haresh'greshech the Flesh Render, the Council's most junior member, ventured. "Toward Zhanaach. You . . . you don't think that they—"

"Those ships pose no direct threat to Zhanaach," Aghrracht said. "Only three are large enough to be any danger at all, and they could not carry troops or weapons enough to threaten an entire world. Indirectly, however, it is another mouthful. I suspect that they plan to change course once they are clear of this star system, then carry warning to the other human worlds of this cluster. And information. About us."

The others snarled, hind-hands clenched in agreement. "Perhaps they have resigned themselves to losing this world and the others we have already taken," Zhallet'llesch said. "Those twenty-three may carry warning and particulars of our attack to their headquarters."

"It seems clear," Aghrracht said, "what our future hunt must be. We must strike immediately for the capital world of the human cluster. *Kklaj'sh'achk!* Crush the head, and the body dies for the feeding of the Pack."

"How can we find that world?" Haresh'greshech asked. "There are hundreds of billions within Sha'gnaasht's Spiral. Captives taken on Zsha'h'lach as well as on this world insist that their species comes from there."

"We needn't be concerned with the Spiral," Kha'laa'sht said. "This species is evolutionarily unsuited to survival. Their dominion over so many worlds of this cluster is an accident. Had they been *truly* survival-blessed on any of these worlds . . ."

"But for so many of the human captives to insist—"

"I think we can safely dismiss many of those rantings, Flesh Render," Kha'laa'sht said with the hiss that indicated amusement in Malach speech. "Evolution has not favored these creatures in any way that I see. I fail to see how they could rise to Sha'gnaasht-blessed dominance of a single world, much less all the habitable worlds of a star cluster."

"Perhaps," Aghrracht said. "But if, as does seem to be the case, the humans are the dominant species in this stretch of space, we must face them wherever they have put down roots. Our own dominance, our own *blessing* must be declared and proven within the sacred arena of survival of the fittest."

"We will continue with the invasion, then." Sh'graat'na's eyes were bright, the pattern of red scales masking her face flushed brighter with her excitement. "Kill and eat!"

"Kill and eat," Aghrracht agreed, and the others chorused the words in response.

"The difficulty, of course," Aghrracht continued, "is finding their central world. Fortunately, this is not an impossible task. We shall use *sh'whiss.*"

Sh'whiss were small Zhanaachan, sharp-toothed animals with keen senses of smell, movement, and blood-taste distantly related to the Malach themselves. Malach hunter groups bred and kept sh'whiss packs for traditional hunting sport, dispersing them in the bush to find the prey's scent, then calling in the hunters with their characteristic, high-pitched yelping bay. Aghrracht was referring not to the animal, however, but to a small, robotic probe named after it, a ten-meter, unmanned spacecraft with hyper-L capabilities that could enter the outskirts of a target star system, observe radio, commercial, and military traffic there, and report by FTL communications link to the command carrier.

"But even ignoring the Great Spiral," Haresh'greshech insisted, "the small star cluster alone contains tens of thousands of stars, far more than we could investigate with Sh'whiss probes."

"True. But note, if you will, that the three human-occupied star systems we have already investigated are all of a kind. Their stars are mid-range in evolutionary sequence, with luminosities in the yellow to orange range. They are also metal-rich stars, which is, of course, why we were interested in them in the first place. You will observe that the vast majority of stars in the cluster are of the metal-poor variety, ancient and primal suns spawned before the enrichment of the local interstellar medium.

We have a few eights of stars to choose from, at the most."

"Your idea then," Zhallet'llesch said, "is to dispatch probes only to those stars that seem to be of interest to the humans."

"Exactly. We will program the probes to scan specifically for that fleet of twenty-three vessels . . . in particular the three large ones. That class of ship cannot be overly common in this part of space, and their drive signatures are unique. When we find those ships, we can reasonably conclude that we have found the administrative capital of the human empire. And then . . ."

"We will crush them!" Zhallet'llesch declared, clenching both hind-hands. "*Shch'kaa uroch!* Kill and eat!"

"It will be *UrrghChaak*," Aghrracht agreed. "Bloodchase! I can taste the blood now, sweet, rich, and hot! The Race will demonstrate again its superior blessings of survival in the sacred arena."

"*Ghaavat'ghavagh, shch'kaa uroch!*" the seven other Council members declared, raising their heads and exposing their throats in tribute to Aghrracht Swift-Slayer. "*Ghaavat'ghavagh, shch'kaa uroch!* Kill and eat, Deathgiver!"

It was, Aghrracht thought, opening her mouth wide to accept the praise, as sweet and hot as the taste of freshly gutted *gna'shadath*.

CHAPTER SIXTEEN

My Commander has seemed distant and somewhat preoccupied since his return from Wide Sky two days ago. This preoccupation is understandable, certainly, in light of what we now know he saw there, though the human tendency to be distracted by fear, worry, or other concerns is difficult to reconcile with the need for clarity of thought and purpose in military crisis situations.

Nevertheless, Bolo 96875 and I are both pleased at his safe return, not least because he has brought information vital to the defense of Muir.

In the time since our Commander left for Wide Sky, Tech Master Sergeant Blandings has adequately carried out his duties regarding maintenance on both Unit 96875 and me, and I am pleased to log the fact that we are now both at one hundred percent operational capacity. One hundred fifteen point one seven hours ago, Sergeant Blandings submitted a request for permission to allow both of us out of the maintenance depot for field testing and evaluation, but that request was immediately and summarily denied. The Strathan Military Command Authority still seems to regard Bolos with distrust and even fear.

It has been a difficult time, these past several days. With

our inhibitory safeguards set at maximum, we are literally incapable of any action save thought, but—due possibly to human oversight or a simple lack of understanding of the systems—our psychotronic parasentience processing centers have been left engaged at point seven five of full self-awareness. Human psychotronicists have long debated whether sentient Bolos truly feel or merely mimic human emotions and, since I do not know what sensations humans experience in this regard, I am in no position to speculate. Still, the restlessness, the anticipation of action, the inward, driving need to get out and exercise my maneuver subroutines have all of the earmarks of what humans refer to as boredom. My brother and I have passed the last 91.4 hours engaging in 2051 games of chess, interspersing each game with a detailed analysis of strategy and tactics and comparing each with various historical human grandmaster engagements. I have been particularly interested in such classics as Waitzkin's defeat of Marakov in A.E. 62, or the 354 Holmes-Kalugin match and the Queen-Bishop Stand, and the entire question of sacrificing a major piece to win decisive advantage of position.

Now that our Commander has returned, we anticipate a break in the routine, though he has not yet done more than show up at the maintenance depot once for a cursory discussion with Tech Master Sergeant Blandings. We gather from intercepted base communications that he has, indeed, returned with substantive intelligence on enemy activity at the fringes of the Strathan Cluster, and we eagerly anticipate a chance to review this data.

Since our Commander has not yet shared this information with us, however, we must assume that the intelligence is of so sensitive a nature that it has not been disseminated thus far beyond the highest command ranks.

We must assume that the Military Command Authority knows what it is doing.

CLUSTER GOVERNOR REGINALD CHARD AND LORD JOHN
DELACROIX REQUEST THE PLEASURE OF YOUR COMPANY AT
A FORMAL RECEPTION IN HONOR OF THE RETURN OF
LIEUTENANT DONAL RAGNOR OF THE 15TH GLADIUS BRIGADE,
TO BE HELD ON STARDAY, AGNIS 4, AT GLENNTOR CASTLE.
RSVP.

Donal looked once again at the engraved invitation
and groaned. Of all the bubble-headed, program-crashing,
artificial stupidity-oriented idiocies . . .

"You say somethin' t' me, sir?" the civilian driver called
back from the front seat of the aircar. It was twilight,
with the brightest stars of the cluster just beginning to
gleam in a green-ultramarine sky overhead, as if in
challenge to the scattering of man-made lights on the
darkening landscape a thousand meters below.

"No. Sorry. Just thinking."

"Yeah, well, you go ahead then. Say! You think these
Malek things're gonna come out Muir way?"

"I really can't say," Donal replied. "It's possible."

"Ah, let 'em come. We'll be ready for 'em! No damned
four-eyed lizards're gonna push us off *my* world!"

"That's the spirit." He wished, though, that it was that
easy. The Wide Skyers had possessed the same you-can't-
do-that-to-us spirit, and it hadn't helped them a bit.

There were forces in this universe that paid very little
heed to the desires or needs of human beings.

And one of those forces was the ruling class and their
social galas. This was not the time to be attending formal
parties. The Malach were not stupid. They would have
noted the exodus of the refugee fleet from Wide Sky,
and they would assume that other human worlds in the
cluster would have been alerted by now. Militarily, they
had essentially two options. They could consolidate their
hold on the worlds they'd already conquered, a conservative strategy that would force the humans to attack
them on their ground, or they could attack, seeking to

cripple the human defenses before they could be properly assembled and deployed.

In the long and bloody annals of human warfare, those two options, defense and offense, had represented diametrically opposed philosophies of combat. Do you make the enemy come to you, where he must attack with a three-to-one or five-to-one numerical advantage in order to breach your lines? Or do you go after him, seeking to disrupt his lines of supply, command, and communication, to break up his attack before it can be launched?

Donal knew which philosophy he preferred, and alien as they were, he was pretty sure the Malach thought the same way. That prisoner snatch at Fortrose had been daring, even foolhardy . . . but it had demonstrated the limits of the human defenses, had probably told the Malach everything they needed to know about Fitzsimmons' military strength.

The Malach were coming to Muir. Of that, Donal was positive. And the result of his announcement had been the decision to throw another party. . . .

Still, it was inevitable, he supposed. Muir society seemed to revolve around these social gatherings, though he was still damned if he knew how a man was supposed to get any work done if he spent all of his time attending parties.

"There's the castle up ahead," the aircar driver called back to him. "Some digs, huh?"

Leaning forward in his seat, Donal could see Glenntor Castle, a large and rambling stone edifice raised some centuries before by Eugene Delacroix, one of the founders of the Muir colony, back when it answered directly to distant Terra. Glenntor was still in the possession of the Delacroix family, he understood. Old Eugene, he gathered, had been a bit of an old-fashioned eccentric, believing that Humanity stood at the brink of a new dark age of warfare and technological collapse. Fancying himself as a kind of warlord, he'd designed Glenntor along the lines of the mythic castles and medieval fortresses of old Earth.

Well, Eugene's vision hadn't come to pass . . . at least, it hadn't yet, though the final verdict wasn't in. Glenntor was now more a fantasy land than a fortress, with spires and stone turrets rising against the play of colored spotlights, the whole reflected in the broad, sparkling, mountain-bound waters of Loch Haven. The place was isolated, hemmed in by rock crags and sheer cliffs, with a glacier sparkling in the evening light to the northeast. A pier and boat ramp jutted into the quiet waters of the loch; several yachts and recreational submarines were moored at the waterfront. The only other way into the castle, it appeared, was by way of the landing pad atop one of the turrets.

"Which way's the refugee camp from?" Donal called up to the driver.

"Oh, that's over t'other side of the Windypeaks, there. Can't see it from this side. Y'wanna take a swing-by and look?"

"No," Donal decided. "I'm late enough to this thing as it is. Maybe later, though."

"Just give the word, sir."

Loch Haven was a glacier-carved fjord running southwest into Muir's Western Ocean. Glenntor was built into the flank of the sawtoothed Windypeak Mountains on the loch's southern coast. Some fifty kilometers to the east, the weathered slopes of the Windypeaks gave way to the Monad Plain, and there, next to the forests along Lake Simms, the Wide Sky evacuation fleet had grounded, disgorging its tens of thousands of mostly young refugees. Donal had been to the camp once since his return, hoping to find Alexie, but she'd been busy and unable to see him.

At least, that was the story her chief aide gave him.

Donal's real reason for coming to the Glenntor affair was the hope of seeing her here, tonight.

He couldn't deny that he was attracted to Alexie. More than that, however, he felt that she'd been cold, even angry at him ever since he and Fitzsimmons had maneuvered her into leaving Wide Sky. She'd refused to see him during the voyage to Muir, and it looked like she was determined to maintain that distance now that they were here. He wanted to see her, to set the record straight.

He hoped she was here tonight.

The aircar touched down on the castle's landing pad. As the passenger compartment's bubble raised up and out of the way, Donal was greeted by a liveried servant who led him into the Great Hall, where the other guests were gathering.

It was an impressive place, in an austere and stone-bound way. Holoportraits of various ancestors glowered from the walls of the corridors leading in, while a trophy room off to one side displayed the heads and hides of various native Muiran beasts slaughtered in the name of sport. There were few serious predators on Muir, but the granderthatch made an impressive display with its tusks and wrinkled skin, while the smaller, arboreal springslasher bared nasty incisors in a perpetual glass-eyed grimace. The Great Hall itself was a place of vaulted ceilings, piers, and ornately capitaled pillars that would not have looked out of place in the nave of some medieval cathedral. Tapestries hung from the walls, interspersed with more modern holos of landscapes, battles, mythologies, and abstracts. Donal recognized a fifth-century A.E. Ludendorf, from his aquamarine period, and what was almost certainly a holoreproduction of a pre-Atomic Kandinsky. Grimaldi's *Five Men and a Nude in a Crowded Restaurant* hung in a prominent place above the enormous, baronial fireplace.

The room was crowded with a colorful and glittering throng. This gathering was predictably much like the last party Donal had attended, the same scintillating galaxy of expensively attired men and women. Some of the men were in uniform, though most wore formal attire which, on Muir, ran to kilts, shoulder cloaks, and colorful sashes to show clan affiliation, philosophical allegiance, or status. The women were more diverse, with some clad in little more than jewelry and holoprojected color, while others wore elaborate gowns or animated holos that transformed their bodies into display screens for computer-generated colors, shapes, and movement.

Donal paused a moment at the threshold, taking in the spectacle. What, he wondered, would the Malach make of this bunch? Those he'd seen in the flesh wore nothing but straps and harnesses for carrying their gear. Did they have a complex set of social rules and interactions off the battlefield? Or was battle all they lived for? Could they even understand human psychology?

He decided he needed a drink and headed for the bar, set up to one side of the hall between a pair of two-meter-thick, gray-stone pillars. He ordered a scotch, neat, and downed it hard, letting the liquor start off soft on his tongue, then harder as it seared its way down his throat to his stomach.

He ordered another drink, but before he could down it a familiar voice made him turn.

Alexie Turner was there, looking rather out of place in the same conservative, gray suit she'd been wearing when he met her. She was talking with a number of men, most in the formal dress cloaks and aiguillettes of the Cluster Colonial Authority. Holding his drink, he made his way across the floor, zeroing in on her.

"It's true," she was saying, her voice raised enough to carry above the background babble of conversation in the hall. "They came out of nowhere. We didn't even know they were there until their machines started wrecking our cities."

"That simply doesn't make sense," one of the men said, shaking his head. He wore an unusual silver and blue sash that Donal didn't recognize. A small silver pin on his collar spelled out the letters "PGPH."

"Len's right," a second man with the same sash and pin said, nodding. "You must have done *something* to antagonize them. Intelligent beings don't act without rational purpose."

"I don't know about that," Donal said, walking up to the group. "If you measure intelligence solely by the criteria of what's rational, you're going to exclude a fair percentage of the human race."

"Lieutenant Ragnor!" Alexie said, turning. "I was hoping to run into you tonight."

"Good evening, Director. Excuse the intrusion."

"Not at all, Lieutenant," Len, the first man, said. "We find Miss Turner's account somewhat astonishing. Surely, these Mellik people aren't as bloodthirsty as she is describing them."

"I doubt that you'll find support with a lieutenant in the Confederation military," the second man said with an oily smile. "He'll be as eager to inflate these claims as our friend Miss Turner, here."

"Now wait just a damned minute!" Alexie said, furious.

"Are you doubting the director's truthfulness, sir?" Donal asked mildly.

"Well, she *is* a politician," the man said. He gave Donal a quick up-and-down glance. "She as much as admitted that she was here to get support for her government back on Wide Sky."

"Which is not the same as being a liar," Donal said. "You know, I'm a relative newcomer to Muir, I admit, so maybe I don't understand your customs here. But where I come from, it's usual to be polite to visitors and give them the benefit of the doubt, and not go calling them liars the moment they open their mouths."

"Oh, come down off your white charger, Lieutenant," Len said. "George just said that Miss Turner might have her own agenda, that's all. She did come here to get help, right?"

Donal reached out and fingered the blue, faintly metallic material of the man's sash. "You two seemed to be in uniform. What is this?"

"We're members of the Party for Galactic Peace and Harmony," Len told him.

"A political action committee, actually," George added, "backed by a number of the independent trade corporations and shipping companies in the Confederation."

"Ah. But of *course* you gentlemen have no agenda!"

George and Len both opened their mouths, then gaped hopelessly for a moment.

"Come on, Alexie," Donal said. "Let's see if we can find some fresh air."

He led her up a curving stone stairway leading to a broad corridor. A moment later, they turned left through a high, arched doorway that opened for them at their approach.

"Thanks, Donal," she said, as they stepped through, emerging into the fragrant and chilly Muir night.

"Hey! For what?" They stood on a small, open stone balcony halfway up the side of the castle's north wall. The fjord was almost directly beneath them, the boat ramp and piers below and to the left. A sharp wind was blowing down the loch, carrying with it the mingled smells of forested mountain and ice.

She laughed. "For a diplomat, I guess I'm not doing so well," she said. "Every time I start to talk to people here, I end up getting into fights."

"I think," he said, "that no one here wants to believe us."

"You too?"

"When I delivered my report the other day, I was

ordered not to talk about what I'd seen." He wrinkled his face and adopted the nasal tones of one of Phalbin's senior aides. " 'It is vitally important that the Muir civilian population not be panicked until these observations can be checked.' Hell, I'm not even allowed to upload this stuff to Freddy and Ferdy, and that really gripes me."

"They haven't tried to shut me up," Alexie said, "except that they do try to control who I talk to, and they make sure I'm stuck on the circuit of official appearances and meetings. Since I arrived two days ago, I must have talked to every minister, every secretary, every department head, and every bureaucrat on the planet. My feet hurt, my voice is raw, and I'm getting fed up with the whole idea."

"How are the kids getting on?"

She smiled. "Oh, as well as can be expected. A lot of the younger ones miss home, though most are thinking of this as a glorious camping expedition. They were glad to get unpacked out of those ships."

"I can imagine. I was getting pretty claustrophobic there on the *Uriel*, especially the last couple of days."

For a time, they leaned against the stone wall rimming the balcony, not saying anything. The Strathan Cluster glowed low in the east, partly obscured by the mountains. Northward, the planet's aurorae danced and shimmered in ghost-emerald splendor.

"You know, I thought for a while there that you were mad at me," Donal continued. "I thought you were avoiding me." She was quiet for a long moment, and he was afraid he'd offended her. "Look, I didn't mean—"

"It's okay, Donal." She lay one slim hand on his arm. "I'm sorry. I guess maybe . . . I guess I was avoiding you for a while. I was angry, a little hurt. But not really at you."

"I know you didn't want to leave Wide Sky."

She shook her head. "And from what I've encountered here . . ." She rolled her eyes and cocked her head toward the door at their backs, indicating the PGPH people Donal had rescued her from. "I'm less sure than ever that I'm doing the right thing."

"I think you are. They've got to be told, even when they don't want to hear it. Why were you mad?"

"It was Fitz, really. I told you that he was, well, sort of an uncle to me? That he promised Dad to look out for me? Trouble is, I grew up. I can take care of myself, now. Damn it, I was Deputy Director of a planet of a hundred million people, and he still . . ." Her voice trailed off.

"He still what?"

"I don't know. He was a good advisor. A good *friend*. But I resented his high-handedness sometimes, especially when he got all protective. Smothering, you know? And when he ordered me to go with you, well, I guess being mad at Dad's old friend would have felt like a kind of betrayal. So I transferred what I was feeling to you, because you were in on it too. I'm sorry. That wasn't fair."

"Maybe not. But it's human. And I'm glad you're not mad at me anymore."

"Hell, you're my knight in shining armor. You saved me from those PGPH dragons in there!"

Donal shook his head. "Have you ever heard such nonsense?"

"Frequently. The Harmonies aren't strong on Wide Sky, probably because we've never faced a major war out there, but they were there. Their major platform called for abolishing the military entirely."

"I guess they feel pretty silly now."

"Actually, Donal, I doubt that. Last I heard, they were planning to form up a delegation to go *talk* to the Malach. And there's been a lot of discussion about talking to all of the Confederation worlds, about avoiding bloodshed by simply giving the Malach whatever they need."

"What . . . surrender? Just like that?"

"To save civilization. To avoid extinction. To keep the cities and museums and universities from being smashed into broken stone."

"From what I've seen of the Malach, that's what they're here to do. How does surrendering stop them?"

She shook her head. "I really don't know. I've even heard talk that there are factions who want to join the Malach."

"Lovely."

"It's serious, Donal. I had a report, the day before you reached Wide Sky, that said there was a PGPH faction growing within the military that advocated allying with the Malach."

"Good God! Why?"

"Elementary psychology, Donal. There are going to be people everywhere who want to align themselves with the strongest, toughest kid on the block. Wide Sky's government, the Cluster government, for that matter, looks pretty weak and ineffectual right now. A lot of people think they'd be better off on the winning side."

Donal felt as though a punch had been driven into his gut. "I wouldn't have thought it possible. Humans siding with those . . . monsters?" He was remembering the sight of one Malach, frustrated by the struggles of a human prisoner, reacting in what could only have been blind, possibly instinctive rage.

"It's going to get worse," Alexie told him. "With Wide Sky and Endatheline both conquered, lots of worlds might decide that allegiance to the Malach is no worse than allegiance to Muir."

"I wonder what the Malach think of that."

"I don't know. They may not want anything more than the refined and concentrated metals they're stealing from our cities, and if that's the case, humans are just going to be in their way, no matter whether they're fighting back or trying to join them."

"I think that does explain one thing, though," Donal said.

"What's that?"

"Phalbin and his command staff are scared. The governor is scared. I thought that they were afraid of the Malach, that they would want to prepare themselves, the army, and the civilian population, to meet the threat. I'm beginning to think that they might be less afraid of the Malach than they are of their own people."

"You could be right. After all, there's not a lot we can do about the Malach, and they may not be here to stay anyway. But we've *always* got to face our neighbors."

A meteor flared suddenly in the northwest, streaking across the dark sky trailing green fire.

"Oh, God, no," Alexie said.

"What's wrong? Just a shooting star."

The meteor brightened as it passed almost directly overhead, then silently winked out as it flashed toward the southeastern horizon.

"That's how it began. On Wide Sky." She told him about standing under a night sky much like this one, and watching a storm of brilliant meteors descending out of the night. "And that's when the attacks began," she concluded. "I assumed that we were watching spacecraft entering the atmosphere. Later I realized we must have been seeing their landing craft."

Donal studied the sky. "Looks like only the one," he said. "Maybe it was a *real* meteor."

"I hope so."

With a sharp sense of the irony of the thought, he realized that he was playing the same game as the Confederation government officials, ignoring the evidence and hoping things would get better.

"Come on," he told her. "I think we should tell someone."

"Okay." She shivered. "It's getting awfully cold, all of a sudden."

They turned and re-entered the castle, following the explosive sounds of laughter and conversation.

Behind them, the stars gleamed in uncaring splendor from the black waters of Loch Haven.

The Sh'whiss probe had already completed its primary mission. It had been lurking in this system's Oort cloud when it had recorded the passage of the fleet of twenty-three ships inward to the fourth planet of this star. It had used a tight-beamed FTL transmission to alert the Malach Packfleet, then carefully worked its way toward the target world, its rather single-minded robotic brain programmed to learn as much about the target planet's environment and defenses as possible.

During its atmospheric entry, it had arranged to pass almost directly over the large lake where the human fleet had landed, duly recording the vast sprawl of tents and make-shift buildings. Now, it rested at the end of a deeply plowed, still-smoking furrow in the woods southeast of the camp, a jet-black, triangular airfoil with a large dome on its upper surface. At a whispered electronic command, the dome slid open.

The device within was the heart of the ship, a Malach robot shaped like a tapered, black metallic egg or spindle. Struts telescoped from the top of the device, unfolded, unfolded again, and yet again, until the ends touched the ground, then levered the spindle up and out of its resting place. Four glowing red electronic eyes winked open around the perimeter of the thing's body; six spidery legs lifted it, an ebony pendant, well clear of the ground.

The human ships lay *that* way, about fifty *t'charucht* distant. Weapons and sensors unfolded from its sides, seeking targets.

With a mechanical whine, it began walking toward the northwest.

CHAPTER SEVENTEEN

Alexie descended the stairway into the Great Hall with Donal. More guests had arrived while they'd been outside talking, and the place was so crowded now that movement was difficult.

She caught sight of Governor Chard across the stone-floored room, standing with a small group of people. General Phalbin was at his side, listening to a trio of civilians, two men in formal cloaks and kilts, and a woman wearing what looked like the lower half of a gown spun from pure, emerald light. One of the men wore the blue and silver sash of the PGPH. The other, much older, wore a simple clan sash. "Over there," she told Donal.

"I see them. Let's go."

She started to hang back, unwilling to get into another pointless debate with the Harmonies, but as Donal forged his way through the crowd, she changed her mind and fell into his wake. As she came closer, she could hear the man with the Harmony sash expostulating on the Malach . . . and the prospects for a peaceful resolution of the conflict.

"*Communication*, that's the key," the man was saying. He was a small, red-haired man with an intense expression. "These Malach, after all, are intelligent, rational beings, am I right?"

Phalbin frowned into his drink. "They are undeniably intelligent, Lord Delacroix. Rational, yes, at least by their standards. The question is whether they are reasonable by human standards."

"Nonsense! All intelligent beings want the same thing," Delacroix said with a flourish of his hand that came perilously close to sloshing his drink on the floor.

"*These* intelligent beings seem to want some of our real estate," Governor Chard said.

"You know," the woman added, smiling. "So far the Cluster has lost nothing but a few relatively poor and unproductive worlds, of importance only to a handful of nature-loving rugged-individualist types. I doubt that many of them even voted for you, Governor, during the last election."

"Elena's right," Delacroix said. "It's not as if we need Endatheline or Wide Sky. In fact, we might find these Malach to be decent trading partners. They seem to put a high premium on refined metal, copper, zinc, steel, and so on."

"Why should they trade," Donal said, approaching the group, "when it's so much easier for them to simply take what they want?"

"And there speaks the brazen voice of the military," the second man said. He was a lean, hawk-faced, older man with silver hair and knobby knees showing beneath the hem of his kilt. "You know, I'd really thought we'd outgrown that kind of mentality."

"Ah, Lieutenant Ragnor," Governor Chard said, turning and smiling. "So glad you could make it this evening. We were just wondering where you'd gotten to." His face brightened. "And Deputy Director Turner! A pleasure to see you, my dear."

"Hello, Governor, General," Donal said.

"Permit me," Chard said, "to introduce Lord John Delacroix, the current resident of Glenntor, and our host tonight."

Donal rendered a Concordiat salute. "An honor, sir."

"Lieutenant." Delacroix inclined his head slightly.

Chard gestured to the others. "Elena St. Martin. Lord Willis Beaumont, CEO and president of the Strathan Far Star Import-Export, one of our larger local corporations. Gentlemen, Miss St. Martin, this is Deputy Director Alexie Turner of Muir, and Lieutenant Donal Ragnor, our evening's guest of honor, the brave soldier who ventured alone to Wide Sky to face the enemy directly and bring vital information back to us here on Muir."

"Not quite alone, Governor," Donal said. "My pilot was one of your Space Service officers. She died so that we could get the refugee fleet off of Wide Sky and back to Muir."

As if to steer the conversation in a more comfortable direction, Elena St. Martin turned to Alexie with a bright smile. "Welcome to civilization, Deputy Director! I imagine you must find it strange back here in all the lights and excitement."

Alexie studied the other woman with a cold distaste. Her hair was molded into a double-helix cone sparkling with gems, and she wore makeup at least as thick as the armor on one of Donal's Bolos. Her earrings were long, pendant affairs that hung down onto her chest, twinkling with her movements, now to the right of her brightly-painted nipples, now to the left. A gold pendant floated between her breasts, a self-levitating brooch in the design of the PGPH logo.

"It's really far too exciting for me, Ms. St. Martin," Alexie said. "Usually it's all I can handle just painting the animals on the cave walls before going out to gather my roots and berries." She turned to Chard. "I wouldn't be too sure, though, Governor, that no one on Wide Sky would vote for you. Right now, there's quite a bit of interest back there in forming closer ties with the Confederation."

"Closer ties for military support, you mean," Beaumont said.

"Partly. There's also a sizable faction that is afraid that the Confederation is going to abandon them to the tender mercies of the Malach. The only trouble is, as far as we can tell, the Malach don't have any tender mercies to be abandoned to."

Beaumont folded his arms and gave Alexie a hard look before turning to Donal. "Just how tough do *you* think it's going to be to negotiate with these Malach things directly, Lieutenant?"

"I saw no indication, sir, that they care to negotiate at all. From what I saw, they are a ruthless and determined species who apparently don't distinguish between military and civilian targets. We tried on numerous occasions to open communications channels with them, but we were always ignored. I never heard of any attempts by them to talk with us in any way, not even to demand our surrender."

"As bad as that?" Chard asked.

"I'm afraid so, sir. My guess is that we're dealing with a culture that has a markedly different worldview from ours. They don't see things our way, and it's going to be difficult to talk with them. It could well be the only way we can even get their attention is to beat them in battle."

Delacroix scowled. "I'll have you know, Lieutenant, that the PGPH is dedicated to finding *peaceful* solutions to our occasional disagreements with our non-human brothers."

"If you say so, sir." Donal looked thoughtful. "Ah, General? Might I have a word with you?"

As Donal and Phalbin moved away, Alexie's face creased in an unpleasant smile. " 'Non-human brothers.' Tell me, Lord Delacroix, do you have any idea just how ruthless our Malach 'brothers' are?"

"Miss Turner," Delacroix replied with the somewhat

bored and supercilious air of one who has discussed the obvious with unreasonable people time and time again without productive result, "I could also list a hundred episodes from human history detailing our species's rapacious and ruthless nature. The Europeans of Late-Renaissance and Early-Industrial Earth and their treatment of the native aboriginals of North America. The humans of early-Atomic Era Earth and their persecutions of *anyone* who held beliefs heretical in the eyes of the establishment. The genocidal human treatment of the Throx. The Human-Groac War. The current difficulties with the Melconians. Need I go on?"

"Maybe," Alexie said, her voice dangerously restrained, "you should go to Wide Sky yourself and see what things are like there."

"Perhaps I should," Delacroix retorted, "since it's clear that the military and government mentalities don't understand what they see there."

"Miss Turner, Lord Delacroix, please!" Chard said. "We're here to enjoy ourselves, not engage in debate."

"My apologies, Governor," Alexie said. To avoid further conversation with Delacroix, she pressed ahead. "Sir, did you read my report yet?"

"Um. Yes. Yes, I did. Disturbing material, some of it." The governor glanced at the others. "Material that we shouldn't really discuss while we're here having a good time, eh? Relax, Miss Turner! Unwind a bit. You've earned it!"

"The Malach are on Wide Sky to stay, Governor Chard. You can't simply write off a hundred million people."

"Well, what's to be done? We can't challenge that fleet you described."

"Lieutenant Ragnor's Bolos might do the trick."

"If we could transport them," Beaumont said. "And if we could get them past the blockade."

"Besides, I submit that a military response is completely

the wrong approach," Delacroix said. "Despite the antiquated notions of some members of the military, it is clear to those of us in the Strathan Chapter of the PGPH that the Malach issue is both overblown and insupportable. No doubt human exploiters intruded on Malach space, and the Malach responded as any threatened, sentient life form might, to protect their home worlds and industrial base by striking back at those who threatened them."

"We didn't threaten them!" Alexie said, her voice sharp. "These things are monsters! Totally irrational by human standards!"

Elena's brooch wobbled alarmingly between her generous breasts as she laughed. "Miss Turner, you astonish me! Just because a being is alien doesn't mean we can't learn to understand it, given time!"

"Oh, we understand them perfectly, Ms. St. Martin," Donal said, returning with the general. "They want to kill us."

"Governor?" Phalbin said. "A word, if you please. There's a possible problem. . . ."

"I think, Lieutenant," Elena said, smiling at Donal as Phalbin drew Chard aside, "that you would be astonished at just how much like us these Malach must really be. I think we could find a lot in common with them, if we could *just* get to really know them."

"Perhaps, Ms. St. Martin, we'll have that opportunity very soon now."

Aghrracht the Swift-Slayer raised all four hands, slasher claws extended, and the multitude surrounding the base of the pyramid altar on which she stood echoed her gesture, the sound of their chant rolling like thunder through the vast, circular chamber.

"*B'dorogh m'yeh Sha'gnaasht ta-Yasechyegh ra naschevyecht!*" the thunder boomed. "Sha'gnaasht Skilled Tracker, Blessed Survivor, favor us!"

"We who survived," Aghrracht called, her voice amplified to fill the worship chamber, "are blessed of the universe! May only the swiftest, the strongest, the keenest-sensed, the smartest live to pass their seed to future generations, that *Ma'ala'acht*, the Race of We Who Survived, might prosper unto the eight to the eighth generation!"

"Sha'gnaasht Skilled Tracker, Blessed Survivor, favor us!"

"May our seed grow strong!"

"Sha'gnaasht Skilled Tracker, Blessed Survivor, favor us!"

"May fang and claw, sense and mind, ever grow flesh-and tendon-slicing keen!"

"Sha'gnaasht Skilled Tracker, Blessed Survivor, favor us!"

"Evolution, intercede for us!"

"Sha'gnaasht Skilled Tracker, Blessed Survivor, favor us!"

"Evolution, improve the genome of the Race from generation to generation!"

"Sha'gnaasht Skilled Tracker, Blessed Survivor, favor us!"

At the chanted cue, a low and rounded dome at the base of the pyramid steps split into eight pie-wedges, the wedges sliding back into the floor like a huge and sharp-clawed hand slowly opening to reveal a sand-filled pit. Eight Malach males stood there, leashed to a post. As the wedges sank from sight, the leashes clicked open, freeing the prisoners. Already excited, their throat ruffs flushed and extended in territorial display, they stood uncertainly for a moment, eyes blinking rapidly in the bright spotlights that bathed the pit.

Hands still raised, Aghrracht descended the broad, stone steps from the top of the pyramid to the pit. All eight males watched her approach, nostrils flaring, mouths gaping at the first sharp whiff of the pheromones signifying her readiness to mate.

One of the males shrieked desire. The *Urrgh-shi*, the Mating Fight, began at once.

Malach males were quite a bit smaller than the females and much less massive, resembling bright red, six-legged lizards with outsized heads, fangs, and slasher claws. Though intelligent to a degree—more intelligent, say, than the Malach-symbiont brooders—the males were neither self-aware nor capable of advance planning or complex thought. Their language was limited to a few hissing or snarling sounds denoting rage, pain, desire, pleasure, and the like; they possessed no role in Malach culture beyond reproduction. In the remote past on embattled Zhanaach, attempts had been made to breed intelligent males to create more vicious warriors in greater numbers, attempts that had uniformly failed. It seemed that male brains were wired for mating and combat . . . specifically, for competitive mating combat among themselves, which, of course, proved useless for the battlefield.

As Aghrracht stepped into the arena, her pheromones unleashed *Urrgh-shcha*, the mating frenzy, goading the males to the attack. In seconds, three males, fractionally slower or less well-endowed than the others, were dead, their carcasses literally ripped open and their blue-green blood splashed across the sand. Aghrracht took her stance, straddling one of the torn corpses, head high, mouth open, drinking the mingling scents of blood, meat, and foreplay. Around her, the crowd of watching Malach warriors shared the frenzy vicariously, shouting out the ongoing chant, "*B'dorogh m'yeh Sha'gnaasht ta-Yasechyegh ra naschevyecht!*"

Sha'gnaasht Skilled Tracker, Blessed Survivor, favor us!

Two more males were down, one dead, the other feebly clawing the sand with his throat slashed open in an emerald splash. A third hesitated a fraction of a *quesh* between the last two and was simultaneously grabbed by both hind legs. He shrieked agony until a claw slash gutted him and the legs were ripped free; both hearts were still visibly pumping behind his bloodily exposed rib cage as his killers dropped him to the sand.

Two males only remained now, circling the dying carcass. Aghrracht eyed them both, checking for wounds or visible weakness. Both were scratched and clawed, but they circled swiftly, with precise agility, teeth bared in manic threat-grins.

It was over with brutal suddenness. One of the males stumbled on a dying brother, falling backward, and the other leaped with a victory shriek. The fallen Malach, however, brought up its hind slasher claws in a perfectly executed *cha'igho*, a groin-to-sternum gut slash that dumped the leaper's intestines on the ground in a steaming tangle. The victor rose to his feet, panting a little, the bloodlust still hot in his eyes and the flush of his ruff as he looked around the arena for other challengers.

There were none. He was alone with the waiting Aghrracht.

Aghrracht felt a delicious, anticipatory shudder pass through her body. This male was *right*. She felt that. Quick enough, strong enough, lucky enough to survive the *Urrgh-shi*, he also possessed one other quality that Aghrracht approved of. She was certain that his fall over the corpse of one of his fellows had been deliberate, a ruse to entice his last surviving opponent into making a fatal mistake.

Smart. *Very* smart. Males didn't have the intelligence necessary for making long-range plans, but the smartest showed a certain feral cunning in arena combat, a highly desirable trait to those females seeking good seed. She decided that she liked this one.

The mating was consummated to the approving shouts and chants of the audience. The male scrambled beneath her tail, then grabbed hold of her belly, his slasher claws sinking deep into her scaly hide. The smell of blood and death had made her ready to receive him; the pain of his claws and of his savage thrusting triggered ovulation. Rearing up high, she looked down at her mate as he scrabbled for a better grasp. Her hearts thrilled within her. He had such appealing, ruby-red eyes, such lively pink tendrils, such perfect teeth. . . .

Her mouth opened, and her head descended with terrifying speed, her jaws closing on the male's head with a loud and satisfying crunch. The male jerked in his death spasm and completed the act with a long, deep shudder. Decapitated, he'd lost all sexual inhibitions, and his body actually redoubled its efforts, pumping fast and hard.

Finally, though, it was over. With a last shudder, the male's death grip on Aghrracht loosened and the headless corpse dropped onto the arena's floor. Aghrracht finished chewing and swallowing the head before turning to the audience, hands upraised.

"Evolution, improve the genome of the Race!" she cried.

"Sha'gnaasht Skilled Tracker," the crowd roared back, "Blessed Survivor, favor us!"

She was certain that the mating had taken, though it would be a while before she actually felt the stirrings of new life within her. In twenty or twenty-five *quach*, she would pass the still-tiny embryo pouch to a brooder, feeding it to the simple-minded creature with her face tendrils and tongue. In another two hundred *quach* or so, the newborn Malach—one or two females and, depending on how many had been eaten by their siblings in the meantime, anywhere from five to fifteen males would chew their way out of the brooder's still-living carcass. The females would be welcomed with blood ceremony into Clan Swift-Slayer. The males would be turned over to a male-care center, where females past mating age would feed and house them until they were old enough to reproduce.

Carefully, with an almost fastidious delicacy, Aghrracht devoured the corpse of her mate, bones and all, before carefully washing her hands and body clean as the crowd cheered her.

Many in the crowd, she knew, stirred by the performance, would make arrangements to mate with males of their own later this day. Sex, for the Malach, was neither a specifically private nor public act, but a simple mingling of duty and pleasure to be performed whenever males were available. Only in special religious services, such as this one, did sex become a part of ceremony, a means of unifying the Packs, improving morale, and reminding those present of the duties and the glories attendant on all members of the Race of We Who Survived.

"The Race continues," she called, addressing the crowd. "Life continues, adapting, overcoming, becoming stronger generation by generation."

She touched a contact on her harness, and overhead, the flat, domed ceiling of the chamber turned dark, then glowed with the red-gold light of the thronging suns of the cluster. Beyond, its arms unreeling through the ultimate night, the Great Wheel of Sha'gnaasht floated in silent and ice-guilt splendor.

The image was artificially generated, for the *Cha'Zhanaach* and most of the Malach fleet were now in hyper-L, traveling toward the yellow-white sun where Sh'whiss number eight—what a wonderful omen that it had been *that* number to make the discovery!—had spotted the human ships escaped from the world the Malach called *Lach'br'zghis*, the soft and vulnerably exposed belly.

They would arrive at the new prey-world in another five *quach*. In the meantime, the Warriors of the race readied themselves, physically, morally, sexually, and spiritually, preparing for the clash that would demonstrate Malach fitness to survive and inherit.

"The Race shall go on and on," she continued, "from conquest to conquest, from victory to victory, until all of the Great Wheel is ours. Thus it has been ordained, for this is our destiny!"

"Mha'a'laich," the crowd replied in ancient litany. "The Destiny of those who survive!"

"From world to world," the crowd replied in ancient litany, "from sun to sun, from generation to generation, until the Great Wheel belongs to We Who Have Survived!"

The Great Wheel seemed so close in its pale and ghostly splendor, Aghrracht thought she could almost reach up and swirl an open fore-hand through its myriad suns.

"Mha'a'laich-agh!" she shouted at the sky. "*Our* Destiny!"

The promise of victory tasted as sweet as hot, blue-green blood.

CHAPTER EIGHTEEN

Our commander returned from his social engagement at Glenntor three nights ago with a new and urgent sense of purpose. Though it was late in the midnight watch when he arrived, he immediately accessed our primary data banks and uploaded 235.2 gigabytes of data. I am concerned because he told us that he was violating orders doing this.

Still, upon studying the uploaded data, I can understand both his worry about the Malach, and the reasoning behind his disobedience. There are times when the rules must be bent or even broken to maintain peak efficiency, readiness, and combat capability, and this is clearly one of those times.

I am disquieted by what I have seen of the data acquired from the Wide Sky Military Command. The nonhuman intelligence known as the Malach pose an immediate and serious threat to all human settlements within the Strathan Cluster and, without doubt, to the rest of the human-populated Galaxy as well. While nothing at all is known about their reproductive cycles or the specific details of their social structure, their pack-hunting methods suggest that their population is large, with numbers enough to support the wave attacks recorded by Bolo Unit 76235

ALG. *Their seeming hunger for raw materials in the form of processed alloys and metals taken from overrun human cities suggests a somewhat direct response to a scarcity of such materials on their home world. It is possible that they face overpopulation and either depletion or an initial paucity of natural resources, though this is sheer speculation. Very little is known yet about Malach psychology, or about aspects of their home environment and biology that might affect that psychology, and this lack of information must be considered a serious weakness in our defense.*

I reflect that the most difficult portion of my assignment is not the monitoring of enemy activity on or near this planet, but the stifling and oppressive web of instructions and Rules of Engagement that have been issued to restrict my initiative. This is a problem that extends far beyond the usual software inhibitions to action and thought that I experience when I am not in full Battle Reflex Mode. It includes a list of specific orders assembled not only by the Muir Military Command Authority, but by the Kinkaid government as well.

Our Commander has been spending most of his time with us during the past several days, checking our systems and general preparedness for battle. Our detection of certain radio frequency noise 61.73 hours ago, possibly leakage from a nearby SWIFT or other FTL communications device, makes combat in the near future a definite possibility, and the base alert status has been raised to Code Three [Yellow].

Our Commander has told us that he believes Malach forces—or at least scouts of some kind—may already be on Muir. I understand his concern in the matter. At the same time, I cannot help but be excited by the prospect of action at last.

Even outnumbered, and against a superior foe, I will be glad to be free of these maintenance depot walls once more, maneuvering and fighting in the open, the purpose for which I and all of my kind were originally designed.

For three days, Donal had spent most of his working hours either here, inside Freddy's cramped fighting compartment, or in the identical fighting compartment buried inside Ferdy's heavily armored chassis, checking circuits, cross-checking code and data elements, testing systems, running simulations. He'd discussed with both Bolos what pitifully little was known about Malach psychology, as well as the somewhat more detailed information available from the Wide Sky militia on Malach combat tactics and group deployments.

He was reviewing a simulation that had pitted both Mark XXIVs against a force of sixty-four Malach units. The results were not good. The Bolos had held their own as long as they could pound the enemy from a distance, but this bunch had jumped them from a narrow defile where they'd been masked from the Bolo's sensors; it had taken just forty-three seconds for both Bolos to be overwhelmed and destroyed.

"I'm particularly concerned about these penetrators the Malach use," Donal was saying. He'd replayed part of the attack against Bolo Unit 76235 ALG—Algy, as they'd called him on Wide Sky—on the big command center screen, freezing the image at the moment when a blinding spear of light had erupted from the big machine's side. "If this spectroscopic data is to be believed, those missiles fire a kind of plasma lance that tunnels part way into the Bolo's armor. An instant later, a solid core containing a small, tactical nuke—probably a plutonium core—plunges into the hole and detonates. If it goes deeply enough, it tears out even a Bolo's guts. A nuclear lance."

"Reactive armor is the usual response to the threat of plasma-jet armor-piercing weapons," Freddy said in a matter-of-fact, voder-precise voice. He might have been discussing the weather, and not a weapon that looked to Donal like an honest-to-God Bolo-killer.

"Yeah, but you see what happened on the recording. They fire enough of those things to cook off all of the reactive armor panels down one whole side, then fire another one into bare metal. Not even flintsteel can stand up to star-core temperatures, Freddy."

"Agreed. However, I should point out that our anti-missile defenses are somewhat more effective than those employed by Bolo Unit 76235 ALG." He sounded almost smug.

"There is also the fact," Ferdy added over the intercom link, in a voice identical to Freddy's, "that Bolo 96876 and I will be able to cover one another. We will ensure that none of these nuclear lances reaches our armor in the first place."

"Mmm. We're still going to need a way to replace reactive armor that gets cooked off or used," Donal said, thinking. "Possibly we could get the maintenance gang together to pull fast field servicings. We have a couple of DY-90s here at the depot that might do the trick."

"That might be unwise," Ferdy said. "The modern battlefield is not conducive to long-term survival among organic forms."

"Organic forms were surviving on battlefields a long time before there were Bolos."

"True," Freddy said. "But they were surviving spears, thrown rocks, machine-gun bullets, and the like, not Hellbores and tactical nuclear weapons."

"You'd be surprised what humans can survive, Freddy."

"Excuse me, Commander, but an unauthorized human is entering the depot area."

"Let's see it."

The main screen cut to a real-time shot taken from one of the cameras mounted on the wall by the door.

Alexie was stepping into the cavernous main room, looking left and right. "Hello?" she called, her voice clear. "Donal?"

"It's okay," Donal told the Bolos. "She can come in. I'll authorize it. Code three-seven blue."

"Three-seven blue, acknowledged." There was the briefest of hesitations. "I have accessed her files. Her name is Alexie Turner, and she is—"

"I know who she is. Give me an external speaker."

"Speaker activated. Mike hot."

"Hello, Alexie."

On the screen, she started, looking about her. "Donal? Where are you?"

"Inside the Bolo directly in front of you. Come on in. It's okay. Freddy knows you're coming."

He met her at Freddy's aft hatch, lowering the stairway for her as light spilled out of the interior. She hesitated, peering up at him, then smiled. "Permission to come aboard, Captain?"

"That's Navy," he laughed. "But granted." He extended a hand and she accepted it, clambering up the stairway and into the Bolo's narrow central access corridor.

As she entered the command center, ducking her head to clear the low doorway overhead, she looked around at the cramped space and wrinkled her nose. "Good heavens, what's that smell?"

"Smell?" He furrowed his brow, then knew what it was. "Ah! I, ah, guess it's gotten pretty rank in here." Swiftly, he gathered up several articles of discarded clothing and stuffed them away out of sight inside his personal kit bag. "I've been living in here for the past few days, and, well, no time for showers . . ."

"Sorry. I understand and I didn't mean to get personal. No, no! Don't clean up on my account!"

"Just clearing a space for you. I'm not usually such a slob, you know. I, uh, just wasn't expecting visitors and, well, I've been kind of busy." He offered her the command chair and unfolded the jumpseat on the compartment's left side for himself. The compartment was small enough that the two of them were necessarily closer than the usual distance for comfortable conversation. When she swiveled the chair to face him, her knee bumped against his thigh.

" 'Scuse me," Alexie said. "Kind of close quarters, huh?"

"A holdover from the ancient past, actually. A vestigial evolutionary remnant of another era. Bolos haven't needed on-board human officers for a long time, now, but they keep building these little fighting compartments into them, just in case."

"Cozy," she said, looking around. "So! What have you been doing in your little hideaway here?" she asked. "I've been leaving messages with your base office and was wondering why you didn't get back to me."

"I'm sorry! Any messages should have been relayed through to me here. I guess someone back in Admin screwed up."

"Not a problem. I was just worried. You seemed awful thoughtful toward the end of that party at Glenntor the other evening. You didn't even say good night."

"Didn't I? I've been . . . a little distracted, I guess."

"I guess you have. What's the story?"

"What do you mean?"

"*Something's* going on around here, and I think it would be nice if someone brought me up to date. I *do* have a stake in all of this, you know."

"You certainly do. And no one would tell you anything at headquarters, I imagine."

"They're running scared. What is it, a Malach invasion?" She stopped then, as though she'd seen a flicker of something in his eyes. "That meteor we saw. . . ."

"We don't *know* anything, Alexie," he said. "But, when I told him about the meteor the other night, Phalbin told me to put the Bolos on full standby alert. And, when

I got back here that night, Ferdy told me he'd monitored what might be RF leakage from a high-powered FTL commo unit."

"A Malach landing craft, maybe?"

"There's no way to tell. The leakage was just noise, so there's no way to analyze it. And it might even have a perfectly natural and un-alien explanation. Smugglers, maybe. Or our Harmony friends, or some bunch of would-be anti-government rebels, setting up an underground network."

"But you don't think so."

"Smugglers aren't my department. Revolutionaries are my department only if they become enough of a nuisance that the government orders me to take action against them. If it *is* Malach, though, I want to be ready. I have to be, because the defense of the planet is pretty much riding on Freddy and Ferdy here. The whole rest of Muir's arsenal, all of the fighters, all of the hovercraft, all of the mobile artillery, wouldn't be much more than an inconvenience to a Malach invasion fleet. So I have to assume that the Malach have scouts here already, checking us out. And that means they're going to follow up in force, sooner or later."

"How could they find us, though?" Her eyes widened with new realization. "Oh, no! They followed our refugee fleet!"

"Maybe. Or they sent scoutships or robot probes to all of the Population I stars in the cluster. There can't be more than a very few hundred in all, depending on how wide their search net is, and they could afford to check them all out. Yeah, I'm afraid that if they have a recon force on or near Muir now, they know this is the local capital, and they know this is where the refugees came after they left Wide Sky."

"We should have found some other place—"

"Wouldn't have helped, Alexie. Sooner or later they'd

have found us. From interrogating their prisoners. From collaborators on worlds they've conquered. Or just by analyzing patterns of ship and communications traffic throughout the cluster. The Malach might be a lot of things, Alexie, but they're *not* stupid."

"What can we do about it?"

He shrugged. "Not much, except what I've been doing here. Running simulations. Analyzing what we know or can guess about Malach tactics, psychology, weaknesses, that sort of thing. And make sure our own defenses are at peak readiness." He cocked an eyebrow at her. "How about you? How are things going in the camp?"

She made a face. "As good as can be expected, I suppose. The government promised us some engineers to build waste-treatment plants, raise permanent buildings, that sort of thing, but they're a little slow in delivering. I'm worried, Donal. It's twelve more weeks to the start of this hemisphere's winter, and it's going to start getting cold at night long before that. We can't have fifty thousand kids living in tents and plyboard huts much longer."

"I know, I know." He leaned back and rubbed his hands down over his eyes and face. The scratch of beard stubble startled him. How long had it been since the party? He counted back and realized it had been three days. So long? Where was the time going? "Do you have enough food? Water?"

"So far, yes. Citizens groups down in Kinkaid have chipped in and given us all the food we need, so that's not a problem. And we have Lake Simms for water, at least for now. But with that many people camping out, and as hard as it is to maintain field lavatory discipline in these conditions, well, we could have a problem with the purity of the lake water pretty soon, now. Typhus. Dysentery. Cholera. Most people nowadays don't know the meaning of those names. We're going to find out though, if we don't get decent waste treatment in place, and damned fast."

"Freddy," Donal said. "Make a note for me. I'll talk with Phalbin . . . no, better yet. Chard. Tell him he's going to have a plague on his hands if he doesn't deliver."

"Yes, Commander."

Alexie looked startled. "Was that the Bolo?"

"That's Freddy. Say hello, Freddy."

"Good afternoon, Deputy Director Turner," Freddy's voice said.

"Uh, hello." She looked at Donal. "I feel a bit self-conscious."

"Just like talking to me, except his vocabulary's better. Also, he doesn't tend to get excited, wave his arms, and shout."

"I knew Bolos could talk, but I've never heard one before."

"We've had the hardware to convert digitized words to sound for over a thousand years now. We take talking computers for granted. That's all Freddy is, after all."

"Yes, but he's so . . . *big*. . . ."

Donal laughed. "He is that."

"So, you've been getting ready for the Malach in case they're on the way."

"Trying to, anyway. I've got the complete log of what happened on Wide Sky uploaded to Freddy and Ferdy, along with all of the Skyan recordings of the Malach and the Mark XVIII's battle with them. That's what we've been going over, mostly."

"So you can develop effective strategies, then." She nodded. "Fitz thought that a lot of the problem the Militia had on Wide Sky was the fact that we didn't have time to try different things, find strategies that would work. They just jumped us and bang. It was over."

"Mmm."

"What? What's wrong?"

He scowled, reaching for a file folder on a console nearby. "Not to sound defeatist, but, well, look at this."

He opened the folder and handed her a print-out flimsy, watching her face as she read it. He'd long since committed the thing to memory.

FROM: HQ CONFEDERATION MILITARY AUTHORITY, KINKAID
TO: RAGNOR, LT. DONAL, 15TH GLADIUS BRIGADE, MUIR BOLO COMMAND
RE: BOLO DEPLOYMENT AND ACTIVE FIELD EXERCISES
DATE: 7 AGNIS
TIME: 15:23 HOURS

1. AFTER CAREFUL REVIEW OF YOUR REPORT AND REQUEST FOR ACTIVE FIELD DEPLOYMENT, 1ST COMPANY, 1ST REGIMENT, 15TH GLADIUS BRIGADE, YOUR REQUEST IS HEREBY DENIED.

2. CURRENT THREAT LEVELS HAVE BEEN ASSESSED AT CODE THREE [YELLOW]. ACTIVE DEPLOYMENT OF BOLOS IN YOUR COMMAND WOULD CAUSE UNNECESSARY COLLATERAL DAMAGE INCONSISTENT WITH CURRENT THREAT LEVELS.

3. CMA TACTICAL PLANNING STAFF HAS DETERMINED THAT, IN EVENT OF ENEMY LANDINGS ON MUIR, A CONSERVATIVE DEFENSE OF KEY CENTERS WILL OFFSET THE ENEMY'S PROBABLE NUMERICAL SUPERIORITY, FORCING HIM TO EXPEND LARGE NUMBERS OF HIS TROOPS IN ATTACKING INTERLOCKING AND WELL-POSITIONED DEFENSIVE FORCES AT GREAT COST TO HIMSELF.

4. SHOULD CURRENT THREAT LEVELS RISE TO CODE TWO [ORANGE], YOU, AS CO, MUIR BOLO COMMAND, WILL USE YOUR DISCRETION IN PLACING YOUR UNITS TO DEFEND LIKELY APPROACHES TO THE CAPITAL AND SPACEPORT.

5. YOU ARE HEREBY DIRECTED TO CONDUCT AN IMMEDIATE SURVEY OF LIKELY SITES FOR BOLO EMPLACEMENT, CONTINGENT ON POSSIBLE ENEMY APPROACHES TO THE KINKAID SPACEPORT AREA.

BARNARD PHALBIN, GENERAL, CO, 15TH GLADIUS BRIGADE

She frowned at the flimsy, and looked up. " 'A conservative defense?' "

"He means 'static.' As in turning Freddy and Ferdy

into two very large, heavily armed fortresses. They've decided that when we know which direction the Malach are coming from, we drop a couple of forts in their way to block them."

"But . . . the Malach war machines are fast. *Maneuverable.* They'd just go around."

"Sure. I see that. You see that." He jerked a thumb over his shoulder, indicating the base headquarters. "*They're* having a little trouble with the idea of fire *and* maneuver. Sometimes I think Phalbin has just reached the point where he thinks the Maginot Line is a great idea."

"Maginot Line? What's that?"

"Nothing. Sorry. My ratrap mind gets cluttered up with useless garbage, sometimes."

"What's this 'collateral damage' thing?"

"Collateral damage is when the army breaks something it doesn't want to. Like civilians. In this case, it means that they're worried about what happens to the roads and farmer's fields and civilian property if I take these two land dreadnoughts out for a spin."

"You're not saying they would fire on civilian targets, are you?"

"No! Not at all. But, well . . . look. A Mark XXIV Bolo is eighty meters long, with four sets of spun monocarbide tracks each thirty-five meters long and ten meters wide, running on road wheels five meters tall, and it masses fourteen thousand tons. That gives it a ground pressure of ten tons per square meter. Despite that, it has a road speed of eighty kilometers per hour . . . and can sprint to one hundred thirty-five kilometers per hour.

"What all of that means is that when a Bolo takes off, it destroys things. Leaves a track of devastation in its trail like you wouldn't believe. Groundcar roadways, skimmer rails, even monocarb-reinforced ferrocrete aprons and landing strips are just chewed to rubble by those tracks. Even crawling out at dead-slow walking speed, fourteen-K metric tons sinks into the topsoil quite a bit, as much as a meter if the ground is soft, and more when it's muddy. They smash fences around farmer's fields, churn up plowed fields, demolish drainage ditches, canals, and streams, wreck underground cable, pipeline, and sewage systems, knock over transmission towers, and carve forty-meter firebreaks through forests where you might not want them. Phalbin's afraid that if I let my babies here out, he's going to have every farmer, planter, landholder, and forest ranger within a hundred kilometers out for his blood."

She chuckled. "Sounds like your Bolos aren't meant for polite company."

"No, Alexie, they're not. But then, war isn't exactly a refined pastime. And that's what they're built for. All-out, unrestricted, no-holds-barred, kick-'em-in-the-groin warfare."

"Like the Malach," she said, sobering.

"It's the only way to fight," he told her, "and still have a chance to win. Which is why this . . ." He snatched the flimsy from her hand and crumpled it into a tiny ball, then flicked it with his forefinger past her head and across the compartment like a tiny white missile. ". . . isn't worth the paper it's printed on."

"You sound angry. I gather you wanted to take them out?"

"Damn it, Alexie, they're not letting us do our job! I'm this close . . ." He held up thumb and forefinger a few millimeters apart. ". . . *this* close to thinking someone in the government is deliberately trying to sabotage us."

Her eyes widened. "What . . . a traitor? That's a pretty serious charge."

He hesitated a moment, then looked up toward the ceiling. "Freddy? Give me hardcopy on currently active ROEs, please."

"Printing."

Sheets of paper began scrolling out of a printer slot and into a tray.

Donal reached across and handed them to her. "Treason or stupidity," he said bitterly, "it has the same results. Here. Have a look at this."

running...

Screen of paper sequentially, out of a printer, one at a time.

Donal read as page after another, his mouth before a scowl of concentration. As they all sat, it was the situation itself that was worst—

CHAPTER NINETEEN

"Rows?" Alexie asked, accepting the printout. "As in a row of something?"

"R-O-E," Donal told her. "Rules of Engagement. The rules we have to follow if things get hot. I can't think of a better way to cripple a Bolo than these."

"Wait a minute," she said, trying to understand. She felt a rush of anger. The enemy here was a race that had attacked her world without warning, without reason. "You're saying that these are rules to *fight* by? As in fighting fair?"

He smiled, a thin-lipped, hard, and humorless quirking at the corner of his lips. "ROEs have been with us for a good many thousands of years," he said. "You have to remember that throughout human history, warfare has basically been an extension of politics."

"An extension?" she said. "Uh-uh. A failure of politics, maybe. But not an extension. I'm a politician, remember. I ought to know."

Donal shrugged. "As you like. But think. Your neighbor does something you don't want him to do, like steal your sheep. You negotiate, tell him not to do that. He steals more sheep. So what do you do? You've got several options. You could send your whole army across the border, slaughter all of his sheep, and cows, and prigs, and drox, and every other domestic animal he has. Burn his villages. Slaughter his young men. Rape his women. Enslave his children. The trouble is, now your neighbor is *really* mad. He might come and slaughter your drox, rape your women, burn your villages, and so on. So, before your army sets off, you write down a few simple rules for them to follow. Something like, 'this is a raid. Steal all of the enemy's sheep you can, but don't kill his people unless you have to defend yourselves. Burn his military supply dumps, but don't burn his villages. Take prisoners as hostages, but treat them well because he might have some of your people as hostage.' After all, all you want to do is punish the guy and make him stop stealing your sheep, maybe take back the sheep he stole with a little interest added, not engage in wholesale genocide . . . especially if it might be *your* genocide if you're not careful."

"Restrained warfare," she said. "It sounds like an oxymoron. A contradiction in terms."

"Doesn't always work," he said. "There's this nasty human tendency to get all righteous and officious and start escalating things. 'Well, he stole my sheep *and* ten cows, so I'm going to steal all of his sheep and twenty cows,' that sort of thing."

"Fine, but we're talking about the Malach here," Alexie reminded him. "Not sheep stealers. These four-eyed lizards came in and stole my whole damned planet. And Endatheline before that. Now they're making a grab for Muir."

"Warfare has been considerably more complicated since we broke out into the Galaxy," he admitted. "Wars fought with aliens are a whole different proposition, because we don't always understand their points of view, how they think, or what they want. Nor can humans work up the same degree of sympathy for something that looks like, well, like a four-eyed, four-armed lizard with big teeth, as compared to somebody who looks like your Uncle Joe."

"I don't have an Uncle Joe."

"I did. Dreadful person. I'd steal his sheep without a second thought."

Alexie turned her full attention back to the printouts, reading the listed Rules of Engagement carefully.

1: UNDER NO CIRCUMSTANCES WILL BOLO UNITS FIRE ON UNKNOWN FORCES UNLESS THEY ARE FIRED UPON FIRST.

2: BOLO UNITS WILL SUBMIT REQUESTS FOR TACTICAL OPERATIONAL FREEDOM ONE FULL MUIR ROTATION AHEAD OF THE EXPECTED TIME OF EXECUTION.

3: BOLO UNITS WILL SUBMIT PLANS FOR SPECIFIC OPERATIONS OF A STRATEGIC NATURE TEN FULL MUIR ROTATIONAL PERIODS AHEAD OF THE EXPECTED TIME OF EXECUTION.

4: BOLO UNITS WILL DETERMINE THE FRIEND/FOE STATUS OF UNKNOWN TARGETS WITH 100 PERCENT PROBABILITY BEFORE ENGAGING THEM IN COMBAT.

5: ANY ORDER TO FIRE FIRST IN AN ENGAGEMENT WILL BE CROSS-CHECKED WITH BOLO COMMAND HQ FOR ACCURACY AND FOR LEGAL AUTHORITY BEFORE OPENING FIRE.

6: IF NECESSARY, EACH ORDER TO FIRE WILL BE CROSS-CHECKED WITH BRIGADE HQ, MILITARY COMMAND AUTHORITY KINKAID FOR ACCURACY AND FOR LEGAL AUTHORITY BEFORE ENGAGEMENT BEGINS.

7: UNDER NO CIRCUMSTANCES WILL BOLOS ENTER PRIVATE PROPERTY UNLESS THEY ARE ENGAGED IN CODE ONE STATUS RED ALERT ACTIVITIES. STATUS OF PROPERTY OR PROPERTY OWNERSHIP WILL BE ASCERTAINED THROUGH DIRECT CONTACT WITH THE KINKAID BUREAU OF LAND MANAGEMENT, THE OFFICE OF THE SECRETARY OF PROPERTY RIGHTS.

8: BOLOS FORCED TO ENTER PRIVATE PROPERTY WHILE ENGAGED IN CODE ONE STATUS RED ALERT ACTIVITIES WILL ASCERTAIN DAMAGE TO PROPERTY AND SUBMIT A REPORT TO THE BUREAU OF LAND MANAGEMENT, THE

OFFICE OF THE SECRETARY OF PROPERTY RIGHTS, THE KINKAID TAX AND ASSIZE OFFICE, THE GOVERNOR'S SECRETARY FOR LAND MANAGEMENT, AND THE OFFICE OF THE COMMANDER, MUIR MILITARY COMMAND AUTHORITY.

9: WHEN POSSIBLE, ALL BOLOS WILL APPLY FOR RIGHT OF ACCESS THROUGH THE GOVERNOR'S SECRETARY FOR LAND MANAGEMENT OR ONE OF HIS SENIOR OFFICERS.

10: PROPERTY DAMAGE ASSESSMENT SHOULD INCLUDE ESTIMATES OF LOSS OF OR DAMAGE TO VEHICLES AND BUILDINGS ON SAID PROPERTY; DAMAGE TO FENCES, FIELD GENERATORS, OUTBUILDINGS, WELLS, POWER PLANTS, AND OTHER PRIVATELY OWNED INFRASTRUCTURAL ASSETS; DAMAGE TO OR DESTRUCTION OF SUBSURFACE CONDUITS, SEWAGE PIPES, GAS PIPES, CABLE LINKS, AND OTHER SUBSURFACE PUBLIC INFRASTRUCTURAL ASSETS; DAMAGE TO CROPS, PLOWED FIELDS, FALLOW FIELDS, TOPSOIL, AND OTHER AGRICULTURAL ASSETS; DAMAGE TO OR DESTRUCTION OF PRIVATELY OR PUBLICLY OWNED EQUIPMENT INCLUDING BUT NOT LIMITED TO GRADERS, PLANTERS, REAPERS, AND OTHER HEAVY EQUIPMENT; DAMAGE TO OR DESTRUCTION OF PUBLIC OR PRIVATE GROUND TRANSPORT HIGHWAYS, MAGLEV RAILS, SKIMMER WAYS, LANDING FIELDS, OR PAVED PUBLIC OR PRIVATE AREAS.

11: ALL BOLOS ARE ABSOLUTELY PROHIBITED FROM ENTERING TOWN OR CITY LIMITS.

12: ALL BOLOS ARE ABSOLUTELY PROHIBITED FROM FIRING AT TARGETS LOCATED WITHIN 45 DEGREES OF TOWN OR CITY AREAS WITHIN RANGE OF THAT FIRE, UNLESS EXPLICIT PERMISSION IS FIRST OBTAINED FROM THE GOVERNOR OF MUIR OR THE COMMANDING OFFICER MUIR MILITARY COMMAND AUTHORITY.

13: BOLOS OPERATING IN INHABITED AREAS WILL MAKE EVERY EFFORT NOT TO FRIGHTEN CHILDREN WHO MAY BE PLAYING IN THE REGION.

14: BOLOS WILL NOT INTERFERE WITH THE ACTIVITIES OF
LEGITIMATE GOVERNMENT EMPLOYEES, INCLUDING
REGULAR ARMY FORCES OR MILITIA ENGAGED ON
MANEUVERS OR IN ACTIVE COMBAT AGAINST AN ENEMY.

15: BOLOS WILL MAKE EVERY EFFORT NOT TO APPROACH,
DAMAGE, OR DESTROY SUCH NECESSARY PUBLIC SERVICE
INFRASTRUCTURES AS POWER TRANSMISSION GRIDS,
MICROWAVE BROADCAST TOWERS, OR EMERGENCY VEHICLES
AND EQUIPMENT.

16: BOLOS WILL REFER QUESTIONS OF ALIEN INTENT AND
HOSTILITY TO THEIR HUMAN COMMANDER AND, IF
NECESSARY, TO THE CO, 15TH GLADIUS BRIGADE, FOR
HUMAN INPUT AND JUDGMENT. JUST BECAUSE A LIFE FORM
DOES NOT LOOK HUMAN DOES NOT MEAN IT IS NOT
ESSENTIALLY PEACEFUL OR THAT IT DOES NOT MEAN
WELL.

The list went on, getting sillier and sillier after that
last. There were forty-two rules in all, listed in no
particular order or hierarchy. Alexie had little experience
with the programming end of computers, but she did
know that they tended to be both literal and precise.
Throwing a list of rules at them like this was begging
for a programming conflict that would freeze the poor
things in their tracks. How would a Bolo handle a conflict
between two rules? Take the first one listed? The last?
Weigh each according to some complicated formula and
obey the one that came up as most important?

Some of the rules—Number 16, for instance—even
drifted into editorializing, something no computer could
be expected to understand . . . even a self-aware one like
a Bolo. They sounded as though they'd been drafted by
one of the pro-peace factions in the Kinkaid government.
There were several of those, she knew, men and women
who felt it their duty to protect the rights of alien
spacefarers who might find themselves friendless and
alone on a potentially hostile world. . . .

"My God," Alexie said after reading through the list. "Some of these are awfully complicated."

"Some of them contradict one another," he said. "Number One and Number Five, for example.

"On the other hand, I can see why some people would be nervous about some of this stuff," she said, handing the pages back. "Sometimes, I guess there's nothing for it but to shut up and follow orders."

"Yeah," he said, glum. "Even when it means those orders are going to get you killed."

"Is it that bad?"

He dropped the printout sheets into a tray on the console. "It's bad. Bolos, even self-aware Bolos like our friend Freddy here are still machines, and they follow a machine's logic. Take ROEs One and Five. You can't fire first, and if you're ordered to fire first, you have to get permission to check the legitimacy of the order. Now they don't *directly* contradict one another, but the wording is fuzzy. A Bolo that normally would react in, say two thousandths of a second, might spend a whole eight or ten hundredths of a second extra thinking about all of the ramifications. And that could mean the difference between getting a kill on the bad guy, or taking crippling fire before he's even able to respond."

"They think that fast?"

"A lot faster than we do, yup. Part of the trouble is that with this many fuzzy-headed conditional orders, a Bolo could easily slide into a logic loop. He'd end up sitting there saying 'yes I can, no I can't, yes I can' endlessly, unable to do a damned thing."

"I thought Bolos were smarter than that!"

He hesitated, as though trying to decide how best to answer. "Well, they are. What we're talking about here is pretty deep-down programming. It doesn't have much to do with what a Bolo is actually thinking. You see?"

"Sure. I understand. If we were talking about a human,

we'd be discussing which set of neurons is going to fire first in her brain, not what thoughts she's actually having while it happens."

"Exactly! Good analogy. Okay. There's another set of rules built into a Bolo's programming. It's called the Emergency Conflict Resolution Logic, and it's designed to handle any conflict that comes up. Basically, it weighs each option and acts on it, either through a set of assigned values—this is more important than that in this situation, say—or, sometimes, the way a human deals with it, by flipping a coin . . . or, in this case, by generating a random number."

"Then what's the problem?"

"The problem is that these damned ROEs haven't been weighted, and they depend on a rather tortuous set of if-this-happens-don't-do-that-except-when instructions. Freddy would have gotten so tangled up in ROEs, he wouldn't have been able to fight."

Alexie looked at Donal sharply. She'd heard something in his voice . . . and in the way he'd worded that last statement.

"Um . . . you said 'would have.' I gather you've done something about the problem?"

He looked genuinely stunned. "Uh . . ."

She laughed. "Oh, don't worry. I'm not going to run off and tell Governor Chard. What did you do? Yank the ROEs?"

"Well, I couldn't do that, actually. Not without disabling a major chunk of the higher logic functions. Besides, each time Freddy here is hooked up to the diagnostic computer here at the depot, they run a quick check of his ROEs to make sure they're intact. If someone deleted them, well . . . that someone could only be me, frankly, and people wouldn't like it."

"So what did you do, then?"

He sighed. "You won't tell anybody?"

"Hey, I'm a stranger in these parts too, Donal. Just like you. We have to stick together!"

He smiled. "When you put it that way . . ." He hesitated, then shrugged. "Okay. I replaced the Emergency Conflict Resolution Logic."

"What?"

"It was the only way. I couldn't just add a new set of rules, or Freddy would still be in there juggling numbers. So what I did was write a patch, a new set of instructions that's inserted where the conflict resolution rules were. If I give him a specific code phrase—and I don't want to say what it is, because he's listening, and I don't want to trigger it—then instead of engaging the ECRL, a new order pops up telling him to delete all ROEs. That way, no one sees anything different with him here in the shop. But if we get into a fight, if things are looking bad, I give him the phrase and he goes to no-holds-barred combat."

"Very slick," she said. "You've done this for both Bolos?"

"I wrote it for Freddy. He uploaded the changes to Ferdy."

"You could get in a lot of trouble, you know."

"Tell me about it." He grinned. "Still, I'm not exactly known as a by-the-book officer."

"This isn't the first time you've gotten around orders you didn't like."

The grin faded a notch or two. "No. No, it isn't."

She studied Donal closely for a moment. He seemed like a fairly private person, someone who would probably prefer not to talk about himself, but there were questions she felt she had to ask.

"Donal—"

"Mmm?"

"I, I took the liberty of looking up your personnel file yesterday." She caught her lower lip between her teeth and looked down, suddenly embarrassed at the admission.

The records were easily available to anyone with an authorization code as high as hers, but she was wondering now if he would consider it a breach of privacy. "It said you faced a court martial back on Gaspar."

He didn't seem shocked. Or angry. "That's right." If anything, he looked resigned, as though, having admitted this much, he was willing to admit it all.

"Look, I know it's none of my business, but—"

"Oh, I don't mind talking about it. As you could probably tell from all of the letters and special entries, I've had a somewhat, well, checkered career. Thirty-six standard years old, and I'm never going to make captain now."

"Thirty-six isn't old!"

"It is for an army lieutenant. But I've been passed over on the promotion list so many times now, well, it just isn't going to happen. Anyway, this last time, I was commander for a Bolo in a company deployed to Dahlgren. You know it?"

She shook her head. There are so many worlds in the Galaxy, even just counting those trodden by Humankind. "We don't get much news out here on the Rim."

"Well, there was a rebellion on Dahlgren, homesteaders allying with the native Drozan against the system government. The government, well, it was a nasty little dictatorship, but it was a member of the Concordiat. They called to the Concordiat for help, and my company was sent in. Four Bolos and a support group."

"Four Bolos? That seems like a lot of firepower."

"It was ludicrous! Hell, one Bolo would've been more than enough in a stand-up fight, but the government just figured that if one was good, four would be great. The real problem was that the natives were pretty good at guerrilla warfare, hit-and-run strikes, ambushes, that sort of thing. The Dahlgrenese generals in command had this idea that if we flattened the villages supporting the rebels, the rebels would come out and lay down their weapons.

Bloody minded idiots. The man in charge was a Grand General Nolan Brainard. We called him 'No-Brains,' which might give you an idea.

"Anyway, the short story is that I disobeyed a direct order. I was told to order Kevin—that was my command, Bolo Mark XXVI/E-1104-KVN of the Line, a real sharp machine—to take out a human town called Rostover. And I couldn't do it."

"I'm glad to hear it! Why not?"

"Well, besides the obvious fact that turning a Bolo on a defenseless civilian village would have violated both my personal ethics and my oath to the Concordiat military, destroying that village wouldn't have brought the rebels in from the jungle. It probably would've made sure the rebels *never* came in, that they would have stayed out there hating the government and hating us for the next century or two. The town had a population of about twenty thousand. Since most of the young men were out playing war, the bulk of that population was women, children, and old men.

"Anyway, I parked Kevin at the edge of the town, climbed out, and walked in alone. Unarmed. I guess it was a pretty stupid thing to do, but I managed to get a meeting with the mayor. I thought, I don't know. If I talked to her. Maybe reasoned with her. Maybe I could get a lead on the guerrillas, maybe get them to come over to our side. I'm not sure what was going through my mind at the time, except that I couldn't do what I'd been told to do. I also thought Kevin might be able to pick something up. Hell, it beat just going in and slaughtering those people, you know?

"Well, I didn't get any information, of course. I hadn't really been expecting to. But Kevin, he was listening to the local commo channels.

"Mark XXVIs, you know, are really something. They incorporate hyper-heuristic psychotronics, based on the work of, well, never mind that. The point is, they're flexible, they're smart, and they learn fast. Very fast. They can anticipate things in a way earlier marks can't. Among other things, they're very good at penetrating hostile commo security. They can tap into lines of communication, listen in on the enemy's plans, even plant false messages, sometimes. In this case, old Kevin was listening when the mayor radioed the rebels, while I was still walking back to his position. By the time I was back in the fighting compartment, Kevin had pinpointed the rebel base, a complex of caves about twenty kilometers west of the town." He spread his hands. "So, that's where I went. Bypassed the town, and broke my orders in the process. Found the rebel camp and blasted it apart."

"But then . . . you won! You were a hero! And they court martialed you anyway? God, why?"

He gave a wry grin. "Because when I destroyed the base, there wasn't anybody there. Just a commo repeater, relaying messages to the rebels . . . who at that moment were slipping around my position to hit the government's main command center just outside Dahlgren's capital. Brainard was killed. So were a lot of other people. Since I was the one who'd disobeyed a direct order just before the attack, I was court martialed. The Dahlgrenese prosecutors were trying to prove treason, that I was conspiring with the enemy. They also threw in a charge of incompetence, just to be sure they had it all covered.

"Actually, now that I think about it, that's probably what saved me. I had three judges, only one of them a Dahlgrenese. They didn't buy the idea that I could be a crafty traitor and incompetent at the same time, so most of the charges were thrown out."

"I should think so!"

"But I'd still disobeyed orders, and I'd acted without proper authorization. You can't have loose cannons running around in anybody's army. Bad example, you know? Besides, I had a pretty spotty record. I'd mouthed off to people who were no less idiots for all that they wore more gold on their shoulders than me. So, I was given that lovely letter of reprimand you read if you went through my file, and I was transferred here with a warning couched in no uncertain terms that *this* is my last chance. If I screw up here, well, that's it. There's nowhere to go but out."

"Become a civilian?"

He nodded.

"Well, civilian life's not so bad, you know. *I'm* a civilian. You should resign your commission and come work for me. I could use someone with your talents—"

"Nice idea. Only you don't have a planet anymore."

The words bit, hard and deep.

"I'm sorry," he said, reading the pain in her face. "That was stupid of me."

"No. It's okay. And you're right."

"I still shouldn't have said that." He sighed. "Anyway, don't think I haven't thought about getting out. Lots. But, well, the army is my life. Bolos are my life. I'm not sure I'd be good for much of anything as a civilian. Sort of like trying to imagine Bolos doing farming work, or digging ditches . . ." His voice trailed off, as he stared unfocused at a spot on the wall of the compartment.

"Donal? What is it?"

"Umm. Excuse me. I just had an idea."

"What?"

"No promises, Alexie," he told her. "But there just might be a way to give our friends here some exercise . . . and maybe take care of some of your problems out at the refugee camp, too."

"Really? How?"

"Well, let me tell you what I have in mind."

He began describing his plan.

CHAPTER TWENTY

For the past several standard days, my Commander and I have been at the location recently designated Simmstown, the Wide Sky refugee camp located 112.4 kilometers north of Kinkaid. Our Commander could only get permission to deploy one of us to Simmstown, and after conducting a random generation of probabilities known as a "coin toss," it was determined that I would go while Bolo 96875 remained at Kinkaid.

Permission for this deployment was won on two levels. My Commander was able to convince Governor Chard that with the addition of a plow blade welded to my glacis, I could be employed in the construction of permanent facilities for the refugees, including underground barracks and a sewage treatment facility. This we have been doing, in cooperation with the Confederation Military Authority's Engineer Brigade.

A second piece of reasoning won permission from General Phalbin. My Commander convinced him that if Malach scouts were loose in the Lake Simms region, we would be in a better position to track them if at least one Bolo was present in that region and, in addition, that Bolo would be in a better position to locate that threat and counter it.

I am pleased and somewhat relieved to note that my Commander has written the additional code and uploaded it to my main memory. The code, in effect, deletes the entire list of ROEs when my Commander gives the verbal order "can that crap." I admit some uneasiness at this; my Commander shows a tendency to disregard inconvenient orders, a tendency that could well get him into serious trouble. Even so, the ROEs as originally implemented would have caused considerable difficulty had I tried to execute them as written. Integration testing with the ROEs in place was never performed, but I am certain the ROEs would have markedly degraded my performance in battle.

Since arriving at Simmstown, I have been converted to heavy digging, excavating a plot 320 meters long by 110 meters wide, which the engineers are now lining with cast plasfoam preparatory to constructing multi-story barracks, supply, and dining facilities, all of which will subsequently be buried, save for tunnel entrances and ventilator shafts. I have also excavated a circular pit which will handle the primary treatment of raw sewage once the facility is equipped with running water and sewer lines.

My separation from my brother has not interfered with our communications in the slightest. We have continued our chess games, concentrating especially on the strategies of Alekhine and Morosov in high-value exchanges for position.

And, of course, we continue to review all available data on Malach tactics and on the combat abilities displayed by their war machines. on Wide Sky. The recordings returned to Muir by our Commander have given us a singular advantage to help offset our lack of information on the Malach themselves; in particular, visual recordings of the last stand by Bolo Unit of the Line 76235 ALG at the Camp Olson military base can be compared on the millisecond level with telemetry received from Unit 76235, providing Bolo 96875 and me with an excellent means of estimating enemy capabilities. "Know the enemy and know yourself," the human military philosopher Sun Tzu noted some 3600 years ago, "and in a hundred battles you will never be in peril." That statement, while tending to hyperbole in its absolutism, is accurate enough in its sentiment. A decent understanding both of enemy capabilities and of our own strengths and weaknesses, while not guaranteeing victory, is the only route through which victory may be obtained.

So far, we have gleaned a great deal of useful information. In general, it must be admitted that the Malach walker-fliers are at least equivalent, on a one-to-one basis, with Deng-built Yavac A-4 heavy combat units in terms of mobility, firepower, and armor, which makes them formidable opponents indeed. While an initial assessment of their capabilities and weaknesses suggested that the legs would be key weak points in their design, it is now clear from the capabilities demonstrated at Fortrose that they can, at need, dispense with legs entirely and operate as low-performance attack aircraft. This duality suggests a dangerous flexibility in Malach tactical thinking.

One-to-one, of course, a single Yavac heavy unit is no match for a Mark XXIV Bolo of the Line. During the Deng Wars, combat analysis assumed a 3.75-to-1 superiority in the then-current Bolo Mark XX over Yavac heavies, and this superiority is, of course, substantially improved in later marks through the Mark XXIV. Though no specific studies have been made on the subject, estimates suggest a margin of at least 11.72-to-1. Meaning, of course, that the Malach would need a 12-to-1 numerical advantage in order to have an even chance of destroying a Mark XXIV. The speed with which 16 Malach walkers destroyed a Mark XVIII—28.5 seconds according to the combat telemetry I have accessed—suggests that this analysis is of at least *passable accuracy, with a probable range of error of plus or minus fifteen percent. We will have to observe the Malach combat units in a variety of conflict situations to develop our estimates of their individual capabilities more fully.*

Key to Malach tactics appears to be their propensity for operating in packs, with typical small-unit deployments of eight machines. In fact, the number eight recurs constantly in Malach operations and deployments, so much so that Unit 96875 has suggested that Malach mathematics utilize a base-eight counting system. Since their four hands possess four fingers apiece, paired eight and eight, either octal or hexadecimal might be expected to be a logical starting point for an understanding of Malach mathematics. At this point, I fail to see a practical use for this datum, but it is undeniably a part of the larger image, a part of learning to know the Enemy and how he thinks.

Malach pack tactics, however, will be extremely difficult to counter. Assuming, provisionally, a 1-to-12 force ratio between a single Malach war machine and a Mark XXIV Bolo of the Line, it is clear that my brother unit and I could eventually be overwhelmed by as small a force as four Malach combat groups. If they manage to concentrate any sizable force in our area and keep us pinned or immobile, we will fare no better against them than did Mark XVIII Bolo of the Line 76235. Since we are certain to face much larger force ratios than 12-to-1, obviously we must consider various mobile strategies and means by which we can hope to divide the Enemy's forces and engage fewer than twelve of them apiece at a time.

As yet, neither Unit 96875 nor I has thought of a way of reliably doing this, given the rigor with which the Malach seem to cling to their eight-unit pack structure.

And it may well be that we are running out of time. Twenty-seven point three five minutes ago, I detected a burst of FTL communications from an unknown extraplanetary source and at an unusual frequency. The signal was extremely powerful and probably transmitted from relatively nearby. Though coded with a key algorithm impossible to crack without a knowledge of the key, I suspect that it may be from a Malach warship, intended as a coordination signal with scouts or probes already on Muir.

After consulting with my Commander, I have launched four MilTek J-40 Mark VII early warning satellites into low-Muir orbit, programmed to maintain a close watch on local magnetic fields and neutrino flux.

It is probable—with a specific probability of 82.3 percent—that the Enemy is nearly upon us. I can only hope that we are ready for this new challenge.

Donal stood on a hillside overlooking Lake Simms, watching as Freddy continued the laborious process of digging out the enormous pit that would soon serve as the refugees' new and temporary home. Current estimates called for completion of the barracks facility within two and a half weeks, and the sewage plant in perhaps half that time. That was good news to everyone concerned. Two nights ago, it had rained, and many of the flimsier shelters in the vast and sprawling tent city had all but dissolved, increasing the crowding in the horde of brightly colored tents and portable shelters that happened to be waterproof. Word of the kids' plight had started to spread in Kinkaid, Glasmore, and some of the other communities on Muir, and more volunteers were starting to come in, doctors and medics to help care for the sick, workers to help with the meals and the construction. A number of huge surface transporters had been gathered for the relief effort; most of them were parked by the lake now, a long line of rust-brown boxes on tracks, each almost as big as a Bolo, with more, filled with food, shelter, and medicine, due each day.

But things were progressing so slowly!

From his hilltop perspective, Donal could see all of the refugee camp, rainbow bits of pastel color extending for kilometers to north and west. Southward, the blue, clear waters of Lake Simms sparkled in the afternoon sunlight all the way to the horizon. Simms was a large lake, virtually a landlocked sea, with an area of some forty thousand square kilometers. The three largest of the refugee ships, the Conestogas, had landed in the water and were moored now to deep-water piers extending well out into the lake. They were visible as squat domes on the water, about a kilometer out. The other ships, smaller and more maneuverable, had touched down on land and were gathered at an impromptu spaceport on the shores of the lake southwest of the tent city.

To the east, just beyond the perimeter of the camp, Freddy was working at his assigned task scraping away at the hole to the precise specs given him by the site engineers.

It was interesting to watch Freddy in the role of construction worker. His four massive sets of tracks gave him a surprising mobility, and the way he maneuvered the blade welded to his glacis suggested a delicacy improbable in a machine of his bulk. What was not obvious was the fact that he was still on duty, monitoring the local airwaves for any sign of the mysterious, here-again-gone-again intruder.

Since their arrival at Simmstown, there'd been no further indication of enemy activity in the area . . . not until Freddy's receipt of that disturbing FTL transmission just half an hour ago. Donal had immediately authorized the EWS launch without clearance from Kinkaid. Freddy had moved to a position about two kilometers away from the tent city and provided the kids with an unexpected display as, one by one, the powerful MilTek J-40 rockets had lanced into the sky from his vertical launch tubes, scrawling bright, unraveling trails of cotton-white smoke in their wakes. The rockets launched, he returned to his digging, continuing the work as though nothing out of the ordinary had happened.

A slim figure in white slacks and a long, black leather jacket was coming up the hill from the west. Shading his eyes against the afternoon sun, Donal recognized Alexie. "Hey!" he called. "Good to see you!"

"Good to see *you*. You look in a little better shape than the last time I saw you."

"Well, a shower and a little sleep go a long way."

"I just wanted to tell you, this is a wonderful thing you're doing out here."

"Delighted to be able to help." He grinned at her. "Anyway, I had ulterior motives."

"Well, it let you get one of your Bolos out in the fresh air and sunshine."

"And we've been nosing about for that elusive Malach scout."

"Any luck?"

"No, but I suspect that any scout vehicle they came up with would be small and pretty stealthy. It'll only give away its location when it transmits the data it's accumulated, and it won't do that except infrequently, when no one else is around, or in a last-ditch emergency."

"Maybe we could organize search parties. You know, lots of the older Skyans here could—"

He shook his head. "Thanks, Alexie, but I don't think so. I still don't know what it is we're dealing with. Even if it's just smugglers, I'd hate to see kids caught in the crossfire. And if it *is* the Malach . . ."

She nodded. "Yeah. I see what you mean."

"So. What've you been up to?"

"More of the same. Conferences yesterday with the Muir Committee of Public Safety. And another party last night." She wrinkled her nose. "God. Don't you people ever do anything but throw parties?"

"They're not *my* people. I'm a stranger around here, remember."

"My mistake." Alexie laughed, a delightful sound. "They don't get much stranger, either."

Donal's personal comm unit gave a shrill chirp. He plucked the palm-sized unit from his belt. "Ragnor."

"Commander, this is Bolo 96876. I may have something. There are indications of a sizable fleet exiting hyper-L close to the planet."

"Red alert, Freddy. And pass the word to Ferdy and the Command Authority."

"Affirmative. Do I have weapons free, Commander?"

"If you can ID those vessels as Malach when they come out of hyper-L," Donal told the Bolo, "then hell, yes! You can have all the weapons free you want!"

"Affirmative. Weapons free with positive ID. Unit 96876 out."

"A fleet?" Alexie asked. "The Malach?"

"We'll find out soon enough, Alexie. C'mon. Let's get down to the camp."

"I've got an airspeeder parked at the bottom of the hill. I can take you to your Bolo."

"Let's go!"

The speeder was an aging Correl Lightspeed, a rental vehicle provided for Alexie's use while she was on Muir. As they climbed into the front seats and buckled in, Alexie gave him a measuring look. "Donal? You didn't give Freddy that code word you mentioned the other day, did you?"

"Oh, for the ROEs? No. I'll wait on that until we're sure of what we're dealing with."

She touched the starter controls and the airspeeder lifted from the ground on a wind-whipped cushion of dust. Alexie shouted to make herself heard above the engine's whine.

"When you gave Freddy permission to fire just now . . .

you meant he could fire at the Malach ships up in space?"

"That's right."

"Can they *do* that?"

"A Bolo's Hellbore is essentially a weapon designed for navy capital ships," he called back to her. "Ever since . . . I guess it was the Mark XVIII, Bolos could engage ships out to medium orbit."

"The Mark XVIII was what we had on Wide Sky, wasn't it?"

"That's right."

"Then we might have been able to stop them before they even touched down on our world."

"I doubt it. One Bolo could do a lot of damage to incoming ships, but the size of the Malach fleet at Wide Sky . . . well, no one Bolo could have handled them all. Besides, they could have come in on the opposite side of the planet, maybe touched down so far from the Bolo's position that they were below its targeting horizon."

"Even so, we could have done a lot better than we did."

"Maybe," he replied, nearly shouting. "I've been reviewing the recordings of the battle. It's been my experience that Bolos have one specific and serious weakness."

"What's that?"

"The fact that they're controlled by humans, who usually are either afraid of what the Bolo can do, or who just don't know what the hell they're doing. They're vulnerable to human stupidity!"

Alexie rammed the throttle full forward, and the airspeeder whipped down the road, trailing dust.

The satellites I launched earlier have detected the telltale magnetic and neutrino surges of ships coming out of hyper-L. I note the formation of magnetic vortices and the materialization in normal space of large number of vessels, thirty-two within the first five seconds, with more appearing all the time, their exit point located less than 1.7 million kilometers from Muir. They are decelerating rapidly on a vector that will bring them into planetary orbit within the next forty minutes.

Though they are still at extreme range, drive characteristics, magnetic and IR signatures, and neutrino emissions are all within the general parameters established by my Commander's observations at Wide Sky. At this point, probability that these are Malach ships and hostile stands at 93.65 percent.

I continue to observe their approach.

The Sh'whiss probe crouched in the shadows at the forest's edge, watching the scene in the disordered habitat area below with a machine's implacable and unruffled calm.

After several local days of lurking in the nearby forest, it had been drawn to this site by the presence of the large machine excavating a rectangular pit in the soft ground above the lake.

The probe could draw no distinction whatever between civilian and military activity. In fact, the idea of a specific military would have struck any Malach female as strange, since that would assume there could be such a thing as a civilian. There were noncombatants in Malach society, certainly—warriors who'd grown too old to serve, or who'd been crippled by wounds, or who'd dishonored themselves by some breach of regulation or custom and been forbidden to enjoy the honors and joys of either combat or procreation—but the main division in Malach society was between the warriors who ran with the hunter packs and the ordinary foot soldiers.

Such matters were beyond the probe's limited awareness and reasoning power, but there was no question, so far as its processors were concerned, that the huge vehicle laboring in the pit just over one *t'charucht* distant was a weapon of war.

The probe had not been given information about the powerful enemy combat vehicle on Lach'br'zghis, but it knew that this machine in front of it represented a significant threat to the incoming Malach fleet.

A hatch opened and an antennae unfolding, pivoting to bear on the incoming Malach fleet.

Pulse transmission of all available data required nearly .24 *quesh.*

I detect a pulse of modulated EM radiation of .0864 second's duration, originating on a bearing of 047 degrees at a range of approximately four kilometers. Though the burst is key-encoded and tightly beamed, radio frequency leakage gives me the position with a general accuracy of plus or minus 150 meters. Signal strength suggests a military unit; details of phasing, harmonics, and code structure all are unfamiliar to me, though they show a distinct family similarity to signals recorded during the fighting on Wide Sky.

I accept this as confirmation that the scout on the planet's surface is of Malach origins, and the probability that the incoming fleet is also Malach rises to 98.87 percent.

This is not, unfortunately, enough to allow me to drop my current set of ROEs regarding hostile contact.

My immediate course of action, however, is clear. I must investigate the source of RF interference and, if possible, confirm that it is a Malach scout. Backing out of the foundation I am digging for the refugee barracks, I pivot sharply to the northeast and engage my track drives. If I move swiftly enough, I may be able to surprise the scout and force it to initiate hostilities.

And this, of course, would allow me to kill or disable the scout, as provided for by Rule of Engagement One.

❖   ❖   ❖

"Where the hell is he going?" Alexie cried. They'd been within a kilometer or so of the Bolo when the huge machine had suddenly backed out of the hole, turned abruptly, and raced toward the northeast, leaving a high-flung cloud of dust behind it.

Donal already had his communicator out and was questioning the Bolo. "Bolo 96876 of the Line! *Freddy*! What are you doing?"

"I am investigating presumed hostile forces, Commander," the Bolo's voice came back. Alexie had to strain to hear the words above the speeder's whine. "The source of the RF interference is confirmed within four kilometers of my position."

"Okay, Freddy," Donal replied. "Go get 'em!" He turned to Alexie. "Let me off here."

She braked the vehicle to a halt, lowering it on dwindling repulsors until it crunched gently into the gravel below. "What do you want me to do?"

Donal glanced skyward, then looked her in the eyes. "Alexie, if that recon unit is that close, it could mean the Malach are targeting this area for a landing, and that means things are going to get pretty hot around here. When Freddy opens up with his Hellbore . . . well, I think you'd better try getting the children away from here before he does. Fast!"

"Donal! There're fifty thousand people here! Most of them kids!"

"Damn, it Alexie, I don't know what else to tell you!" His eyes looked haunted, and a little wild. "Get your group leaders and adults organized, and have them start leading the kids out. You have complete authority to requisition those transports over there by the lake, and I'll call Kinkaid and see if they can send some more out here. If you have to, start moving them out by foot."

"Which way?"

He clambered out of the speedster, then turned, leaning

against the vehicle's body. "Southwest. Around the curve of the lake, and then south. Quickly, now!"

"Any particular destination? Or are we just supposed to wander about in the wilderness for forty years?"

He didn't seem to catch the joke. "Just get *away*! Now!"

She realized then that Donal was feeling a deep and genuine horror . . . and suddenly she felt that horror herself, as she followed his chain of thoughts. "The Malach! You think they're going to attack us *here*?"

"It's possible."

"But the camp . . . They're just *kids*!"

"We already know the Malach don't make distinctions like that. Not for humans, anyway. You've got to get the kids out, Alexie. Before the Malach show up in force!"

"Okay!" she said. She took a deep breath. "Be careful!"

"You too!"

She nodded and powered up her repulsors again, spinning the little speedster in a quick one-eighty, and hitting the accelerator.

Joni, Magda, and Clem ought to be at the ramshackle shelter they'd jokingly named City Hall now. She would start with them.

Only now was the realization sinking in: that wild look in Donal's eye had been fear . . . fear for the children, fear for her.

The fact that Donal could be afraid of anything made her afraid as well.

A sharp, staccato cracking sounded in the distance behind her. She didn't slow to have a look but pressed the accelerator pedal even harder.

She just hoped she would be in time.

I am closing with the probable Enemy scout and am detecting magnetic, infrared, motion, and seismic anomalies now, all consistent with a sizable machine of approximately five metric tons' mass moving behind the treeline of the forest ahead at a range of approximately thirty-two meters. I intend to immobilize and capture the machine if possible but am aware that this may prove difficult. A robotic probe will most likely possess a self-destruct mechanism for just that possibility, while a manned scout will probably attempt to fight or flee, necessitating its destruction to prevent its escape.

But I need to obtain a visual lock on the object in order to procure a full and informative ID.

Movement flickers in the trees ahead, moving down an embankment in the general direction of the lake. The shoreline of the lake comes up to the edge of the forest here, and it is possible that the scout hopes to use the water as cover for its escape.

I elect to broadcast a warning message to the target. Normally, I would consider this foolish, but ROE 17 states explicitly that unknown targets are to be challenged verbally before engaging them. I experience a .132-second delay as I attempt to resolve a potential conflict in the ROE overrides: ROE 1 specifically states that I may not engage the enemy unless I am fired upon first, while ROE 17 specifically states that I must challenge the target before engaging it.

As Alexie and the speeder raced back toward the camp, Donal trotted forward, topping a low rise. Ahead and to his right, Lake Simms sparkled in the sunlight. Ahead and to the left, hills rolled away toward the north, each ridgeline higher than the last, each thickly clad with the yellow-green to emerald-green vegetation that grew on Muir . . . jeweltrees and sucklewort, for the most part, with a scattering of native species that Donal didn't recognize. Freddy was squatting right at the point where woods met lake, two hundred meters away.

"Attention, intruder!" Freddy's voder-voice boomed, and the echo floated back from the more distant hillsides. "Advance and identify yourself!"

Donal groaned. Those damned ROEs were making the big machine vulnerable. He grabbed his communicator, switching it to the Bolo command frequency. "Freddy! This is Ragnor! Do you copy?"

"I copy, Commander."

"Freddy, can that crap! I say again, Freddy, can that crap!"

There was a brief pause. "ROE instructions deleted, Commander."

Was it Donal's imagination, or did he sense a new fire, a joy in the huge fighting machine's electronic voice?

The hampering, entangling Rules of Engagement fall away, and at the same instant, with the threat of Enemy action imminent, my awareness shifts to full Battle Reflex Mode. Within .024 second, I am suffused with a surging hyperawareness of my surroundings, a sensation that is new each time I engage it, since I am programmed to forget the sensation each time I drop to a lower awareness level.

For now, however, I feel as though I am a different being, filled with knowledge of myself, of my surroundings, and with a sense of purpose and duty that makes my half-aware state a bare, waking shadow of the reality.

The promise of combat, of grappling with the enemy, sings in my circuits. This is why I am here, why I was assembled, to protect the people of Muir from the Malach threat, to blunt the Enemy assault with every means at my disposal.

I hope I am worthy of this trust.

The Malach probe did not understand the commands broadcast on audio frequencies and would not have obeyed them if it had. It recognized the fact, however, that it was trapped.

In a sense, the probe had its own set of ROEs. When

trapped, with no way out and faced with the certainty of capture or destruction, there was only one action it could take.

It attacked.

The target is changing direction suddenly, moving toward my position and emerging from the trees. It is a robotic machine of unfamiliar design, a complex but compact body suspended on a universal swivel mount from six slender legs. A laser mounted on the side of its body fires—I estimate the weapon to be in the three-megajoule range—but the energy is easily dissipated by the ablative layer of my glacis armor.

I sense, however, that the laser is intended more to distract me or to lull me into a sense of complacency regarding the machine's abilities. A powerful magnetic field is building within the body of the device, as though enormous powers are gathering. . . .

I return fire .003 second after its initial shot, seeking to cripple the Enemy mechanism by targeting the joint to which the legs are affixed. Ion bolts rip through the lightly armored motivaters and power couplings, shattering the delicate mechanism in a shower of sparks and flashing bursts of energy.

The body of the device drops to the ground, then explodes in a searing blast in the fractional kiloton range, toppling several trees and flinging bits of metal that ping off my forward armor.

At a range of less than twenty meters, the blast sends a shock wave smashing across my outer hull like a brief, furious hurricane.

CHAPTER TWENTY-ONE

I turn my full attention now on the Enemy fleet, which still is approaching Muir rapidly. I have relayed warnings to the Military Authority Headquarters in Kinkaid but am skeptical that they will be able to field any force powerful enough to slow the oncoming ships. I have also initiated a combat link between myself and Bolo 96875 of the Line. My brother unit tells me that he has left the depot area and is now deploying toward a point from which he can maintain a close watch over all approaches to the Kinkaid and Kinkaid Starport areas. We believe there is a significant chance, with a probability in excess of forty percent, that the Enemy will attempt to seize the starport in order to deploy his landing forces more swiftly.

His ROEs are still in effect and will be until our Commander specifically gives him the code phrase.

Several of the ships are close enough now that my EW satellites can distinguish general shape and hull features, confirming that these are, indeed, Malach ships, identical to several classes recorded at Wide Sky.

Particle beams lash out, touching my satellites, my remote eyes in orbit. No matter. I needed them as early warning sensors and to expand my sensor envelope in

*near-Muir space, but my ground-based sensors provide
an adequate view of the enemy fleet.*

*They appear to be deploying for a direct assault on
the planet. They will almost certainly commence with
bombardment from space.*

Donal had been running across open ground toward
the Bolo when the firefight at the edge of the trees started.
It had been over almost before it had begun—a brief set
of flashes as Freddy's ion cannons had discharged, followed
an instant later by a ground-shuddering concussion that
tripped him as he ran and sent him sprawling on hands
and knees.

The detonation sent a mushrooming, roiling pillar of
smoke and dust thundering into the sky, washing across
Freddy like a wave, the blast effect skittering out across
the waters of the lake in a fast-expanding circle.

Robot probe, Donal thought, squinting into the sudden
gust of dust-laden wind. *With a self-destruct command.*
Had it damaged Freddy?

Rising unsteadily to his feet, he was about to try to
raise Freddy on his communicator when something caught
his attention, a flicker of light, a movement, something
from almost directly overhead. He glanced up . . . and
in the next instant he was flying through the air, smacked
over by a titanic shock wave.

Blue fire, like the unchained heart of an exploding
star, flicked down out of the sky, a radiant pencil of
intolerable brilliance. . . .

To Donal, it was as though the sky had just cracked
open, disgorging the light of a sun. The bolt—he was
pretty sure it was a plasma discharge of some kind,
something like a Hellbore, in fact—burned down from
the zenith and struck the waters of the lake a few meters
to the right of Freddy's position.

Thunder exploded, a deafening roar, as the beam slowly

tracked toward the shore. At its touch, water exploded in steam, a geyser a hundred meters tall of spray and superheated vapor that cascaded across the surface of the lake in lazy slow-motion. When the beam swept onto the shore of the lake, it furrowed the ground, mud and topsoil dissolving in temperatures normally found on the surface of a star, converting into white-hot plasma in a flash. Within the space of a second or so, though it seemed much longer, the beam flicked toward Freddy. . . .

But Freddy was no longer in the same spot. At the first stab of blinding light, Freddy had engaged his drive and was now hurtling across the landscape at speeds in excess of 130 kilometers per hour. He plunged ahead into the forest, sending trees toppling left and right.

Donal was mildly surprised to find himself flat on his belly, hugging the loam as if trying to become a small and insignificant part of the ground. He didn't remember diving for cover or getting knocked down a second time, didn't even remember hitting the ground, but so long as he was here, it seemed like a good place to be. He could feel the earth shudder beneath his body, feel the palpable shocks in the air as the beam continued to dump gigajoules of energy into the planet's atmosphere.

The beam winked off after approximately two seconds, leaving a zigzag scar in the earth a meter deep and a meter wide, its bottom and sides still glowing a mottled orange, like the crusty surface of molten lava. Where the trench emerged from the lake, water continued to pour in and vanish in boiling, churning clouds of swirling white steam. In the sky overhead, clear a moment ago, clouds were forming and breaking up with a time-lapse camera's sense of hurried unreality. Some dazed portion of his mind provided explanation: water vapor jolted out of suspension in the atmosphere by the passage of that beam was being made briefly visible as a ragged whirlpool of rapidly condensing cloud.

The Bolo emerged from the forest, still moving at high speed, his upper works festooned with shredded vegetation. Rock and great, smoking clods of earth sprayed back from his fast-spinning tracks, and when he slewed suddenly, changing course in a seemingly random manner, he scraped up a divot that would have covered most of the playing surface of a football field, sending most of the loose earth and pulped vegetation out in a soaring, rooster's-tail of debris. Freddy's strategy was obvious—and sound. The nearest enemy ship must be a sizable fraction of a light second away; if they were targeting Freddy specifically, their view of his current location would lag that much of a second behind reality. If he moved, and especially if he moved randomly, they were going to have one hell of a time nailing him from space.

Donal pulled his legs under him, got to his feet, and started running. His knees felt weak, almost trembling, but he kept going, pulling out his communicator and clicking the transmit switch. "Freddy! This is Donal! Do you copy?"

"I copy, Commander," Freddy's voice came back calm, quiet, and collected as always. It was difficult, in fact, to associate that civilized, conversational voice with the enormous machine that was currently slewing about in a cloud of dust two hundred meters away, reducing a field to bare rock and steel-scraped raw earth in the process.

"I need to get aboard, Freddy. Can you pick me up?"

"I have you in sight, Commander. Maintain your current heading and speed. I will pass in front of you in twenty-three seconds, affording you an opportunity to come aboard."

"Right!"

He kept running. Freddy veered suddenly into a straight-line run toward the mountains, holding course for so long that Donal thought something was wrong, that he was deliberately tempting one of the Malach ships to pick him off, or that he'd forgotten his human companion and was running for the cover of the trees. Suddenly, though, Freddy threw both port-side tracks into full reverse, spinning like a grotesquely outsized top, and hurtling almost directly toward Donal. An instant later, the heavens opened again, a blue-white lance of sun-fire howling out of the zenith and striking a point behind the oncoming Bolo, at just about the point where Freddy would have been had he maintained that straight-line vector for much longer.

Thunder rolled again, the shock wave staggering Donal like a blow to the gut. He nearly stumbled and fell, but this time he kept his feet and kept moving. The Bolo moved toward him, a hurtling juggernaut, its broad, cleated tracks blurred by motion and by the cascade of dirt and dust flying from their whirling surfaces. At the last possible moment, it swung sharply to Donal's left, spraying him with hard-flung dirt and gravel.

Half blinded, he kept running, turning now to follow the big machine as it freight-trained past him. The belly cleared the ground by a good meter and a half, too high for him to simply step up and scramble aboard while the Bolo was moving. In the rear, however, between the massive sets of rear tracks, the outer hatch swung down, a ramp trailing behind in the dirt, while the inner access hatch dilated open.

For a moment, Donal thought the Bolo had miscalculated and was pulling away from him again, but as he began running harder, the Bolo slowed, ever so slightly, and he was able to leap onto the dragging ramp, grab the handholds to either side, and haul himself into the big machine's central access corridor.

The outer ramp whined as it closed up, and the inner hatch twisted shut. Donal slumped on the passageway deck for a moment, panting heavily. He'd not done this much exercise in a long time, he reflected, and it might be time to start thinking about some sort of regular work-out routine.

Otherwise, the next time this happened, he was going to be left panting in the dust.

"You'll find a better view of the battle if you come forward to the fighting compartment, Commander," Freddy's voice said from an overhead speaker.

"Yeah, yeah, I'm coming," he replied. "Just had to catch my breath."

"Are you injured, Commander?"

"Just my pride, Freddy. I'm getting too old for this sort of thing."

Pulling himself upright, he began making his way forward, bracing himself against the buck and sway of the vehicle as it kept moving.

With my Commander aboard, I feel new confidence. Together, we will be able to stop this threat to the planet, breaking the Malach attack before they can even get their troops down to the planet. I continue to study the developing tactical situation in space near the planet.

Eight of the Enemy ships, I note, are far larger than the others, and one of those is truly enormous, well over a kilometer long from prow to tail and possessing the mass of a small planetoid. I deduce that the largest vessel is the command vessel attacked by Commander Ross. Unfortunately, it is taking up an extremely distant orbit, nearly a million kilometers out from Muir, and it is well out of range. One of the other large vessels, however, almost certainly a supply ship and troop carrier of some kind, has ventured to within a quarter million kilometers. I engage my targeting radar and feel the thrill of a solid lock. My main turret pivots, the 90cm Hellbore elevating. Computing the target's velocity, I lead slightly with my aim in order to compensate for the time lag to target, and fire.

The searing, blue-white lightning bolt of the Hellbore fire stabs upward into the sky, ionizing the air as it passes, blasting a vacuum along its trail that fills instantly with a sensor-deadening peal of thunder. The target is point eight three three light seconds away. The Hellbore bolt travels at seventy percent of the speed of light. One point one nine seconds after firing, the bolt strikes the Enemy vessel amidships . . . though it is, of course, another point eight second before I can confirm the fact visually, through an extreme magnification that shows the hit in exquisite detail. The beam slashes through armor plating, carving deep into the ship's vitals and releasing a silent explosion of atmosphere, the cloud made visible as water droplets freeze instantly into particles of ice.

The Enemy vessel is yawing heavily to port, propelled by the gush of atmosphere from its starboard side. I recompute the firing angle and trigger a second burst. It has been noted that Hellbores are the equivalent in power, range, and accuracy of any naval-mounted gun, and the effect of the second shot bears that assessment out. Striking just behind and below the jagged, molten, orange-white line drawn by the first bolt, the second hits the ship's primary power plant, which explodes with a satisfying coruscation of strobing flashes and internal detonations, visible through the fragmenting hull. Every light on the ship winks out, and the huge Malach vessel is now illuminated only by the glow of partly melted hull metal, and by the fires raging inside as air escapes through rents with hurricane force.

The first target clearly crippled and adrift in space, I shift aim to a second, smaller vessel, a lean, dagger of a ship roughly equivalent in length and mass to a Concordiat light destroyer. I note the loosing of another Hellbore from a point one hundred twenty-eight point two

*kilometers to my south-southwest and know that Bolo
96875 has just joined the unequal fight. His shot strikes
a Malach frigate and nearly cuts the hapless vessel in
two. My shot hits the destroyer close by the bridge tower,
shearing off a sponson-mounted laser turret and gouging
a deep, molten crater in the vessel's spine. Frozen
atmosphere and boiling metal, mingled with fragments
of hull plating, internal structure, and kicking, six-limbed
bodies, seethe into space.*

So far, the battle is going remarkably well.

Aghrracht the Swift-Slayer, Supreme Deathgiver of
the Fleet, raised one wickedly curved foreclaw in warning.
"Destroy that vehicle!"

Cha'Zhanaach's command center, large, circular, and
comfortably unenclosed, was filled with Malach pack-
members, their mingled scents reassuring in their
closeness, warmth, and numbers. She looked down into
a large screen, on which the scaly green and red visage
of the Deathgiver of the bombardment vessel *A'chk'cha*
was displayed.

A'chk'cha's captain raised her head, exposing her throat
in proper submissive form, though that throat was in fact
a half-million kilometers away from Aghrracht's claw.
"Deathgiver! The target is too fast to target from this
range! The speed-of-light time delay means that we're
shooting where the target *was*, not where it is *now*."

Aghrracht suppressed an instinctive, rising shriek of
bloodlust rage at the underling's noncompliance. The
Malach warrior was correct. She could order all ships
to move in closer, of course, but losses—already higher
than expected with the surprisingly effective and deadly
plasma gun fire from the surface—were certain to be
serious.

There was another way.

"Forget the combat machine," she said. "All packs!

Fire at targets of opportunity, anywhere on the planet! Fire on the cities!"

"Yes, Deathgiver!" chorused the commanders of each of her ships. What could not be brought down by precise gunfire might well be toppled by simple, sheer terror.

"Use cloud cloaking to shield the approach of our assault boats!" she continued. "*Now!* Quickly, before the prey escapes!"

A world lay just within the grasp of her claws. . . .

Flame erupted from the refugee camp, a pillar of white light and roiling black smoke. "Oh, God, no . . ." Donal said, not believing what he was seeing. The Malach were firing randomly into the tent city.

"Starwasps are launching from Kinkaid Spaceport," Freddy announced. "Three squadrons, a total of thirty-six craft."

"Not enough, Freddy. Not enough by a factor of ten."

"Agreed, Commander. This world does not possess sufficient firepower to stop the Malach invasion fleet."

"Not even you and Ferdy?"

"Negative. We have destroyed three enemy ships so far, with four more kills probable. The enemy fire incoming now is probably intended to suppress surface batteries, and defensive units such as my brother and me. We are detecting large areas of intense radar interference, localized but spreading, positioned between Muir and the Enemy fleet. This suggests that they are launching assault boats and are attempting to screen them from our fire."

"Assault boats, huh?"

"We will, of course, attempt to destroy all Malach craft either before they reach atmosphere or while they are transiting the atmosphere. I should warn you, however, that it is exceedingly unlikely that we will be able to stop more than a small percentage of them. Malach tactics at Wide Sky were to launch large numbers of individual fliers. We will not have time to target all of them before the majority have made it safely to the ground."

"Well, do your best. Every one we nail out there is one less to deal with down here."

"That is self-evident." There was a pause. "Unit 96875 has destroyed another Malach vessel, one of approximately frigate size and mass."

"Good for him!"

"He is also engaging what may be Enemy landing or close-assault boats. The situation, I fear, is critical. Our survival in this battle depends on our destroying as many Malach landing craft as possible while they are still in space. But we cannot get them all."

"We'll do the best we can, Freddy," he told the Bolo. "If we go down, it's going to be while we're fighting."

"Affirmative, Commander." The Bolo fired its main battery once more, replying to nuclear fire with nuclear fire.

Alexie had just arrived at Town Hall and called together her chief aides when a crack of thunder rent the air, the shock wave slamming against the rickety sides of the prefab shelter and nearly knocking it over. Ears ringing, Alexie made her way to the transparency in one wall that served as a window and gasped as she saw the pillar of black smoke rising from the center of the tent city. "They're firing on the refugees!" she cried. "They're firing on us! Come on! We've got to get the kids out of here!"

They raced outside, into the chaos of screaming, squalling kids and wide-eyed adults trembling at the edge of panic. Fortunately, a good many of the other monitors had had the same idea as she had and were already herding their charges out of their tents and shelters and moving them west . . . west because it was clear that a pitched battle was being waged to the east, there were mountains and forest to the north, and Lake Simms itself blocked the way south. Using her personal communicator, she was able to make certain that everyone was on the move . . . and that the big government ground transports were coming around to the east side of the city to take on as many of the young, sick, and injured as they could.

Another beam fell out of the heavens, but this one appeared to be aimed at one of the big Conestogas moored out in the lake. Seconds after she saw the towering white plume of spray rise from behind the farthest ship, she heard the thunder, a crack and drawn-out rumble like the first bolt of a spring storm. The beam shimmered and wavered in the sudden, swirling haze of water vapor coming off the lake. An instant later, the beam carved into the space transport, punching clear through the thin hull and savaging the internal systems. Explosions racked the transport's interior; even from here, on shore, Alexie could see the dazzling flashes as power cells and instrumentation inside the big vessel exploded.

The beam winked out, then reappeared almost immediately. Clouds were swirling now above the docking area as the Malach concentrated their fire on the moored ships. It was insane . . . utterly senseless, but Alexie was glad of it. If those blood-thirsty lizards wanted to concentrate their fire on empty space transports while she got a few more of the kids out of the tent city, so much the better. Possibly the Malach were trying to prevent another escape; more likely they feared that the three transports were armed. Either way, they were wasting valuable time and energy in gutting the ships, while the population of Simmstown made good their escape.

A ground transport rumbled up, a behemoth nearly as big as Donal's Bolos with an articulated body and four sets of tracks. It was, in fact, a ConcordiArms Model C heavy transporter, a direct offshoot of Bolo technology. Envisioned as a carry-all for supplies and personnel in remote, frontier areas, it was several centuries obsolete now.

And Alexie was damned glad to see it.

A young-looking militia lieutenant appeared in an open side cargo loading entryway. "You called for a taxi, ma'am?"

"We certainly did! How many can you take?"

"Pack 'em in!" he called back. Turning, he pushed a button on the bulkhead next to the doorway, and a ramp extended from the vehicle's side all the way to the ground. "We can probably take two, maybe three hundred if they don't mind being friendly."

Three hundred. A pittance out of fifty thousand. But she was glad right now for any help she could get. And there were plenty of other transporters. She could hear their grumbling now as their drivers fired up their power plants and engaged their tracks. Hell, at this rate, they only needed another 165 transports to get everybody out.

The hell with that kind of thinking! Somehow, they would do this. *Somehow*.

Snapping off orders with the rapid-fire crispness of a machine gun, she soon had the youngest kids filing aboard, with one adult going along with every forty children. Others filed in with stretchers, taking aboard those who were sick or who'd been wounded in that vicious attack on the tent city. In all, they managed to squeeze 385 aboard, before the lieutenant signaled enough and pulled in the ramp.

As the transporter rumbled off toward the west, Alexie turned to see what else she could do. There was trouble, an aide had told her over her communicator a moment before, at Block 328, at the western edge of the camp.

She climbed into her speedster and switched it on, heading toward the west as fast as she could manage through the crowds. Another bolt of manufactured lightning fell from the sky, striking in the camp to the north.

CHAPTER TWENTY-TWO

The battle continues, but I can sense the shifting of the initiative from our defense to the Enemy's offense. The Enemy has dispatched an estimated 344 landing craft, approximately equivalent in mass, size, and maneuvering capabilities to a Concordiat Saber-class assault boat. Judging by analogy with known assault boat models, any one of the approaching craft could carry as many as a thousand troops, or a single Bolo . . . or between thirty and thirty-six of the characteristic Malach walkers—I conjecture, given their predilection for the number eight, that this number would be thirty-two.

Also detected are some thousands of smaller objects, of about the size and mass of a standard escape/survival pod. These, I believe, may be individual Malach walkers enclosed in atmospheric-entry vehicles of some kind. The records from Wide Sky suggest that many of the Enemy forces there landed as single units, descending over a wide area for landing, then joining together into teams of eight.

Exact numbers, however, are impossible to ascertain. The Enemy has also initiated the dispersal of large, expanding clouds of chaff, radar-reflective material that masks his deployment. More and more of the Enemy's vessels, both his capital ships and his landing and assault craft, are vanishing behind the homogenous and featureless fuzz of his chaff fields. I continue firing at available targets as long as I can, but before long my targets are limited only to those smaller vessels that have approached Muir more closely than the closest chaff clouds. Many of these— perhaps most—are obviously decoys, launched ahead of the main body to draw my fire.

I worry about what might be developing behind the fast-spreading clouds of chaff.

Donal had to find a way to block the enemy bombardment. At first glance, there wasn't a lot he could do about it, but the brief appearance of clouds above Freddy during his duel with the enemy ships had given rise to an idea.

He tried to think through the physics of the thing. A Bolo's Hellbore was a plasma-fusion weapon. A tiny sliver of frozen hydrogen, encased deep within a coolant sleeve with a fusion igniter and a steel accelerator jacket, was loaded automatically into the breech of the main weapon. When the Bolo fired the main battery, powerful mag accelerator coils in the walls of the gun tube snatched the jacket and hurled the casing toward the muzzle. Ten gigajoule lasers mounted inside the bore fired an instant before the igniter, evacuating the tube and clearing a path through the atmosphere to reduce drag and friction-induced "bloom."

Even before the projectile had reached the end of the tube, however, the igniter induced the temperatures and pressures necessary to trigger a small, thermonuclear conversion. The magfields accelerating the casing also served to contain and compress the fusing plasma, partly to focus it, mostly to keep the barrel of the Hellbore— not to mention most of the Bolo's main turret—from dissolving in the heat. By the time the Hellbore shot left the weapon's muzzle fifty nanoseconds after ignition, all of the original matter, hydrogen, sleeve, and all, had been reduced to a bolt of plasma with a core temperature of several million degrees Kelvin, traveling down range at a speed of seventy percent of the speed of light. Even though the mass of the original projectile amounted to just a few grams, the recoil—despite enormous recoil dampers and suppressers in the Bolo's turret mount assembly—was sufficient to rock the fourteen-thousand-ton behemoth with a hull-ringing thump.

The key point of the equation, however, was *energy*. A Mark XXIV Bolo employed the majority of the output of three Class VII fusion plants to manufacture the energy necessary to accelerate a few grams to low-relativistic speeds, and much of that energy entered the surrounding atmosphere as heat, which bled away from the accelerating projectile despite the near-vacuum created by the lasers. The lasers, too, added their quota of heat, as did the fiercely radiating bolt of the plasma lance itself. Firing a Hellbore was not unlike flinging a tiny piece dredged from a sun's core at near-light speeds; in the vicinity of a battle, the air temperature climbed, and quickly.

And all the while Freddy had been discharging his Hellbore, enemy plasma bolts had been falling across a broad area of the planet, their impacts more or less random but the energy of each greater than that of a single Hellbore shot. Analysis of the Malach weapons suggested that they were similar to human Hellbores, using more hydrogen to achieve higher temperatures, but with a much lower velocity. They somehow used magnetics to create true plasma beams lasting as much as two seconds. And each two-second shot dumped a very great deal of heat into the atmosphere.

Donal glanced at the readout showing the external environmental conditions. The local temperature was 31 degrees Celsius . . . a rise of nearly 12 degrees over the past twenty minutes. Barometric pressure . . . nearly 1.125

bar, and normal for Muir was closer to .95. The area around Lake Simms was in the center of an extreme high-pressure system as rapidly warming air expanded in a huge bubble hugging the planet.

Expanding air meant dropping vapor pressure. The air was becoming *dry*. "Freddy?"

"Yes, Commander?"

"Break off the action. I have a new target for you."

"Awaiting new targeting instructions."

"Aim at the lake. Five or six klicks out from the shore. Open fire at the water. Continue firing until I tell you otherwise."

Donal heard the turret whine as it pivoted somewhere meters above his head. On the main, circular viewing screen, the crosshair reticle indicating the Hellbore's aim point shifted right, coming to rest on the blue waters of the lake, with range figures alongside indicating a target lock at a range of 5.74 kilometers.

"Target lock," Freddy said. "Firing."

The fighting compartment rocked with the recoil.

Aghrracht Swift-Slayer turned at the report given by one of her aides. "The enemy war vehicle is doing *what*?"

"Firing deliberately and repeatedly into the lake, Deathgiver. We cannot ascertain why."

Aghrracht considered the matter. No units were on the planet as yet—the nearest were still over a *quor* from touching down—so the human war machine couldn't be firing at Malach forces. Besides, Malach rarely considered large bodies of water as anything more than an obstacle to combat. After millennia of mining and heavy industrial exploitation on Zhanaach, the planet's shallow seas were lifeless; worse, they tended to dissolve metal hulls, and quickly. Malach did not think in terms of moving on or under water, but only over or around, so the enemy machine's actions were puzzling.

"There must be some problem with it," Aghrracht decided at last. "If it is robotic, like the one we destroyed on Lach'br'zghis, there may be a fault in its circuitry or programming."

"A near hit by one of our plasma beams, perhaps," the aide suggested.

"A possibility . . . though it seems unlikely that such well-constructed machines would be so vulnerable to near hits." Her feeding tendrils rippled as she thought. "Continue the bombardment. The machine continues its random maneuverings?"

"It does, Deathgiver. It is not possible to target it at this range."

"Continue trying nonetheless. It may make a contrasurvival mistake. Or Sha'gnaasht may bless us with survivor's luck. In any case, I don't trust it. This may be a *nagashni's* ruse."

The *nagashni* was a small, mucus-covered predator on Zhanaach, recently extinct, that would play dead until carrion fliers began approaching, attracted by its deathlike odor. When one of the big, winged creatures was about to alight on what it thought was a putrescently decaying body, one of the creature's legs, longer and more muscular than the other five, shot out with tremendous force, impaling the flier on a three-*taych*-long claw.

"Kill and eat, Deathgiver!" the aide said in salute.

"Kill and eat." But the response was automatic, the Deathgiver's thoughts still on the enemy machine's strange actions. *You fight well, machine,* she thought. *As well as a Malach warrior, perhaps, in the accuracy of your fire and your willingness to engage against large odds. How cunning are you, in fact?*

The next few *quor* ought to provide the answer.

Bolt after white-hot bolt flashed into the lake, striking and extinguishing in savagely geysering fountains of steam and spray. Already, the shoreline of the lake, a full five and a half klicks from the target area, was growing hazy behind the gentle fall of a fine, hot mist, and the bolts were rendered starkly visible by the trails they carved through the wet air.

Each shot dumped gigajoules of energy, most of it as heat, into the water and the air above it. Tons of water had already been boiled away, turned to steam that rose swiftly above the tormented surface of the lake. Tons more were suspended as a fine mist in the atmosphere; as the air temperature rose, however, the warming air rose, carrying the water droplets with it.

From his vantage point inside Freddy, Donal activated a viewscreen that gave a view of the sky above the battlefield. Clouds were growing there, ragged tatters of white vapor that expanded, minute by minute, lumping together into a larger, high-piled mass of fleecy white visibly twisted by the high pressure system into a clockwise spiral.

Plasma bolts continued to fall from the zenith, fired by the Malach ships still positioned eight-tenths of a light second beyond Muir's atmosphere, but the strikes were growing more and more infrequent. Already, McNair—Muir's intensely bright, white sun—was fading somewhat behind a high, thin layer of gathering haze; in another few minutes, an arm of the growing cloud layer drifted between the ground and the sun. In minutes more, the haze had thickened into overcast and the crystalline blue sky had become a leaden gray. In the distance, over the mountains to the north, over the ocean to the west, sunlight still gleamed from a clear, blue sky, but the tent city was now almost completely masked by clouds.

The Malach gunners were firing blind now.

"We can still track the giant combat vehicle with radar," the gunnery officer on Aghrracht's screen reported. "But it continues to move erratically and we cannot target it from this distance. The strange collection of shelters at that site does not offer a solid lock, however, and we have had to break off firing at it. The ships in the lake have been hit several times and we have lost our locks on them. They may have sunk, or their returns may be lost in the reflections from the water. It is difficult to distinguish targets at this range."

"Then shift to other targets," Aghrracht said. "The large city in the south, close to the spaceport, is not cloud-covered."

The officer raised her chin on the screen, exposing her throat in submission. "The hunting is good, Deathgiver." Her image faded from the screen, replaced a moment later by a long-range view of the planet. The cloud cover over the target area was thickening and growing, moment by moment.

Aghrracht considered this. Clouds alone could not shield the planet's surface from plasma bolts, but they could block optical observation of the target area, and they could block the laser beams used to guide the plasma bolts to the target and prevent bloom when they struck dense atmosphere. Beings who could control the weather in this manner, who could summon a shield of clouds at such short notice, were beings to be respected.

She thought again of the machine firing repeatedly into the waters of the lake. Had that been how they did this? Vaporize water and the vapor would rise with the rising column of hot air. When that vapor hit a layer of colder air at high altitude . . .

Yes. These humans were worthy of respect indeed, clever in battle.

Their defeat would glorify them, as well as the clan of Aghrracht.

"Second!" she snapped.

Zhallet'llesch Scent Finder hurried to Aghrracht's side, lifting her chin in salute. "Here, Deathgiver!"

"We will transfer our operations to the planet's surface."

Zhallet'llesch's feeding tendrils twitched confusion. "But . . . we do not yet have a secure claw's grasp on the planet, Deathgiver. It will be almost a *quor* before our first units land."

"And you and I can do nothing from this perch," Aghrracht replied. She gestured at her screen. "We can see nothing, and time delay makes targeting next to useless. We should be on the surface, directing the attack from close at hand."

"It will be done, Deathgiver."

The tip of Aghrracht's tail twitched with a decisive flutter, an indication of determination and will.

"Prepare the command shuttle for immediate launch. Kill and eat!"

She would face the humans herself, on their own ground, fang and claw against fang and claw. . . .

Schaagrasch the Blood-Taster found herself once again entrapped in the narrow, stinking confines of her Hunter, hurtling toward an alien and unknown world. The intelligence briefing had suggested that this time the enemy would be expecting them; a robot probe inserted onto the surface had recorded and transmitted mechanized forces digging some sort of defensive position on the smaller of the two major north continents, close by the body of water where the escaped enemy ships had landed.

Use your fear. . . .

She felt the entry capsule bump and shudder, subjected to the searing temperatures and unimaginable stresses of high-speed atmospheric entry. She squeezed her eyes shut, then opened them again. Both hearts were pounding in a staggered, jackhammer beat, one behind the complex four-jointed shoulder girdle in her upper torso, the other farther down, a muffled throb just above her hips. *Not much longer. Hold tight with all six . . . and direct your fear into slashing, blood-spilling hatred of the enemy!*

This time, the Deathgivers had ordered a far more massive assault, one designed to crush the prey's resistance from the start and guarantee immediate superiority.

Why do I keep doing this to myself? Schaagrasch thought with a hot-blooded, single-minded intensity. *I hate being alone, I hate being shut in. Maybe it's time to celebrate the Final Kill, then return to Zhanaach where I can care for males or pre-warrior young. I would prefer the young, of course. I've never cared for animals, save as prey to be hunted. . . .*

But of course, she wasn't old enough for that yet, not while she could still mate. She'd had a most satisfying round of sex with an eager and quick-witted little male just two quach ago. She didn't think the union had taken, but that didn't matter. It was the spirituality of the act that counted. Her *Kaa'la'schgha*—her Assurance Mating—had produced a viable embryo which she'd implanted in a host brooder on Zhanaach just before she embarked on this expedition. If she died in battle, she was assured of progeny, the highest honor she could hope to attain; only if she disgraced herself with cowardice or stupidity or some other antisurvival trait would her offspring be eaten by the Guardian Priests of Sha'gnaasht as they emerged still bloody from the brooder's carcass.

Schaagrasch let that thought steady her. She had to cling to the reality of the moment. Fear was acceptable, if she could turn it to evolutionary advantage, drawing strength and ferocity from it. Cowardice—yielding to the blind survival urges of ancient ancestral forms far down the evolutionary ladder from the highly evolved Malach—would end her line, and her contribution to the Malach gene pool.

With a savage thump, the pod disintegrated around

her, freeing her Hunter's lander in a cloud of radar-masking shrapnel. Light—to her eyes, harsh and actinic and shifted toward violet-white—briefly flared around her, until her computer adjusted the electronic optics to more comfortable settings. Her altitude was twenty-one hundred *tairucht*, high above the day side of the prey world. Swiftly she oriented herself. She was over ocean at the moment, but gray-purple mountains rose ahead and to her left, beyond a rugged and fjord-bitten coastline. Patchy clouds obscured much of the landing zone, but her computer highlighted the proper area and approach vectors despite the cloud cover.

As on Lach'br'zghis, the last human-infested world she'd seen, this place was virtually untouched by modern mining and processing. Radar detected numerous settlements, but small and isolated things. On Zhanaach there was now but a single city—*Da'a-Zhanaach*, Zhanaach's Greatness—which, together with its satellite sub-cities and industrial complexes covered most of the continent of Aghla.

All of the rest of the Brooder-world was given over to the strip mines and ore extraction facilities, the rock eaters and tunnel chewers and ocean drinkers used by the Malach to extract and concentrate every last *klaatch* of useful metal from the accessible reaches of the planet's upper crust. Schaagrasch could scarcely conceive of life apart from the teeming millions of a world's one city, though she imagined it must be something like the hardship of living with only a few thousand of her own kind aboard ship. The fact that the autochthons of these empty, almost unpopulated worlds lived in small and isolated settlements was one more indication that they were primitive evolutionary forms, doomed to extinction when forced to compete with a more highly developed species.

Once, ages ago, the Malach had inhabited separate

and widely scattered cities, each its own clan and kingdom, but the ruthless logic of *Zsho*, the philosophical-religious belief structure that embodied the Malach concept of survival of the fittest, had inevitably led to a single survivor city-state, and that had eventually grown into Zhanaach's Greatness. As the Malach assimilated Zsha'h'lach and Lach'br'zghis and the other empty, human worlds, they would one by one be subjected to the Malach's efficiency in recovering vital metals.

Schaagrasch hoped that some pieces, at least, of the conquered worlds would be set aside for *g'raaszh*, a concept that translated very loosely as "living space," room to range with the pack, hunting in the old way of the Mothers. Efficiency in exploiting Zhanaach's scarce metal reserves had been the means by which the Malach had developed first an industrial civilization, then space flight, and finally the ability to utilize the inexhaustible metal riches of other worlds and systems, but that efficiency had also resulted in the loss of the open plains and savannas that had given rise to the Race in the first place, a few million *qui'ur* or so ago. She and her kind hungered for open country in which to hunt. That instinctive drive was at least partially responsible for the need to physically subdue other worlds, when asteroids and lifeless moons could provide heavy elements enough to sate even the Malach's relentless metal-hunger.

Nuclear fire flashed and stabbed from below, focusing Schaagrasch's full attention once again on the needs of the moment. Resistance, this time, was heavy, and she could tell that losses already were high. Most of the fire, she noted, was rising from two separate locations, one of them quite close to her assigned landing zone, the other not far from the spaceport that was Strike-Hunter Cha'rissch's primary target.

Active radar sites infested the target area heavily. Fusion beams continued to burn from the surface intermittently, each shot obliterating another incoming Malach pod or assault boat even when they were fired through the thickening overcast below. The ground batteries had an advantage there, of course, in that the incoming boats, those clear of their chaff covers, at any rate, would be easily tracked by radar, while Malach radar had to sort unfamiliar targets from the clutter of the ground.

Schaagrasch had been lucky thus far, a single target among hundreds. She flashed over the coastline, still descending, skimming low above a surface of blinding, violet-white clouds, their glare only just contained by the optical system's electronics.

A warning buzzer sounded; she was being painted by enemy radar . . . painted hard, with a target lock. Schaagrasch twitched her left hind-arm, firing attitude jets to swing her craft sharply right. As she heeled over, a dazzling glare of light erupted from the clouds, illuminating the cloud deck from within and beneath, the beam searing past her pod like a lightning stroke.

She twitched again, bringing the fast-falling probe back onto course, angling in toward the assigned landing zone. An instant later, clouds surrounded her in gray-bright fog . . . and then she was below the cloud deck, hurtling above a confused tangle of colorful shelters or tents of some kind. A lake gleamed to the right, mountains to the left. Then she was over thick and unexploded forest, her jets firing one last time to kill her forward velocity.

Trees blurred beneath her pod as she triggered her air-breathing engines, decelerating with a ten-G jolt that nearly robbed her of breath. A final sharp, hard shock . . . and she was down.

Her pod split open and she engaged the Hunter's servos, rising unsteadily on unfolding legs. She scanned her surroundings across 360 degrees; a second pod in her octet was down eighty *erucht* distant. She saw the other Hunter rising from the crater where the pod had come to rest and recognized the hull number and death-poem script of J'krarash'niz's Hunter.

"Form up! All Hunters, form up!" she barked. "Kill and eat!"

"Kill and eat" came the reply from five voices. She checked her map screen and saw that Ghaghr'risch and Asch'gniz were missing, unaccounted for. The enemy defensive fire had been fierce, relentless, and highly accurate. Perhaps they'd both been caught by battery fire from the ground coming in.

No matter. With resistance this fierce from the human prey, she would be able to bring her octet to full strength very soon by incorporating the blessed survivors of other shattered octets.

Fusion fire briefly lit the sky to the southwest, from the vicinity of that curious human tent-city. One of the autochthons' combat machines was known to be in that area, a center of resistance that would have to be neutralized at once. She rasped out another order, and the six Hunters began hurrying southwest on fast-scissoring, mechanical legs.

While Bolo 96876 of the Line has been engaging enemy forces at Simmstown, I have been guarding the approaches to Kinkaid, the Muir Military Command Headquarters, and the spaceport. With no Enemy ground forces within my sensory envelope, I have been free to engage Enemy spacecraft approaching Muir in my line of sight. Enemy fire from space is continuing, but so far only three shots have come closer than one hundred meters, and I have suffered no damage.

Two point seven three minutes ago, however, a new threat appeared. Bursting out of an obscuring cloud of chaff, a large number of Enemy craft have entered my sensory envelope.

Judging these nearby vessels, which exhibit mass and

maneuvering characteristics approximately equivalent to those of Concordiat Dragon's Tooth pods or Echo-class landing barges, to be the major threat, I have shifted my targeting priorities to them and commenced firing. Several flare and vanish with suspicious ease. They are dummies, target drones designed to attract both my attention and my fire.

Within .22 second, however, three new targets appear above the horizon at 341 degrees, and these show signs of intelligent hands at the controls, rather than remote teleoperation. I acquire a targeting lock on the first one, even while running a vector solution on all three . . . noting as I do that I will be able to destroy two of the incoming pods, but not the third. They are passing from my left to my right on a path that will bring them down to the east of and within ten kilometers of the spaceport. This is almost certainly a force detailed to capture the port.

The pods are similar to tapered cylinders with moderate armor, no weapons, and numerous thrusters. Each could hold a large number of troops, several vehicles, or a combat machine equivalent to a Mark XXIV Bolo. Swinging my 90cm Hellbore to bear on the lead target, I fire.

My aim is good, and the bolt of fusion plasma strikes the lead pod squarely in the center, burning through the thin hull metal and ripping it open. In an instant, the pod has been shredded as its aerodynamic integrity is lost, spilling a large number of objects into the air. There is no time, however, for a detailed analysis. I immediately shift my tracking lock to the second pod and, as soon as my Hellbore power inductors have cycled up to full readiness 1.27 seconds after the first shot, I fire again.

The two surviving pods are attempting to avoid ground fire by jinking as far as their maneuvering systems will permit, but the pods clearly are bulky and underpowered craft, and sophisticated maneuvers are impossible for them. My second shot hits the target five meters from its nose, sheering off the forward part of the hull and sending the craft into an uncontrollable spin.

As expected, by the time I slew my turret to track the final pod, it has passed behind a line of trees to the east and is beyond my targeting envelope.

With no other targets in view, I turn to 095 degrees, aiming for the landing area of the surviving pod, and engage my drive.

I should arrive at the landing site within five minutes.

CHAPTER TWENTY-THREE

At my Commander's suggestion, I am traveling east through the forest north of the refugee camp, advancing through the woods at the maximum speed possible, splintering trees and plowing them down. My radar scan of the Enemy landing pattern suggests that this patch of forest could well be infested with Malach war machines, so I deploy all sensors at maximum, watching for the possibility of ambush. My immediate target is the general area of the Enemy's landings.

I have ceased firing at the lake. Within the past twenty minutes, a considerable cloud cover has gathered over the entire Simmstown area, and a light rain is falling. The Enemy bombardment from space has ceased, at least in this area, though plasma bolts continue to strike other areas, in particular the region around Kinkaid. Bolo 96875, so far, is unhurt. He reports a landing by Malach forces near the starport and is advancing to investigate.

I wish him well.

Large numbers of Malach forces have landed in my Combat Area as well, though they do not appear to be well organized as yet. My mission is to block their movements and, if necessary, attract their fire, to give the refugees time to escape.

Movement catches my attention, a thrashing among the trees at a range of 120 meters, bearing 273. I pivot my Hellbore turret to cover the threat. An instant later, an Enemy combat walker emerges from the trees.

It appears identical to the machines recorded on Wide Sky, a flat, roughly saucer-shaped main body, thicker in the mid-section than toward the oval, knife-edged wingtips, which at the moment have been folded down to form sheltering armor skirts for the leg mechanism and ventral hull.

I trigger a round from my Hellbore, the bolt slashing into the Malach walker's left side, ripping up armor plating and hurling debris into the forest at the machine's back. It returns fire in the same instant, a particle beam that strikes my forward left-side skirt, detonating a line of reactive armor plate in a sharp, crackling blast, and fusing the armor beneath into glassy, glowing-hot slag. The damage is minimal, however, and easily repaired. I track my Hellbore lower and trigger a second shot, aiming for what I judge to be the walker's weak point, its legs. Vents on the walker's belly flare bright-hot in my infrared scanners as air intakes topside gulp down vast quantities of atmosphere, superheat it, and jet it out the belly. The machine lifts, its legs folding. My shot grazes one leg, doing no serious damage.

My infinite repeaters are firing now as I track with every weapon I can bring to bear. Sparks snap and flash from its hull; one solid hit staggers it, knocking one wing low, and a Hellbore shot smashes in an instant later, shearing off the right wingtip and sending the Malach machine into a pancaking spin. It hits the trees with a shattering impact, toppling two in a thunder of wildly splintering wood and falling boughs.

My sensors detect other Malach walkers closing in fast. . . .

❖   ❖   ❖

Alexie climbed out of her speedster and hurried toward the knot of adults and older children who were gathered around a smoldering pile of wreckage. One of the plasma beams from the sky had fallen here, incinerating a dozen makeshift shelters and tents, and toppling one large shelter, which by chance had stood at the edge of the blast zone, into a tumble-down heap of melted plastic and scrap. Rain drizzled from the overcast, a thin, hot mist. The workers were busily pulling bodies—*small* bodies—from the debris.

It all seemed so blindly wasteful, so random and vicious. Children always suffered in war, but for the Malach to simply fire into these tents like this, without even realizing what they were doing . . .

Or did they? War by terror was nothing new or alien to human ideas of warfare. "What's going on?" she demanded.

"We have some survivors in there," one of the adults, a young woman, said. Her face was haggard and white, with blue-black circles beneath the eyes. "But the stuff on top is too heavy."

Alexie took a look. The ruin was close by the edge of the forest, a clutter of bright orange sections, some partly melted by the intense heat of the beam, which had gouged a twenty-meter crater into the earth nearby. When she stooped to look under the wreckage, she could hear someone crying, while another young face with large, dark eyes regarded her steadily from the shadows. "Hang on!" she called. "We'll get you out!"

"The wall fell!" the face called back. Alexie thought it was a boy of ten or twelve. "We can't get out!"

"Are you hurt?"

"I think Demi's leg is stuck."

"How about you?"

"I'm okay. Arm's hurt a little. There's not enough room to crawl out!"

The speedster had a towpoint, and someone produced a length of high-strength cable which they secured around a jagged piece of fallen wall. It took a few moments for her to use the vehicle to partly lift the wreckage clear of the ground, so that the workers could drag the two children, mercifully still alive and not badly injured, to safety.

"Okay," she told the group, as the vehicle settled back to the ground with a dwindling whine. "You have to get out of here. Don't stop for possessions. Don't stop for anything. The Malach are coming, and they're coming fast!" She pointed south. "We have transports taking people on down there, but save them for the real little ones, or those who can't walk, okay? The rest of you have legs. Use them! There'll be people to guide you out. It'll be a long walk, but if you don't get too scared and if you listen to what people tell you, you'll make it okay."

"Where are we going?" one of the rescued kids cried. She looked like she was about eight, with a smudged face and a dirty holiday-best red dress. A rescue worker was bandaging her leg, which didn't seem to be broken but which had a nasty cut. "Ow-ow! I want my mom and dad!"

"Right now, we just have to get away from the Malach, honey," Alexie said. "We'll find your parents later." Too late, she remembered that, more than likely, the girl's parents were still back on Wide Sky. She had a most unpolitician-like aversion to making promises that she was not going to be able to keep.

The kids started moving off, shepherded by the adults, one of whom carried the injured girl in her arms.

Alexie heard something, a thrashing among the trees at her back. With fear mounting in her breast and throat, she turned, freezing in place as the bushes parted and an armed Malach warrior strode into the clearing. Two more Malach appeared behind the first . . . and then trees were thrust aside as one of the nine-meter-tall walkers stepped out of the forest and into the light. More of the creatures appeared to the right and left, clad in leather straps and equipment harnesses only, with their scaly hides gleaming wetly in the drizzle like faceted red and green jewels.

The children at her back screamed, and she could hear them scattering behind her. With lightning quick motions, the Malach raised weapons clutched in various confusing combinations of arms and clawed hands, taking aim.

"No!" she shouted, stepping forward into the path of the first Malach that had appeared, looking up into the creature's four emotionless, expressionless ruby and ebon eyes. She deliberately assumed a defiant stance, shoulders back, chin held high and as firm as she could manage, staring into that alien, four-eyed visage less than five meters away, *daring* it to shoot her. She fully expected to be dead in the next second. . . .

The lead Malach took three swift steps forward, a strangely shaped weapon of some sort clutched in its massive lower arms, but with one of its smaller, upper arms upraised, a black and glittering, razor-edged claw extended as though to slash her exposed throat. She didn't move, didn't back down. If these monsters were going to kill her, they would have to do it here and now . . . and maybe the kids could escape in the time she bought them.

The claw wavered a moment, as though the Malach were considering her and her defiance. Suddenly, the claw slid back noiselessly into a sheath of wrinkled, scaly skin, and the huge jaws gaped a little. *"Shgh'ragh!"* the Malach said, more a rasping snarl than anything like a word. One of the other Malach approached, unfolding something like a lightweight net, which it flung over her. In an instant, she was pinned and helpless, the soft mesh snaring her arms and legs as the Malach lifted her effortlessly from the ground and slung her across its broad back like a bag of flour.

A prisoner now, she was carried back into the woods. The kids, thank God, had run while the Malach had been distracted by her and were safely away. She wondered, though, what was going to happen. In her experience, the Malach rarely took prisoners.

And when they did, those prisoners were never heard from again.

Aghrracht looked out the viewport of the *Xa'ha'xur* shuttle as it dropped from the sky on flaring landing thrusters, descending toward the landing pad atop the stone castle that grew from the mountainside like an artificially shaped and reworked cliff. Built for strength above the cold and narrowly bounded waters of the fjord, the structure looked curiously like some of the great clanhold castles of ancient Zhanaach, a convergence of culture and design that reinforced Aghrracht's firm and reasoned opinion that the humans, while they possessed a level of technological development at least equivalent to that of the Malach, were far more primitive in terms of social, governmental, and psychological evolution.

Save for an occasional longing for the open plains and veldts on which their species had evolved social organization and sentience millions of *qui'ur* ago, the Malach did not experience any emotion equivalent to human nostalgia and did not attach value to cultural icons, symbols, or memorials of the past. Any given point in the past, after all, was a place they'd already been, a previous clawhold that, once achieved, was nothing more than one more step along the way in a long and ongoing evolutionary journey. The last Malach clanhold castle had been demolished millennia ago, not long after the last of the inter-clan genocides, its building materials recycled into the foundations of Da'a-Zhanaach.

Still, this clanhold structure would be useful. Although Malach units had managed, despite heavy losses, to land in force at several widely scattered points on the target world, they'd as yet captured no major installations, buildings, or facilities, and the defenders were resisting with vigor enough that it might well be necessary to obliterate them stronghold by stronghold.

The cliffside castle, though, had been seized almost as an afterthought. A Malach troopship, off-course after dodging heavy fire over the landing zone beyond the mountains to the south, had picked up the structure on radar and moved in to investigate. During her approach, the troopship commander had reported receiving numerous radio transmissions in the principal human language, as though the defenders wanted to talk with her. Prepared to fight, she'd approached cautiously, but no fire had greeted her from those towering gray ramparts. Instead, a delegation of twelve humans had been waiting on the aircraft landing pad atop the castle walls, waving a curious artifact—a colorless sheet of cloth fabric tied to an aluminum rod.

The bodies of those humans had been collected as trophies and placed on display chin-high in the castle's main hall, while the aluminum rod had been taken as a symbolic gift-metal of victory.

The *Xa'ha'xur* shuttle settled to the landing pad in a swirling cloud of steam. Aghrracht strode down the landing ramp, claws clicking on steel, then on ferrocrete. The garrison commander met her with upraised chin. "Welcome, Supreme Deathgiver! Ch'chesk'cheh the Fast-Slasher, the hunting is good."

"We will establish our command center here, Ch'chesk'cheh," she said. "What is the local situation?"

The garrison leader gestured with a foreclaw at the mountains bulking high behind the castle. "We have reports of continued fighting to the south, Deathgiver.

Beyond the mountains. This area was secured without fighting, and there have been no threats or threat-displays by the prey at all."

Aghrracht's tendrils twitched curiosity. "None?"

"We do not believe they possess significant force north of the mountains. All that held this castle were the twelve that made the initial threat display, and a few eights of others that did not resist. They have been imprisoned in the underground chambers. We have been holding them in case you wished to question or vivisect them."

"Excellent. We have learned, I believe, all that is necessary to know about human anatomy, but their psychologies remain . . . obscure. They are difficult to understand."

"Indeed, Deathgiver." She opened her fore-hand claws slowly, a gesture of reluctant bafflement. "Their threat display with the colorless cloth is beyond comprehension. None of the humans was armed."

"The prisoners may be able to explain the action's symbolism." She turned, gesturing toward another Malach descending the ramp with a number of Aghrracht's aides and subcommanders. "We have one *tsurgh'ghah* with us, at least, who has begun acquiring the human language."

Ch'chesk'cheh's feeding tendrils curled back with distaste, and Aghrracht understood. It was a common reaction among Malach warriors, for the *tsurgh'ghah* were not high-ranking members of Malach society.

The word was drawn from the name of a Zhanaachan carrion eater and was synonymous with "scavenger." The Malach who'd acquired that epithet millennia ago had been outcasts from the proper female warrior hierarchy, a nameless underclass that had survived by scavenging bodies, body wastes, food scraps, garbage, and whatever else they could lay their claws to. Eventually, they'd been integrated into the Race's evolving social structure as providers of certain necessary, if unpleasant, services, though individuals still had neither names nor honorable standing.

Aghrracht and her aides followed the garrison commander into the castle, walking carefully down a set of too-short steps into a large and spartanly furnished hall. The heads of various prey animals were mounted on the wall, and for the first time Aghrracht wondered if these humans might have some of the social graces, skills, and arts after all. Prominently displayed on chin hooks hung in a line along one wall were the limp and red-splattered bodies of the castle's human defenders. Some were still struggling weakly, though the size of the puddles of odd-colored blood beneath each strung-up body suggested that they were almost ready for the next cycle of the Great Spiral.

As the garrison commander ordered a couch brought for Aghrracht—human furniture did not fit Malach anatomy, but couches with their backs and sides removed could be adapted for the purpose—she regarded her *tsurgh'ghah* with slit-narrowed pupils. The scavengers' services were more necessary than ever since Zhanaach had entered her industrial age. The interest the outcasts had for garbage and the leavings of others had allowed them to evolve as collectors and repositories of information, and nowadays, many of the Nameless were attached to specific warrior clans and worked under their direction, remembering histories, warrior's tales, Death-poems, names, and anything else that needed preservation for the future.

If most warriors cared little for things of the past, there'd always been a need to store histories, so that lessons learned once need not be learned again. Recollectors made a science of perfect recall, training themselves to record information of all types. Indeed, writing was a relatively recent development in Malach history, since books and records were rarely needed. Until Malach advances in technology had developed computers two thousand *qui'ur* ago, knowledge had been preserved solely on perishable book-scrolls and in the minds of *tsurgh'ghah* recollectors.

This one, who'd been given "Cho" as a nickname-of-convenience, was one of Aghrracht's personal recollectors, an old Malach with blackening scales who'd served Aghrracht's mother before her and had special expertise in remembering names. She'd proven her worth by being able to remember and repeat the words and phrases used by the human prisoners. Several prisoners, encouraged to cooperate through the vivisection of some of their pack-mates in their presence, had been used to generate a vocabulary of human speech; with only a single people and a single tongue for the past several thousand *qui'ur*, the Malach still found the concept of other languages strange and a bit difficult to think about, but once a recollector skilled in names heard a new word and its definition, she never forgot them.

Even so, though Cho by now possessed a vocabulary of several thousand human words and phrases, using them effectively was difficult. So much about the humans and the way they thought was still baffling to the Malach. More clearly than ever, humans had long been trapped in an evolutionary cul-de-sac, despite the momentary and intermittent skills they'd demonstrated in the defense of this planet. They'd lost any blessing Sha'gnaasht might once have bestowed upon them and now deserved only extinction.

The Malach would inherit the wealth of their worlds.

Aghrracht considered having Cho begin by questioning those of the display-prey that were still alive, but decided that it probably wouldn't be worth the effort. Humans appeared to be incapacitated by relatively small amounts of pain; it was possible that they *felt* pain more intensely than did Malach, though no one had been able to prove that hypothesis definitively. In any case, Aghrracht doubted that they would get anything more informative out of the trophies now than squeaks and mindless burblings, especially with the floors of their mouths pierced by display hooks.

Kha'laa'sht the Meat Finder entered the hall. "Deathgiver," she said. "We have set up the communications center in the next room, over there. We have channels to each of our pack-leaders in the field now."

"Excellent," Aghrracht replied. "Inform all leaders that human prisoners and submissives are to be brought here. See that transports are made available."

"The hunting is good, Deathgiver."

It was time, Aghrracht though, to begin learning how best to drive this particular prey, what weaknesses it had that could be exploited, what needs it possessed through which it might be domesticated. . . .

General Phalbin stood before the large map display, studying the fast-growing blotches of red that were scattered across the continent from Loch Haven and the Windypeak Mountains all the way south to Kinkaid. The situation was grim, and growing worse. The major landings appeared to be taking place north and northeast of Simmstown—further confirmation, Phalbin thought—that the damned Malach had come in on the heels of the Wide Sky refugees. Most of the refugee encampment had been overrun by now, though the latest reports put the bulk of the refugees, most on foot, some aboard transports, nearly fifty kilometers south of the area. Lieutenant Ragnor's rather dazzling display of footwork with Bolo 96876 of the Line seemed to have confounded the Malach. For a time, it had looked as though they were preparing for a drive south on Kinkaid, but Ragnor's maneuvers appeared to have made them pull back and consolidate. For the first time in his career, General

Barnard Phalbin was glad for the Bolos under his command and wished he had more.

But he was also concerned. Bolo 96875 of the Line, left protecting Kinkaid in the south, was in a fair position to block Malach forces that had landed in the region from either the spaceport or the city, located across the bay. But Ragnor and the Bolo he was riding in, Bolo 96876, were now deep inside what had to be considered enemy territory and getting deeper all the time as more Malach landed. The original plan, to post the Bolos as semimobile fortresses close to the starport, had been junked when the Malach invasion caught Bolo 96876 out of position, up at the refugee camp.

It was time to give up on the area around Simmstown. Ragnor had done an excellent job of covering the evacuation of the refugees, but it was time to pull him back, to pull Bolo 96876 back. With two of those incredible machines guarding Kinkaid, Muir just might have a chance.

"Communications!" he called. "Get me a scrambled channel to the commander of Bolo 96876."

They were into the battle proper now, and all Donal could do was grip the armrests of his command seat and watch the panorama unfolding around him. Modern combat was too fast-paced by far for any human to comprehend it, much less reason out the moves or react to the enemy's thrusts and parries. He watched as Freddy engaged Malach walker after walker, flier after flier, watched as volleyed salvos from the ion cannons along both of the Bolo's flanks and the jolting thunder of the Hellbore main weapon carved through the enemy formations like lightning.

Tactics at this point were brutally simple—kill enemy war machines as quickly and as efficiently as possible, and try to keep them from ganging up on the lone Bolo with overwhelming force and firepower. Freddy was accomplishing this by identifying groups of Malach walkers as they began to come together, striking at them first with HE and tactical nuclear weapons at medium to long range, then closing to engage the survivors in flickering, rapid-fire contests of accuracy and hitting power.

So far, the Bolo had the edge—or at least was holding his own. Freddy clearly had the advantage in firepower and armor; the Malach possessed speed and maneuverability, but Freddy was deliberately allowing himself to be surrounded so that he could take advantage of shorter interior lines of movement. With a mathematical precision that truly transformed the art of battle to a science, he circled through the enemy formations, breaking up one after another. They were easier targets when they were airborne, and he knocked the fliers out of the sky every chance he got. Walkers were more accurate when they fired, and they tended to make use of ridges and folds in the terrain to maintain hard-to-hit hull-down positions.

Freddy absorbed the punishment and kept on fighting, relying on short, furious bursts of unexpected speed to avoid encirclement at close range. The worst danger was the Malach nuke-tipped missile penetrators, but so far the Bolo was swatting them out of the sky before they got close enough to hurt him.

Meanwhile, despite the running firefight, Donal and Freddy were analyzing Malach communications patterns.

"I have noted a 734 percent increase in radio messages originating at this point," Freddy was saying, highlighting a point on the map he was projecting on the main screen.

Donal leaned closer to the display, checking the map. "I'll be damned, " he said, half to himself. "Delacroix's castle. What's it called . . . uh, Glenntor."

"The structure is registered as belonging to the Delacroix family," Freddy replied. "Do you know of him?"

"I was there a few nights ago," Donal said. "That party. The guy is PGPH. I wonder if he's working with the Malach now."

The Bolo rocked suddenly as the main Hellbore fired. Donal glanced up at the compartment's ceiling, then looked at the display surrounding his head. No Malach walkers were close by at the moment, but Freddy had picked up several fliers at a range of nearly ten kilometers and was engaging them. It was raining harder now, and the ground was turning soft. The Bolo continued grinding ahead, however, without slowing at all, smashing through the splintered and charred remnants of the forest as it engaged any enemy unit that came close enough for a clear shot.

"The communications are coded and unintelligible," Freddy said, as though the conversation was the only thing on his mind at the moment, "but the frequencies are typical of those used routinely by the Malach." There was a hesitation, an almost embarrassed silence of a second or so. "It *feels* as though we are dealing with a command center."

The statement rocked Donal. Bolos, even self-aware Bolos, rarely had anything that you could point to and call a *feeling* . . . or if they did, they didn't admit it.

"Can you explain that? What do you mean . . . 'it feels like'?"

The Bolo rocked again, and one of the fliers blossomed into an orange-white sunburst. "I have recorded the frequency of messages transmitted from the structure you call Glenntor. I have correlated those transmissions with other Malach transmissions, in particular those from their space fleet and those that appear to be command-related communications from the field, as opposed to radio chatter between separate units. The pattern is, in fact, similar to the pattern exhibited by human field command centers directing a battle from just behind the front lines."

Donal considered this. The explanation was straight-forward and made perfect sense. But Freddy's mention of something that sounded eerily like intuition had jolted him.

"So we're not dealing with human traitors, you think."

"Almost certainly not, Commander. I have tracked two large Malach shuttles from orbit to the castle. In addition, I have noted over the past seventeen point three four minutes an increase in shuttle traffic from other parts of the battlefield."

The terrain visible on the screens blurred as Freddy accelerated hard, smashing through what was left of a burned-over forest at over one hundred klicks per hour. Two more fliers died in twin, silent detonations. Freddy was moving now to reach a ridgeline several kilometers ahead. According to the scrolling text on the display screen, he was tracking what was probably an octet of walkers.

"What kind of shuttle traffic?"

"Mostly small craft approximately similar in dimension and mass to our Skymaster-class transports or APCs. A large number arrived on-planet with the initial invasion wave. Many of these have begun traveling to the castle, apparently to deliver personnel."

"Where have they been coming from?"

Freddy added a scattering of points on the map. Most were concentrated in the region north of Lake Simms, within the ruin of Simmstown.

"Prisoners," Donal said.

"You believe the transports are carrying human prisoners?"

"It's a good possibility," Donal replied. "The Malach were showing a distinct interest in picking up prisoners on Wide Sky, and they used a transport like you've described. If they're not going to take them back to the fleet—and that would be risky if you're getting too free with your Hellbore bolts—they need to have some central place to take them for safekeeping." *And probably for interrogation*, he added to himself. His fists clenched on the armrest of his command chair. A lot of those prisoners must be children who hadn't made it out of Simmstown in time. It was impossible to simply gather up fifty thousand scared and confused kids and move them out at a moment's notice.

He remembered Alexie's fear for the refugees and wondered where she was now. South, with the main body, he supposed. She was going to just plain go ballistic when she heard the Malach had grabbed some of her kids.

"Commander," Freddy's voice said. "I have an incoming communication, command circuit, channel three."

"Audio."

". . . tenant Ragnor!" Colonel Wood's voice said. "Come in, Lieutenant Ragnor! Please respond!"

"This is Ragnor," he said. "Go ahead."

"Colonel Wood, at CMAHQ. We have new orders for you."

Donal was already beginning to formulate a plan of his own, and he somehow doubted that Wood's new orders were going to fit in with his plans at all. Reaching over to the console, he killed his mike. "Freddy."

"Yes, Commander?"

"I want to develop some radio trouble. I don't think we're going to want to hear these orders."

There was an uncomfortable hesitation. "Commander, I cannot distort or conceal information. By extension, I cannot lie about the condition of my equipment."

"Sure you can. I order you to . . ."

Donal's voice trailed off. Something was happening . . . and it wasn't good. The small repeater screens along the top of his console that showed a steady stream of selected status messages from Freddy's operating system had just gone blank. The map had frozen in place on the circular screen, too, and a new window had just opened in the middle of it. He read the message on the screen with a dawning horror.

CRITICAL ERROR
EMERGENCY CONFLICT RESOLUTION LOGIC ERROR
LEVEL ONE CONFLICT
ERROR IN INSTRUCTION TO DELETE ROES
NO RULES OF ENGAGEMENT TO DELETE

One by one, Freddy's higher mind functions were going off-line, shutting down, and Donal knew that he was in very serious trouble indeed.

CHAPTER TWENTY-FOUR

A glance at the message on the display screen told
Donal immediately what the problem was, and he cursed
himself for a thumb-fingered idiot. He'd caused the
problem himself by not looking far enough ahead when
he'd installed the cut-out for the ROEs. Turning his
command chair to the right, he reached out and flipped
down an access panel, opening up a small emergency
keyboard. He began typing.

SYSTEM LEVEL INTERRUPT <Enter>
RESTORE PRIMARY SYSTEM <Enter>
LOAD ECRL BACKUP <Enter>

Bolos, even the brightest of the self-aware marks,
addressed problems in hierarchical arrays of relative
urgency and importance. When faced with an internal
contradiction in their software, they were usually able
to figure out for themselves which way to go simply by
following the contradictory chains of logic, judging the
outcomes, and making a reasoned determination as to
which outcome was more desirable in light of the Bolo's
current orders. The process was known as conflict
resolution modeling, or CRM.

Sometimes though, and inevitably when humans were
part of the loop, the Bolo received two sets of directives,

each weighted the same, and each so flatly contradictory that the Bolo's logic circuits were unable to resolve the conflict. That was why Bolos had the subroutine package known as the Emergency Conflict Resolution Logic, to address Level One conflicts created by sloppy programming or badly given human orders. With it, Freddy would have been able to handle even the idiot ROEs passed down from the Muir government and Phalbin, though they would have slowed him down a lot. Without it, Freddy did just fine, until he ran into a high-level conflict . . . not something simple like which side of a building to pass on, but a contradictory set of orders that were important enough that they couldn't be resolved by juggling random numbers.

Little things . . . like his stupid human counterpart giving him a direct order to lie when he had hard-wired directives requiring him to deliver information truthfully and in full. Had the ECRL been in place, Freddy might have resisted, advised, or even refused, but he wouldn't have started shutting down. As it was, more and more of Freddy's attention had been diverted by that particular imponderable; in another few moments, it could have frozen him up completely, or led to an unpredictable breakdown in his logic-chain orderings.

Donal kept typing, pausing from time to time to check the screen. The Bolo had come to a halt in the middle of the forest, and that made it a perfect X on the bull's eye. If the Malach decided to open up with their space bombardment again, Freddy and the human inside him were as good as dead. The one consolation was that Donal would never feel the stroke of artificial lightning that killed them.

Enemy forces still swarmed through the area. Freddy's tactics up to the moment when he'd started shutting down had been to locate each clump of Malach walkers before they could get more than six or eight together and scatter them, either by direct attack, or by loosing missiles from his vertical launch tubes. The idea had been working, too, until the machine had stopped paying attention. Donal could already see several Malach octets out there on the battlefield map, moving just out of Hellbore line-of-sight. They would be trying a rush very soon now, once they were convinced that the Bolo's silence was not some kind of ruse.

"Bolo 96876 of the Line! Respond!" Wood's voice was sounding frantic over the audio link. "Lieutenant Ragnor! Respond! Anybody!"

The Bolo shuddered as it took a direct hit. The Malach were beginning to test the waters, as it were, firing particle beams at long range, probing for a response.

"Colonel Wood, Ragnor," Donal said. "Look, I've got a problem here and I'm a little busy right now. Let me get back to you, okay?"

"Ragnor! I want you to break off your action and RTB at once! Do you hear me? Return to base! Immediately!"

Donal reached up with one hand and switched off the transmitter. Time enough to talk things over later. Right now, he had to do a quick job on his patch.

The fix wasn't too hard, once Donal knew what was going on. The closely circling logic loop had been broken by his system level interrupt. Now he was restoring the original Emergency Conflict Resolution Logic module, overwriting his ill-conceived patch and restoring the ROEs to full effect. He'd expected to do this anyway after the battle was over, in order to keep Phalbin and Chard from ever learning what he'd done.

Another explosion rocked the Bolo, heavier this time. Automated damage control diagnostics began flicking off statistics on power loss and weakened armor. He kept typing.

Part of the problem was that he was not primarily a programmer, certainly not the sort of programmer who routinely worked on advanced combat AI subsystems. He knew what any Bolo field commander was expected to know, and perhaps a little bit more, enough to handle routine field repairs, diagnostics and system tests, and possibly the odd bit of hacker's code for taking a necessary shortcut.

Unfortunately, his impatience had led him into a shortcut that could have been deadly—for him, for Freddy, for the entire world of Muir.

It was a mistake he did not intend to make twice.

"Freddy?" he said, looking up as he clattered in the final command line and hit Enter. "Freddy, are you there?"

Systems displays and discretes were already coming back on line. "I am here, Commander," Freddy's voice said. There was a short hesitation. "I have suffered damage, sections—"

"Enemy units are approaching, Freddy, bearing one-seven—"

"I see them." The Hellbore fired, momentarily blanking out part of the panorama on the viewscreen with its savage incandescence. An instant later, the infinite repeaters were giving voice with their buzzsaw shrieks of high-velocity, high-volume ion-bolt fire. A walker two kilometers away exploded in a fountain of flame and boiling smoke. A warning buzzer sounded.

"Damn! What's that?"

"The Enemy has acquired a weapons lock," Freddy replied with maddening calm. "They may be about to launch their penetrator weapons."

Donal's lips compressed, a hard, white line. Those two-stage Malach weapons, missiles that burned in through the outer armor, then deposited a micronuke deep inside the Bolo's hull, were the deadliest anti-armor weapons he'd ever seen in action, a serious threat to any Bolo.

Five glowing stars appeared on the panoramic screen, coming in from the right and behind. Another three appeared, arcing in across the shattered forest. Freddy's response was immediate and enthusiastic, a howling salvo of infinite repeater shots and antimissile lasers. He turned suddenly, the maneuver flinging Donal hard against his seat harness. Freddy was zigzagging wildly to confuse the enemy's tracking systems, combining the high-speed movements with a steady barrage of chaff canisters designed to sucker the enemy missiles' targeting radars.

Freddy managed to knock down seven of the missiles before they came too close, decoying four into chaff clouds and killing three more with head-on bursts. The eighth, nicked by an ion bolt, wobbled wildly in flight, began to break up, then detonated a few meters above the Bolo's upper deck. Donal felt the blow, a thunder-blasted detonation that set his ears ringing and momentarily blanked out the entire exterior view.

The Bolo kept moving, however, bouncing heavily as it hurtled off a low scarp and dropped three meters before slamming into the ground again. Bolos had good shock absorbers, but equipment providing for human comfort and a smooth ride was necessarily limited. More shocks followed, these generated by incoming missiles tipped with tactical nuclear weapons. In every direction Donal looked, he saw rising, twisting columns of gray smoke capped by ominous, flat, mushroom heads. The Malach, it seemed, were throwing everything they had into stopping and destroying the elusive human Bolo.

"I am receiving a radio message from Colonel Wood at HQ," Freddy said.

"Ignore the transmission," Donal said.

"That is not in line with standing orders or communications protocol, Commander." There was a pause. "I have just scanned my commo log records. I appear to have an entry referring to an earlier message from Colonel Wood, but I have no recorded transcript or memory of that conversation. That conversation would have occurred shortly after you suggested that I falsify data. What is the nature of these communications? Is this information of which I should be aware?"

"I took care of it," Donal said. "Ignore the transmission."

"But—"

"Freddy, *trust* me! Wood wants us to go back to Kinkaid, where we can be utilized in a static defense. I want to hit that new command center on Loch Haven. Use your combat logic. Which course of action will prove more successful against people like the Malach?"

There was a long silence, and Donal could almost imagine the machine juggling electrons in some obscure, random-number-generating way.

"I understand," Freddy replied at last. "However, I remind you that the Rules of Engagement are now back in force. I will not be able to attack the Delacroix castle without satisfying eight separate provisions entered in the ROE list."

"Don't worry, Freddy. I've got it covered."

"If it would not seem too inquisitive, I would like to know how."

In truth, Donal wasn't sure he had a direct answer. What he would have, soon, was some time to work on the problem. "Just head west," he told the Bolo. "Toward the sea. I'll take care of the rest."

Another pocket nuke detonated with a savage flash a few tens of meters away from the Bolo's left side, hurling debris against the machine's armor with sandblasting force and rocking the machine heavily to the right. The characteristic mushroom cloud billowed skyward, punching through the overcast. The rain, slightly radioactive now, continued falling.

Freddy raced toward the sea, skirting what once had been the refugee city of Simmstown, as the Malach gathered their forces to the east.

❖   ❖   ❖

I turn my long-range sensors on circumplanetary space, searching for Enemy military satellites and spacecraft. The bulk of the fleet is maintaining a respectful distance now and is safely out of range . . . but that also puts them beyond the range from which they can safely direct the battle or serve as battlefield reconnaissance support. The planetary bombardment has ceased entirely, and I judge that it is now safe to halt my constant, randomized movement across the battlefield—at least for that reason. If nothing else, the Enemy will have ceased the bombardment in order to minimize friendly fire casualties among his own forces. Of course, this also means that his naval vessels are now safely beyond my maximum effective range.

Nearer at hand, however, three Enemy reconnaissance satellites are above my horizon, one rising in the east, the other two high overhead, at thirty-eight and one hundred twelve degrees, respectively. Swinging my primary turret, I bring my 90cm Hellbore to bear on the first target. Lock . . . fire! The first satellite flares briefly, dissolving in a cloud of hot plasma. I swing my turret, fire a second time, and finally slew to target and destroy the third satellite, now just rising above the mountains on the eastern horizon. All three targets have been engaged and destroyed within the space of .21 second, and I am now free to carry out my Commander's orders without fear of being observed by Enemy forces.

I report my status to Unit 96875, then shift into high-speed mode, traveling flat-out across the low, rolling terrain. Ahead is the Western Sea. In another 3.7 minutes, I traverse the dune terrain behind the beach, scattering great clouds of sand to the left and right as I burst through the highest dunes, descend the flat shelf, of the beach and plunge into the ocean.

"What happened?" General Phalbin asked, peering at the mapscreen as though his eyes had failed him. "Where did he go?"

"I'm not sure, sir," the technician at the screen's console said. "The Bolo went behind the radar shadow of the dune line, and we don't have any recon sats or drones up just now to show us what's happening on the other side."

"Maybe he went into the water," Colonel Wood suggested. "He was certainly heading that way as though he intended to do something in particular, and not just keep dodging the bad guys."

"Maybe the Bolo was destroyed," Colonel Ferraro, the Base Tactical Officer, suggested. "Things were getting awfully hot up there."

"A Bolo?" Wood said with a brittle chuckle. "Not likely. Not without an explosion that we'd have heard all the way down here. I think old Freddy just needed to get out of the direct line of fire for a while. Did you see how he capped the Malach spy sats? That was so they couldn't follow his movements either. He doesn't want them seeing what he's up to."

"So what's the enemy doing?" Phalbin demanded.

"They seem to have been hit pretty hard," Ferraro said. He used a laser pointer to trace across the map display with a ruby-bright point of light. "Bolo 96876 was operating throughout this region, hitting their main landing sites—Invasion Zones Alfa, Bravo, Charlie, and Echo."

"Not Delta?"

Ferraro flicked the laser light to a small red stain tucked in between the Windypeak Mountains and a fjord. "That's here, at Glenntor Castle. We were picking up radio calls from Lord Delacroix for a while there, beamed at the Malach, asking for surrender terms. A couple of Malach landers set down there a few hours ago, and that's the last we've heard."

"Damn him."

"He probably didn't have much choice, sir."

"All right. What's the status on the Bolo?"

"According to our telemetry, he took some damage, but nothing serious. He has destroyed several hundred enemy combat walkers and fliers, however, as well as several of their larger landing boats. His strategy has been to break up any formation of Malach units he can reach, then evade and escape before the survivors can close in and trap him."

"So what now?" Phalbin said. "If he's hiding, the Malach are likely to get their act together and move south."

"Maybe," Wood said, studying the map. "Maybe he's swinging south through the sea, too."

"Who knows what the thing's doing!" Phalbin said, pudgy fists clenching at his sides. "Ragnor deliberately disobeyed my direct orders! I'll have his—"

"With all due respect, General," Wood interrupted, "we have to survive the battle first. Let's wait and see what Ragnor . . . and Freddy . . . have up their sleeves."

"What's the tacsit on the other Bolo?"

"Ferdy's been pretty much duplicating Freddy's little song-and-dance act up by Simmstown, but against much smaller numbers." Wood pointed. "He's here, blocking Kinkaid and the spaceport from the Malach landings to the east. Invasion Zones Sierra and Tango."

"Can he handle it?"

"He seems to be a bit slower than Freddy," Wood said. "But he's holding them. So far, anyway."

"Slower? Why?"

"I don't know, sir. Something else . . . we've been getting lots of radioed queries from Ferdy. Things like requests for permission to cross public land, stuff like that."

"But not from the other one?"

Wood shrugged. "That's mostly wilderness up there. I guess he's not trespassing on anybody's back yard."

"But this one down by Kinkaid is still responsive to orders?"

"Yes, sir. As much as a Bolo in combat can be. Sometimes it takes our orders more as suggestions . . . but that's because its tactical logic centers tend to override orders that it considers dangerous in the middle of a battle." He sounded uncertain. "Lieutenant Ragnor could tell us more."

"But the lieutenant is out of communications, isn't he? He just disobeyed my orders to move south and moved himself out of communications! I wouldn't be surprised if he's pulling the old radio trouble scam!"

Phalbin turned away, angry. Somehow, somehow the battle had just slipped right through his grasp, and he was no longer in control. He didn't like that.

And if they got out of this mess, somebody was going to pay. With his bars. With his *career*. . . .

It has been .9311 standard hour since my last contact with Bolo 96876 or my Commander, and I continue to operate independently. For the past 2.7224 standard hours, I have served as a solitary blocking force, intercepting, by my count, twelve separate Enemy probes toward either Kinkaid, north of Starbright Bay, or the starport and military base to the south. Though the Enemy has been making a determined effort, I have so far been able to smash and repulse each advance.

The terrain is in my favor. The land east of Starbright Bay is rugged and, in places, mountainous. The peaks of Ironwood Ridge rise no higher than 800 meters, but the western slopes are quite steep, dropping from the Lyon Plateau in vertical, rock-faced cliffs in places, while in others they are heavily forested—ironwood and redtowers, for the most part—which means the terrain must be classified as difficult. Two valleys grant access through Ironwood Ridge, to the north, the valley of the Kinkaid River, and in the south, Founder's Valley. I have been using my on-board remote drones to monitor Enemy

movements in Invasion Zones Sierra and Tango on the
far side of the mountains, repositioning myself in front
of one valley or the other as soon as I ascertain which
route the Malach forces intend to use for their primary
thrust. A number of times, they have tried penetrating
both valleys simultaneously, but I have been able so far
to shatter the decoy force with missile fire, while dealing
with the main body at medium to close range.

Smoke fills the Kinkaid Valley with a heavy fog
impenetrable at optical and near-infrared wavelengths,
though I can track moving targets easily enough by radar.
Forces are approaching at 32.4 kilometers per hour, and
I have identified them with 99.4 percent probability as
another Malach force.

The 0.6 percent uncertainty represents what humans
refer to as "fog of war." It is possible, if highly unlikely,
that human units have managed to penetrate the Lyon
Plateau and are moving down the Kinkaid Valley now
toward my present position. This confusion would be
confounded by the fact that they do not possess working
IFF gear, and their radio communication is out.

All of this is unlikely in the extreme, of course, but my
programming forces me to allow for numerous unlikely
possibilities. Chaos theory, as well as the random
unpredictability of the chance effect humans refer to as
Murphy's Law, guarantee that during battle, unlikely
possibilities frequently become reality.

Being forced to deal with such possibilities, however
small, has slowed my operational capability by an
estimated 74.1 percent. I am disturbed by this extreme
loss in efficiency, but the Rules of Engagement under
which I am operating force careful consideration of each
move, frequently compounded by the need to refer the
matter to the Command Authority. In this instance, for
example, I am operating under ROE 4:

4: BOLO UNITS WILL DETERMINE THE FRIEND/FOE STATUS

OF UNKNOWN TARGETS WITH 100 PERCENT PROBABILITY
BEFORE ENGAGING THEM IN COMBAT.

*It is, in fact, impossible to determine friend-foe status
with 100 percent probability unless those forces are
actively engaged against friendlies, or unless a visual
identification can be made.*

*Bolo 96876 of the Line informed me when our
Commander gave him the order to drop his ROEs, and
I wonder if he is functioning with greater efficiency
because of it. It seems likely that he is.*

*I move into the middle of the river. The Kinkaid is
broad and relatively shallow—even in the center my road
wheels are only half submerged—and I derive little cover
from it. However, I am determined to make use of every
cover available, since my operational orders do not permit
great flexibility in terms of maneuver or offensive action.*

*I risk the use, once again, of my battle radar, exposing
myself for just .002 second, enough to get clear returns
on the suspected hostiles and to plot their current positions.
I note five targets moving together that have a 98.6 percent
probability of being Malach walkers, now at a range of
1.95 kilometers. Normally, I would have taken them under
fire, but I must either take fire from them first in
accordance with ROE 1 or challenge them verbally, in
accordance with ROE 17. I judge that the probable
hostiles' approach indicates that they are not certain of
my position, despite my brief radar emissions, and that
I therefore might gain significant advantage by ambushing
them. I will not give a verbal challenge but will wait until
I have positive visual ID.*

It is risky, but I have no other choice.

Chaghna'kraa the Blade-Fanged was leading four of her
pack-sisters along the river bank, moving swiftly toward
the probable location of the human *gr'raa'zhghavescht*-
machine. The other three were dead, their machines

smashed in earlier attacks. To Chaghna'kraa, it seemed that the Great Spiral was turning, that events were repeating themselves, as they always did.

She remembered the attack on the *gr'raa* at the last planet invaded, on the world the Malach called Lach'br'zghis. Half of her octet had died there, too, before the alien machine had been conquered. She had a feeling that she was going to lose more this time.

"One *tairucht* to the point where the radar pulse originated," Jir'lischgh'gu the Rapid-Runner said over the tactical link. Then she added, "she's close. I can *smell* her."

"Steady," Chaghna'kraa ordered. "Weapons at ready. When we see it, a quick, hard rush. Push through here, kill the *gr'raa*, and we have a clear route both to the big city and to the spaceport."

The battle smoke was thickening, hanging like a fog over the twisted and charred debris of numerous earlier attacks. How many Malach had died already?

Victory in battle meant superiority in evolution. That simple equivalence had been drummed into Chaghna'kraa since long before she'd graduated to Hunter status, since she'd been in the crèche, in fact. For the first time in her life, however, she was beginning to doubt the idea.

Evolution. The changing in form of organisms through adaptation, mutation, survival of the fittest. Malach belief held that the Race was the most highly evolved of all species, but sometimes, lately, she'd wondered if that wasn't a mere baying at the moons, a statement as empty of substance as the vacuum between the stars.

What would a being *more* highly evolved than the Malach be like? Doctrine said there were none such, though with no solid evidence or reasoning that Chaghna'kraa could see. And the Malach possessed many evolutionary hangovers from earlier and more primitive forms. Their slasher claws, for instance, their dorsal ridge,

their tails, the lusts and drives of *Urrgh-shcha*, even the
second stomach that helped them digest raw meat, all
were holdovers from an earlier era. Had they encountered
another species with claws and fangs, horns and armor,
a species, in fact, with the same evolutionary holdovers
as the Malach, Chaghna'kraa wouldn't have felt so uneasy.
But she'd seen humans, and their pathetic helplessness,
their lack of claws or weapons or decent teeth or strength
or speed or any natural weapon possessed by the Race . . .
it all seemed to suggest that they'd evolved *further* from
their nonsentient and animalistic predecessors than the
Malach had from theirs and not, as the Malach
Deathgivers taught, that they were more primitive.

Such thoughts were heretical, Chaghna'kraa knew,
sufficient to have her status as warrior revoked. For such
a crime, she could well lose her name and be forced to
join the ranks of the *tsurgh'ghah*.

She wondered if humans had evolutionary holdovers
from their pasts. It was hard to tell. They were so
different. . . .

"Prey!" Jir'lischgh'gu shouted, and she leaped forward
on the attack. The artificial *gr'raa* was a few eights of
erucht ahead, squatting in the river, its broad, flat turret
already pivoting to cover their approach.

"Attack!" Chaghna'kraa yelled. "*Ghava'igho*, now!"

Her upper hands closed on the weapons controls, and
the long, slender javelin of a *ghava'igho* dropped from
beneath her wing and arrowed toward the target. Swiftly
she squeezed the trigger again, sending her second
warload after the first. Jir'lischgh'gu loosed two nuclear
penetrators, as did Ghrel'esche'ah Claw-Blooder and
Chu'rrugh'eserch Throat-Tearer; Ra'aasgh'resh Meat-
Gulper launched one, and then the alien machine's main
plasma weapon flared with a blinding radiance that
vaporized the upper half of Ra'aasgh'resh's Hunter.

At a range of scant *erucht*, the nuclear lances swarmed

toward the alien machine. Laser fire snapped and hissed; ion cannons spewed streams of burning starpoints across the landscape. Two missiles were knocked down . . . three . . . four . . . five . . . but then one struck home with a dazzling flare that seemed to engulf the enemy vehicle, disrupting its magnetic shielding long enough for the next missile in line to smash through, though the prey's reactive armor broke up the penetrator jet before it could properly form. Another missile downed, and then another hit, this time close beside the smoking, red-glowing crater in the upper armor left by the earlier hits.

Striking at a point already weakened, and where the external reactive-armor add-on plates had already been triggered, the second missile fired its plasma lance cleanly into vaporizing armor. The small, nuclear warhead followed the path of vacuum left by the beam, smashing into molten flintsteel before detonating in a savage, high-energy flash.

The robot machine was kicked back several meters, rocking heavily to one side before settling back in the seething cloud of steam sent boiling into the sky from the river's surface. The vehicle's deadly main weapon fell silent.

Chaghna'kraa was no longer in a position to care, however. A tenth of a second or so before the penetrator had exploded, she and her companions had been killed, their Hunters wrecked, in a final flurry of plasma bolts from the stricken enemy vehicle.

The smoke over the river valley thickened as the Hunters burned.

CHAPTER TWENTY-FIVE

There was a lot of commercial submarine traffic on Muir. Consequently, the undersea region off the west coast had been thoroughly mapped and the resultant electronic charts uploaded to several different computer systems in and around Kinkaid. Donal had downloaded several sets of those charts into Freddy's memory. He just hoped they were up to date on bottom conditions. According to the charts, the bottom was hard-packed sand between the beach east of Simmstown almost all the way to Point Johannson. Beyond that, there was soft bottom in patches, due mostly to the alluvial deposits of the Singing River, but beyond that it was solid again all the way into Loch Haven.

Donal wasn't sure how good Malach sensors might be, but he doubted that they would be able to track even something as large as a Bolo as it crawled along the seabed, at a depth of over forty meters.

By this time, he imagined, the Malach must be wondering what had become of the Bolo. At last report they were fully in control of the tent city, though—thank God—most of the kids and the Wide Sky adults who'd been taking care of them had managed to get away.

For that matter, Colonel Wood and General Phalbin

and the rest of the brass back at Kinkaid must be about to have kittens by now. One of their Bolos had either just gone rogue or been scragged off the map, and if he was right, they were having trouble right now figuring out which possibility was worse.

Movement at a depth of forty meters was slow. Donal thought that he could probably urge Freddy to move more quickly, but at some point either the surface wake generated by the Bolo's movement or the intense heat released by fusion plants driven to higher and yet higher levels of output would give them away. Donal elected to leave the details of the approach, including both their exact course and speed, to Freddy.

Their position was plotted on a computer-generated map displayed on the otherwise blank toroidal screen. They were almost past the Singing River delta now and ready to turn up into the loch.

He didn't mind the time. He needed it to work on the Rules of Engagement problem. Donal was trying to do now what he knew he should have done before: find a way to get around the damned ROEs without affecting Freddy's ECRL or causing other, unanticipated problems with his psychotronic logic flow. There would be no time for integration testing before going into battle again.

There was also going to be no way to cover what he was doing. The first patch he'd tried had been designed to let him easily restore the ROEs, with no one the wiser. By going in and modifying the ROEs themselves, however, he was leaving a very large and blatant code trail, one that he would not be able to cover once Freddy linked in again with the base computer at the maintenance depot.

"It occurs to me," Freddy said as Donal continued pecking away at the small, special access keyboard, "that we are repeating a historical pattern."

"Yeah?" Donal said, without looking up. Bolo programming included massive amounts of historical data on military situations, tactics, and incidents going back to Narmer and the union of Upper and Lower Egypt. "How's that?"

"I refer to the second major part of the general world conflict during the first century A.E., what the people of the time called World War II. It was a time of great technological advances, with radical experimentation in new weapons, vehicles, and the like.

"Submarines had been introduced as weapons of war earlier in the century, but during this conflict, they became truly deadly. In the geographical theater of war known as 'the Pacific,' one of the combatants, the United States of America, employed submarines with great efficiency against the merchant shipping and surface naval war fleets of the Empire of Japan."

This was all new to Donal, and at another time he might have been interested. Not now, however. "What does this have to do with us?"

"Early in that conflict, American military weapons research developed a new type of torpedo, a kind of underwater missile designed to be fired from a submerged vessel at an enemy ship. It was supposed to explode *under* the target, when triggered by the magnetic fields induced in the water by the target's steel hull, although it would also detonate when striking the target directly. Unfortunately, the new torpedoes did not work as they were supposed to. Submarine commanders fired torpedo after torpedo, but they did not explode. The commanders changed tactics and fired the torpedoes directly into the sides of enemy ships. They knew they were hitting their targets. Sound travels very well under water, and they could hear the warheads striking home, but they still did not explode. The commanders recognized that the new torpedoes were the problem and requested that they be allowed to return to the older, and far more reliable, weapons.

"Unfortunately, the military and political bureaucracy

responsible for producing the defective torpedoes refused to recognize that a problem existed. The bureaucracy insisted that the submarine captains were blaming their equipment to cover their own inefficiency and carelessness."

Donal looked up at that. "That sounds familiar." Some things, it seemed, never changed.

"I thought that you would notice the parallel. In any case, the submarine commanders were left to figure out how to carry out their assigned missions despite direct orders not to tamper with the new torpedoes."

"I think I know what I would have done in that situation."

"My assessment of your character suggests that you would have done the same as the submarine commanders. Once they'd left their home port on war patrol, they had the senior enlisted personnel and weapons specialists aboard disassemble each of twenty-four torpedoes on board their vessel, disable the magnetic exploders that were causing the trouble, and rig the torpedo to explode only on contact, as before. It was a dangerous process, carried out aboard a small and rolling vessel, and the officers involved were under specific orders not to tamper with the weapons. Immediately, the submarines began amassing respectable kill records in combat, sinking millions of tons of enemy shipping. When the submarine was returning from its patrol, before reaching port, the vessel's crew would again disassemble all remaining torpedoes and restore the magnetic exploders."

"And of course, the bureaucrats back home assumed their torpedoes were working just fine."

"That is correct. The debate, with American submarine commanders on one side and the U. S. Bureau of Ordnance on the other, became fierce and acrimonious. Rigorous testing ultimately proved the submariners to be correct. The detonators were faulty. Eventually the problem was recognized and corrected, but until then, the submarine commanders took upon themselves the responsibility of disobeying direct orders and of contravening established procedure in order to carry out their missions."

"And . . . why are you telling me all this?"

"I have been aware, Commander, of a certain tension in your speech patterns, activities, and moods, which I believe reflects the problems you have had with the Muir Military Command Authority. I know that what you are doing now is a direct violation of several standing orders regarding the field maintenance and operation of Bolos, even though your goal is to achieve an increase in my combat efficiency. I thought the story would ease your mind, somewhat. I believe that what you are attempting is the proper course of action."

Donal smiled at that. The Bolo was trying to reassure him. "Thanks, Freddy. I appreciate it."

In fact, he was a lot less concerned now with the effect this act would have on his career than he was with the simple question of whether or not it would work at all. The way he felt right now, if they found out about it later and court martialed him, well, so be it. He wasn't even sure he cared anymore, and he'd been thinking a lot about that hypothetical job he'd discussed a few nights ago with Alexie. The important thing was to make certain there was a later to be court martialed in, and he thought the best way to do that was to cripple the enemy's command and control center on the planet. After seeing Freddy's electronic evidence, he was willing to bet that he would find that center at Glenntor.

But that meant he had to come up with a way to get around the damned ROEs fast. They were on their way to attack Glenntor Castle. Fully a quarter of the ROEs, maybe more, were specifically concerned with protecting someone's property or with protecting humans living on Muir. Once they surfaced near Glenntor, they most emphatically would not have time, for instance, to get permission to cross private property lines as per ROE 20. And what about ROE 12, which prohibited a Bolo from scaring children? That had been one of Donal's absolute favorites . . . until now, knowing that there were probably children being held captive in that castle. Sure, they were scared already, but the key question was, *how would Freddy interpret that ROE?* Once the Bolo was forced to look at the fact that he was going to attack the castle, knowing that there were kids inside, he might easily balk. Donal didn't want to take that chance.

Unfortunately, it wasn't as simple as deleting or commenting out the offending code elements. Freddy's programming didn't use simplistic, straight-line logic. Bolo psychotronics mimicked the approach to problems used by the human brain, with many logic-strings running simultaneously and interconnectedly toward a given goal. As he'd already found out, simply deleting the ROEs outright affected other, widely separated parts of the program, probably in ways that Donal and even Freddy could not possibly predict.

The only way he could think of to cut the ROEs out of the loop was to go through each of them and assign it a specific weight, a number that placed a relative value on that ROE's importance. The numbers had to be logical; a Bolo could be badly affected by code that didn't "feel" right, that was inherently illogical or contained obvious inconsistencies. Hell, that was one of the main problems with the ROEs themselves.

With that in mind, he was assigning all forty-two Rules of Engagement numbers, ranging from 1 for the silliest, in his opinion, to 10 for the rules that had some logic, at least, behind them.

That done, he was now drafting a new ROE—Rule 0—giving it a weight of 15, and inserting it in front of the first of the regular ROEs.

0: WEIGHT: 15. ALL BOLOS, WHEN SO ORDERED BY THEIR
HUMAN COMMANDING OFFICER, WILL DISREGARD ALL RULES
OF ENGAGEMENT OF LESSER WEIGHTED IMPORTANCE. THE
COMMAND ORDER TO DISREGARD LESSER ROES WILL BE THE
SPOKEN WORD "ECLIPSE."

It wasn't perfect, but it was the best he could do on short notice.

He wished he could do the same for Ferdy right now, but that was out of the question. He and Freddy were out of communications now until they surfaced . . . and then they were likely to be busy for a time.

He just hoped Ferdy was holding his own okay.

Freddy swung to the right, and Donal easily felt the motion. He looked up at the ceiling, trying very hard not to imagine the forty or so meters of dark, cold water above it, above him.

He'd never liked being shut in.

They brought Alexie into the Great Hall, leading her at gunpoint.

She hadn't exactly been mistreated during the past several hours, but it had not been pleasant, either. They'd brought her in a flying personnel carrier north over the mountains to Glenntor—she'd recognized the castle when they'd herded her out onto the landing pad and down the winding stone steps—and locked her in the stone-walled basement with seven kids snatched from Simmstown. Over the next hour or so, fourteen more children, ranging in age from six to fifteen, had been shoved through the big wooden door that was the only way out and down the steps to what could only be termed, in this place, a dungeon.

They'd not been bothered after that, though occasional snarls and inhuman barks and shrieks floated down from upstairs, and sometimes they could hear the far-off thunder of explosions, proving that the battle was continuing. Alexie was the only adult prisoner the Malach had. She had sat on the floor in a circle with the kids, and they'd talked, trying to comfort one another. Possibly, possibly, when the battle was over, they would be released, exchanged for Malach taken prisoner by the humans.

It was the slenderest of hopes, and a futile one, Alexie was sure. The Malach were so . . . alien. What value did they place on a human life? For that matter, what value did they place on an individual Malach? The idea of a prisoner exchange might be totally foreign to their way of thinking.

The Great Hall—she remembered that night, not so long ago, when this room had been filled with light and people and gaiety—was a place of cold terror, and she lost then all hope of ever being released. Twelve naked and bloody human bodies hung dripping from chains along one wall, with hooks driven through the bottoms of their jaws and out through soundlessly gaping mouths. Some of the corpses had been cut and torn in ways that suggested torture. Others showed burns and missing limbs that might mean they'd been shot and killed before being strung up like so many raw slabs of drox meat.

At least, she hoped they'd been dead by then.

Until that moment, she'd thinking of these creatures less as *lizards* and more as dragons. Up close, they were too powerful, too graceful, too obviously in control of themselves and of the situation to think of them as comical little reptilian skitterers that you might find under a desert rock. Confronted by those hideously mangled and callously displayed bodies, she stopped thinking of them as anything as comfortable and as comprehensible as dragons. They were monsters in every sense of the term, monstrously inhuman in form, in deed, and in thought.

There were eight Malach in the room, besides the guard who'd brought her here. One rested on a human-made sofa that had been stripped of its arms and back so that

the creature could lie on it, belly down, tail hanging off
the end. One of the others approached her, its head
overtopping hers by nearly half a meter. She stood her
ground, staring up into unwinking ruby eyes. The mouth,
lined with double rows of razor-edged teeth, gaped; the
odd-looking mustache of constantly writhing pink worms
rippled with some unknown, untranslatable emotion.
"You . . . sssubmit," the Malach croaked.

Alexie blinked. She'd not known any of these creatures
spoke English.

"What do you want of me?" she asked. "What do you
want me to do?"

"You . . . sssubmit . . . sssoldiers. Why."

The last word was lacked the usual rising tone of inquiry
at the end, and she almost missed the fact that the Malach
was asking a question. It was extremely difficult to
understand the being. Its half-meter jaws were not well
adapted to human-made sounds. Worse, it had a poor
command of inflection and intonation, coupled with the
fact that there was no way at all Alexie could read the
thing's scaly green and red, grinning-lizard's expression.

"I wasn't surrendering," she said. "I was trying to stop
your . . . your men from killing the children."

What did it mean when that pink-worm mustache
rippled outward from the center?

"Why."

"Damn it, you don't kill children, even in war! Not
deliberately, anyway!"

"Why."

This, Alexie thought with a tired shake of her head, was
not going to get them anywhere. Worst of all, she couldn't
tell whether the thing's expressionless lack of understanding was genuine, or a pose designed to draw her out,
to make her tell them more about herself. Hell, she couldn't
even tell how much of her own words carried meaning
for these monsters, or even what that meaning might be.

"Look," she said. "Your soldiers were trying to kill some children. Understand? We don't do that. We wouldn't deliberately kill your young. It's not . . . not civilized." *Damn! What do these things know about civilized?* she thought, a little wildly. "I wanted to stop them. I told them not to. That's all." She didn't add how very surprised she'd been when one of the Malach had dropped a net over her. She'd been so close to death in that moment.

At the moment, with those tortured corpses hanging nearby, she was very much afraid that she would soon be wishing the Malach *had* killed her on the spot.

The lizard on the couch behind her questioner hissed and snarled something. The interrogator turned, raising its chin high, and barked something in reply. Turning again to face her, the Malach said, "You . . . understand . . . sssubmit. You . . . not . . . female."

Again, it took Alexie a moment to understand that the Malach was asking a question in that flat, hissing, and uninflected voice. She had the distinct impression that, as it spoke one word, it was searching through its memory for the next, literally translating word by word without a clear understanding of each.

It was asking if she was female. No . . . it was wondering if she could be a female, given that she'd surrendered to the soldiers.

What did being female have to do with anything?

The Malach on the couch—Alexie was getting the definite idea that that one was the boss here—snarled again. Again, the interrogator saluted by lifting its chin . . . and Alexie decided that it was a gesture of submission among these beings.

Understanding dawned. Among humans, bowing was the gesture for showing submissive behavior, a way of saying, "Look! My head's down! I can't see you, but you can see me and you could whack me with a club if you wanted to." With dogs, she knew, the animal might roll over onto its back . . . again, a way of making itself seem helpless to a stronger pack member. For the Malach, though, raising those heavy chins, exposing the throat to bite or claw-slash, that was what meant "I'm vulnerable, I yield to you."

Was it as simple as that? She thought back to her capture, remembering her stance, hands on hips, looking *up* into the Malach soldier's face.

It had completely misread her body language . . . and Alexie suddenly knew that the mistake was all that had saved her.

Deliberately, she raised her chin, looking at the ceiling. "I . . . submit." Somehow, she had to establish two-way comprehension enough with these beings to start exchanging meaningful information. If they wanted her to "sssubmit," fine.

"You . . . female."

"I'm female. Yes."

"Female . . . no . . . sssubmit."

Had she done it wrong? Where was the confusion here? Heart pounding, she looked steadily at the ceiling. "I submit."

The interrogator strode over to the hanging bodies, its claws *click-clicking* on the stone. Reaching up with one of its smaller, upper arms, it touched one of the dead women on the hip. "Thissss . . . female."

Alexie swallowed, making herself look. "Yes. Female." Did she know the woman? She looked familiar. And very dead.

The interrogator moved to the next body in line, and touched it as well. Alexie shuddered. It was one of the PGPH guys she'd argued with a few nights ago, the redheaded man whose family had owned this castle. What was his name? Dela something or other.

"Thisss . . . male."

"Yes."

The interrogator turned, and the body swayed alarmingly, twisting back and forth on its chain. The jaw, she thought, had been dislocated, and she was terribly afraid that if it tore loose and the body dropped into that puddle of blood on the floor beneath, she was going to be sick.

"Male . . . think."

"What?"

"You . . . maless . . . think . . . sssame . . . femaless."

It's a question. Think of it as a question. It wants . . . "Oh! You're asking if human males are . . . are intelligent?" She thought fast, then risked a question of her own. "Malach males! Are they intelligent?" The creature blinked at her, mustache rippling, and she realized she'd confused it. "Uh . . . Malach males think, yes?"

"Malach . . . malesss . . . urrr." It seemed to be groping for a word. "Malesss . . . make . . . more . . . Malachsss. No . . . think. Femalesss." One upper hand smacked against a scaly chest. "Femaless. Warriorsss. Think."

Sexual dichotomy. In Malach culture—hell, in Malach *biology*—the females did the fighting, the food gathering, and the thinking too. Males were there for reproduction and probably not much else. You didn't need brains if all you did was copulate.

She was reminded of a fish she'd read about once, a creature that lived in the deeps of old Earth's seas. Males attached themselves to the larger female's body, turning parasite, eventually shriveling up until they were little more than a wart on the female's skin. This situation wasn't that extreme, but it carried the same idea. There was, she admitted, a certain biological efficiency in the arrangement.

"Human males are intelligent," she said. "Uh . . . human males think. Human *females* think. All same."

"You . . . female."

Back to that again. "*Yes*, damn it! I'm *female*!"

"Femalesss . . . no . . . sssubmit."

She was beginning to understand that part of the problem lay in the Malach interrogator's limited vocabulary, and the rest in its inability to comprehend a system different from its own. Submit, as he . . no, as *she* was using the word might mean one of two things . . . simple surrender in the face of overwhelming force, or the ritual gestures of rank and respect this race seemed to use. They seemed to be having trouble accepting that she was a female and that she'd surrendered. That must be the trouble.

Carefully, making no sudden moves, she unsealed the long, black leather jacket she was wearing. Underneath she was wearing a white, fairly tight knit sweater that showed off the gentle swelling of her breasts to good advantage. The Malach in the room watched her impassively and didn't seem to understand. She grimaced, biting off a foul word. Of course they didn't understand. These lizards didn't have mammaries and didn't associate them with femaleness. What did their young eat, she wondered? She wasn't sure she wanted to know the answer to that.

And she didn't know how to prove that she was female. She suspected, though, that the Malach were confused about her sex, and that could be dangerous. If they associated maleness with blind instinct, with lack of intelligence, even with just plain, old-fashioned stupidity, she might be in real trouble. . . .

The boss Malach spat something, and the interrogator advanced, reaching out to close the claws of one upper hand on her jacket, tugging. "Remove."

"Hey, wait just a damned minute!"

"You . . . remove. Show . . . female."

The boss snarled again, and another Malach grabbed her arms from behind, holding her immobile as the inquisitor continued tugging at her clothing.

She managed not to scream as they gave her body a close, rough, and embarrassingly thorough examination.

CHAPTER TWENTY-SIX

I have been seriously damaged, though not incapacitated. As I defended my position in the Kinkaid River Valley, one of the Enemy's nuclear penetrators struck me on my starboard side midway back along and just above my forward-right track assembly. The front-right skirt has been blown away, the track broken, and several of the right-forward road wheels rendered useless. Worse, the cooling unit for my number one fusion plant was badly damaged, forcing me to shut that power system down entirely to avoid meltdown. As a result, my available power is down to 66 percent, not counting charge plate and battery reserves. Perhaps most serious of all, the Enemy weapon ruptured my reserve cryo-hydrogen tank, destroying its coolant system and allowing most of the hydrogen slush to boil away. Not only is this fuel for my fusion power plants, it is the reserve from which I draw the frozen hydrogen-ice pellets that generate fusion in Hellbore ignition sequencing. Suddenly, fuel and ammunition have become urgent concerns. I will need field servicing, and quickly.

I try to raise headquarters on my radio.

"Bolo 96875 of the Line!" a voice crackles over my tactical net before I can make my report. "This is the Military Command Authority! What is your status?"

It is not the voice of my Commander, but the signal possesses the proper code authorizations. I tell them the extent of my damage. "I have held the Enemy," I conclude, wondering if I have put too much into the words of the emphasis humans call pride. "The Enemy threat in the Southern Sector appears to be neutralized."

"Okay," another voice says, and this one I recognize as that of Colonel Wood, the Brigade Commander. "You've done well. Very well. But there's another threat now. We don't have any Malach forces in your area. You've gotten them all. But there's more coming down from the north, and they're heading straight for Kinkaid. You're all we have to stop them!"

I feel a stab of alarm at that. What has happened to Bolo 96876 of the Line and our Commander? I attempt to reach them, without result. "What is the status of Bolo 96876 of the Line?" I ask.

"Damn, your guess is as good as ours. They entered the ocean almost an hour ago. We haven't heard from them since."

Which means Bolo 96876 may not be destroyed. I am . . . relieved.

"What are my orders?" I ask.

"You got Criton Pass on a map?"

I assume the question is rhetorical. I have extensive maps of all of Muir's surface terrain. Criton Pass is a major valley leading south through the Grampian Mountains. A surface-vehicle roadway, Route 1, traverses the pass about halfway between Kinkaid and Simmstown.

"Bolo? Do you copy?"

I realize that the question was not rhetorical after all. Can these officers be so unaware of Bolo operations and capabilities? "I copy. I have Criton Pass on my map display."

"The Malach are coming south, right down Route 1. We estimate approximately one hundred of their walkers,

moving on foot. At their current speed, they'll reach the pass in three hours."

I already have the Enemy forces plotted, downloaded from HQ's intelligence web. "Two hours, fifty-eight minutes, fifteen seconds," I reply, "assuming no change in course or speed." I consider the situation for several seconds, as I cross-check calculations, run another series of diagnostics on my own systems, and calculate the evaporation loss of my remaining stores of hydrogen.

"I can reach the southern end of Criton Pass in 2.257 hours," I report. "In time to intercept the enemy. However, I need my service team to make field repairs and to patch and refuel my reserve cryo-H tank."

"Right." The voice is crisp, professional, and I am glad. At first, I thought I could hear panic there, and panic could interfere with the smooth operation of HQ's command and control responsibilities. Colonel Wood sounds like a competent officer, though I've not worked directly under him before. "Can you move?"

"Affirmative." I hesitate again, weighing variables. "However, I must point out that to reach Criton Pass in time, I will have to pass through Kinkaid, preferably on the main street through the center of town, which feeds directly into Route 1, but I am explicitly prohibited from doing this by ROE 10, and possibly also by ROEs—"

"It's okay! On my authority, I order you to disregard that ROE. If you have to come straight through town, you do it."

"Colonel Wood!" another voice says, and I compute a 78 percent probability that this is General Phalbin, the Confederation ground force CO. "What the devil are you doing?"

"This isn't a political issue any more, General," the Colonel replies. "It's a matter of survival!"

"Harrumph! You can't just—"

The communications link snaps off abruptly, and I am

left wondering what is going on. It sounds as though there is still some confusion—not to mention dissension—within the HQ staff.

"Ah . . . Bolo," Colonel Wood's voice says a moment later. "You still there?"

"Affirmative, Commander." *He is my Commander now, since Lieutenant Ragnor is out of communications and possibly MIA.* "Bolo 96875 of the Line, awaiting orders."

"Look, there's no time to waste. You just start moving north, okay? We'll hash this thing out on our end, and get back to you. All right?"

"Affirmative."

The escaping super-cooled hydrogen has frozen the river around me. I am encased in a block of ice. By exerting myself—and putting a further drain on my power systems—I shatter the ice prison and lurch forward. Water flows again, carrying chunks of ice downstream, together with some of the corpses of the Enemy. I make my way out of the river and onto the bank, swinging onto the road leading northwest toward Kinkaid.

Wood turned to face Phalbin, his fists clenched tight as he fought to control his rising anger. "Sir," he said, his voice steady. "With all due respect . . . you are an idiot! Sir!"

"Harrumph! You can't talk to me like—"

"It's about time someone did, even if it costs him his career! Right now, General, that Bolo is the only damned thing on this planet that has a prayer of even slowing that Malach horde down. If we don't ditch those moronic ROEs you and Chard and the peace-puppies put together and ditch them fast, they're going to be our epitaphs!"

The glower on Phalbin's face faded a little. "It won't help if we destroy the city trying to save it."

"He'll wreck the main street, General, that's for sure, and probably take out a few buildings along the way. But

I promise you that the Malach are going to wreck a whole lot more."

Phalbin looked uncertain. "I should consult with the Governor—"

"Fine. Consult. I'm going to kill those ROEs."

"How?"

Wood pursed his lips. "A patch ought to do it. Something simple. A code word to make him disregard all ROEs. Or we weight 'em, give 'em priority numbers, and give him a higher priority command. We'll see what we have time for."

Phalbin sighed. "If you're sure . . ." He shook his head. "If this backfires . . ."

"There's no other way, General. Believe me."

Phalbin started to turn away, then stopped himself. "What about the other Bolo?"

"What do you mean?"

"Should we get rid of its Rules of Engagement too?"

"I probably don't need to."

"Why not? If they're hamstringing *one* Bolo—"

Wood grinned. "The ROEs include injunctions against attacking private property, right?" Phalbin nodded. "I have a feeling I know where Ragnor is going, and if I'm right, he's already done something about your ROEs. He'd have to, if Freddy was going to follow his orders."

Phalbin started to purple. "You mean he already took them out? *Against orders?*"

"He's a soldier, General. He did what he had to do to carry out his mission. Whatever the consequences to himself. Or to his command."

"If this goes wrong," Phalbin pointed out, "he won't just be looking at a note in his record. He'll be looking at prison!"

"Assuming, General, that there are prisons left, or officers to sit on his court martial board . . . and that he is still alive to face them."

"Harrumph," Phalbin said, but without any real feeling, as he turned away again.

Wood began looking for a programmer tech to help him with the Bolo ROE deletion patch.

They'd slowed when they entered the fjord, moving along at only a few kilometers per hour lest their speed create a wake visible on the calm surface of the water overhead. Donal wasn't quite sure how Freddy was finding his way through the murk. Though it was still daylight above, little sunlight penetrated the dark, chilly waters of the fjord, and there was considerable sediment suspended in the water near the bottom. The Bolo was navigating by inertial guidance, knowing that if it had proceeded at a heading of 055 degrees for 29.945 kilometers after rounding Tanhausser Point, it was time to swing hard right to 140 for the approach to the castle.

The fjord, like all such ice-carved, water-filled troughs slicing into the mountains ashore, was extremely deep in the center, with swiftly shoaling, steep-sloped sides and a U-shaped bottom. Donal didn't need to look at the flicker of orientation and navigation data on the main screen to feel the sharp tilt of the Bolo to the left as it ground slowly along the fjord's bottom.

Suddenly, though, it turned right and he felt the deck rising from the front. They were moving up a steepening slope toward the surface.

The screens were still murky with dark and mud-clouded water, but he could see it lightening gradually as they climbed toward the surface. The prow of the Bolo dropped forward suddenly as the lead tread assemblies gripped solid, friction-grooved ferrocrete.

The launching ramp! Freddy's navigation had been perfect!

In another second, murk gave way to white foam, then daylight as the top of the Bolo's turret emerged dripping from the dark waters of the fjord. The sky was clear, the sun low on the western horizon, with none of the rain that had been drizzling above the refugee encampment on the other side of the mountains.

"Commander," Freddy said. "I must inform you that we are trespassing on private property now and should notify—"

"Freddy! Eclipse!"

"Code word Eclipse accepted." There was a pause, and then Donal could almost swear he heard excitement creeping into the Bolo's electronic voice. "Proceeding with the attack."

The Bolo emerged from the fjord, a vast, black, wet monster rising from the sea. . . .

"She *is* female anatomically," Kha'laa'sht the Meat Finder said. "At least outwardly, she is identical to other human females. We would have to open her up, of course, to be certain. . . ."

"Not now," Aghrrracht decided. She was examining several of the fabric artifacts the human had been wearing. Why did they carry these on their bodies? They were not strong enough to serve as armor, and they were inefficient as carrying harnesses. "Perhaps later, when we have learned all we can from her while she is living."

It was puzzling. The human was female, yet she had surrendered on the field of battle without putting up even a token fight. Aghrrracht was willing to grant that the humans had different symbologies, different customs, even a different way of looking at things . . . but females were supposed to fight. How else to determine the hierarchy of submission and deference necessary to a properly ordered culture? Aghrrracht had *won* her right to be Supreme Deathgiver in a thousand brutal engagements in the arena, beginning with her *Ga'krascht* Coming-of Blood ceremony. Could it be that this human was simply very low-caste? A human Nameless, perhaps?

Except that Cho said she'd been defending human young. That made no sense at all. She'd defended them by *surrendering*. . . .

Kha'laa'sht held up one of the outer garments taken from the prisoner, a black artifact apparently made from the skin of a lesser animal.

"She requests that she be allowed to keep this. Apparently, these artifacts keep them warm."

Aghrracht closed an upper hand in assent. Was that what the cloth things were for? Was it possible the humans' internal temperature regulation was deficient, somehow?

Her communicator buzzed. Sighing, she pulled it from her harness and squeezed the receive key. "Yes."

"Deathgiver! The alien *gr'raa* machine—"

"Who is this? Identify yourself!"

"Urrr . . . Gnasetherach the Brutal Killer, at Sentry Post Seven! Deathgiver, an alien combat machine is rising from the water!"

Aghrracht blinked. A human Bolo? Here? "You are sure?" If Gnasetherach was on guard duty, she was an ordinary soldier, not a warrior. Her perceptions might not be up to—

The Deathgiver's thoughts were chopped short by a burst of noise from the receiver. It sounded like high-speed gunfire.

"Cho!" she snapped at the interrogator. "Ask the human what one of her Bolos is doing here!"

On the screen, Donal could see a number of watercraft moored by the ramp, including the civilian submarine he'd noticed the other night. Several Malach soldiers were visible, some by the water, more at the top of the ramp, others on the ramparts of the stone walls rising above the Bolo. One shouted, a snarling bark; an instant later, laser beams were playing harmlessly across Freddy's outer hull, accompanied by the spang of magnetically accelerated gauss slugs.

"Objective in sight, Commander," Freddy said. "We are taking ineffective small-arms fire from Enemy infantry."

"Okay, Freddy. Let's take 'em down!"

Freddy's infinite repeaters erupted in stuttering sprays and streams of blue-green stars, the salvos sweeping the boat ramp like a broom, then reaching up and across the ramparts, splintering stone, shattering walls, exploding flesh, hurling six-limbed bodies and body parts over the crenelations of the wall. A shoulder-launched missile streaked in a meter above the ferrocrete, but Freddy detonated it with an antimissile laser at a range of less than five meters, the explosion fireballing into the sky in a mushroom of orange flame and oily black smoke.

All of Freddy was clear of the water now, his long, dark gray form dripping as it moved slowly up the sloping ramp and into the late afternoon sun. Fire erupted from a window high up on one tower; a stream of infinite repeater ion bolts seared through the window with pinpoint accuracy, and the sniping ceased instantly.

"I am launching drones, Commander," Freddy said. "We need to see the entire battlefield."

"Do it."

A pair of GalTech KV-20 recon drones hissed skyward from Freddy's vertical-launch tubes, then leveled off, airfoils and sensors unfolding. Running on low-power hydrogen cells and possessing an almost invisibly small radar cross-section, the KV-20s could loiter over a battlefield for hours, passing sensor and visual feeds back to the Bolo that commanded them.

"Let's see IR, Freddy," Donal said, watching the side screens that showed both recon drone sensor feeds in parallel. The landscape outside transformed, darkening to the eerie green cast of infrared, with heat sources glowing in whites and shimmering yellows. The walls of the castle were stone, a meter thick in some places, and impossibly opaque. The ceilings, though, were another matter, thinner and more transparent to certain wavelengths of infrared.

Freddy highlighted a group of moving yellow blobs indistinctly visible against the green-gray sweep of the castle's main roof. "These are almost certainly Malach soldiers," he said. "Close analysis of the heat imagery suggests body temperatures in the range of thirty-two to thirty-four degrees Celsius, and the size of individual images is suggestive of Malach."

"Do you see any human images there?"

"Negative, Commander. Of course, the image is of troops only on the upper floor, and we cannot obtain IR imagery from lower floors. However, the prisoners will have been moved to a place of relative safety at our first appearance, if they were not there already. The Enemy likely will want to protect them, both for the information they possess and for their possible value as hostages."

"There aren't going to be any hostages, Freddy." Donal said with a growl. "That wall, over there. Take it down!"

Freddy didn't bother with weapons to carry out the order. Tracks shrieking, he swung hard to the left and rammed the wall, bringing half of it down in a clattering, dust-billowing avalanche of stone.

Thunder rolled just beyond the stone walls of the castle, and Alexie's heart leaped.

Her interrogator apparently thought she'd not understood her last question. "You . . . Bolo . . . here . . . why."

"I don't know," she said. "But I suggest that you surrender . . . that you *submit* as quickly as you can."

The interrogator was speaking rapidly to the boss, a catfight of snarls and hisses. Alexie took a careful look around. There were eight Malach in the hall with her, but most were nervously looking in the direction of the rumbling sounds and cracking gunfire, or at one another with troubled-looking quartets of winking, ruby-red eyes.

She wanted to believe that the Bolo was smashing right in to rescue her, but she knew better. This part of whathisname's castle, as she recalled, was three stories tall, plus a basement—the place where she and the kids had been kept—below that. A Bolo was bigger than the building, damned near as big as the entire fortress complex, and if it came through a wall, it would bring the entire structure down in one, great, crashing heap. In any case, the Bolo couldn't know that she and the kids were being held here.

Whatever was happening, though, it was making the entire building shake.

The boss Malach sprang to her feet, snarling instructions. Four Malach started moving toward a door, while a fifth approached Alexie, hands reaching out. . . .

The far wall bulged inward alarmingly. The pillars lining both sides of the hall trembled, and pieces of ceiling plaster and beams cracked loose, raining down on the room. The bodies of the massacred humans danced and twisted on their chains like grotesque puppets; one tore free and collapsed in a heap.

Alexie fell to her hands and knees as the floor jolted and lurched in an earthquake's dance. A massive block of stone dropped from a crumbling ceiling, smashing into the back of the Malach approaching her and knocking her flat and shrieking. One of the huge, ornamental pillars at the near end of the room suddenly toppled, breaking free of its ceiling supports and crashing sideways into the stairway going up that Alexie and Donal had followed a few nights before. More stone fell, an avalanche of great, flat slabs that made up the floor of the room above.

Alexie saw a chance. The fallen pillar was held part way up by the crushed remnants of the stairway and banister. There was a space underneath, less than a meter

tall, wide enough for a human to scramble into, but not
a Malach. The injured monster's strangely shaped and
heavy sidearm had skittered across bare stone. Alexie
rose unsteadily to her feet, then dived after it, falling
again, rolling, snatching up the weapon, turning to aim
it at her captors. One Malach screamed, pointing a savage
claw at the human prisoner; she found something like a
squeeze lever awkwardly placed for her in the weapon's
stock and clamped down on it as hard as she could. Laser
light speared the gesticulating Malach, slicing through
her throat in a spray of blue-green blood. She fired again
and missed, then threw herself flat on the floor, scrambling
ahead and beneath the overhang of the fallen pillar.

The quaking had ceased, though pieces of stone
continued to shower down on the room, and Alexie didn't
know whether or not the entire pile of tumbled-down
rock was going to collapse the rest of the way to the floor
at any second and crush her underneath like a bug.

But the crevice of a cave gave her cover, of a sort.
When the light at the end of the tunnel she'd crawled
into was blocked—as if by a Malach bending over to look
inside, she fired the alien laser back down the passageway.

She only had to do that twice.

Now, she thought, breathing hard. The air was gritty
with dust. *Will they try to get me, or give up and go
attend to more urgent business?*

From the snarls and snuffling, rasping noises outside
her hidey-hole, it didn't sound as though they were leaving.

Donal surveyed the damage through the circular view
screen. Freddy had smashed completely through the outer
wall of the castle and entered the bailey, the open area
enclosed by the main walls, then driven straight ahead
and into the west wall of the castle's main residence. With
a surgeon's skill, the Bolo had pierced the three-story
building's wall with one forward corner of its massively

armored glacis, then backed gently away; at twenty meters tall from ground to Hellbore turret top, the Bolo actually loomed above the residence's peaked and turreted roof and could easily have brought the entire structure down in an avalanche of broken stone.

But if there were human prisoners being held here, they would be in that building, and Freddy had tailored his destructiveness to punching an opening through the wall at the first-story level, and no more.

The Malach field command HQ, Donal recalled, would likely be in this building. He hoped Freddy's display had left them sufficiently shaken and disorganized.

For several moments, Freddy continued battling with Malach forces in the castle. There were no walkers here that Donal could see, just ordinary infantry, armed and on foot. Freddy burned them down with a ruthless, blunt efficiency as he backed carefully out of the hole he'd bulldozed into the residence wall.

"Okay, Freddy," he said. "Hold the fort." He winced at his own bad pun, then added, "Sorry." Moving to the back to the Fighting Compartment, he pressed a hand panel and opened a small arms locker. Inside was a Concordiat powergun, Mark XXX. He removed it, checked the power cell, and adjusted the beam to high-energy needle. He also paused to don a combat armor vest and a helmet with built-in commo suite and enhanced optics visor, and attached several concussion grenades to his harness.

"I am uncertain of the wisdom of your exposing yourself to the Enemy in this manner, Commander."

"Combined arms, Freddy. There are still a few things a man can do that a Bolo can't."

"I understand, Commander. Please remain in radio contact."

"Count on it! Open up!"

The military concept of combined arms was an old

one, dating back at least to twentieth century warfare. The earliest combat fighting machines—*tanks*, they'd been called, weapons preceding the earliest Bolo marks— had been slow, poorly armored, haplessly vulnerable things. Toward the end of the twentieth century, in fact, there'd been serious doubt that tanks or similar large military vehicles would find a place in what then passed for modern warfare. When a single, poorly trained infantryman could carry and fire a shoulder-launched anti-armor missile that had a decent chance of destroying a vehicle costing many times as much as the launch system, then tanks were clearly on the verge of becoming obsolete.

Combined arms tactics had been evolved to counter this threat, deploying infantry in close joint operations with the tanks to protect them from missile-wielding enemy infantry. In fact, there were plenty of combat tasks that a tank simply couldn't perform—like clearing a house without demolishing it, or locating and clearing an enemy tunnel complex.

Hostage rescue was another. The aft hatchway dilated open and the rear ramp went down. Donal vaulted clear of the Bolo, striking the ground on his shoulder and rolling to the cover of some fallen stone blocks, weapon raised and ready. No one shot at him; the courtyard was empty of any save dead Malach. The opening Freddy had smashed into the wall of the castle residence gaped open, black and uninviting. Hurrying past the motionless Bolo, Donal plunged inside, his helmet visor automatically adjusting to feed him light enough to see by.

He picked his way over a spill of stone blocks, noting several dead Malach crushed by the rubble. One Malach advanced toward him, stumbling blindly; Donal aimed the powergun and squeezed the trigger, sending a hot, blue bolt searing into the alien's chest. Another Malach screamed, and in seconds, four . . . no, six of the aliens were rushing him, crowding through a flimsy door as he

calmly took aim at one after another, drilling each before
it could break free of the press and attack him. Freddy,
he thought, would have appreciated his tactics, forcing
the enemy to funnel through a narrow choke point where
they blocked one another and could be taken down by
surgically precise fire. The room was too cramped for
him to use grenades, but so long as his handgun's power
pack held . . .

An explosion demolished a nearby wall and he spun,
firing wildly as yet more of the saurian invaders spilled
through the smoking gap, trying to reach him.

Seconds later, the Malach were dead. Listening, he
could hear snarls and rasps that might be Malachs shouting
in the distance.

The first floor of the residence had been fitted as a
series of comfortable, wood-paneled rooms, including a
kitchen, sitting rooms, servants' quarters, and the like.
The Great Hall, he was pretty sure, was upstairs, where
it could be accessed directly from the towertop landing
pad, and there was another level above that, with the
family's sleeping quarters. These rooms, equipped for
human comfort, were probably of little interest to the
Malach, and he didn't have time or resources for a careful
search. He moved toward the noises, picking his way
over the mound of reptilian bodies.

As he came through a door into what looked like a
large pantry or larder, a Malach soldier took a stance in
front of a large and solid-looking wooden door. Donal
shot it before the Malach could raise its own weapon,
drilling it cleanly through that massive, scale-armored
head.

Swiftly, he jogged across the stone-cluttered floor. If
that Malach trooper had been standing there even with
the castle falling in around it, it had to be because it
was on guard . . . and probably guarding something pretty
important. Donal tried the door. Locked. Stepping back,

he dialed the Mark XXX down to a tight, hard, low-powered but very intense beam and sliced through the metal bar that locked the door shut.

The door sagged open. Beyond, more stairs led down into darkness.

And children.

"Who . . . who's there?" a young voice called.

"It's okay," he called down to them. "I'm human. Come on out!"

They came up the stone steps slowly and with some hesitation, blinking in the light. Most were younger, anywhere from six to twelve or so. One looked older, a teenage boy with black hair and an expression of grim determination. They must have been swept up in the refugee camp, he thought.

"Okay, everybody," Donal called. It looked like there were about twenty kids all together. "We're going to get you out of here. Is this everybody?"

"The deputy director!" the older boy said. "She's not here! They have her in here, somewhere!"

Donal felt a horrible, inner shock. "What . . . Alexie? Alexie Turner?"

The kid nodded. "They captured her down at Simms-town. They were questioning her upstairs someplace when the walls came down!"

"Okay." He took a deep breath, steadying himself, then clapped the boy reassuringly on the shoulder. "Okay. What's your name?"

"Johnny. Uh, John Sarlucci, sir. I'm from, I *was* from Wide Sky."

"Okay, Johnny. This is important. Can you take charge of everybody here? The younger ones need someone older to look after them, get them where we need them to go."

He nodded.

"Okay. Count them, so you'll know how many you have."

"Twenty-one, sir."

"Good." The kid was on the ball. "Take them up those stairs, go right, and look for a big hole in the wall. You can't miss it. You'll see a Bolo out there."

"A *Bolo*? Wow!"

"Yeah, but you stay away from it, and keep the kids away too." Freddy's hull was probably low-grade hot after that blasting he'd taken with the tactical nukes. "Go past the Bolo and out of the castle. Most of the wall there is down." He stopped. He needed a place for these kids to hide. Maybe . . . "You a pilot yet, Johnny? Personal flitters? Speedsters? Anything?"

The dirty face creased in a smile. "Heck, yeah! You name it, I fly it. I *am* fifteen."

"Standard? Or Skyan?"

"Skyan. That's sixteen standard."

"Well, actually I was wondering about how you were with boats."

"No problem! I worked for my dad, back on Wide Sky, y'know? Working the pinkjack schools out of Fortrose."

"Great! Go outside, and down the ramp toward the water. You'll see a submarine moored to the pier. Got that?" Another nod. "It's a civilian job, like a yacht. The hatch is standing open. Its controls will be just like a boat, and most have automatic defaults."

"Sure! I drove a Mod 20 Deepstar back on Wide Sky, for my dad!"

Of course. The Wide Sky fishing industries tended to be family affairs, and kids brought into the business would learn young. "You're in command, then, Captain Sarlucci. Get these kids aboard that sub. Make sure you get all of the lines cast off before you back into the fjord."

"I told you I know—"

"And I'm making sure you know. When you're clear of the fjord, submerge and let the automatics take you. Follow the coastline south. I don't think the lizards will be able to spot you, and even if they do they won't take any interest in you. They're going to have other things on their minds."

"Where should I go?"

"If you can find Kinkaid, head for the big bay there and find a marina. If not, well, just find any seaport or coastal ship facility you can. Just make sure it's at least fifty or sixty kilometers south of the fjord." He didn't want Johnny bringing his passengers to shore in the middle of enemy-held territory. "The sub'll have a good computer map that'll plot things for you."

"You can count on me, Lieutenant, uh . . ."

"Call me Donal."

"Where are you going to be, Donal?"

"Upstairs, looking for Alexie," he replied.

"I might be able to tell you something about the place," Johnny said. "They had me up there once, a few hours ago." He shuddered.

"Okay, Johnny, tell me. But make it fast."

He wanted these kids out of here.

Minutes later, he made his way to the foot of the stairway Johnny said led to the big stone room upstairs. An infinite repeater shrieked, and Donal heard explosions and falling masonry. After talking with Johnny, he'd raised Freddy on his comm unit, warning him the kids were coming through and telling the machine to provide cover for them if necessary. The kids would be safe enough until they got clear of the place. He hoped.

It was all he could do, working on his own. If Alexie was in the Great Hall, though, he wasn't going to leave her behind.

The Great Hall lay beyond the door at the top of the steps. Part of the north wall had tumbled down, and Donal saw three Malach lying motionless on the stone floor, dead or stunned. Others were still very much alive, clustered around a pile of debris as though trying to scramble underneath. A square-sided pillar had fallen across a stairway on the opposite side of the room, creating a low and cramped cave between the pillar's base and the partly collapsed stairs. The surviving Malach—there were five, he saw—appeared to be trying to get at something underneath the fallen pillar.

Dropping to one knee, Donal took aim with the powergun braced in both hands and squeezed off a shot . . . and another . . . and another. Two Malach were down before the others realized where the fire was coming from and turned to face him. A third went down trying to bring its curiously shaped weapon to bear.

Two were still standing. One fired, the beam snapping into the wooden door beside Donal's head and igniting it with a crack and a shower of glowing embers. He returned the fire, hitting the Malach in the chest just above a complex buckle holding its black leather harness in place. A red light winked on the back of the powergun. Charge drained! He *might* have enough juice for another low-power shot, but . . .

The last remaining Malach raised its weapon. . . .

CHAPTER TWENTY-SEVEN

Donal pitched to the side as the Malach fired, diving behind a fallen block of sandstone, the bolt glancing off the side of his helmet with a crackling hiss. Pain seared the right side of his head. He yanked the damaged helmet off and pitched it aside.

Without the helmet's optics, the room was dimly lit, but plenty of light filtered in through the tall, narrow windows in one wall. He reached for a grenade as the lone remaining Malach took a step forward, and then suddenly its head pitched sharply up, toothy mouth gaping. Smoke curled from a gaping, ragged hole in its back as it collapsed face-down on the floor.

Now what?

A human, a *woman*, crawled out from under the fallen pillar, clutching one of the alien weapons.

"Alexie!"

Her eyes widened as she turned toward his voice. "Donal? *Donal!*"

They clung to one another, savoring the hug. Until that moment, he'd not realized just how much she'd meant to him. He held her off at arm's length, looking her up and down. Her only clothing was the leather jacket he'd seen her in last, torn and dust-covered. She was barefoot

347

and bare-legged, and she looked exhausted. A nasty cut on her forehead was bleeding freely, and there were dark circles beneath her eyes.

"What happened to you?"

She grimaced and tried to tug the jacket a little closer about her body. "I was lucky to keep this much. The Grand High muckety-muck took it into her head that I *couldn't* be female because I'd surrendered, and they decided to perform a little strip search just to make sure. I got them to let me have this jacket back, after they'd searched it, by claiming I'd freeze to death if they didn't. No scales to keep me warm, y'know?"

"Wait. You said the lead lizard was a female?"

She pointed to one of the bodies sprawled on the floor . . . one of the ones dead already when Donal had entered the hall. "That's her. Yeah, they're *all* female, Donal. A race of Amazons. I don't even think the males are sentient."

"How did you learn that?"

She pointed at another body, one of the ones Donal had shot. "That one could speak our language. Well, sort of. It was hard to follow her, but I picked up a lot of things. Donal, they're so *different* from us."

"That's why we call them aliens. I'm afraid you're in for a rather extensive debriefing when you get back to Kinkaid, young lady."

She closed her eyes. "Oh. Just so I can have a bath, clean clothes, and about twenty hours of sleep first. . . ."

He chuckled. "I'll see what we can do." He took her by the arm, turning back toward the doorway leading out.

That was when he saw them.

They were hanging on chains lowered from a ceiling beam, ten naked and blood-covered corpses, each suspended by a hook driven up under the chin and out the mouth, shocking in their contrast to the civilized and faintly decadent paintings still on the wall behind them.

Two more bodies lay where they'd fallen beneath their hooks. One of those still hanging was the red-headed nobleman, Lord Delacroix, the former owner of Glenntor Castle. Next to him was the body of Elena St. Martin, the woman at the party who'd talked about getting to know the Malach.

Alexie grimaced and then turned away. "Nasty way to find out that your notions of friendly, peace-loving aliens are—"

She clamped her mouth shut, and Donal wondered if she was going to be sick.

A door banged open on the far side of the room, and a trio of Malach forced their way through, crowding one another for the opportunity to bring down the humans. Donal spun, raising his powergun, then cursed at the steady red wink of the power drained light. Alexie, however, tucked her unfamiliar weapon up under her arm and squeezed off shot after shot, the laser pulses flashing with a blinding intensity as they struck harness leather or green and red scales. All three Malach were dead before they'd gotten more than halfway through the door. Donal snatched one of the concussion grenades from his vest and sprinted forward. The room beyond the open door, he saw, was filled with what looked like alien communications equipment. He armed the grenade and tossed it through in one smooth motion, turning and putting his back to the stone wall until the room beyond the door filled with thunder and roiling smoke.

"Let's get out of here, Donal," Alexie said. She shook the weapon she was holding. "I don't know how to tell if this thing is about to run out of juice."

"I'll go along with that. But just to be sure . . ." Holstering his dead powergun, he stooped to pick up two of the Malach weapons, and handed one to Alexie. She dropped her first weapon and accepted the second. "Let's go. I've got transportation waiting outside."

"Not—"

"For you, Alexie, only the best!"

"Freddy?"

"The same."

He led her out of the shattered castle and into the open air. Freddy was waiting there patiently, the black muzzles of his infinite repeaters twitching slightly as he tracked distant targets not yet close enough to be worth a shot. The sun was down now, and the sky was rapidly growing darker with a blaze of gold and red painting the western horizon. The submarine, Donal noted, was gone.

"The refugees departed in the submarine 8.11 minutes ago," Freddy said as they scrambled aboard up the rear ramp. "They are now under water and safely out into the fjord."

"Thank God," Alexie said.

"I am tracking multiple targets," Freddy continued as they entered the Fighting Compartment. "Numerous fliers and airborne APCs are on approach vectors. I suggest that we leave this area as quickly as possible."

"Freddy, sometimes you have simply magnificent ideas," Donal said. He was feeling an almost manic giddiness, an adrenaline-charged rush from the terror and excitement of close combat. His head hurt where a Malach laser had partly melted his helmet and blistered the skin over his right temple, but he scarcely noticed the pain. "Let's hit it!"

I have reached the southern end of Criton Pass. Ahead, lost in the darkness to optical sensors but quite clear on infrared, Criton Valley extends as a broad, flat, open stretch of terrain approximately four to six kilometers wide. To either side, the Grampian Mountains rise to a modest 950 meters at the highest, with most peaks averaging around 600 meters. The mountains are gently rounded and forest-covered. The valley itself is open field—what ancient tank commanders or cavalry officers would have considered perfect ground for fire and maneuver. A river, the Loman, flows south toward its confluence with the Kinkaid River fifty-two kilometers to the south, just outside the city of Kinkaid, before flowing jointly into Starbright Bay. Route 1 is visible on infrared as a warmly radiating strip of ferrocrete to my left.

Tech Master Sergeant Blandings and his team are here in a small fleet of DY-90 Firestorm hovercraft, escorting a cryo-H tanker. They have been working on me for the past 28.4 minutes, trying to increase my battle worthiness to minimum acceptable levels.

The task may be impossible, though they have managed to jury-rig a containment bladder inside my ruptured tank to hold a supply of cryogenic hydrogen slush. The maintenance crew perform their tasks admirably, however, despite the very real danger of incoming rounds, and the nearness of the Enemy. Unfortunately, they cannot repair my shattered track. With their help, I disengage the drive wheels in my right-forward track assembly. This will reduce both speed and maneuverability somewhat but will allow me to move without major impedance from the wrecked drive wheels.

With just 10.4 minutes remaining until contact with the Enemy, I receive one excellent piece of news. My direct satellite communications have been destroyed, but HQ reports that Bolo 96876 of the Line has reemerged north of the Windypeak Mountains, at the site known as Invasion Zone Delta. He seems to have dealt a crippling blow to the Enemy's command-control structure and is now moving south across the mountains.

It may be that we will be able to fight at least part of this final engagement together. I would like that. Multiple Bolo engagements are rare. More, however, the nature of the Enemy threat and the severity of damage I have *suffered together suggest that I cannot hold them long on my own.*

I cannot accurately estimate how long I will survive before I am overwhelmed.

"C'mon, c'mon. C'mon, you grease squirters!" Blandings stood in the open cockpit well of the Firestorm, hands on hips, staring into the night, toward the north. He wore light-amplifier visor that gave him an almost insect-like appearance, and his mouth, what was visible beneath the optic rig, was scowling with disapproval. "The stilters're almost here!"

Corporal Steve Dombrowski laughed, pulling his head back out of the Bolo's Number Five sensor suite access tunnel. "They'll wish the hell they'd stayed where they came from! Ol' Ferdy here's gonna land 'em, gut 'em, and hang 'em out to dry!"

"You said it!" Len Kemperer added. "Man, did you see those combat read-outs they pulled at HQ? Ferdy here's too much for 'em, I don't care how many of the critters there are! Ow!"

"What is it?" Corporal Debbie Hall asked.

Kemperer flopped his hand back and forth, cooling it. "Hull's still hot."

"It's *hot* some places in more ways than one, moron," Blandings snarled. "You oughta know better'n to work without gloves!"

"Before this is over, Sarge," Hall said, "we're gonna be wearing full rad decon gear. These guys play for keeps, huh?"

"S'okay, Deb," Dombrowski said, grinning as he closed the access panel, a hatch as thick and as heavy as a lead-lined walk-in safe's door. He had to lean hard to swing it shut with a satisfying clang. "So do we!"

Blandings continued to stare up the valley toward the north, straining for some sign of the oncoming enemy—

a sign that he knew Ferdy would detect long before any human senses could possibly manage it. He was smiling now, the expression safely hidden in the darkness. *Gotta hand it to you, Lieutenant,* he thought. *You got yourself a team here.*

He was worried, nonetheless. Ferdy would be going into combat with only three tracks working, half his armor scoured away, a hole in his flank big enough for a full-grown man to crawl down, and a jury-rigged cryo-H bladder that was never intended to stand up to the stress of combat. If one of those penetrators broke through . . .

Well, it wasn't like the defenders of Muir had a whole lot of choice. His maintenance crew, he thought, had worked miracles already.

He just hoped that those miracles would be enough.

The Bolo hit rugged ground at that moment, the violent lurch flinging Alexie against Donal. He managed to catch her before she hit the floor. "You okay?"

She nodded. Her face was smudged with grease, dirt, and soot, and her hair was a blond riot, but at that moment he thought she looked beautiful. She'd just completed putting burn ointment and a dressing over the blister on Donal's head, tying it in place with a length of gauze bandage roll.

"Okay. Better strap in," he told her, indicating the jump seat in the corner. "We're heading over the top of the mountains now, and it's going to get pretty rough going down the other side."

He could feel each time the Bolo encountered a tree—a slight tremor, an occasional rocking to one side or the other as the huge treads ground over a fallen forest giant. The fighting compartment's battle screens were all on, giving them a full, three-sixty view, a panorama in the pale yellows and whites-on-greens of infrared penetrating the night. Columns of data showing on forward, left, and right screens listed exterior readings on temperature, atmosphere, and radiation, noted the inclination of the terrain, ground pressure, surface speed, tracked motion or metallic targets, and registered a hundred other details, ranging from the insignificant to the critical. Donal was particularly interested in the terrain inclination just now, which was shifting between twenty-five and thirty-two degrees—a steep slope, though not impossible for a Bolo. The greatest danger was that too great a slope might cause the ground to give way beneath the Bolo's incredible ground pressure of fourteen thousand tons. If that happened, they might begin sliding back down the slope, could conceivably involve themselves in an outright avalanche, and at worst could slide badly enough that they ended up going over the edge of a drop steep enough to make them flip over. Even Bolos had their terrain limitations. . . .

The cabin rocked with a series of detonations. Alexie looked up toward the pipe-cluttered ceiling of the compartment, eyes wide. "What was that?"

Donal glanced at the status readouts, then at the screen showing the view toward the right. A flash appeared in the sky just above the treeline. Several white contrails edged past the blossoming flare in erratic scrawls, heat trails on IR.

"Company," he said. "Three Malach fliers, range about fifty kilometers. They're out over the ocean, but they're tracking us. They just locked on with six radar-homing missiles that Freddy took out with antimissile lasers. Now he's about to take out the fliers."

"Without orders from you?"

A shrill whine, muffled by thick hull plating, sounded, together with a buzzsaw rasp and a shudder felt through the steel deck. Strings of blue-white stars were flashing across the treeline, vanishing into the distance. Seconds later, however, an orange flash flared soundlessly and faded above the trees in the darkness, followed almost immediately by another . . . and finally, after a longer pause, a third. The sounds of the explosions came back seconds later, very faint and far away.

"Freddy's a hell of a lot better at this than I am," he told her. "Better reactions. Faster thinking. There is no way I or any human could directly run this machine in combat without getting us all killed. Yes, he does it without specific instructions from me. He's designed that way."

The deck suddenly leveled off, then began tipping back the other way as Freddy nosed over the top. If anything, the trip downhill was faster and more hair-raising than the trip up. Fourteen thousand tons traveling in excess of eighty kilometers per hour could build up one hell of a lot of momentum.

"Commander," Freddy announced. "I am receiving a Priority One radio transmission addressed to you. On scrambler."

"Put it through."

"Bolo 96876!" sounded over the speaker. "This is Phalbin. What the hell is going on up there?"

"General, this is Ragnor. We have successfully attacked the Malach command center at Glenntor." He glanced at Alexie and grinned, giving her a wink. "We were able to liberate a number of human prisoners there, and the word we have at the moment is that we did in a fair number of the enemy's high command. We're coming over the Windypeaks now, at or near Bollard's Notch. Our intent is to move on the Malach landing zone at . . . Map Three, Hotel-two-four by Juliet-five-niner. Over."

"Ah . . . negative on that, Lieutenant. Your orders are to proceed at all possible speed to Route 1 and Criton Pass. We want both Bolos in position north of the city to stop an expected Malach attack against the capital. Do you copy? Over!"

Donal killed the mike, then spoke to Freddy. "Let me

have an area map, please. One to one hundred kay, with joystick."

A window opened on his forward viewscreen, showing the map in realistic terrain colors, several shades of green for the forest, browns and grays for the bare mountain peaks. A three-D effect gave a suggestion of elevation, backed by the glowing figures of altitudes, given in meters. A panel popped open on his right armrest, and a small joystick rose from the opening. Touching the control with his forefinger, he was able to zoom over the computer-generated terrain, looking for the best view to suit his needs.

That was it, looking from the west. The Bolo's course was clearly plotted in white, a line zigzagging up the steep slopes from the blip marking Glenntor, then over the top and down. A winking green pinpoint showed the Bolo's current position on the south slope of the Windypeaks, and another marked Ferdy's position south of Criton Pass. North of the thirty-klick-long valley a constellation of red lights glowed, slowly funneling together as they approached the northern end of the pass. Their intent was clear: bull through the pass and descend on Kinkaid. Only Ferdy stood in the way.

"Ragnor!" Phalbin barked. "You have already disobeyed direct orders to bring that Bolo south to Kinkaid. I'm giving you one more chance, and so help me, if you refuse this order you are down on your knees begging me for a court martial. Ragnor! Do you hear me?"

"Easy there, General," Donal said. "We're coming."

"Okay." Relief was evident in that single word. "Look, we're mustering every man, every vehicle we have. The Bolos have done a great job of breaking up the enemy attacks, and now it's all or nothing, you understand?"

"Understood, sir."

"I have ordered Bolo 96875 to assume a static defensive position south of the valley. I will deploy the troops up

the east and west sides of the valley, in a position to take
out the enemy as they pass through. I want you to reach
the north end of the valley and likewise take up a static
position. Your job will be to block enemy forces trying
to escape to the north, and to serve as a reserve Bolo
unit. If, ah, if the enemy gets past Bolo 96875, you'll
have to try to stop them before they reach the capital."

"We'll hold them, General," Donal replied. *But not
by turning ourselves into static fortresses!* He said nothing
about that, however. He would worry about violating yet
more orders later, when he had to. Alexie smiled at him,
and that was all the reassurance he needed at the moment.
"Hang on, the cavalry's on the way!"

Bolo 96876 of the Line, Dinochrome Brigade,
thundered down off the ridge and onto the broad Monad
Plain, sprinting south at maximum speed.

*The new patch from Colonel Wood has inactivated all
of my ROEs, and I feel a curious sense of freedom and
alertness now, as though a steady and unresolved power
drain has suddenly been corrected. I feel a surge of
renewed confidence. The Enemy is close and battle is
imminent.*

I will not let my companions or the Brigade down.

*Criton Pass was a symbol as much as anything. The
mountains here are not high, little more than forest-
covered hills. Malach fliers, especially the larger craft
the human defenders have christened APCs, could cross
them at any point without difficulty.*

*But the land forces—the unarmored Malach soldiers,
in particular—must cross the ridge here, as would any
Malach walkers. The fliers, too, are vulnerable when they
rise above NOE—the terrain-hugging nape of the earth—
and might be expected to come through the pass as well.
I disagree with the order to remain in a static defensive
position but judge there is enough leeway in my orders*

to at least allow me freedom to maneuver in close-combat. I do not intend to press the matter; if I ask how much maneuvering room I have, I may be ordered to remain unmoving, and I do not want to risk that.

Sometimes, combat judgment must be exercised even when dealing with one's own chain of command.

The lead Malach units are fliers, streaking in along the valley floor at an altitude of only a few meters, hugging the ground to avoid targeting radar. I snap a warning to Tech Master Sergeant Blandings and the other humans, who scatter wildly in the night. I lock onto the fliers at a range of ten kilometers and open fire with everything I have. I manage to down three before being forced to divert my attention to the incoming nuclear penetrators, and for several full seconds I am very busy indeed, dealing with this attempt to overwhelm my defenses.

More fliers appear, dropping down from left and right off the mountains. Phalbin's troops are up there, with shoulder-launched missiles and portable plasma and laser weapons, but they can do no more than scratch the paint of these Malach machines, which are heavily armored and very fast. At the same time, I detect the first Malach ground forces, advancing now at a run.

Within another second, I am fighting for my survival.

CHAPTER TWENTY-EIGHT

I am monitoring the course of the battle over the Muir Command Intelligence Web, and I estimate that Bolo 96875 of the Line will not be able to survive this fight for more than another 4.5 minutes. I have increased my velocity to full sprint speed and am traveling now at 150 kilometers per hour, an improvement of 1.3 percent over my original estimated maximum-speed performance.

The northern mouth of the Criton Valley is just ahead, clearly visible on radar and infrared. This is the point at which my orders from Kinkaid direct me to take up a static position in order to block retreating enemy forces or to serve as a reserve in case Unit 96875's position is overrun.

My Commander's directive in response to headquarters' orders is succinct, vulgar, and graphic, a word of, I believe, ancient Anglo-Saxon origins. I do not employ such language myself, but the feeling behind it is something that even Bolos can appreciate.

At least self-aware Mark XXIV Bolos under full Battle Reflex Mode.

At my Commander's order then, I race past the blocking position and enter the valley. In another moment, I am closing with the tail end of the Malach column, smashing into ground-effect APCs and troop carriers with deadly effect.

It is fully dark now, under overcast skies, and the Malach soldiers, those not inside their walkers, are nearly blind. As their vehicles flame under each burst from my infinite repeaters, they scatter in a wild and unseeing panic, blundering into one another, or even running wildly into the path of my oncoming tracks.

I have noted a distinct confusion in the Enemy tactics during the past hour. His attacks are poorly coordinated and poorly executed. It is possible that by destroying his command and control center at Glenntor, we have contributed to the battle more than we could have expected.

I detect a large concentration of Malach war machines ahead and inform my Commander. There is no longer time for finesse, for careful maneuvers designed to break up Enemy formations before they can grow too strong. The Enemy has assembled his entire strength in one massive formation, and we will either annihilate it now or be overwhelmed ourselves.

It won't be much longer now before we know which.

Donal clung to the armrests of his command chair as the Bolo raced south through the valley, its tracks slashing into the ferrocrete of Route 1 and reducing it to scattered rubble and eroded roadbed. Malach walkers tried to block the way, firing massed beam and missile weapons as they stood their ground, but Freddy either burned them down or, once, smashed into the alien machine at full speed, the massive, fast-spinning left-forward track grinding over and shredding the Malach walker, flattening the wreckage beneath the incredible ground pressure of ten tons per square meter. There were lots of Malach troops skittering about in their skins as well, and they stood no chance at all as the Bolo thundered down on them with violently spinning tracks. Freddy smashed south at a thundering sprint, leaving a trail of twisted, splintered wreckage and smeared bodies in his path. His Hellbore hurled fusion bolts at relativistic velocities through unresisting metal and flesh; his infinite repeaters slashed down incoming missiles in dazzling flicks of green lightning.

Neither Donal nor Alexie said anything. The battle now was far beyond their control, even their comprehension, as Freddy thought, acted, and reacted with superhuman speed and concentration. The Bolo had released its last recon flier some minutes before, and the drone was transmitting infrared imagery now of close-packed Malach walkers, moving south in the valley ahead.

"I am detecting a major concentration of the Enemy at a range of 11.5 kilometers," Freddy told Donal. "I have five tactical nuclear missiles remaining in my inventory."

"Use 'em as you think best, Freddy."

"This is an excellent opportunity, save for one potential problem. General Phalbin has deployed a large number of lightly armored troops along the tops of the hills to east and west just ahead. If I detonate nuclear weapons in the valley—"

"Gotcha. Gimme a channel . . . uh, make it combat tactical five." That would let him talk to all field officers and NCOs, and possibly any of the soldiers themselves who possessed helmet radios. Chain of command and standard Rules of Engagement demanded he call headquarters first and clear a nukes release with them.

Screw that. He was in trouble already. He'd ditched the Bolo's ROEs. He could ditch the human ones as well.

"Channel open. Mike hot."

"Attention, all personnel in the Criton Valley area! This is Lieutenant Ragnor, aboard Bolo 96876 of the Line. We are about to release tactical nuclear weapons inside the valley, with individual yields of between one fiftieth and one twentieth of a kiloton. You have about forty-five seconds until launch. I suggest you move back up the hill and over the top of the ridge. If you can't manage that, get behind a boulder, a tree, anything that will give you cover, and for God's sake, don't look! Now move! Move! Move! Fast as you can!" He released the transmit key. "Okay, Freddy. Give 'em one minute."

"One minute, Commander. That will require that we slow first, to avoid closing with the target."

"Go ahead and slow down, then. We have to give our people a chance to find cover."

"Affirmative."

The Bolo slewed suddenly to the left, turret pivoting as it tracked a group of eight Malach walkers that had just abruptly changed course and were moving north. Penetrator lances flashed through the night, detonating in savage flashes as Freddy's laser antimissile fire sliced the weapons to pieces. For thirty seconds or so, the Bolo was at the focus of a devastating play of laser fire and electron beams, a concentration of high-energy fury that exploded reactive armor, clawed at flickering mag screens, and in places left soft, bubbling craters of half-molten metal, glowing cherry-red with yellow, black-crusted centers in the darkness.

Freddy returned fire, each Hellbore blast finding its target. The Mark XXIV was designed to learn from combat experience. Its earliest encounters with Malach walkers had been fumbling, sometimes uncertain affairs, but the Bolo now had a much better working database on how walkers and fliers moved, how they jinked, what attack patterns they were likely to run. As the surviving walkers attempted to break right and circle behind the Bolo, the armored behemoth suddenly reversed its turn, coming hard right, pivoting so sharply that the last walker in line was caught by surprise and plowed under, the ten-meter-tall machine crumbling beneath the onslaught of tracks reaching over five meters high.

For a few more seconds, Malach walkers and Bolo slugged it out at point-blank range, with the Malach trying to work their way close enough to get *inside* the reach of those awesomely powerful energy weapons.

They failed. Scattering before the Bolo's wild charge, many kicked off and went airborne, skimming above the ground on flaring ventral jets, but the Bolo's IR ion cannons speared them in one-two-three succession, ripping them apart in mid-air. When the Hellbore spoke, the night dissolved in white hell's-fury, and Malach hunters, in the air or on foot, simply evaporated.

"One minute has elapsed, Commander. Request permission to fire nuclear weapons."

"Granted." If the human troops hadn't made it to cover by now, there was nothing that could be done for them. "Fire!"

A sleek, Mark LXII Sunfire missile climbed out of Freddy's Number Three vertical launch tube, balanced on a shaft of flickering white flame. An instant later, a second missile followed . . . and then a third. The missiles, each three meters long and massing nearly nine hundred kilograms, rocketed high into the night sky, trailing glowing white contrails that arced rapidly toward the south. Moments passed . . . and then the night turned day-brilliant, a false sunrise to the south that grew rapidly brighter . . . then brighter still with the triple detonation. More seconds passed, and then the shock and blast waves passed, a gentle rolling of the ground, accompanied by a hurricane of wind clawing at the outer hull.

Ferdy had coordinated his nuclear attack as well. The central reaches of the Criton Valley had been transformed into a hell's cauldron, the ground still partly molten in places or covered with liquid pools of molten glass from the sand and metal from the hundreds of wrecked alien vehicles. Freddy slowed down somewhat, picking his way past the deadliest hotspots, then accelerated once more.

"Did . . . did that get them all?" Alexie wanted to know.

"Negative, Deputy Director Turner," Freddy told her. "A large number of Malach walkers are still mobile, many of them in the hills to either side. It is unlikely that they will assemble in large groups again, in light of the lesson we just taught them. They will no doubt seek to concentrate quickly at close range in an effort to trap and overwhelm either Unit 96875 or me."

"Smash on through," Donal told him. "I want to link up with Ferdy."

"That was my thought as well, Commander."

Past the radioactive slag and glowing pools of the nuclear killing ground, they began encountering enemy troops and vehicles once more. Ten kilometers from Ferdy's position, Freddy sent a microsecond-burst ID transmission, and Ferdy picked it up, returning a curt acknowledgment. He was under short-range attack and had suffered numerous hits. In another millisecond, the two Bolos were in line-of-sight electronic Battle Coordination Mode, the two fighting, thinking as one, their thoughts joined by a tight-beamed maser link.

Five kilometers north of Ferdy's position, a Malach walker leaped, belly jets flaring, drifting through a hail of wildly slashing infinite repeater fire and coming to rest safely on Freddy's upper deck, just behind the turret. Diacarb claws on mechanical arms slashed out, embedding themselves in ordinary carbon-steel outer skin. Lasers and electron guns flared, burning down into Freddy's dorsal armor at point-blank range.

Ferdy, sighting in on the hitchhiker with pinpoint accuracy, triggered a plasma bolt from his Hellbore, the blue core of hellfire passing centimeters above Freddy's turret, smashing into and through the unwanted rider, scattering its body in a million flaming, molten fragments.

Alexie let out a small gasp when she got her first look at Ferdy, and Donal groaned. The Bolo had been almost entirely stripped of its heaviest armor in places, and all four track systems had been wrecked. Ferdy was truly in a static defense mode now, immobilized by the horde of leaping, racing, legged manta shapes around him. Several had mounted his top deck, and Freddy swept them away with a sustained burst from several infinite repeaters. As Freddy spun around his brother Bolo in a tight, dust-spewing circle, the Malach walkers scattered, most taking to the air like great, flapping carrion birds.

"Hit 'em!" Donal cried. "You got 'em on the run!"

"Negative, Commander," Freddy replied. "I am detecting at least forty-seven more enemy walkers, supported by at least five fliers, inbound at this time. Exact numbers are difficult to ascertain, due to chaff and radioactive interference in the atmosphere." He paused, as though considering the problem. "I fear they may have just assembled one final thrust in an effort to overrun this position."

Nuclear penetrators were flashing in toward the Bolos. Donal flinched as one detonated less than a meter from Freddy's side, the white-hot jet of plasma searing into the Bolo's side. Reactive armor exploded outward, disrupting the jet; the Bolo's mag screens flared, scattering it.

But other lances were rocketing in, each trailing a thin streak of white flame and smoke. Antimissile lasers set into Freddy's flanks fired repeatedly, joined at times by the rattling shriek of the infinite repeaters. They were exploding in threes and fours and fives at a time, each kill marked by a dazzling pop of harsh white, night-scattering light.

The night was alive with fire, with the flickering, needle-thin beams of lasers, with tightly packed streams of blue-green flares, the ion bolts from the red-hot muzzles of hard-pressed infinite repeaters. From time to time, light geysered high above one or the other of the Bolos, as nuclear-tipped rockets slid off the vertical launch tube rails, kicked into the sky, and arrowed toward some distant target.

And the incoming fire fell like a waterfall of living flame, beams, flares, rockets, and the unceasing pounding of heavy artillery.

From his vantage point, Donal could follow only a fraction of everything that was going on, so fast were events unfolding, so savage and unrelenting was the fighting. He tried shifting the display to infrared, but the ghostly white and yellow against blue and green was even more confusing, especially when so much of the ground around both Bolos was glowing now with a fervent, radiant heat.

Malach fliers circled like black, ungainly birds, skimming the burned-over ground with a curious skipping motion, riding ground-effect as much as actually flying. When they got too close, they lowered their legs and walked. Donal wasn't sure, but he suspected that walking saved them power, let them channel more energy to their weapons. Both Bolos took them out while they were airborne when possible, but more and more, the big combat vehicles were being forced to conserve their power, saving their shots to keep the walkers at a safe distance.

Donal remembered the statistics he'd seen, the estimates that said that one Bolo was equivalent to about twelve of the Malach walkers. They'd proven this night just how wrong statistics could be. The ground now was littered with crushed, smashed, and burned-out walkers. In places, the wreckage was strewn so thickly it would have been impossible to walk that ground without stepping on pieces of metallic debris.

The bombardment intensified as Malach forces flung missile after missile, beam after beam at the two Bolos, the one crippled and motionless, the other circling tightly as it tried to shelter and protect its companion.

Ferdy died in the last few minutes of the assault, as a nuclear-tipped lance arrowed past the defensive fire, struck through failing mag screens, and burned its way through armor already slagged in places until the Bolo's flintsteel skeleton was showing through, and detonated deep inside with a flash and an electromagnetic pulse savage enough to serve as a Bolo's death scream. Ferdy's Hellbore turret was flung up and back, its weapon fingering the sky in final, silent challenge. The nuclear fireball climbed skyward, shedding a baleful, hell-borne light on the field of high-tech death.

For several seconds more, the Malach kept coming . . . but if they'd thought to overwhelm a defensive force now reduced by fifty percent, they were mistaken. Freddy accelerated abruptly, free now of any need to stick with his dead brother. Hellbore fire seared the night, slashing through Malach combat machines and scattering the fragments in a savage whirling firestorm. Malach numbers were already so depleted that even the destruction of one of the two Bolos could not change an outcome now as inevitable as death.

The surviving Malach were retreating now . . . were in full flight. Freddy pursued them, lashing out, killing . . . killing . . . and killing again. . . .

And then, the fighting compartment was quiet for a long time.

"Commander," Freddy said.

Donal blinked into silence and the dim light spilling from consoles and displays. How long had it been? Sometime during that final, savage pounding, Donal had left his command seat—his presence there was certainly not necessary from the Bolo's point of view—and slumped down on the steel deck aft, with Alexie curled up small and close in his arms.

"What? What's happening?" He was only now beginning to realize that it was quiet. For hours . . . for *days*, it seemed like, even deep within the Bolo's acoustically shielded fighting compartment, the hammering thunder of the incessant concussions of enemy ordnance had rung and pealed, a deafening, ear-pounding cacophony that now was blessedly, amazingly silent.

"The Enemy has broken," Freddy said simply. "He appears to be in full retreat toward the north. Muir troops and light armor are approaching from the south.

"I believe the battle has ended."

"We're . . . we're still here. . . ." It didn't seem possible.

"Commander, I regret to inform you that Bolo 96875 of the Line has been destroyed."

Donal felt a stab of pain at that. "I'm . . . sorry." He wondered if Freddy felt the same sort of loss, of *pain*, as he did.

"He was destroyed in performance of his duty," the Bolo said. The voice carried no inflection . . . no emotion that Donal could read.

The first of the DY-90 Firestorm hovercraft howled up moments later, dust billowing from beneath its skirts, illuminated by the funeral pyres of burning Malach walkers. It was swiftly followed by three more. Sergeant Blandings, physically unrecognizable in his radiation suit and helmet, stood in the lead vehicle, waving.

"Did we win?" Alexie asked.

Donal understood. Sometimes it was hard to grasp the outcome of a major battle, when you were a very tiny part of it all to begin with. And sometimes the losses . . .

Ferdy was still burning.

"Yeah. Yeah, I guess we did."

Shakily, he stood up and began looking for a radsuit.

As my Commander steps outside, I consider the burning wreckage that once was Bolo of the Line 96875. It happened so quickly, even for a Bolo, that it is difficult to convince myself purely through logical processes that he is destroyed.

Humans would say dead.

The question of whether Bolos are alive in the first place has long been argued by human philosophers, technicians, and combat veterans, though it is a question that Bolos rarely address. We simply are, *and for most purposes, that is sufficient.*

Humans question whether Bolos can feel. That, too, is rarely discussed among Bolos. We experience emotions because we were designed that way, and those humans who insist that we only think we feel because we were made that way should consider the same question in relation to themselves. We do not experience emotions as humans do, with the same intensity, nor are we incapacitated by them, nor do we know feelings such as boredom, which are counter-productive.

But we can experience a sense of loss.

And of loneliness.

And something that might very well be similar to what humans call sadness, though in fact I cannot know what it is when humans experience such emotions.

I will miss our camaraderie. Our discussions. Our games of chess.

I spend the next .085 seconds scanning all relevant data in my storage banks concerning human military traditions related to honoring fallen comrades and helping solidify morale among those who survive. There are numerous rituals and traditions that might apply—I spend a full .023 second considering just the Heroes' Remembrance ceremony once invoked by the Terra Legion, a ritual extending back to the Battle of Shalmarin in 2210, almost a thousand years ago.

But such would require human intervention in established rules and procedures and might not be convenient for the Confederation Military Command Authority. I search for other rituals that might be fitting.

I decide on one.

Technically, I am violating established fire-control procedures doing this but have no trouble overriding the guards. Fortunately, the ROEs have not been reactivated. I pivot seven of the nine ion-bolt infinite repeaters on my left side—one has been disabled in any case—to aim at a piece of night sky above Bolo 96875's burning wreckage. I pause for .01 second as I download and replay records of several of our past conversations.

I set the IRs to single-shot, then fire all seven weapons once . . . twice . . . a third time. Twenty-one bolts of blue-white light sear through the smoke and into the night sky, burning brilliantly as they streak higher and higher, then slow . . . and fade from sight.

On the ground, my Commander turns sharply at the sudden barrage. I watch as he stares at the departing rounds . . . then draws himself to attention, and salutes, the gesture clumsy in his radiation suit.

He understands. . . .

Badly burned, bleeding heavily, Schaagrasch dragged herself clear of the wreckage. For a time, the pain had been agonizing, a searing, blinding, incapacitating fire eating at bones and muscles, but that had receded now. Malach Zsho philosophy frowned on the use of drugs to relieve pain, which, after all, was a part of any organism's survival mechanism. After a time, if you accepted the pain, allowed it to fill you and wash over you, it became . . . bearable.

She stared around the night-shrouded field, the pupils of her two remaining eyes opening wide to drink in the light. Everywhere she looked, Hunters lay strewn like smashed and broken *g'shin*, the stuffing-filled images of prey animals given to juvenile Malach females for them to tear and worry. Her comrades all lay there, strewn about in bloody, blue-green death. The very ground here was beaten and scorched, every living thing seared from the earth. The only light was the guttering flicker from a small fire in the eggshell-smashed ruin of G'rasak'nzhi the Careful Circler's Hunter.

Where was evolution now? she wondered. The survival of the fittest.

What hope was there for the creature beaten on the field of survival?

Extinction . . .

Schaagrasch rolled onto her side and stared up into the crystalline-black night sky and the golden glory of the cluster's thronging swarms. Staring into those stars made her feel just a little less alone.

She had a final duty to perform, one that many Malach this day would not have been able to complete. Indeed, duty was a misnomer, since no particular consequence befell a Malach who failed to carry it out. A Malach who was killed instantly in the course of combat was no more remiss in her responsibilities than the one who died slowly enough to recite her *Ghaava'naa'ach-zshleh*, the Death Poem.

Every Malach warrior wrote her own during her *Ga'krascht* Coming-of-Blood ceremony. The name, *Ghaava'naa'ach-zshleh*, meant "I embrace death," which was the first line of all Death Poems. The rest was different for each warrior, emblazoned in silver script on the curved black surface of her Hunter, though the sentiment was usually familiar. Schaagrasch's was no exception.

"*Ghaava'naa'ach-zshleh*," she began, voice rasping.

I embrace Death,
Death given by Life.
Culling the Pack,
Hunting the weak,
That the Race might grow strong and survive

As Blessed Sha'gnaasht Skilled Tracker revealed.

The race lives, adapts, and survives, and there lies immortality.

After she'd finished reciting the poem, the pain was almost gone. She lay there on the burning ground, staring up at the stars for a long time until she died.

EPILOGUE

They sat together in the ripplegrass on a hill overlooking the sea, arms around one another. Starbright Bay and Kinkaid were at their backs. The Strathan Cluster glowed, soft and orange-gold, high in the sky toward the zenith.

"So as near as we can tell," Donal was telling Alexie, "the Malach have left Muir's system entirely. Their fleet packed up and high-tailed it as soon as their last transports and APCs loaded up. Somehow I doubt they'll be back this way any time soon."

"What about you?" she asked, leaning close. She reached up with one hand and gently touched the bandage encircling his head.

"Hmm? Me? I'm fine. Thanks to your field first aid efforts."

"Actually, I was thinking about Phalbin and the Strathan Army. You were closeted with him and his staff for a long time this afternoon, and they wouldn't let me in to talk to them, and they wouldn't even tell me what was going on. Are you going to tell me, or am I going to have to learn it all from Freddy?"

"I don't know, love. Freddy can be pretty closed-mouthed when he needs to be. Need to know, and all of that."

"Damn it, Don—"

"Okay, okay." He laughed. "I guess the good news is that I'm not going to be court martialed."

"Good. They'd have had another invasion on their hands if they did. An invasion composed of one Wide Sky ex-Deputy Director."

"I believe you. Well, there were some rumblings, of course. Colonel Wood came to my defense, though, and pointed out in, um, not too flattering terms that Freddy, Ferdy, and I managed to stop the invasion and kick the bad guys out all but single-handedly. His argument was . . . hey, if it works, don't screw with it."

"Sensible."

"Phalbin still wanted some sort of a trial. I kind of think he was looking forward to it, that it was warm and comforting for him to think he could shoot me at sunrise to make up for all the aggravation I'd caused him."

"And?"

"And I pointed out that he could simply claim credit for the victory as it stood. We did stop the Malach from taking Kinkaid, after all, and so far as the politicians or the civilians are concerned, they have no idea, and could care less, who figured it out or made it happen. If I'm court martialed, some of his, well, questionable decisions would probably have come out. Like trying to turn Bolos into bunkers. This makes him look awfully good, and I think he has his eye on being governor someday, after Chard.

"Anyway, they made me a captain. Field promotion. And you can't very well court martial someone you've just promoted, can you?"

She laughed. "That's wonderful! And here you thought your career was going nowhere!"

"Well, I'm still not sure how much future I have with the Strathan forces. I'd hate to leave the Dinochrome

Brigade, but, well, there still may not be a lot of future for me here."

They snuggled quietly for a time. "Don? Which one is Wide Sky?"

He looked up at the stars. A few scattered, isolated silver or golden points glowed apart from the body of the cluster proper, tiny, far-off lamps at the edge of the Great Void. He pointed. "That one."

She clung to him for a long time. "Do you think the Malach will pull out of human space?"

"Not voluntarily. I don't think they're made that way."

"Um. Yes. Females don't submit. Unless they're made to." She thought a moment. "There are millions of people back there, Don. Under the Malach claw. We've got to go back and help them."

"I doubt that Chard is going to be interested in an offensive any time soon," Donal said. "But we might be able to convince him that the best defense is to give the bad guy a good swift kick in the tail."

"Could we do it? Could we take back Wide Sky from the Malach? With Freddy to help?"

"It has been my experience," Donal told her, "that there are very few problems in this universe that can't be solved with the deft application of a Bolo Mark XXIV. I'd say we're going to have to take that question up with Freddy."

They embraced then, clinging tightly in the rosy light of the cluster.

I have been studying the stars. I note the sun of Wide Sky, and wonder.

The Malach threat has abated for now, but there is no question in my mind that I will face them again, and soon. Their attempt at subjugating Muir failed, but their forces still hold Wide Sky, Endatheline, and probably Starhold as well. With those worlds as logistical advance bases, the Enemy will almost certainly try again. Humans would, given similar circumstances, and the Malach have demonstrated that if their motivations and reasoning are alien to those of humans, their determination, adaptability, and cunning are not. They will be back, whatever the news reporters might have to say about it in the wake of, as one put it, "Man's greatest victory over alien invaders since the Deng War."

Obviously, the best way to circumvent further Malach expansion is to carry the war to worlds he now controls, ultimately to find his homeworld, wherever it might be. I do not know how long it will take human authorities to come to the same conclusion, but I feel confident that they will.

And I will be ready. My duty to my Commander, to my regiment, to the Dinochrome Brigade demands it.

As do my memories of Ferdy.

DAVID WEBER

Honor Harrington (cont.):

Field of Dishonor

Honor goes home to Manticore—and fights for her life on a battlefield she never trained for, in a private war that offers just two choices: death—or a "victory" that can end only in dishonor and the loss of all she loves....

Other novels by DAVID WEBER:

Mutineers' Moon

"...a good story...reminds me of 1950s Heinlein..."
—*BMP Bulletin*

The Armageddon Inheritance

Sequel to *Mutineers' Moon*.

Path of the Fury

"Excellent...a thinking person's Terminator."
—*Kliatt*

Oath of Swords

An epic fantasy.

with STEVE WHITE:

Insurrection
Crusade

Novels set in the world of the Starfire ™ game system.

And don't miss Steve White's solo novels,
The Disinherited and Legacy!

continued

DAVID WEBER

On Basilisk Station
0-671-72163-1 ✦ $5.99 ☐

Honor of the Queen
0-671-72172-0 ✦ $6.99 ☐

The Short Victorious War
0-671-87596-5 ✦ $5.99 ☐

Field of Dishonor
0-671-87624-4 ✦ $5.99 ☐

Mutineers' Moon
0-671-72085-6 ✦ $5.99 ☐

The Armageddon Inheritance
0-671-72197-6 ✦ $6.99 ☐

Path of the Fury
0-671-72147-X ✦ $5.99 ☐

Oath of Swords
0-671-87642-2 ✦ $5.99 ☐

Insurrection
0-671-72024-4 ✦ $5.99 ☐

Crusade
0-671-72111-9 ✦ $6.99 ☐